LAST FLIGHT TO STALINGRAD

BY THE SAME AUTHOR

DI Joe Faraday Investigations

Turnstone

The Take

Angels Passing

Deadlight

Cut to Black

Blood and Honey

One Under

The Price of Darkness

No Lovelier Death

Beyond Reach

Borrowed Light

Happy Days

FICTION

Rules of Engagement

Reaper

The Devil's Breath

Thunder in the Blood

Sabbathman

The Perfect Soldier

Heaven's Light

Nocturne

Permissible Limits

The Chop

The Ghosts of 2012

Strictly No Flowers

DS Jimmy Suttle Investigations

Western Approaches

Touching Distance

Sins of the Father

The Order of Things

Enora Andressen thrillers

Curtain Call

Sight Unseen

Off Script

Spoils of War

Finisterre

Aurore

Estocada

Raid 42

Last Flight to Stalingrad

Kyiv

NON-FICTION

Lucky Break

Airshow

Estuary

Backstory

LAST FLIGHT TO STALINGRAD

GRAHAM HURLEY

HEAD
of
ZEUS

First published in the UK in 2021 by Head of Zeus Ltd
This paperback edition first published in 2021 by Head of Zeus Ltd

9 7 5 3 1 2 4 6 8

A catalogue record for this book is available
from the British Library.

ISBN (PB) 9781788547567
ISBN (E) 9781788547536

Printed and bound by CPI Group (UK) Ltd,
Croydon, CR0 4YY

Head of Zeus Ltd
5–8 Hardwick Street
London EC1R 4RG

WWW.HEADOFZEUS.COM

To Jenny and Pete with love

'The wildest life is the most beautiful'

Joseph Goebbels, *Diaries*, 1937

PRELUDE

Levitation. Werner Nehmann told her he'd first seen it in a circus ring erected in a meadow outside Svengati. He'd been a kid, immune from disbelief, and later he swore he'd experienced it himself, a kind of magic, his soul leaving his body, everything you took for granted viewed from a different angle. He also said that Hitler understood it, practised it, had fallen half in love with it. Obvious, really.

She'd spent the night with Nehmann, here in this apartment in the Wilhelmstrasse. The apartment belonged to Guramishvili, a fellow Georgian who'd made a fortune importing wine. Nehmann said Guram, as he called him, was out of town just now and had left him the keys. Hedvika had never met Guram but knew that, unlike Nehmann, he'd never bothered to disguise himself behind an adopted German name. Too proud, he said. Too Georgian. And very rich.

The apartment was on the first floor. The tall window in the bedroom offered a fine view of the Wilhelmstrasse, the broad boulevard pointing at the heart of the Reich. The Chancellor's train was due at the Anhalter station at three o'clock. According to Goebbels, whom Nehmann had seen last night, every allotment in Berlin had been ordered to supply a

1

tribute of flowers to brighten the route from the station to the Chancellery. As a result, the boulevard was ablaze with colour.

After waking late, Hedvika had got up and stationed herself at the window, offering Nehmann a running commentary on the hundreds of busy hands unloading the carts and barrows below. Trays of crimson begonias and delicate gladioli. Handsome stands of lilies, nodding in the breeze. Even the Führer's name, prefaced with the obligatory *Heil*, picked out in yellow roses on a first-floor balcony across the street. Minutes later, with the city's trains cancelled and swimming pools closed, long queues of workers began to appear, marching from their workplaces to swell the crowds along the Wilhelmstrasse.

Senzacni, Hedvika had murmured in her native Czech. *Wonderful.*

Nehmann agreed. In a handful of weeks, Hitler had crushed every Western European country that mattered except Italy and Great Britain. In the case of the Italians, Nehmann told her there'd be no need because Mussolini was simply Hitler with a bigger chin and a fancier wardrobe. And as far as the British were concerned, he added, it was simply a matter of time. In a month or two, once Goering had dealt with the RAF, there'd doubtless be an even noisier homecoming. Maybe they'd lock Churchill in a cage and parade him through Berlin. Assuming, of course, they hadn't already put a gun to his head.

Now Nehmann emerged from the kitchen, fully dressed, with a bottle of champagne and two glasses. Ever since they'd first met on set in the Ufa studios, he'd called Hedvika *Coquette*. The scene she was shooting had required her presence on a tiger-skin rug in the palatial setting of a rich man's weekend retreat. She'd been naked under a mink coat the colour of virgin snow and

2

Nehmann, assigned to do an interview, had afterwards spent an hour or so in her dressing room. The woman who attended to her make-up, a Czech cousin, called her *Koketa*. Nehmann liked the sensation of the word on his tongue but thought it sounded even better in French. And so *Coquette* she became. It meant 'temptress', with undertones of 'tease'.

'What time is it?' Naked but for a silk blouse, Hedvika was still at the window, her back to the bedroom, her elbows on the windowsill, looking down at the street.

Nehmann put the two glasses on the windowsill, moved his precious pots of chilli plants into the sunshine, and then knelt on the carpet and nuzzled the soft cleft between her buttocks. He was a small man, slight, nimble. After a while, gazing out at the street, she began to move under his tongue. Over the past few months, whenever he was in Berlin, Nehmann had become more than familiar with the repertoire of tiny grunts and sighs that signalled pleasure. The Georgian had a gipsy talent for lovemaking. It went with his origins, and his rumpled face, and the mischief in his eyes, and his reputation for a certain reckless charm that had opened countless doors across this wonderful city, but as far as women were concerned he'd never met anyone so responsive, so eager and so candid in her many demands. Remarkably for an actress, in bed or otherwise, she never faked it.

'Time?' she asked again.

Nehmann was on his feet by now, unbuttoned, moving sweetly inside her.

'Two minutes,' he said. 'The man is never late.'

'You're lying.'

'I am. It's what I do.'

'*Ja... ich kenne...* so why am I not surprised?' She looked to the right, towards the station, and reached for one of the glasses. 'Any ideas?'

She glanced backwards, over her shoulder. Nehmann smiled at her and then shrugged. She knows I lie. Everyone lies. That's the currency you use in this place. Spend your lies wisely and you might end up as rich as Guram. In Prague that might count as a sin. Here, it keeps a head on your shoulders and buys you champagne.

Outside the window, the gigantic crowd was beginning to stir. Over Hedvika's shoulder, across the street, Nehmann could see balcony after balcony crowded with faces and flags, children fighting their way through a forest of legs to get a better view, heads turning towards the oncoming growl of the motorcade.

Nehmann paused for a moment, reaching for the other glass, then began to quicken. A moment like this, he'd decided, deserved every kind of tribute.

'Don't,' she murmured. 'Not yet.'

The crowd was cheering now, thousands of voices, Berlin at full volume. Nehmann began to move again, deep, slow, taking his time, then he murmured an apology and withdrew for a second or two. Hedvika, he suspected, had barely registered his absence. At a moment like this, like every other spectator, she was in the hands of a quite different experience, no less overwhelming.

Nehmann was right. The blouse she'd thrown on earlier had become unbuttoned, but she didn't care. She leaned forward over the windowsill, her slender arms outstretched in welcome. Hitler's open Mercedes was barely metres away, at the head of the huge motorcade. He was standing at the front, beside the driver, both hands gripping the top of the windscreen, looking neither to left nor to right, grim, implacable, victorious.

Other women might have wanted him to smile for once, to risk one of those natural moments of warmth the newsreel cameras sometimes caught at the Berghof when he was playing with somebody's children, but not Hedvika. Berlin had been a good swap for Prague. Her heart was bursting for this man-God who'd shown the rest of Europe just who was in charge. Berlin, indeed the whole of Germany, was getting no less than it deserved. Thanks to the unbending figure below her window.

'*Heil!*' she screamed. '*Mein Führer!*'

The Mercedes moved on towards the Chancellery and the Brandenburger Tor and in its wake came the long procession of equally sleek limousines, each one laden with more of the faces that Hedvika had come to know from their lingering visits to the studios. But these men she regarded as mere walk-ons, riffraff, nobodies, bit-part players in the unfolding triumphs of the Reich. Hitler, to his great credit, never stooped to studio visits.

She peered to the left and offered a last wave to her departing Führer, and then – as the crowd began to thin – she looked down towards the pavement. Hitler gone, there was an emptiness deep inside her and she knew exactly how to fill it.

'Faster,' she murmured.

Nehmann obliged as he always did. She pushed back against him, finding the rhythm, then a single face among the crowds below caught her attention. Everyone was still on tiptoe, looking at the last of the cars, but this single face had no interest in the motorcade. Instead, it was looking up. At her.

For a moment, she couldn't believe it. The curly hair he deliberately wore long. The suntan he worked so effortlessly to maintain. The simplicity of the open white shirt. The lumpy peasant contours of his face. The broadness of his grin. Even the champagne glass, nearly empty, lifted in salute. Werner Nehmann.

But wasn't he behind her? Making love to her? Perfectly *à deux*?

Still moving sweetly, she looked over her shoulder. It was Guram, Nehmann's friend, his fellow countryman. She'd met him twice before, once here in Berlin, and once in Munich, both times when she was with the little Georgian. He was a large man, with a belly to match, and he had Nehmann's talent for making her laugh. In Munich, an evening in one of the city's bierkellers had ended with all three of them in bed, a night she remembered with great affection. Generous people, she thought. In all kinds of ways.

Now, Guram's perfectly manicured hands had settled on the tops of her hips. Two rings, one featuring a showy bloodstone.

'*Guten Tag*.' Georgian accent. Pleasant smile. '*Wie geht es dir?*'

'I'm fine. Why aren't you in Paris? Making lots of money?'

'Business called me back.' He smiled. 'Faster?'

She held his gaze for a moment, then nodded.

'*Ja*,' she said. 'I'll tell you when.'

She turned back to the street, trying to work out how a thing like this could ever happen, trying to catch the rhythm again. Nehmann, she knew, loved practical jokes, pranks, any kind of mischief, but this had to be in a league of its own. Nehmann's friend owns the flat, she thought. He has every right to be here. The two men grew up together. Brothers-in-arms. He may have been expecting something like this. Nehmann may even have planned it. Who knows?

She shook her head, enjoying the ride, knowing she was seconds away. She closed her eyes for a moment, letting it happen, exulting in the long spasm of orgasm and then she arched her back and gasped one final time before her gaze fell on Nehmann again and she held her limp hands wide in a gesture than needed no translation. You fooled me. I give up. But thank you all the same.

Nehmann was laughing now. He handed his glass to a man beside him and then cupped his own hands.

'Levitation,' he shouted, before asking the stranger for his glass back.

1

GRAMMATIKOVO, KERCH PENINSULA, CRIMEA, 20 MAY 1942

Oberstleutnant Georg Messner occasionally wondered whether he'd fallen in love with his boss.

Generaloberst Wolfram von Richthofen was the legendary chief of *Fliegerkorps VIII*. In half a decade he'd routed the Reich's enemies in Spain, Poland, France and the Balkans. His Stuka dive bombers, with the terrifying siren he'd invented himself, had become a battlefield code for instant annihilation, and even the vastness of the Soviet Union hadn't daunted him. On the day German armour poured into Russia, *Fliegerkorps VIII* had destroyed no less than 1,800 enemy aircraft for the loss of just two planes. Even hardened *Luftwaffe* veterans couldn't believe it.

Now, Messner – who served as an aide to *Generaloberst* Richthofen – was sitting in a draughty tent on a scruffy airfield on the Kerch Peninsula. The meeting had started barely half an hour ago. Messner had flown in last night, anticipating a celebration at the end of Operation *Trappenjagd*. General Manstein was rumoured to be arriving in time for lunch.

In ten exhausting days of incessant bombing, Richthofen's *Fliegerkorps VIII*, working hand in hand with General

Manstein's 11th Army, had kicked open the back door to the priceless Caucasian oilfields. One hundred and seventy thousand Russian soldiers stumbled off into captivity. Two full Soviet armies, plus the greater part of a third, were destroyed. In raid after raid, the Heinkels had seeded the Soviet formations below with the new SD2 fragmentation bombs, tiny eggs that exploded feet above the pale earth and tore men to pieces. Coupled with bigger ordnance, Richthofen called it 'giant fire magic'.

On the first Sunday of the campaign, most bomber pilots had flown nearly a dozen sorties. A handful had gone three better. Fifteen take-offs. Fifteen landings. All in one day. Unbelievable. This was the way Richthofen organised his campaigns: violence without end, ceaseless pressure, an unrelenting urge to grind the enemy to dust.

The results had been obvious from the air. Towards the end of the first week, personally supervising the carnage from two thousand metres, Richthofen had emerged from his tiny Fieseler Storch to tell Messner that the jaws of Manstein's trap were about to close around the hapless Slavs. 'Unless the weather stops us,' he growled, 'no Russian will leave the Crimea alive.'

And so it went. By the third week in May, after a difficult winter, the road to the Crimean fortress at Sevastopol lay open to Manstein's tanks and Richthofen's marauding bomber crews. After a victory of this magnitude, Germany was once again on course to advance deep into the Russian heartlands. Messner himself was a Berliner and it wasn't difficult to imagine the relief and rejoicing in his home city. Moscow and Leningrad were still under siege, but the real key surely lay here on the southern flank. The seizure of the oil wells would keep the Panzers rolling east. Grain from Ukraine would fill bellies back home. Yet none of the euphoria Messner had expected was evident around this makeshift table.

Messner had first served under Richthofen half a decade ago in the Condor Legion, fighting the Republican armies in the mountains of northern Spain. He knew how difficult, how outspoken this man could be. He treated superiors and underlings alike with a rough impatience which brooked no excuse when things went wrong. His men feared him, of that there was no doubt, but he brought them comfort as well because he was – more often than not – right.

The story of war, as Messner knew all too well, was the story of things going wrong, but Richthofen had an implacable belief in willpower and the merits of meticulous organisation. In his view there was no such thing as defeat. There'd always be setbacks, certainly, occasions when plans threatened to fall apart, but the men under his command were expected to be masters of both themselves and the battlefield below. For Richthofen, the undisputed *Meister* of close air support, there was no sweeter word than *Schwerpunkt*, that carefully plotted moment when irresistible wrath descended on the heads of the enemy and put him on his knees.

Messner knew the faces around this table. Like him, they'd expected – at the very least – a word or two of appreciation for their collective efforts over the last ten exhausting days. *Fliegerkorps VIII* were rumoured to be Hitler's favourite *Luftwaffe* formation, a tribute no doubt to the sternness and brilliance of Richthofen's leadership, and as a result Richthofen had been awarded Oak Leaves to go with his *Ritterkreuz*. But now, in the aftermath of yet another triumph, he seemed anything but satisfied. How many medals did a man need,

Messner wondered. Just what kind of acknowledgement would slake his thirst to crush everything around him?

They were discussing the shape of the campaign over the coming days. No one doubted for a moment that the Soviets manning the fortress at Sevastopol would be the next to receive the attentions of *Fliegerkorps VIII*. This, the key to the Soviet position in the Crimea, was rumoured to be impregnable, a phrase for which Richthofen had no time at all. A priceless naval base. Cliffs falling sheer to the Black Sea. One hundred and six thousand Soviet front-line troops. Reinforced concrete fortifications. Strongpoints dug dozens of metres into the bedrock limestone. Artillery protected by twenty-five centimetres of armour plate. One by one, Richthofen tallied the Soviet boasts. Then, for the first time, he smiled.

'Operation *Storfang*,' he murmured. 'Remember what we did to Warsaw? *Storfang* will be all of that and more. No quarter, no letting up. We'll hit the Slavs until they beg for mercy. Think opera. *Trappenjagd* is just the overture. *Storfang* will have the audience on its feet.'

Trappenjagd meant 'Bustard Hunt'. *Storfang*, 'Sturgeon Catch'. There was an exchange of nods around the table. The war in Russia was still in its infancy. Nothing excited these men more than the prospect of another slaughter. From two thousand metres, regardless of what the Russian air force could muster, it would be a fresh chance to play God.

Richthofen briefly consulted a file that lay open in front of him. Six bomber groups flying in formations of twenty to thirty aircraft. Close support from Ju-87 Stukas dive-bombing Soviet formations. Rolling attacks, one following another. A torrent of high explosive falling on the luckless Ivans below.

A raised hand caught Richthofen's attention. The *Major* in charge of intelligence wanted to know about artillery support on the ground. The question sparked a brief frown from Richthofen.

'They're bringing up a Gustav *Dora*. It's showing off, of course, and completely unnecessary because we can finish the job ourselves, but it might give our Russian friends a fright or two.'

The image sparked a ripple of laughter around the table. The Gustav *Dora* was a monstrous piece of railway-mounted artillery. From a siding forty-seven kilometres away it could bombard a distant target with surprising accuracy and the thought of sharing a subterranean bunker with the thunderous arrival of a seven-tonne shell would do nothing for the Ivans' peace of mind.

'Questions?'

The Bavarian engineer responsible for maintenance wanted to know about the spares situation. After *Trappenjagd*, engines on the Heinkels badly needed servicing before an operation of this magnitude. Another officer at the table had concerns about supplies of aviation fuel. To both questions Richthofen grunted monosyllabic replies, scribbling notes to himself on the pad at his elbow. He seemed indifferent to the smaller courtesies of a meeting such as this but by now these men knew that both matters would be resolved. That was the way Richthofen liked to operate. Decisions taken in a matter of seconds. Action guaranteed.

He glanced up from his pad as a figure appeared at the mouth of the tent. Messner recognised the adjutant who'd been with Richthofen since the early days in Spain. He paused beside the table and handed over a single sheet of paper torn from a message form. Richthofen scanned it quickly, nodded. Then he looked up again and brought the meeting to a close before beckoning Messner to accompany him to the nearby hut he was using as his makeshift headquarters.

Messner settled himself in the only other chair with intact legs, doing his best to avoid the draught through the ill-fitting door, and waited while Richthofen attended to a number of telephone calls.

He'd first caught the *Generaloberst*'s eye back in the days when he was assigned to the Führer's special squadron. Messner's task was to ferry Nazi chieftains around the Reich and from time to time the passenger manifest had included the flyer who'd turned *Fliegerkorps VIII* into a legend. Richthofen, cousin of the great Red Baron, knew a good pilot when he saw one and had – as it turned out – made a note of Messner's name. Aside from his skills in the air, he liked the way Messner handled himself: unshowy, highly organised, with little time for small talk. In short, Richthofen's sort of man.

Then had come the accident, and the weeks of surgery, and the months of slow recovery, and Messner's days in the Führer's cockpit were over. With his mutilated face and a deep chill where his heart had once been, he'd emerged from convalescence a different man. His wife had left him for his best friend. His only daughter had become a stranger. He had no one he could truly call close.

But none of this meant anything as far as Richthofen was concerned. Messner was still a fine pilot. Richthofen demanded an aide's undivided loyalty – total dedication – and in this respect he was never disappointed. Over the last year or so, he'd become Richthofen's eyes and ears as *Fliegerkorps VIII* pushed east, and his growing reputation as the *Generaloberst*'s snitch barely registered. Recently, in a gruff gesture of thanks for all his work, Richthofen had secured his tireless aide a promotion. *Oberstleutnant* Messner had yet to spare the time to celebrate.

The last phone call had come to an end. Richthofen produced the sheet of paper and put it carefully to one side.

'Your days in the *Reichsregierung*,' he said. 'You flew our Leader on countless occasions. What did you make of him?'

Messner frowned. Questions like these were rare. Richthofen rarely troubled himself with other people's opinions.

'Well?' Richthofen never bothered to hide his impatience.

'The Führer is a man you'd treat with a great deal of respect.'

'You think he's clever?'

'Very.'

'Ruthless?'

'Yes.'

'Did you ever trust him?'

'Of course not. But that didn't matter.'

'Why not?'

'Because I was the one at the controls.'

Messner's answer drew a nod of approval. Then Richthofen glanced at the message on the desk.

'Read it.'

Messner picked it up. It appeared to be confirmation that the *Generaloberst*'s personal Storch would be readied for take-off by first light tomorrow. He always flew it alone, shuttling from one forward airfield to another, urging his commanders to yet greater efforts. On this occasion, an extra fuel tank had been fitted.

Messner looked up. 'Somewhere special?'

'Berlin.'

'Am I allowed to ask why?'

'Of course. Our Leader wants a conversation tomorrow night. It's a long way to go for a shit meal but let's hope he makes it worthwhile. Something else, Herr *Oberstleutnant*.'

'Sir?'

'Goebbels' film people are still at work. I'd take the latest footage to Berlin myself but they say they need an extra day. These pictures will do us nothing but good. Can you sort this out, Messner? Make sure the film is in the right hands as soon as possible?'

2

BERLIN, 21 MAY 1942

Werner Nehmann was summoned to 20 Hermann Goering Strasse in an early evening phone call from the Ministry of Propaganda. The call came from one of the secretaries in Goebbels' private office, an old-stager in the Promi called Birgit.

'Why the invitation?' he asked on the phone.

'I've no idea. The Minister said ten o'clock. He's still on the way back from München. I'm sending a car to Tempelhof.'

Nehmann was still living at Guram's apartment on the Wilhelmstrasse. His Georgian friend's business empire had lately expanded to France and he was currently occupying a handsome three-storey house in Tours while he cornered the market for quality vintages from the Loire Valley.

Nehmann hung up and glanced at his watch. Still early, barely seven o'clock. For the next couple of hours or so, over a glass or two of *Sekt* from Guram's personal cellar, he worked on a couple of articles he owed *Das Reich*, Goebbels' weekly offering to neutral countries abroad. Then, as darkness fell, and the city centre's *Blockwarten* began to police the nightly blackout, he checked his own curtains and headed for the street.

Goebbels' official Berlin residence was a ten-minute stroll away. With no raids anticipated, the late evening traffic was slightly heavier than usual and staff, uniformed or otherwise, were still emerging from the Reich ministries at the upper end of the Wilhelmstrasse. Hermann Goering Strasse was on the left, two streets from Hitler's Chancellery.

Number 20 lay behind a high wall, a three-storey building with the faux-classical features favoured in the upper levels of the Reich. Nehmann paused a moment to light a cheroot, acknowledging the nod of recognition from the sentry who stood guard at the iron gate. After a multimillion Reichsmark renovation, the Minister of Propaganda had been living here since the beginning of the war. Add three more properties outside the city – two on Schwanenwerder, an idyllic island on the River Havel, and another at Bogensee – and Nehmann began to wonder how Goebbels ever made up his mind where to sleep at night.

Recently, out of curiosity as well as a sense of mischief, Nehmann had acquired a copy of the Minister's first and only published novel, penned when he was twenty-five. It featured a troubled hero called Michael Voorman and it was, everyone quietly agreed, a pile of *Scheisse*, but what had caught Nehmann's eye was Voorman's principled rejection of materialism. What really mattered to the apprentice novelist was faith, and justice, and the pathway to a better future. What the author sought to avoid were the showy baubles of contemporary German life.

Nehmann ground the remains of his cheroot underfoot and stepped towards the gate. An early fantasy, he thought, amused as ever by where this level of deceit might lead a man.

A member of Goebbels' staff, alerted by the sentry, was already waiting at the mansion's open door. Another familiar face.

'He's back, Hildegard?'

'Ten minutes ago. He's in his study. You know the way.'

She stood aside and let him into the house before closing the door behind them. The ground floor offered a banqueting hall, reception rooms and the overpowering scent of furniture polish. Nehmann, who had no taste for public events, had successfully resisted a number of invitations in the early days of the war without damaging his access to the master of the house. He knew that Goebbels had assigned him the role of court jester, as well as maverick journalist, and he was more than content to keep the grind of official business at arm's length. He also knew from contacts deep in the Promi that Goebbels regarded his take on the world as scurrilous, subversive and frequently brilliant, three reasons – he suspected – to explain the immunity he appeared to have won for himself. Recently, the Minister had given him a nickname, *der Über*. It was shorthand for *der Überlebende*. The survivor.

The grand staircase, the signature boast of so many Berlin renovations up and down the Wilhelmstrasse, was hung with fine art looted from galleries in France. Nehmann, as ever, paused beside a canvas by Courbet. He'd first seen this masterpiece a decade ago. It was hanging in a gallery on the Île Saint-Louis in Paris, and even then – barely able to eat on his meagre earnings from satirical scribblings – he'd regarded it as sublime. The fall of light on the white bones of the cliff face at Étretat. The seemingly artless brushstrokes that gave the rearing breakers both depth and menace. The scurry of clouds on the far horizon. You could taste the wind, smell the ocean, and every time he took another look it seemed to offer a fresh message. Tonight, he thought, it carries a warning. Never take anything for granted.

Goebbels was working in a small study on the second floor, a private space he regarded as sacrosanct. Nehmann knocked and announced himself.

'Come...'

Goebbels was sitting in a leather armchair beside a desk, leafing through a sheaf of notes. He was wearing a suit but he'd discarded the jacket and rolled up his sleeves. He glanced briefly up, then waved Nehmann into the other chair. No words of welcome; nothing to break his concentration.

Nehmann knew better than to interrupt his master. With his senior staff at the Promi, the Minister had never been less than imperious, and recently he'd been insisting on regular 11 a.m. meetings to tighten his grip on every full stop and comma that emerged from the Ministry. Nehmann was mercifully spared this daily inquisition but word around the building suggested that the pressure on Goebbels was beginning to show, and, looking at him now, Nehmann knew that the rumours were true.

Although they'd spoken on the phone a number of times over the past weeks, he hadn't seen Goebbels in the flesh since mid-April. The Minister had a face and a slightly skeletal physical presence you wouldn't forget: high forehead, thin lips, coal-black eyes. For a small man, his voice was surprisingly deep and at his many public appearances he used it to some effect. With his repertoire of gestures – the pointing index finger, the clenched fist, the hammering on the lectern, the planting of arms akimbo – he had the ability to transcend the confines of both his body and his trademark leather jacket. For Werner Nehmann this was yet further proof of the powers of levitation, but here and now, watching Goebbels' pencil race from line to line, he sensed the Reich's favourite dwarf was in serious trouble.

He looked even thinner than usual and scarlet shell bursts of eczema had appeared on the bareness of his forearms. There was another sign of stress, too: one highly polished shoe tap-tapping on the looted Gobelin carpet.

'You're lucky, Nehmann.' The Minister didn't look up.

'Tell me why?'

'I like it that you don't dress for dinner.'

'I'm here to eat?'

'You're here to listen. And to drink. And as it happens I brought back some fine *Weisswurst* from München.' He glanced up at last. 'You think that might be acceptable?'

Nehmann nodded. *Weisswurst* was a Bavarian sausage, an irresistible marriage of minced veal and pork back bacon. Goebbels knew that Nehmann adored it.

Goebbels lifted a telephone on the table by his chair and muttered an order. Then he gestured at the notes on his lap.

'We're running out of grain seed. Can you believe that? I can explain anything within reason. I can turn defeat into victory, I can make angels dance on the head of a pin. Offer me enough money and I can even raise a thin cheer for that snout-wipe Ribbentrop. But a loaf that turns out to be half-barley? In a country like this?'

Nehmann mentioned potatoes as a substitute for grain seed. At short notice it was the only suggestion he could muster. *Kartoffelbrot. Kartoffelomelett.* A Spanish *tortilla* on every man's table.

'*Nein?*'

'*Nein*. This swinish weather has done for the potatoes, too. So far we've had the measure of every single enemy. And now we surrender to the fucking *rain*?'

Nehmann could only agree. Lately, the weather had been evil. Even back home in Svengati, where the mountains made for serious weather, he'd never seen so much water.

One of the kitchen staff appeared at the door with a tray. As well as a pile of fat *Weisswurst*, Goebbels had ordered a bottle of champagne. He gave it to Nehmann to pop the cork and then watched him pour.

'A toast, my friend.' Goebbels reached for a glass.

'To what?'

'To *Trappenjagd*.' He frowned. 'The Kerch Peninsula? Key to the Crimea? You haven't heard? Manstein cleaned out what's left of the Soviets yesterday afternoon. The Führer's planning a major speech. I may even say something myself.'

The two men clinked glasses. Then Goebbels sat back.

'You don't listen to the radio any more?'

'Not today.'

'But I thought your *Coquette*' – a thin smile – 'has been otherwise engaged?'

Goebbels, who lived for gossip, obviously knew that Hedvika had started an affair with an Italian film director but Nehmann didn't rise to the bait.

'She's shooting in Franconia.' Nehmann nodded at a pile of scripts on Goebbels' desk. 'I have my life to myself.'

Goebbels held his gaze, said nothing. Every night, to Nehmann's certain knowledge, the Minister devoted time he couldn't afford to going through pre-production movie scripts. The sight of the ministerial green ink in the margins of scene after scene in these scripts had driven a whole generation of film directors crazy yet in this corner of his empire, as in the others, the little man insisted on total control. A disease, Nehmann thought. And at this rate, probably terminal.

Goebbels was talking about his unhappiness with the Propaganda Companies, yet another innovation for which he claimed sole credit. Nehmann had accompanied one of these outfits during last year's lightning descent on the luckless French. Goebbels, who treated everything in life as a lamp post, wanted to cock his leg and put his personal scent on the probability of a quick German victory. The Propaganda Companies – film crews and journalists – bounced along in the wake of the Panzer columns, raiding the battlefield for images and interviews to send home. Thus, within days, cinema audiences across the Reich would be treated to victory after victory, an epic movie told onscreen in real time, and all of it thanks to the little genius at the head of the Promi. Given the cannibalism within the upper reaches of the Reich, rival warlords were quick to spot the countless benefits of sharing these spoils of Hitler's war, and now, it seemed, Goebbels was facing a serious turf battle with Foreign Minister Joachim von Ribbentrop.

'The man's a fool, an impostor,' he said, reaching for a sausage. 'He has the ear of Hitler because he bought off the Russians for a couple of years, but tell me this: what on earth does the man know about propaganda?'

'He lies,' Nehmann pointed out. 'All the time.'

'Yes, but what lies. Paper lies. The thinnest of lies. The most *obvious* of lies. Ribbentrop is an impostor. He married his fortune. He stole his title. He has a dentist's smile. Even his staff say so.'

Nehmann nodded and emptied his glass. He hadn't been summoned here to listen to Goebbels beating up his many enemies. There had to be another reason.

'So what happens next, Herr Minister?'

'What happens next, my friend, we owe to General Manstein. The Führer believes that *Trappenjagd* is just an *hors d'oeuvre*. The main course is yet to come. He's as sensitive to the grain crisis as I am, and he believes the people deserve a little glimpse of what awaits us. The news footage from the Crimea arrives tomorrow. Ribbentrop is trying to get his hands on it. He won't succeed. He thinks it's due at Tempelhof just before noon and that's because we've planted all the clues. In reality, it'll arrive at Schönwalde around nine in the morning and you, my friend, will be on hand to collect it. I'll be supervising the edit myself. The music is already written, and the earlier battle footage is already cut. Half a day's hard work and we can start sending out the prints. Radio is fine. Radio is a godsend. But in the end, it's pictures that count. You agree?'

'I'm a writer.'

'I know. Tact was never part of my job. I speak the truth as I see it. Not a particle more, not a particle less. Pictures, Werner.' He made an oblong frame with his long fingers. '*Pictures. Ja?* You agree?'

3

Nehmann spent that night with a woman called Maria.
He'd met her a couple of weeks ago in a Moabit nightclub
where she played the piano. She said she was Austrian, from
a village near Villach. Her orphan looks were, to be frank,
Jewish – sallow complexion, a fall of jet-black curls, perfect
mouth, enormous eyes – but Nehmann had met a lot of Italian
girls and when she said that her grandparents had lived in
Bolzano before heading north to Austria he was very happy to
believe her.

To date, unusually for Nehmann, they'd yet to make love.
She'd asked him to be patient, to wait until circumstances were
right for both of them. She'd made the suggestion the first time
she'd stayed with him in Guram's apartment and to his own
slight surprise, Nehmann had agreed. He was transfixed by her
face, most of all by her eyes. They had a depth and a candour
that he found close to hypnotic and, in no time at all, she'd
become an important presence in his life.

They talked a great deal late into the small hours after her
return from Moabit. They were both outsiders in this teeming
city. They compared notes, and drank Guram's wine, and
agreed that much of Nazi Germany was an essay in swagger

and bad taste. Complicity in this small conversational act of treason was drawing them ever closer, and Nehmann liked that. In truth, though he'd never admit it to Goebbels, his Czech *coquette* had begun to bore him and, now that she'd taken her favours elsewhere, he felt nothing but relief. Hedvika was too loud, too easy, too coarse, too suggestive. On the keyboard, and in real life, Maria had an altogether lighter touch.

Daylight came early at this time of year. Maria was still asleep and Nehmann got up and dressed without a sound. The rain had cleared at last and when he descended to the street to meet the car despatched from the Promi, the city was bathed in sunshine. At this hour in the morning there was still the faintest chill in the air but, among the secretaries spilling off the trolley buses, Nehmann saw a couple of older folk carrying rolled-up towels. They're off to the Lido to make friends with summer again, he thought with a pang of jealousy. He swam there himself whenever he got the chance.

The journey out to Schönwalde took no time at all. At the sandbagged airfield checkpoint, Nehmann wound down the window and offered his Promi pass. The officer in charge consulted a list of names on a typed list.

'You're here to meet *Oberstleutnant* Messner?'

'I am.'

'Met him before?'

'Never.'

'You're in for a treat. He's due in about half an hour. He's blaming headwinds over Poland so I expect God will be paying the bill.' He stepped back to wave him through. 'Good luck, Herr Nehmann.'

Nehmann exchanged looks with the driver as the car began to move.

'God?' he queried.

'Messner has a reputation for never being wrong. If there's no one else available, he gives God a mouthful.'

Nehmann nodded, none the wiser. The airfield lay before them, littered with heavy plant. Between the bulldozers and the trucks was a wilderness of puddles.

'I thought this belonged to the *Luftwaffe*?'

'It does. They're laying a hard runway for the day the *Regierung* move in.'

'So where's Messner supposed to land?'

'God only knows. Which is why the bloody man needs to watch his tongue.'

'You know him?'

'I've met him.'

'And?'

'Wait and see.'

They parked beside a barely finished single-storey building that seemed to serve as a rallying point for the army of labourers assigned to the new runway. The driver thought there was a chance of decent coffee inside and left the car to find out. After a while, bored, Nehmann got out to stretch his legs. A frieze of pine trees edged the flatness of the airfield on three sides and he was watching a distant gaggle of tiny stick figures pouring concrete when he heard the faintest mutter of aero engines, throttled back in anticipation of a landing.

Away to the east, below a scatter of fluffy white clouds, he could see the Me-110 dropping a wing and then settling gently on the final descent. From where he was standing it was difficult to be sure but Nehmann had the impression that some of the workmen out there would be wise to get out of the way. Seconds later came the blast of a whistle and the men began to scatter in all directions.

By now, the Me-110 was barely feet from touchdown. Messner lifted the nose, gunned the engines one final time to avoid three men running into his path, and then let the aircraft settle among the puddles. Spray from the main undercarriage sparkled briefly in the brightness of the sunshine, confirming Nehmann's conviction that he'd just witnessed something remarkable. A big aquatic bird, he thought, totally at home in this sodden stretch of Brandenburg turf.

The Me-110 had come to a halt. Another burst of throttle brought the nose round before the plane began to taxi towards him, weaving its way without hesitation through the thicket of heavy construction vehicles. Cautiously, the workmen were returning to their tasks. One was shaking his fist in Messner's direction.

'Here—'

It was the driver. Nehmann took the proffered mug. Coffee with sugar. Better still.

The Me-110 was only metres away, the roar of the engines drowning any longer conversation. Up in the cockpit, Nehmann could see a white disc of face behind a large pair of aviator glasses. Two ground crew in overalls had appeared from nowhere, each pulling a big wooden chock for the main wheels. The taller of the two men glanced up and drew a finger across his throat and the propellers began to windmill before coming to a halt.

In the sudden silence, Nehmann was aware of the

aircraft rocking slightly as the pilot released the canopy and clambered onto the wing. From the rear cockpit, he extracted two canvas mail sacks and handed them down to the ground crew.

He was tall, much taller than Nehmann. He climbed down onto the wet grass, and one hand swept the glasses from his face as if to get a proper look at this modest welcoming committee.

'*Oberstleutnant* Messner,' he introduced himself. 'And you are…?'

'Nehmann. From the Ministry.'

'*Guten Tag, Nehmann.*' He extended a gloved hand. 'Do you mind?'

He wanted Nehmann's coffee. A man could die of thirst flying out of the zoo that was Russia. Once, under different circumstances, he said he could rely on flasks of the stuff, the real thing, Turkish or Arabian, and perhaps a cake or two to keep his spirits up. But those days had gone.

Nehmann gave him the coffee. He'd never seen a face like this before. Once he must have been good-looking, even handsome, but someone – certainly not a friend – seemed to have rearranged all the constituent parts without keeping the original in mind. The sunken eyes sat oddly in the tightness of the flesh. A scar looped down from one corner of his mouth, while more scar tissue, raised welts of the stuff, latticed his forehead.

Messner, who must have been all too familiar with the curiosity of strangers, paid no attention. He bent for the bigger of the two sacks and gave it to Nehmann.

'Compliments of *Generaloberst* Richthofen,' he said. 'Fuck it up and he'll have your arse.'

'These are the film cans?'

'*Ja.*'

'And the other sack?'

'A Russian chicken for my lovely ex-wife. And a Ukrainian rabbit with the compliments of Kyiv. You know Kyiv? Been there ever? No? I thought not. Fine rabbits, my friend. You have a car here by any chance?'

'Of course.'

'Excellent. In which case, the rabbit might well be yours.'

Nehmann passed the sack containing the cans of undeveloped film to the driver. The other one appeared to be moving.

'The rabbit's still alive?'

'*Ja.*' Messner nodded at the aircraft. 'Alas, I have no refrigeration.'

'And the chicken?'

'Dead, I'm afraid. But yet to be plucked.' Messner checked his watch and then gestured at the Promi car. 'I need to get to Wannsee. Do we have a deal?'

*

They did. The driver returned to the Promi, where Nehmann handed over the cans of film from the Crimea. On the Minister's personal instructions, the undeveloped footage was rushed to a processing plant elsewhere in the city. 16mm prints, he was assured, would be ready for the editing suite by early afternoon. Nehmann was expected to attend the edit, where Minister Goebbels – familiar with the footage already cut – would supervise the final version.

The Promi car was still parked outside in the Wilhelmstrasse. Messner, in the front passenger seat, appeared to be asleep.

Nehmann opened the rear door to check on the rabbit and then slipped behind the wheel.

'Still alive?' Messner had been watching him in the rear-view mirror.

'Very. Where are we going?'

'Wannsee. I thought I told you. Get me to the waterfront and we'll take it from there.'

They set off. Nehmann's driving skills were rudimentary. He didn't possess a licence and strictly speaking he should have returned the car to the underground garage, but Birgit said that everything would be fine as long as he was back in time for the edit.

'We've got three hours,' he told Messner. 'You want me to drop you off at Wannsee or take you back to the airfield afterwards?'

'The airfield. Beata was a wife to be proud of, but a man runs out of credit if he doesn't watch his step.'

'So what happened?'

'I didn't watch my step.'

Nehmann glanced across at him, surprised by this small moment of intimacy. Then, from nowhere, a truck appeared, *Wehrmacht*-grey, two lines of soldiers squatting on benches in the back. Heads turned to look down as Nehmann braked hard and swerved to the right. One of the soldiers was laughing.

'Pull in, for fuck's sake.' Messner's muttered oath had the force of an order.

Nehmann came to a halt beside the pavement. Messner waited for a cyclist to pass and then opened the passenger door and stepped out into the road. For a moment, Nehmann

31

thought he'd baled out for good but then the tall figure in the leather flying jacket was pulling his own door open.

'Move over, Nehmann. You drive like a Russian, my friend, and that's not a compliment.'

Chastened, Nehmann did as he was told. Messner adjusted the rear-view mirror and rejoined the traffic. From the back of the car came a series of snuffles and then a brief mew. The rabbit, Nehmann thought, didn't like his driving either.

They drove in silence for a while, following the trolley bus wires out towards Charlottenburg. For no apparent reason Messner slowed at a major intersection. Beyond, on the right, was a branch of the Dresdner Bank.

'Just here...' he said '...if I'm to believe all the stories.'

'Just here what?' Nehmann hadn't a clue what he was talking about.

'The accident. Me and the windscreen.' One gloved hand touched his face. 'This.'

He'd been driving his wife's car, he explained. He'd had the devil of a toothache for three whole days and she'd managed to find a dentist. It was a winter evening, blackout, and a raid was expected. There was a deadline for the dentist, and he must have taken a chance or two.

'You don't remember any of this?'

'I remember nothing. I'd been flying Goering and a couple of his people that day. Next thing, I'm in the Charité hospital. You know anything about hospitals, Nehmann?'

'No.'

'Just as well, especially these days. Put a woman in a uniform and she thinks she owns the world.'

'You're supposed to feel grateful. They probably saved your life.'

'I know. And that only makes it worse. I was months in that place. Pilots and confinement don't mix. As soon as I was mobile again, I tried to escape. After that they locked me up and threatened me with Himmler.'

'You flew him, too?'

'I did. On the Führer Squadron. Next you're going to ask me what he was like, so I'll spare you the effort. The man's a creep. Take it from me.' He glanced across at Nehmann. '*Ja?*'

The rest of the journey passed in silence until they reached the outskirts of Wannsee.

'Are you married, Nehmann?'

'No.'

'Very wise. My wife was a scientist. She worked at the Kaiser Wilhelm Institute. That made her very intelligent indeed. She had a huge brain and that was probably vital to our war effort, but she was no fun. No fun around the house. No fun in public. No fun anywhere. You understand what I'm saying, Nehmann?'

Nehmann nodded. No fun in bed, he thought. Behind the mask that used to be a face, this man is strange. So remote. So stiff. And then so abruptly confessional.

'You're divorced now?' Nehmann asked.

'Yes. Beata lives with a very good friend of mine, a *Kamerad* from the old days. Merz. Dieter Merz. He and I flew in those air pageants before the war. He was like a film star. On the squadron in Spain we always called him *der Kleine*, the Little One. He flew like an angel, no fear, and Beata always loved him. They may even be married by now. Remind me to ask her when we get there. You'll do that for me?'

The marital home turned out to be a modest wooden house with rows of tiny pot plants on the windowsills and glimpse of a garden that stretched down to the lake. From the road, Nehmann could see a rusting child's swing marooned in knee-high grass and a line of washing drying in the breeze. An air of faint neglect extended to the front door, though someone had recently been at work with a blowtorch on the blistered old paint.

Messner rapped twice, peremptory, unbidden, announcing his presence. Nehmann was wondering whether this visit was supposed to be some kind of surprise when he heard footsteps inside. Moments later the door opened and he was looking at a middle-aged woman, plain, barefoot, with a baby in her arms. She was wearing a pair of paint-stained dungarees and a savage haircut did nothing for the faintness of her smile. The last thing Nehmann had expected was this forbidding figure. Beata, he thought. The ex-wife.

'This one belongs to Merz?' Messner was looking at the baby. No greeting. Not a hint of warmth. Just a curt check on the child's paternity.

'Her name's Annaliese.' Beata kissed the top of the baby's head and held her a little closer. 'And the answer's yes.'

'I see...*die kleine Kleine*.' The little Little One.

For Messner, Nehmann thought, this had the makings of a joke, though it didn't seem to amuse his ex-wife.

'And my Lottie?' Messner asked.

'Upstairs.'

'You gave her the doll I sent from Kyiv?'

'Doll?'

'It never arrived? A Russian doll? Green eyes and a little painted skirt?'

Beata stared at him for a moment, and then shook her head. It was obvious she was lying but the really hurtful thing was the fact that she didn't care. In any marriage, Nehmann thought, indifference must be the real killer.

Messner had opened the canvas mail bag. His hand disappeared inside as he cornered the rabbit, then he hauled it out by the scruff of the neck. The softness of its belly and the sight of the long legs kicking and kicking seemed to fascinate the baby. She wriggled in her mother's arms, wanting to reach out and touch this strange creature.

'This is for me?' Beata was staring at the animal. 'For us?'

'It is. I can kill it and skin it now, if you want. There's something else, too, with the compliments of our Russian friends. Nehmann? You want to show Beata our little surprise?'

Our little surprise? Nehmann, who wanted no part of this conversation, reached deep into the canvas bag. The chicken was cold to his touch, the head and neck floppy beneath his fingertips. Beata stared at it.

'It's dead?'

'Very.' Messner nodded. 'Scalding water's best for getting rid of the feathers, as you probably remember.'

Beata nodded. Then she said she had no use for a dead rabbit. Better to keep it as a pet. Nehmann swore he saw the baby nodding. Messner was astonished.

'You don't want it for the pot?' he asked. 'In times like these?'

'No, thank you.'

'But you're serious? About keeping it?'

'I am. Wait. I have a box inside.'

'Don't worry. Here—'

Messner dropped the rabbit back into the canvas bag and handed it over. Then he said he needed a favour.

'You remember those little model aeroplanes I had as a kid? Biplanes? Triplanes?'

'Upstairs,' she said again. 'I know exactly where they are.'

Messner stepped towards the door but Beata shook her head.

'Stay here,' she said.

'You won't let me in?'

'No. Any plane in particular? Or the whole lot?'

'The whole lot.'

Still nursing the baby, Beata disappeared inside with the bagged rabbit, closing the door with one foot. Minutes passed. Nehmann wanted to know more about the property, whether they'd swum in the lake, how cold it got in winter, but Messner didn't seem to hear him. Instead, he was staring at a corner of the front garden where clumps of daffodils softened a little area of raised earth. On top, Nehmann thought he could make out a makeshift wooden cross.

When Beata finally opened the door again, she was carrying a bulging pillow slip. Of the baby and the rabbit there was no sign.

'Seven.' She gave Messner the pillow slip. 'I counted them.'

'And the red triplane?'

'That's there, too.' For the first time, a genuine smile. 'We'll call the rabbit *Schnurrhaar*. What do you think?'

Schnurrhaar meant 'whiskers'. Messner stared at her for a long moment and for the first time it occurred to Nehmann that he might want a little privacy. He handed the dead chicken over and stepped back towards the gate. At the airfield he'd got the impression that the rabbit had been offered in exchange for the lift out to Wannsee but having met Beata he decided that it deserved a good home. A little walk, he thought. A chance to size up the rest of the neighbourhood.

Out on the pavement he turned to wave goodbye, but the front door was already closed again, Beata gone, and Messner's tall figure was striding down the path towards him.

At the kerbside, Messner carefully stowed the pillow slip on the back seat of the car and told Nehmann to get in the front. Nehmann didn't move. He wanted to know what was so special about the stands of white daffodils in the corner of the front garden, and the little mound of earth surmounted with a cross.

'Where?' The question appeared to take Messner by surprise.

'There.' Nehmann took him by the arm and pointed out the daffodils. Messner stared at them again. Then he frowned.

'We kept a rabbit in the early days,' he grunted. 'And that's where we buried her when she died.'

Nehmann nodded. He thought he understood.

'This rabbit had a name?'

'Of course.'

'*Schnurrhaar?*'

'*Ja.*'

*

With Messner at the wheel they drove back to the airfield. Nehmann was good with difficult people. One of the reasons he'd won Goebbels' favour was his talent for getting inside other people's heads, having a good look round and then stealing away with whatever took his fancy. This talent for breaking and entering had served him well in assignment after assignment, as well as with a small army of women, but in the shape of this mutilated air ace he knew he'd met a special challenge. The man was so unpredictable, silent one minute, terse the next, then offering sudden unexpected moments of near-intimacy.

Take the nest of toy aeroplanes on the back seat. They'd skirted Berlin and were barely ten minutes away from the airfield where Messner's Me-110 had been refuelled for the return flight to the Crimea, but a queue of traffic had lengthened behind a farm cart and everyone was travelling at the speed of the horse.

Nehmann, aware of Messner's impatience at the wheel, asked about the model aircraft. Was he young when he'd put these things together?

'I was seven. Just.'

'And you knew how to do it?'

'Of course. Every child wants to be a bird. Wood. Glue. Time. That's all it took.'

His face contorted at the memory and it took Nehmann a moment or two before he realised he was looking at a smile.

'Your father was a flier?'

'My father was a drunk. We lived in Hamburg, an old house, freezing cold. The place had been in the family forever but my father was hopeless with money, and with everything else as far as I remember. Evenings and weekends, it paid to lock yourself away because he could be violent, too, so you had to have something to do.'

'Planes.'

'Indeed. My mother used to cut photos out of magazines. Those little Fokker monoplanes. Big Gotha trainers. A Junkers float plane, way ahead of its time. Once my father bought a medal from a man he met in a *Bierkeller*. He gave it to me for Christmas. He said it was really valuable but it turned out to be a cheap copy. Not that it mattered. I wore it day and night for the rest of the winter. My own campaign medal. *Pour le Mérite*.' He barked with laughter. 'Bravery in the face of impossible domestic odds.'

The queue of traffic had come to a halt. Nehmann twisted in his seat and reached for the pillow slip.

'Do you mind if I take a look?'

'Go ahead. Should I be flattered?'

Nehmann didn't answer. One by one he fetched the toy aircraft out. Each one was a work of art, neatly put together, beautifully painted. No wonder he'd asked for them back.

'You were really seven?'

'*Ja*, to begin with. They came in pieces. All you had to do was glue them together. After a while I had a flight, then a squadron, then a whole wing. As a kid you can invent any fantasy you like.' He nodded down at Nehmann's lap. 'They were mine.'

'But you turned it into real life? Later?'

'Yes.'

'And now?'

'It's still a fantasy. Except in real life there's usually someone trying to kill you.'

'I meant the models. They're beautiful. You'll take them back to the east?'

'Yes, they'll keep me company. All except one.'

39

One? Nehmann looked down at the spread on aircraft on his lap, then asked for a clue.

'A clue?' Messner looked briefly amused. 'The best things in life always come in threes. Think about it, *ja*?'

Nehmann nodded. Then he remembered Messner's query on the doorstep back at Wannsee. His fingers crabbed towards a tiny Fokker triplane, painted a fierce red.

'This one?'

'*Ja*. And you know why? Because that one belonged to the Red Baron. Manfred von Richthofen? You've heard of him? I work now for his cousin, Wolfram. Another legend.'

'You're giving it to him? This is some kind of present?'

'No. Better than that.'

The traffic was on the move again, faster this time, and Nehmann glimpsed the back of the farmer's cart disappearing into a field of potatoes. He still had the Fokker, the fuselage gripped lightly between his thumb and forefinger, and when Messner suggested he tried a loop or two, he held it at arm's length, the tiny fighter silhouetted against the brightness of the sun through the windscreen.

Ahead lay the airfield at Schönwalde. Messner wanted to finish his story. Very recently he'd flown a *Wehrmacht Oberst* on a recce over the Caucasus. The *Oberst* had a regiment of mountain troops under his command and he wanted to take a look at some of the bigger peaks.

'The highest is Mount Elbrus: 5,633 metres. It's cold at that height, very thin air, but he was pleased with what he saw. When the sun's out, the glaciers glow green as well as white. He was looking for a route to the summit and he found one.'

'He's going to climb it?'

'*Ja.*'

'When?'

'In the summer. After we've dealt with Sevastopol. Imagine a single flag up there on the very top. Can you picture that? *Das Hakenkreuz?* Up there among the ice fields?'

Das Hakenkreuz. The swastika flag. Scarlet and white and black against the surrounding peaks. Irresistible, Nehmann thought. A perfect coda after all that spilled Soviet blood.

'And this?' He was looking at the tiny triplane.

'I'll give it to the *Oberst*. He's agreed to find a place for it on top of the mountain.'

'Why?'

'Because this was the Red Baron's plane.' That strange rictus smile again. 'And his cousin is winning the war in the south.'

4

BERLIN, 22 MAY 1942

Nehmann was back at the Promi an hour ahead of his deadline for the edit. He'd delivered Messner to his Me-110, helping him stow the collection of model aircraft below the spare seat in the cockpit. A final handshake, a gruff farewell and *Oberstleutnant* Messner was gone. Watching the tiny black speck climbing away towards a line of distant clouds in the east, Nehmann wondered what lay in store for this solitary man. Rarely had he met anyone so damaged, both inside and out.

At the Promi, the film Nehmann had delivered earlier had already been developed. The Ministry's three editing suites were in the basement of the building, dark, cell-like rooms perfectly suited for the editors to work their magic on the footage from the Kerch Peninsula.

In charge this afternoon was a youngish Rhinelander called Erich, who'd learned his trade at the Ufa newsreel studios across town. He knew instinctively how to tell a story onscreen, weaving that subtle mix of interview and action shots, telling close-ups and lingering pans across the ravaged landscapes of Hitler's wars, and his work had caught Goebbels' eye within weeks of his arrival at Ufa.

Now, he was running yet another roll of rushes on the editing table, pausing to mark up a series of cutaways with his yellow chinagraph pencil. Already a line of these telling little vignettes hung over the big green bin beside the editing table, glimpses of yet another *Wehrmacht* triumph that would find their way into cinema after cinema across the Reich.

'Here, Werner. Look at this.' Erich rolled the spare chair in front of the editing table. 'Thank fuck we're not Russian, eh?'

Werner took the proffered seat and found himself gazing at a line of Soviet tanks, two of which were ablaze. Crewmen were scrambling out of the closest turret, their hands already raised, only to be scythed down by German bullets. More corpses ringed a neighbouring tank.

Nehmann shook his head. He knew that none of this material would ever bother German domestic audiences who preferred to think of their kinsmen as gallant, fearless, and – above all – sternly compassionate. The Minister, on the other hand, liked nothing better than a taste of the war's darker side. Victory, he often said, would in the end go to the side which showed the least mercy. Which was presumably why Erich was saving these little treats for a personal viewing.

Goebbels turned up nearly an hour later. He favoured Nehmann with a brief nod, clapped Erich on the shoulder and demanded a look at progress to date. Erich had just completed an overlength rough cut, a provisional assembly of shots which would end the half-hour newsreel covering the entire Kerch campaign. As yet there was no soundtrack, but the moment the grainy black and white images appeared on the tiny screen Goebbels bent forward, eager, excited, Hitler's favourite alchemist when it came to transforming the base

43

metal of live combat into an experience cinema audiences would never forget.

The rough cut began with cockpit footage from a diving Stuka, the grey steppe resolving itself into columns of Soviet armour and the hunched infantry that followed every tank. This tableau was filling the screen before the pilot hauled back on the controls, and the steppe was suddenly flattened at an alarming angle as the Stuka banked and pulled out of the dive. At this point, Erich had cut to footage shot from ground level, the aircraft climbing again and one of its two bombs exploding in a fountain of earth among the luckless Soviet troops. Then, in the blink of an eye, came a third angle, and yet another explosion, a direct hit this time on the tank itself.

Nehmann had seen enough of Erich's editing to know that this was sleight of hand, a conjuring trick, three separate incidents artfully compressed into one, but what really fascinated him was Goebbels. He, too, understood the dark arts of newsreel compilation yet he was like a child watching his favourite magician. He'd suspended disbelief. He had total faith in every frame. And in his bones he knew that what worked for him would work for millions of fellow Germans.

Recently, in a fawning article in *Völkischer Beobachter*, a once-honest Berlin journalist had described Goebbels as 'the Heinz Guderian of mass propaganda'. Guderian was the architect of blitzkrieg, the battlefield genius who'd perfected the lightning uppercuts that had knocked out nation after nation across Western Europe. Even Nehmann had to admit that there was some merit in the comparison and, watching Goebbels now, as Erich's next sequence pictured a wave of Heinkels, wingtip to wingtip, it was impossible not to share the raw power of these images. After a close-up of the pilot, lantern-jawed, a camera inside the belly of the plane caught the slow, lazy descent of yet another stick of bombs. Then came the wide shot, ground level, seconds later as each of these parcels of high explosive erupted in a storm of torn metal and warm enemy flesh.

At the end of the rough cut the screen went blank and there was a moment of total silence before the Minister sat back and clapped his hands in a gesture of both delight and approval. On these occasions he never made notes, but his recall was perfect. He'd prefer a more brutal cut between this sequence and that. Erich was to be careful about the sheer length of a particular pan. But, overall, once he'd laid the sound effects against the action and thought hard about music, the effect would be mesmeric.

'Try *Tannhäuser*,' he said, 'for that sequence at the very end.' He turned to Nehmann and got to his feet. 'Come.' He nodded towards the door. 'Ten minutes of your precious time?'

*

They talked in Goebbels' office on the first floor. Through a single window Nehmann could see the three secretaries who policed his ever-expanding empire. Goebbels certainly inspired a degree of loyalty but Nehmann knew it was based largely on fear. Over the past few weeks, everyone agreed that the Minister had become more and more unreasonable, barking at minions and quick to assign blame when a word or two of encouragement or at least understanding might have been wiser. Just now, though, much to Nehmann's surprise, he was almost gleeful.

'Wolfram von Richthofen dined with the Führer last night,' he announced. 'Alone.'

'Meaning?'

'Meaning that the Fat One is shitting his pants.' He nodded at the phone. 'He called earlier. I think he might have been drinking. He said he had no choice but to take this insult personally. Richthofen is *Luftwaffe*, of course. He's working miracles down in the Crimea, as we all know, and nothing makes the Führer happier than a man who delivers. That's why Richthofen has personal access. That's why Hitler gives him everything he asks for. The Fat One has at last understood that. But it's far, far too late.'

The Fat One was Hermann Goering, father of the *Luftwaffe*. His downfall, according to Goebbels, began at Dunkirk when he failed to bomb the British Army into oblivion, and continued over the following months when the RAF wrecked Hitler's plan for landings along the English Channel coast. Since then, he'd retreated to his lavish new ministry and sulked, testing Hitler's patience to its limits.

'And now Richthofen,' Goebbels repeated. 'If this was a novel, I wouldn't change a sentence.'

'You think he's in trouble?'

'I think he's fucked. What he wants is a big fat slice of Richthofen's glory, but he knows there isn't a chance in hell. Good things happen in the *Luftwaffe* in spite of the Fat One, not because of him. Very troubling...and you know why? Because vanity and disappointment never mix. Fucked. And fucked good.'

Nehmann could only nod in mute agreement. Lately he'd become a sounding board for Goebbels' wilder outbursts, and it was becoming tiresome. Hitler quietly encouraged murderous turf wars among his courtiers but Nehmann was beginning to resent getting caught in the crossfire.

'Any ideas?' Goebbels was watching him carefully.

'About what, Minister?'

'Us. This.' Goebbels' gesture took in his own office and the secretaries beyond. 'The Fat One is wounded. Ribbentrop needs putting out of his misery. Hess has gone mad and fled. We have the advantage, Nehmann. The stars are shining down upon us. Thanks to people like Richthofen and Manstein, we could be sitting on a great deal of oil within months. That, believe me, will transform everything. Hitler knows it. Stalin knows it. Roosevelt knows it. Even that drunkard Churchill knows it. So now is the moment to cash in on all that glory. Something inventive. Some initiative that will really bring it home to people. The winter was hard. The food situation is a real problem. Fuel is even worse. The home front is where this war will really be lost or won. The people deserve a bit of good news. And the summer is exactly the right time to let them have it. So...' he tapped his desk '...any ideas?'

Nehmann took his time. Goebbels, in common with a number of other Nazi chieftains, loved the sound of his own voice but for the last minute or so Nehmann had been paying special attention. Not simply because his lord and master was putting him on the spot but because, thanks to Georg Messner, he realised he had exactly the answer the little dwarf was after.

'How much do you know about Mount Elbrus?' he asked.

5

BERLIN, SATURDAY 18 JULY 1942

The fortress at Sevastopol fell to Manstein's 11th Army on 1 July 1942. An ecstatic Führer received the news at the Wolf's Lair, his headquarters in East Prussia. Four weeks of ceaseless bombardment and heavy fighting had reduced whole areas of the fortifications to rubble, killed tens of thousands of Soviet troops and humiliated Stalin. The threat to German armies in the south had ceased to exist and the road to the oil fields lay open. That very same day, by radio message, Hitler promoted Manstein to *Generalfeldmarschall*, news that left a sour taste in the mouth of *Generaloberst* Wolfram von Richthofen.

Two and a half weeks later, Werner Nehmann was summoned to the Ministry of Propaganda. Lately, Goebbels had been sleeping especially badly and it showed. The pools of darkness around his eyes were deeper than ever. He occupied one of two armchairs in the office and he had one leg crossed over the other. If his foot was beating time with his pulse, Nehmann thought, then the Minister needed medical attention.

Goebbels told him to shut the door and pull up the other chair.

'Richthofen,' he said, 'has been appeased. The Führer announced his promotion this morning. Chief of *Luftflotte 4*. He flies to Mariupol tomorrow morning to take charge. Rostov should be ours within the week. You want to guess how much operational territory Richthofen now controls? Think of the Reich and treble it. Think Napoleon with wings.'

Nehmann did his best. It was an awkward image.

'And Mount Elbrus?' he asked. 'Messner's little triplane?'

'I talked to Manstein. A detachment of one of his Mountain divisions will be on the summit in weeks before they push on down towards the Black Sea. You were right; it's the tallest peak in Europe. Plant the war flag on the top and you're looking at an image we'll be sending round the world. My congratulations, Nehmann, a brilliant concept on your part. Messner's little triplane, as well? Consider it done.'

The prospect of yet another propaganda coup seemed to brighten the Minister's mood. Then his hand strayed to a pile of paperwork on the carpet beside his chair and he picked up the top document before tossing it aside.

'Children, Nehmann, everywhere. Novices, incompetents, grains of sand in the machine. You'll know about the Ministry for the East. A sensible idea. But put someone like that lunatic Rosenberg in charge and we end up with the Ministry of Chaos. All these people have the same problem. With every particle of good news, every next victory, they think the war's over. They think we've won. These clowns should learn to read a map. Russia isn't small. The winters are evil. We have a very long way to go. And then you get someone like von Choltitz. He did well at Sevastopol. Everyone did well at Sevastopol. But who in his right mind pays tribute to the Bolsheviks for their "fighting spirit"? Am I the only one who has to take this up with the Führer? The Ivans, like most animals, have a primitive survival instinct. Confusing that with courage, with something you respect, is a simpleton's error.'

The bobbing foot, for a second or two, was still. When a secretary tapped lightly on the door, Goebbels waved her away. Then he rearranged his legs and leaned forward, his elbows on his knees. It was an intimate gesture, increasingly rare, and Nehmann wondered what was coming next.

'Loneliness, Nehmann. Have you ever felt that? Has it ever crept into that life of yours? Have you ever woken up one morning, regardless of who might be lying beside you, and realised just how alone you are?' He paused a moment, his eyes holding Nehmann's gaze, his voice soft. 'You're shaking your head. Am I surprised? No. You're resilient, Nehmann. You come from the toughest stock and I admire that. You're also the master of adaptation, of camouflage, of hiding your real self away, and I admire that, too. We make a good team, Nehmann, and in times like these that knowledge can keep a man afloat.'

Nehmann was astonished. More to the point, he was also extremely wary. Over the years that he'd known him, he'd recognised that Goebbels was far less sure of himself than he liked other people to believe. You could read the clues on his face, in the pallor of his skin, in the occasional eruptions of eczema, in unguarded moments when his whole body seemed to sag. At times like these, it paid to listen very hard because intimacy was always the prelude to something else. Support in some arcane turf war. Sympathy over the unceasing workload here in the Promi. Or, it seemed in this case, a favour.

'Hedvika, Nehmann. Your little Czech *coquette*. I know about the business in Italy. The spoils of war, Nehmann. Here today, gone tomorrow. Am I right?'

'Yes.'

'Have you seen her lately? Talked on the phone, perhaps? Exchanged billets-doux?'

'No.'

'But you could. The tingle, the electricity, is still there. Am I right?'

'On my part?'

'Yes.'

'Then the answer has to be no. On hers? I've no way of finding out.'

'Really? Then allow me to tell you. The film director's name is Emilio. He's tall, and good-looking and quite able in his way, but he's also a man who can't pass a mirror. Vanity, Nehmann, is too small a word. He's in love with himself and he's also hopeless in bed. Your *Coquette* is used to proper rations. Emilio offers nothing but crumbs. Does she regret those nights in the Wilhelmstrasse? She does, but only because they're over.' A chilly smile. 'Am I making sense, Nehmann?'

Nehmann said nothing for a moment. Then he stirred.

'A man moves on,' he said.

'Of course, and what a talent she has, what breadth of taste. Schubert impromptus? Kurt Weill? Just a little hint of Negro music on Friday nights when the clientele at that club of hers seem in the mood? My congratulations, Nehmann. I've seen the photos. As ever, you have impeccable taste and – to be frank – your courage has never been an issue. Just one question, do you mind?'

'Of course not.'

'Are *both* her parents Isidors?'

Isidor was Promi-code for Jewish. Nehmann, who should have seen this coming, shook his head.

'Goyim,' he said.

'You know that?'

'Yes.'

'How?'

'Because she told me. Her father hated Jews and priests alike. Her mother is a devout Catholic.'

'Paperwork? Birth certificates? Dull, I know, but it might pay to take a precaution or two.'

'In case...?'

'In case you fall in love with her, Nehmann. In or out of bed, life is a battle. I'm your friend, your *Kamerad*, your brother-in-arms. Maria's a pretty name. I don't want to see either of you hurt. And I want you to believe that.'

'I'm flattered.'

'Don't be. There's also another matter, I'm afraid equally delicate. You can keep a confidence, Nehmann?'

'Of course.'

'Good' – the smile again – 'because we'll need to trust each other.'

At this point there came another delicate knock at the door. Birgit, one of the secretaries, reminded the Minister that he had an important visitor waiting downstairs. Goebbels waved the appointment aside. He'd attend to matters when he was ready. Birgit nodded and withdrew.

'I want to talk about Baarova.' Goebbels had turned back to Nehmann. 'My Lida. You have time, Nehmann?'

'Of course.'

Another interruption, this time a phone call. Watching Goebbels' face, Nehmann sensed it was someone important. The Minister tapped his watch, mouthed an apology. Give me time, please. Have patience.

Nehmann nodded. He knew a lot about Baarova, Indeed, half the nation did, partly because she'd been a leading Czech actress in countless movies, but mainly because Goebbels had made no secret of the fact that she'd become his mistress. Before the war they appeared together in public on countless occasions. They shared an extensive love nest in the woods north of Berlin. Then came the moment when Herr Goebbels, patriarch and husband, had proposed a *ménage à trois*, hoisting his mistress into the very middle of one of the Reich's showpiece families.

Magda Goebbels had been unimpressed by the proposition but what had truly shaken her husband was the wrath of Adolf Hitler. The Führer had a great deal of time for Frau Goebbels and doted on the three children, and when he told Goebbels that his affair with the Czech actress had to end, Goebbels had no choice in the matter.

The final reel in this heartfelt little romance was far from pretty. Goebbels worshipped his Führer. Hitler, as far as he was concerned, was the voice of providence, God's presence on earth. And so he summoned Baarova to tell her that their life together was over. Days later, at Goebbels prompting, Berlin's Chief of Police forbade her to apply for any other roles in German cinema.

With her private life and her professional career in ruins, Baarova attended the premiere of her latest – and last – German film. The movie was called *Der Spieler*, The Gambler, an adaptation of Dostoyevsky's novel. Paid thugs wrecked the screening. Their jeers and abuse drove Baarova from the theatre and ended the movie's public run before it had even begun. Hounded by the Gestapo, Lida Baarova had a nervous breakdown and fled to her native Prague.

Nehmann knew all of this, as did most of Germany, but Goebbels' phone call was coming to an end now and it turned out that there was a great deal more to the story.

'The Führer.' Goebbels gestured at the phone. 'His needs are many. As are mine.'

Nehmann didn't know quite what to make of this.

'Baarova?' he ventured.

'Indeed, my friend. Fate has dealt us both a poor hand. In life you seldom get a second chance, but I see no point in not trying. We Germans should make more room in our lives for the possibility of forgiveness. It can happen, Nehmann, and if it does it can be sublime. My wife will never forgive. My Lida? Here—'

From a desk drawer he produced a white envelope, heavily sealed, and gave it to Nehmann. It contained, he said, a letter for Lida Baarova.

'You're apologising?' Nehmann was staring at the envelope.

'I'm explaining. It may be the same thing.'

'But to what end? Why now?'

'Why now?' Goebbels stared down at him. 'Because I miss her.'

'And?'

'I don't know. Would I like to see her again? Of course I would. Would I like her back in my bed? In my heart? Yes, again yes. Look at me, Nehmann. Tell me I'm right. Tell me this is what must happen.'

'I'm telling you you're crazy. This is madness.'

'I know. But does that make any difference? You know me, Nehmann. You know the way I am. Be honest. A man is a man. There are things he has to do. This is one of them.'

'Get in touch with her again?'

'Make sure she knows the truth.'

'About what happened?'

'About me.'

Nehmann was looking at the envelope, weighing it in his hand. Three sheets of paper, he thought. At least. Then his eyes were back on Goebbels.

'You know where she is?'

'In Italy. Rome, I think.'

'You have an address?'

'No' – he'd put a hand on Nehmann's shoulder – 'but your *Coquette* does.'

*

Nehmann left the Promi nearly an hour later. He owed Goebbels two articles. They were both confections pitched at the outer edges of credibility, but they'd have Nehmann's trademark brio which was, after all, what Goebbels seemed to value. He'd done all the interviews for the first and most of them for the second, but the deadline was still a couple of days away and just now he needed to think.

Ten minutes in the late afternoon sunshine took him back to Guram's apartment. An unmarked van was parked illegally outside and Nehmann was wondering how soon before the authorities arrived. He was still on the pavement trying to find his key for the door when he heard a voice behind him.

'Herr Nehmann?'

He turned around. Three men were standing beside the van. Nehmann recognised the black uniform of the Ukrainian Auxiliary Police, drafted in to help Berlin's regular force.

The taller of the two men stepped forward.

'With the compliments of Graf von Helldorf.' He nodded back towards the van. 'Which floor?'

For a moment nonplussed, Nehmann hadn't got an answer. Then he remembered. Von Helldorf was Berlin's Chief of Police. More importantly, he was hand in glove with Goebbels. A couple of days ago Nehmann had been looking for a grand piano and had mentioned it in conversation on the phone. Goebbels told him to call off the search. The matter, he said, would be resolved. And so here he was, bareheaded on a Berlin street, watching three burly Ukrainians wrestling the body of a grand piano out of the back of the van. The legs, it seemed, would follow.

Nehmann opened the main door of the apartment block and stood aside as the policemen hauled the piano up the first two flights of stairs. Nehmann had left the windows open in the apartment itself and the moment he stepped inside he could smell the frangipani that Maria was cultivating on the sill.

'Just there.' He indicated a patch of carpet in the middle of the room. A Steinway, he thought. Perfect.

Two of the men returned to the street to fetch the legs and the stool. The officer in charge had produced a notebook.

'One box of Chablis. Five of claret. Ten of champagne.' He looked up. 'Agreed?'

'This is for the piano?'

'For the boss. Another box of champagne for the workers would be thoughtful.'

Nehmann nodded. He'd no idea what the barter rate for a grand piano might be but Guram's cellar was extensive.

'My pleasure,' he said. 'Where does the piano come from?'

'House clearance.'

'It belonged to an Isidor?'

'Of course,' he smirked. 'We'll be going back for the rest later.'

The men returned with the legs and the piano stool. Once the Steinway was in one piece again, Nehmann cleared a space against the back wall, beyond the reach of the sunshine. Then he led the way to the closet where Guram kept his wine. Seventeen boxes. Just over a hundred bottles. For a grand piano? Nothing.

The officer in charge was the last to leave. His men were still ferrying the boxes down to the street.

'You play?' He nodded at the piano.

'Of course.' Nehmann patted him on the shoulder. 'Why else would a man part with so much champagne?'

In truth, Nehmann was a stranger to the keyboard. The piano was a gift for Maria. Nehmann went across to the window. The Ukrainians had levered open one of the wooden boxes there on the street and were helping themselves to a couple of bottles each. He shook his head and then glanced back at the piano. Week by week, Berlin was emptying of Jews but if you looked the other way and asked no questions you'd hardly notice. Just another vacated apartment, stuffed to the brim with a lifetime's possessions. Just another dusty space where a grand piano had once been.

Goebbels had another term for these looted treasures. He regarded them as rightful tribute for the master race, payback for centuries of usury. A Jew, he'd once told Nehmann, had the soul of a banker and the conscience of a thief. Only National Socialists knew how to deal with such vermin.

Conscience? Nehmann settled at the piano, deep in thought. Since the last days of peace had brought him to Berlin, he'd been aware of the special place he'd won for himself in Goebbels' boiling wake. Articles he'd published in the handful of independent publications to survive the Party's chokehold had caught the attention of the Minister for Propaganda. He'd liked Nehmann's tone of voice, the way he let his imagination off the leash, even his adopted name. Mikhail Magalashvili would have carried a troubling gust of Slavdom in certain quarters of the Reich. Werner Nehmann – bold, simple, declamatory – was near-perfect.

So far, so good. Goebbels had always been the prisoner of his own schedule, forever criss-crossing the country to roar at his millions of followers, but somehow he'd managed to find the time and the private space to build a relationship with the little Georgian. There was more than a decade between them, but the age difference had never seemed to matter. They both took liberties with the truth. They both loved the company of women. And they were both happy to push their own luck to breaking point. Most important of all, at a level of government where trust and friendship carried serious risks, Nehmann's company became not only welcome but invaluable.

Sounding board? Drinking companion? Raconteur? Nehmann was never quite sure of his precise role in this relationship but as the war began in earnest, and the men in field grey helped themselves to country after country across Western Europe, the dizzying series of victories felt like a party without end. Nehmann had loved this interlude, wild, full of opportunities, ungoverned by anything but a crushing workload and a raging thirst, but as that first proper winter came and went, and the attention of the Greater Reich turned towards the east, the mood had become a little more sombre.

Sevastopol had certainly fallen, and there seemed no reason why the oil wells beyond the Caucasus wouldn't soon be in German hands, but Moscow and Leningrad were still offering stubborn resistance and the sheer size of the Soviet Union defied the gods of resupply. Hitler's appetite for yet more conquest, yet more territory, was insatiable. Yet the tanks and the aircraft were running out of fuel and ten thousand horses needed more fodder than anyone had ever suspected. And now, remember, it was still summer.

Was this why Goebbels had launched this afternoon's conversation? With that acute intelligence of his, could he sense events running out of control?

Nehmann thought it more than possible. The Goebbels he knew better than most men was extremely thin-skinned. He lived on his nerves. He wanted, needed, the approbation of others. He lived for praise, for the constant assurance that he was the mastermind behind everything true and necessary and worthwhile that drove the resurgent Germany forward. A handful of men, all of them visionaries, had shaken the recumbent nation awake, but the Minister of Propaganda – in his own eyes – was the only one with the truly magical touch. *Deutschland erwache!* – Germany awake! – was the chant that launched a thousand newsreels. And all of them, one way or another, were the work of Joseph Goebbels.

And yet the man was lonely. And forlorn. And just occasionally lost. And on these occasions, like this afternoon, he had only one name on his lips.

Lida Baarova.

*

Maria arrived within the hour. It was early evening by now, but she didn't have to be at work until nine o'clock and Moabit was only half an hour away on the tram. One of her fellow musicians at the club owned part shares in an allotment in Charlottenburg, and she had a basket half full of fruit.

'Cherries,' she said, 'and blackcurrants, and some early apples at the bottom.'

She was standing in the middle of the room, the last of the sunshine caught in the thickness of her hair. She'd yet to notice the piano.

'And that' – Nehmann nodded at it – 'is for you.' He helped himself to a cherry. 'Fair exchange?'

She glanced round, then looked properly. She wanted to know what it was doing here, where it came from. She was like a child, tiny gasps of surprise and delight.

'Really?' She'd settled on the stool, already flexing her fingers. 'For me?'

'Yes.'

'Why?'

'It doesn't matter.'

'But it does. This is a Steinway. You don't understand. They cost a fortune. Where did you get it?'

Nehmann mumbled something about a specialist shop off the Ku'damm. It was a lie, of course, but he didn't think it would matter.

'Just play something,' he said. 'For me.'

She held his gaze for a moment, visibly troubled, then inched the stool a little closer to the keyboard and played a chord or two.

'They tuned it for you?'

'I didn't ask. What do you think?'

'Not bad. I have a tuning fork at home. I'll bring it tomorrow. You have some wine? I'd like that.'

Nehmann fetched a bottle of claret from the closet, making a mental note to account for the missing cases. By the time he'd drawn the cork and returned to the lounge with a couple of glasses, she was poised to begin.

'Schubert,' she said. 'An impromptu. You want to know the number?'

'No, thanks.'

'It's number three. If you don't like it, I can play something else.' She accepted the glass and took a tiny sip.

Nehmann made himself comfortable on the sofa and asked her to start. At the club in Moabit, and now here, she always seemed to defer to the music, barely moving on the stool, using her hands and feet to tease out the composer's intentions, an almost invisible presence on the margins of the performance. Nehmann, who had become used to a degree of showiness in his women, loved this about her. Listen to the music, she seemed to be telling him, because I'm only here to do its bidding. So modest. So *respectful*.

He leaned back, half closing his eyes, enjoying the last warmth of the sun on his face. The impromptu, like the wine and the sunshine, seemed to settle deep within him. After the opening – reflective, plangent – came a ripple of something a little more urgent, and he watched her as she caught the rhythm, rode the wave with the faintest backwards motion of her head, then stilled it again. When she'd finished, he asked her what 'impromptu' meant.

'It means improvised. It means the composer's making it up as he goes along. It means free form. It's a joke, of course, but in good taste. The piece is perfect. Schubert thought hard about every note. Everything is there for a reason. You liked it?'

'Very much.'

'And this?'

She began to play a jazz piece Nehmann had first heard barely weeks ago when he'd gone down to the club on the recommendation of one of the secretaries from the Promi. Very pretty girl, she'd warned him. And she'd been right.

Nehmann got to his feet and fetched the bottle. When he offered her more, she shook her head. Then, in the middle of a deeply promising riff, she stopped playing.

'Where did it really come from?' She was looking at the piano.

'I told you. Little place off the Ku'damm.'

'Not true. There are no little places off the Ku'damm. Not with room for something like this.'

'Does it matter?'

'Of course it does. It matters that I know where it came from. And it matters even more that you tell me the truth.'

Nehmann nodded, recharged his own glass, remained silent.

'You're not going to tell me?' She was frowning now.

'No.'

'You don't know?'

'I think I can guess.'

'Then tell me.'

'Why? Would it make a difference?'

'To what? To me sitting here playing it? Or to us?'

Us. Nehmann acknowledged the word with a smile. So far he'd told her nothing about the Promi. About the life he led feeding the propaganda machine. About the lengths he'd happily go to, gleefully twisting the truth in the service of God knows what. Instead, he'd told her about growing up in the mountains back home in Georgia, about the father who'd left the family to fend for itself, and about the uncle who'd owned the abattoir in Svengati, and had insisted that his little cast-off nephew become a butcher. His uncle, he told Maria, had paid him well. He'd hated butchery but by the time he was seventeen, he'd saved enough to take the bus out of the mountains. He'd made his way first to Istanbul, and then to Paris, and there he'd discovered a talent for writing that began to shape the rest of his young life. Language, he said, had become his friend, his passion. And on good weeks, when he was lucky, it even paid a bill or two.

Listening to these stories of his, half true, half not, Maria had shown endless patience and what he liked to believe was a genuine delight, but the more he got to know her, the more he sensed a fellow traveller. She guarded her own secrets with a playful deftness he rather admired. One day, if he was lucky, she might tell him a great deal more but for now she seemed happy to enjoy his versions of what might, or might not, have happened. Which, in the light of her next question, was deeply ironic.

'I met someone last night who knows you,' she said. 'She was in the club with her boyfriend. They bought me a drink. We talked.'

'She has a name? This person?'

'Birgit. She works in the Promi and when I mentioned the apartment, she said she knew it.'

Nehmann was staring up at the ceiling. The gods of coincidence had always treated him gently. Until now.

'And what did she tell you?'

'She told me you work for Goebbels. Is that true?'

'Yes.'

'What do you do for him?'

'I lie.'

She nodded, unsurprised, and then one hand reached for the keyboard again. A single chord. Dark. Ominous. Slightly out of tune.

'And the piano?'

'It probably came from a Jewish family.'

'At a fair price?'

'I doubt it.'

She turned to look at him. Then she smiled and beckoned him closer.

'There.' She kissed him on the lips. 'Not so painful, after all.'

6

VENICE, 9 AUGUST 1942

It took Werner Nehmann nearly three weeks to track down his *Coquette*. A telephone call to the Cinecittà film studios in Rome confirmed that Hedvika had recently finished a movie under director Emilio Brambilla and was expected back from a well-earned vacation any day now. Nehmann left his name, and a hint that Hedvika might welcome a conversation, and waited for the phone to ring.

When nothing happened, he tried again. This time he got through to an executive in the publicity department who'd recently read an article of Nehmann's in *Das Reich*. The piece, typically playful, had made her laugh. Nehmann had set out to ponder the current appetite in both dictatorships for show and spectacle, for huge parades, for wardrobes of fancy costumes, and for the public's apparent willingness to go along with this pantomime. As always, Nehmann had trodden the high wire between treason and entertainment with immense panache, though his first draft, submitted to the Minister, had drawn a caustic response. 'Publish this shit,' Goebbels had scribbled in green ink, 'and we'll both end up in the KZ.'

Nehmann, of course, had no intention of getting anywhere near a concentration camp and half an hour in the Minister's office, late at night, had produced a second draft, and then a third. This was the version, carefully salted with dutiful nods to the many glories of the Reich, that had landed on the publicity executive's lap.

'I was at the dentist,' she explained on the phone. 'It made perfect reading.'

Nehmann mentioned Hedvika.

'You know her well?' she asked.

'Very.'

'How well?'

'Ask her. That woman never lies and neither do I.'

'I don't believe you,' she laughed. 'Everyone lies, all the time.'

'OK, so try this. Tell her the trick really works.'

'What trick?'

'Levitation. Just say it. Levitation. That's all you need.' He paused. 'So, where is she?'

'On vacation. I thought you knew.'

'I did. How long a holiday does she need?'

'It's complicated. You know about Emilio? I'm guessing you probably do. He threw her off the set last week as soon as she'd done her final scene.'

'Am I allowed to ask why?'

'I'm sure you can guess. Who gets to see her in close-up? Who controls her lighting? Who makes her look truly beautiful?'

'The cameraman.'

'You're right. And his services didn't end there.'

'He's with her now?'

'He's in hospital. Emilio has rough friends. You want me to talk to Hedvika? Give me your number. I'll do my best.'

Nehmann didn't have to wait long. That evening, Guram's

phone rang. Maria was playing in the club at Moabit. Nehmann lifted the receiver and waited for the long-distance crackle to recede. Finally, an Italian operator checked his name and asked him to stand by for a call.

Nehmann was sitting at the piano, newly tuned. He walked his fingers along the keyboard in a slow arpeggio, a trick that Maria had taught him. Finally came a voice he recognised.

'Hedvika?' he asked.

'Ja.'

'Where are you?'

'Venice.'

*

Next day, Nehmann took the train south. Goebbels had given him five thousand Reichsmarks two weeks ago. He'd already spent nearly four hundred on presents for Maria, but he had plenty left. The southbound express left the *Hauptbahnhof* at six minutes past nine. He changed trains at Munich and dozed through the Alps in a sleeping compartment he had to himself, woken only by a cheerful Italian customs official at the border.

Dawn found him crossing the lagoon towards the distant promise of a city he'd never seen before. He stepped into the corridor and hung out of the window, savouring the rankness of this inland sea. Already, Venice smelled of decay and corruption. Perfect.

Hedvika had given him instructions to her hotel. He was to find a vaporetto and ask for the Palazzo Grassi. Three streets away from the water, look for another tiny canal on the right. Maybe a hundred metres, a once-imposing front door with a brass plate that badly needs a polish. Alla Vite Dorata. Top-floor room with a fine view of a neighbour's yard. *Gute Reise*.

Safe journey. Nehmann didn't bother with the vaporetto. He had money in his pocket and the city at his feet. In any movie, he thought, this opening scene called for a gondola and a boatman with a half-decent voice. The dock at the railway terminus was emptier than he'd expected. Maybe it was the hour, he thought. Still barely seven in the morning.

The first gondolier he tried was a hunchback who had trouble meeting Nehmann's eyes as he gazed down from the dock. The man's face had acquired a wistful bitterness that Nehmann loved at first sight. Someone had done a startling job on the perfectly ironed whiteness of his shirt and, when Nehmann asked him for a song before embarking, he obliged with a *fortissimo* version of the 'Horst Wessel'. Nehmann blinked. The gondolier was stamping one boot, the tiny barque trembling beneath him. For just a moment, Nehmann wondered about hiring one of the other gondoliers but decided his new friend was making a point and was happy to accept a helping hand as he clambered aboard.

'Welcome to Venezia,' the gondolier said. 'I am Benito. You will be Adolf. The world is crazy, *si?*'

Nehmann, blissfully content in such company, settled on the upholstered banquette in the stern. Benito, braced on the platform behind him, handled the gondola with dismissive aplomb. Sweep after sweep of the long paddle took them away from the railway terminus towards the heart of the city. Wherever he looked, Nehmann thought, history had its feet planted deep in the murk of the Grand Canal. A frieze of houses, as perfect as a theatre set, impossibly old, impossibly crooked, impossibly beautiful. Elegant palazzos, their windows half shuttered against the brightness of the morning light. Only this morning, before leaving Berlin, Maria had warned him that Venice would be the sweetshop of his dreams. A temptress city full of impossible delights. A city that played tricks with you. A city that led you deep into a maze you simply couldn't comprehend. She'd been there herself in circumstances she might one day share but for now she just wanted him to let the city cast its spell.

'You'll have no choice.' She'd reached up to kiss him. 'Nobody has.'

She was right. They were approaching the landing stage at Palazzo Grassi. The gondola bumped gently against the rope fender and Benito reached down to help him off. The sight of a fifty Reichsmark note briefly sparked what might have been a smile.

'Take care, my friend.' Benito carefully folded the note into a pocket. 'The lady isn't as sweet as she looks.'

'Lady?'

'Venezia.'

Nehmann left the landing stage without a backward glance, aware that the city was already drawing him in. Barely metres from the water, the buildings closed around him, towering walls of windowed brick and stone, each subtly different. There was no sign of the war here, no indication that vast armies were fighting to the death, that millions of city dwellers were spending every night underground, that a family could starve without a ration card. Instead, he was looking at lines of washing hanging across the narrowness of the street, at women kneading dough in open bakeries, at flocks of starlings swooping busily over a street-corner market stall. Nehmann paused to check his bearings. A conjuring trick, he concluded. Normal life restored by sleight of hand.

He found the Alla Vite Dorata without difficulty. The building had the air of a beggar in the street, unkempt, neglected. The grey stucco was crumbling. The windows were still shuttered. He stepped back and shook his head, bewildered. Movie stars earned good money. If you'd come to Venice to spoil yourself why would you ever stay here?

Nehmann tried the door. It was locked. There was no bell, no knocker, and so he hammered on the peeling paintwork with the side of his fist. At length, he thought he heard movement inside, then the door opened and he was looking at a man in his thirties, white shirt, black trousers, bare feet. His face was heavily tanned beneath several days of stubble.

'Hedvika…?' Nehmann gestured inside.

'*Lei parla Italiano?*'

'*Nein.*'

The man looked at him a moment longer, then came a voice Nehmann recognised from the depths of the building. She was shouting something in Italian.

'That's her,' he said. 'Hedvika.'

He found her, as promised, in a bare room on the top floor. Naked from the waist up, she was sitting up in bed, stroking a fat tabby cat. Nehmann settled at once on the side of the bed. He knew about cats.

'She's got a problem with her eye,' he said at once. 'Try a weak vinegar solution. She'll hate it but it might do the trick.'

'He,' she said. 'He's a he. He fights all night and comes back for attention. Sometimes it's an eye. Sometimes other places.

There isn't enough vinegar in this city to make him better. He lives to fight. Sometimes I think he must be German.'

Nehmann wanted to know about this pension of hers. With all those movies behind her, why end up in a dump like this?

The word 'pension' amused her. The house, she said, belonged to a friend of hers. He'd bought it before the war as an investment and one day he'd come back and tidy things up, but for now that was difficult.

'He's in hospital, your friend?'

'He is.' She looked surprised. 'How did you know?'

Nehmann shook his head. Wouldn't say. Instead, he asked about the man downstairs.

'He's Carlo's brother, Fabio. Not bad, but Carlo's twice the man. Fabio's been here for a while. He thinks the war's stupid and he's got no time for dying.'

'He's in hiding?'

'He doesn't go out much.' She got rid of the cat and moved to the side of the bed. Then she asked Nehmann to shut the door. 'A fuck might be nice.' She smiled. 'If you're offering.'

*

Later, she took him to lunch at a trattoria on the Piazza San Marco. The exchange rate between the lira and the Reichsmark was very good just now and she had more money than she could possibly spend.

'So, fifty Reichsmarks…?' Nehmann asked.

'A fortune. Fifty will buy you the evening of your dreams. *Tosca* at La Fenice. Dinner at the Danieli. Grappa by the bottle. Whoever said war was a bad idea?'

Nehmann grinned, thinking of his little gondolier. Fifty marks, he decided, was cheap. The biggest gestures were always the best. He should have made it a hundred, maybe two. Goebbels, early on in their relationship, had put his finger on it. Whatever the challenge, whatever the difficulties, you go as fast as you can, you be as bold as you can, and you ignore all advice to the contrary. Because the wildest life is the most beautiful.

'Lida Baarova,' he murmured. 'You know her?'

'Of course. I'm Czech. I'm an actress. As it happens, we even share a couple of schoolfriends, back in Prague. Why do you ask?'

'Because I'd like to meet her.'

'But why?' She beckoned him closer. 'I've given you a taste for Czech movie stars? You like the way we treat our men? Is that it?'

'It might be. It depends.'

'On what? On her? Just now, she's seeing no one. In fact, she hasn't had a man for a very long time.'

'Should that be a surprise? Given what happened?'

'Of course not. The poor woman had a breakdown. Your friend Goebbels set the dogs on her, chased her out of Berlin. First he frightened her, then he put her in an asylum. You couldn't write a story like that. No one would ever believe it. And you know what makes it even worse? She loved that man, she really did. They were together for two whole years. She believed everything he told her, every promise he made. It wasn't just the money, the fame, the presents, the attention. He said it was about her. He said he needed her wholeness, her specialness. He said she was the only woman, the only *person* in the world who could bring him peace.' She paused. 'Does any of that sound familiar?'

Nehmann was watching an elderly couple hugging the shadows at the edge of the piazza as they walked their dog. They were arm in arm, discreetly turning their backs as the little spaniel squatted on the warm marble.

'Maybe he meant it,' he said softly. 'Maybe it was true.'

'And now?'

'Maybe it's still true.'

'And is that why you're here? An envoy from the dwarf?'

This was uncomfortably close to the truth and Nehmann sensed she knew it. Had someone been sent earlier? Had Goebbels tried to contact Baarova in person? Was this mission his last throw of the ministerial dice?

Hedvika wasn't giving up. She wanted to know more.

'You know this man well,' she said. 'At least that's what you always told me. You think he's lonely? Might that be a clue?'

'Everyone's lonely at his level. Goebbels, Ribbentrop, Himmler. The only one who copes is probably Goering and that's because there's so much of him.'

'You mean he's fat?' She was laughing.

'I mean he's big. Big-hearted. Lots of soul. He's been through one war and he's helping to win the next. Hitler's the same. It takes a lot to frighten men like that.'

'And Goebbels?'

'Goebbels is clever. In the company he keeps, that can be a handicap. He's also insatiable, just like the rest of them. He wants more and more. Of everything. By and large that seems to work. He reads this war like no one else but the one thing he can never guarantee is a good night's sleep.'

'Maybe Lida gave him that.'

'Maybe she did. If he could put her in a bottle, a spoonful a day after meals, I'm sure he would. In the meantime, she's a couple of countries away and all he's left with are his memories.'

'Hence your phone call?'

'Yes. He wants me to see her, track her down, meet her, talk to her.'

'Get her back?'

'I doubt it.'

'Then what?'

Hedvika was waiting for an answer, tapping her perfect fingernails on the zinc-topped table. In these situations, as he remembered far too late, she could be remarkably shrewd. In bed, in the middle of a particularly vigorous session, she'd once told him she could read him like a book. You think you can hide from me, she'd said. Wrong.

'Well?'

'I just need a conversation. An address? Maybe a phone number? That would be kind.'

'And if she says no?'

'She won't.'

'How can you be sure?'

'She just won't. When did I ever lie to you?'

'All the time, but we both know that. Your little friend leaves nothing to chance. I've watched him, remember. I've been there. He was often on set in Berlin. He wanted to control every detail. The way you delivered a particular line? What the make-up people had done to your eyebrows? How he'd rescued the fourth version of a shit script and turned it into a proper

74

movie? He's like that bloody cat. He can't help himself. He has to mark his territory. As poor Lida found out.'

Nehmann resisted applauding. This was exactly the Goebbels he knew – thin-skinned, hopelessly ambitious, but a slave to his own neuroses.

'He thinks no one likes him,' Nehmann said. 'He's found success beyond his wildest dreams. He's been clever with money. He owns far more houses than he needs. He drives the fastest cars. He's got a couple of boats on the lake. Hitler loves his wife, adores his children. He can snap his fingers and get on a plane and thousands of people will be waiting in some hall in God knows which shitty little town to listen to his every word. But it's still the same face in the mirror every morning. And he knows nothing will ever change that.'

Hedvika reached for her glass. They were both drinking Campari and soda, an aperitif before the waiter appeared with their order.

'He'll have written her a letter.' Hedvika was running her fingertip around the rim of the glass. 'And the man probably trusts no one else in the world to deliver it.' She looked up. 'Don't bother denying it. Just nod.'

*

They were back in the Alla Vite Dorata, back in bed. Hedvika was still straddling him, moving very slowly as he wilted inside her. Afternoon sunshine flooded in through the window and of the cat there was no sign. Heaven, Nehmann decided, tasted of *osso buco*, lightly flavoured with parsley and thin splinters of garlic.

'I think I'm in love.' He closed his eyes. 'Did I mention that?'

'Name?'

'Maria.'

'Italian?'

'Austrian. She says.'

'You don't believe her?'

'I don't know. And that makes her even more promising. She plays the piano like an angel. You can't fake that.'

'And she's good at this, too?' Hedvika was smiling.

'Very. You can't fake that, either.'

'Lucky you, then.'

Nehmann nodded. Hedvika's bluntness had limited appeal but at least she was honest.

'It's in my jacket.' He nodded down at the pile of discarded clothing on the bare boards.

'Goebbels' little missive?'

'Yes.'

'You agree we should open it?'

'I'm not sure.'

'Another envelope for afterwards? White? Standard size? That shouldn't be a problem.'

'You're right.'

'So, what's stopping you? We open the envelope. Then we read whatever's inside.'

'Exactly. And afterwards?'

'And afterwards you get on the train and take it to Rome. That's where you'll find Baarova. She has an apartment near the Piazza Navona. She's living alone. She's had some movie offers from Italian studios. You apologise for the intrusion. You introduce yourself. You present the great man's compliments. And then you give her the letter.'

'And leave?'

'Of course. Unless you can't resist another Czech actress. She has the most wonderful mouth, incidentally. My guess is that Goebbels can't leave that memory alone. Have you ever met Frau Goebbels? The sainted Magda?'

'Many times.'

'And?'

'Great presence.'

'And her mouth?'

'Stern. Pursed. The tightest lips.'

'Exactly. Had she been born in Prague, maybe his marriage would have worked out, *ja*?'

She slipped free and then leaned forward. Nehmann could smell the Valpolicella on her breath.

'You want me to get the letter?' She kissed him. 'Or will you?'

7

MARIUPOL, UKRAINE, 9 AUGUST 1942

News that Army Group 'A' had taken the oil wells at Maikop reached Wolfram von Richthofen's headquarters the same day. When the *Generaloberst* called for maps, Messner obliged within minutes. Richthofen was on the phone to Jeschonnek, the *Luftwaffe*'s Chief of Staff. He was at the Führer headquarters at Vinnitsa with Goering and Hitler. When Hitler was especially pleased, he had a habit of performing a little impromptu jig. This afternoon, according to the *Luftwaffe*'s Chief of Staff, the jig was in danger of becoming a full-blown waltz.

Only yesterday, *General* Paulus – still ambling far too slowly towards Stalingrad – had managed to encircle major Soviet formations at Kalach. Army Group 'B' had seized 50,000 prisoners and more than a thousand tanks, and Richthofen had only just returned in his tiny Storch. From two thousand metres, he said, he'd had a perfect view of *Fliegerkorps VIII*'s Stukas and other close-support aircraft cleaning out the pocket. This news, too, had made the Führer dance.

Now, Messner had spread the campaign map on the big conference table that dominated Richthofen's office. Maikop and the oil wells lay in the foothills of the northern Causcusus. The news from Army Group 'A', on the face of it, was very good indeed, but Richthofen counselled caution. His respect for the Soviets was growing by the day. Barely a week ago, Stalin had issued an order – No. 227 according to German intelligence sources – that had chilled senior German staff officers on the southern front. The *Vodzh*, the great Leader, was still at his modest desk in Moscow. *Ni shagu nazad!*, he'd said. Not a step back!

The warning to both sides in this cut-throat war couldn't have been clearer. The notion of retreat no longer applied anywhere on the front line. Every square inch of territory still in Soviet hands was to be defended at all costs. Deserters would be shot on sight. Mother Russia, in short, would prevail.

Messner left the campaign map with Richthofen and returned to his own office. In the early evening, he was summoned back. A long phone conversation with an officer on the spot at Maikop had confirmed Richthofen's worst fears. Soviet troops had destroyed hundreds of wells, wrecked oil storage facilities and crippled the refineries around Maikop by removing key components. Most of the oil wells had been set ablaze and would burn for days. Concrete had been poured down other boreholes, setting solid within hours.

'You want to know Goering's solution?' Richthofen glanced up. 'He wants someone to come up with a gigantic corkscrew. What's good for a bottle is good for an oil well. I'd love to say we're working on it, but the engineers are in despair. Most of them want to lock Goering in that cellar of his. What the rest are saying is unprintable.'

Richthofen waved Messner into the chair in front of his desk. He rarely smoked in his office, but tonight was clearly an exception.

Messner enquired whether the *Generaloberst* wanted him to fly down to Maikop and file a report.

'Not yet.' Richthofen shook his head. 'Maikop is a disaster but it might pay to look on the bright side. The Soviets down in the Caucasus are still falling back. In my judgement, whatever Stalin had to say, they're finished. By the end of the month we could be on the Black Sea. The other oil wells are in Grozny, and the Ivans will wreck those, too, but if we ever get that far it'll be time to stop. We're at the end of the line here, as you know. Resupply is already a nightmare. In my view we only have one option, which might serve us very well. Tomorrow morning, I shall conference with Jeschonnek. The time has come to concentrate our forces, Messner, and I'm sure he'll agree. That slowcoach Paulus has finally sprung a trap on the Ivans at Kalach. He should be over the Don and driving hard for Stalingrad within days. I want you to fly up there. By the time you arrive, God willing, we'll have declared a new transport region. It will extend as far as Stalingrad and receive our full attention. The Ivans got a taste of the *Schwerpunkt* at Kalach. Stalingrad should be the real thing.'

He waved his hand in the direction of the map on the table, an unvoiced gesture that spoke volumes about command decisions at the very top of the Reich. Hitler and Goering, he seemed to be saying, should get their heads out of their arses and understand the brutal mathematics of a supply chain that reached back thousands of kilometres. Infantry needed food in their bellies. Guns needed ammunition. Tanks needed fuel. And the big Ju-52s, most important of all, needed luck and good weather, as well as full tanks, to bridge the gap between the end of the single railway line and the slow advance of Paulus's Sixth Army.

'How many tons a day, Messner? Take a guess.' Richthofen was looking at a series of pencilled calculations on his desk.

Messner did a rapid calculation. Over a quarter of a million men. Hundreds of tanks. Thousands of guns.

'Fifteen hundred tons,' he said.

'Double it.'

'Three *thousand*?' Messner shook his head. 'Impossible.'

Richthofen looked up, a thin smile on his face.

'My thoughts entirely,' he growled. 'You take off at first light. One way or another, we have to make this happen.'

*

Messner retired early, telling his orderly to rouse him before dawn. He enjoyed a dreamless sleep and was up and shaving by the time the orderly appeared at his door. He'd organised transport out to the airfield where he found himself looking at a spare Fieseler Storch that Richthofen had acquired from Kyiv. Messner's usual Me-110, it turned out, consumed far too much fuel. As a portent of things to come, thought Messner, the message couldn't have been clearer.

It was years since he'd last flown an aircraft this light and this responsive. He turned it into the wind and nursed it into the air after barely a hundred metres, glad to spare the fragile undercarriage any more punishment, and shaded his eyes against the orange spill of the rising sun as he climbed into a cloudless sky. To his right, the blueness of the Sea of Azov as it began to narrow. Beyond, the silver gleam of the River Don as it wound beyond Rostov towards Kalach.

Half an hour's flying time from the landing strip, he banked to the west and lost height, uncertain about the weight of enemy air activity. The Russians were flying Lend Lease aircraft now, English Hurricanes, American Tomahawks, and even their own fighters – mass-produced by the hundreds in factories beyond the Urals – would feast on a little insect like the Fieseler Storch. With Kalach at last in sight, he stole a look towards the east. Stalingrad lay less than a hundred kilometres away across the interminable flatness of the steppe. With Sixth Army at full throttle, thought Messner, and the whole of Richthofen's 4th Air Fleet at Paulus's disposal, the city should fall within weeks.

He dropped a wing to find the airfield and, as he did so, a square packed with tiny black dots swam into sight. At first, he mistook them for livestock of some kind, then he realised he was looking at thousands of uniforms, dark brown, huddled together. Soviet prisoners, he thought. The fruits of Paulus's labour, now disarmed and penned in behind strands of barbed wire to await the long march westwards. Beyond the caged prisoners lay the debris of the battlefield, dozens of burned-out tanks scattered at random like a child's discarded toys. The bareness of the steppe was pocked by thousands of craters, each one with its signature ring of charred grass.

Messner began to lose height. Kalach itself, like so many Ukrainian towns, was nothing to look at: a scattering of small workshops, rusting tractors, a railway station that seemed to be falling apart, and dozens of shacks, each with its scrap of tended garden. The airfield was rudimentary, a flattish space that seemed to double as a meadow for a handful of bony cattle. On landing, Messner did his best to avoid the deeper potholes, finally coming to rest beside a battered army command vehicle. The driver who helped him out of the Storch was to drive him to a command facility where a briefing had been hastily organised. The driver was an older man, a Rhinelander, companionable, friendly. Unlike most strangers, he paid no attention to the state of this newcomer's face and when Messner asked him how he was coping with the campaign, he said his wife would never believe it.

'Just over seventy kilograms.' He patted the flatness of his stomach under the grey serge tunic. 'She'll think she's married a stranger.'

They drove through the town. Wherever he looked, Messner saw more debris, more abandoned tanks, more evidence of the recent battle. Half a dozen prisoners, stripped to the waist, were hauling heavy wooden boxes towards a line of waiting trucks. When Messner enquired about the supply situation, and evacuation flights for the wounded, the driver admitted it was tricky. Most of the army were regrouping for the final push across the Don. Closing the Kalach pocket hadn't been easy. Whatever the odds, the Ivans fought like lions.

'Our guys are tough, though,' he added. 'If you can get through last winter, you can get through anything. Stalingrad should give us everything we need. When it gets below minus thirty, it pays to be in a city.'

Messner said he understood. *Luftwaffe* boys, he was the first to admit, had a sweet time of it. A proper bed for the night. Decent food. And the prospect of playing God from two thousand metres.

'Sounds wonderful.' The driver was smiling again. 'Me? I like to keep my feet on the ground.'

*

They'd arrived at a sizeable tent, pitched beside the dirt road. This was where the briefing was to take place. Messner pushed aside the tent flap and stepped into the gloom. The air was thick with cigarette smoke, harsh, acrid, and the fuggy heat under the canvas was close to unbearable. Half a dozen faces looked up from a makeshift table. Messner, who could smell paraffin from the single lamp, didn't recognise any of them. No one got up. Not a hint of a welcome.

'And you are…?'

'*Oberstleutnant* Messner. From 4th Air Fleet HQ. And you gentlemen?'

No one said a word. At first Messner put this seeming truculence down to poor morale and worse leadership but then it occurred to him that these men were probably exhausted. Springing a trap that had netted tens of thousands of Soviet troops didn't happen by accident and it was obvious that any euphoria that accompanied a victory such as this had quickly vanished. At ground level, the stone-hard steppe would be endless. Another day of bouncing into nowhere. Another week of heat and dust. Yet more Ivans offering themselves for slaughter.

Messner tried to put some of this into words in a bid to break the ice but the *Oberst* in charge dismissed his clumsy sympathy with a wave of his hand.

'Our boys love it round here.' He stifled a yawn. 'Some of them dream of coming back as farmers once the war is over. Can you believe that?'

There was a ripple of laughter around the table. The *Oberst* wanted to know whether Sixth Army could rely on the Stukas again.

'When? Exactly?' Messner queried.

'Next week. We'll be crossing the Don and the Ivans will jump us the moment we move. The Katyushas are the worst and those T-34s deserve a bit of respect. Stukas, Herr *Oberst*. The Ivans hate them.'

Messner said he understood. The Russians fired Katyusha rockets from the back of flatbed trucks. Like the T-34s, their equipment was rugged and rarely broke down. If intelligence reports were accurate, they also seemed to have more and more of them, inexhaustible supplies that appeared from nowhere and could make life on the steppe extremely difficult.

'We have well over a thousand aircraft, gentlemen, and you'll be pleased to know they'll all be available on your behalf.'

There was an exchange of nods around the table. One officer even permitted himself a brief smile. Messner sat back, wondering just how much more he should reveal. The total of serviceable aircraft had come from Richthofen last night. He'd also said that most of them would be overflying Sixth Army to bomb Stalingrad. Of the Don River crossings, he'd made no mention.

'And resupply?' The *Oberst* again. 'You have good news on that front as well?'

'I do.' Messner paused, looking round, taking his time. 'Three thousand tons a day. How does that sound?'

The officer nodded. He made a rapid calculation on the pad at his elbow, crossed out a line of figures, arrived at a new total, showed it to his neighbour, then looked across at Messner.

'This assumes a fighting advance? Until we get to Stalingrad?'
'Yes.'

'Then three thousand tons might suffice. Assuming, of

course, that we can rely on a figure like that. You're offering us a guarantee?'

Messner shook his head. He could recognise a trap when he saw one.

'Of course not,' he said. 'We can't predict the weather. We might have mechanical problems with some of the aircraft.'

'And the Ivans? Up in the air?'

'We have fighters of our own. And some excellent pilots.'

'So still three thousand tons a day? Or thereabouts?'

'We'll do our best.'

The officer nodded, seemingly satisfied. For a brief moment there was silence. A truck ground past on the dirt road outside. Then another of the figures around the table stirred. For the first time, through the fog of cigarette smoke, Messner realised that he didn't belong to Sixth Army. Instead, he was wearing the *Feldgrau* uniform and lightning flashes of an SS *Standartenführer*. His cap, with its unmistakeable death's head symbol, lay on the table in front of him. His hair was beginning to recede over a bony forehead, and he had a cast in one eye.

'You're here on behalf of *Generaloberst* Richthofen? Is that what we are to understand?'

'Yes.'

'So when will he pay us the honour of a personal visit?'

'Very soon. I suspect.'

'Before we move out of here? Before we cross the river?'

'I imagine so. You have a question for him? Can I help at all?'

'Maybe yes. Maybe no. You have plans to bomb Stalingrad?'

'Of course.'

'And do you know when?'

'Soon. Very soon. Maybe you saw what we did to Sevastopol. Stalingrad isn't a place you'd want to be just now.'

'Good.' The *Standartenführer* produced a handkerchief and mopped his face. 'Very good. How many aircraft?'

'As many as necessary. If we can smash the city before you get there, I imagine it will save you gentlemen a great of time and effort.'

Messner paused. He'd no idea where these questions were leading, and he suspected the rest of the officers around the table were equally mystified.

The *Standartenführer* returned the handkerchief to his pocket and reached for his cap before checking his watch and getting to his feet. He had a face, Messner later realised, that was bred for madness: the cast in his eye, the tightness of his mouth, the thin sprout of unrazored hair beneath his nose that appeared to serve as a moustache.

'One aircraft, Messner.' He tried to force a smile. 'That's all we'd need.'

'We?'

'Myself. And my *Gruppenführer*. It will be a pleasure to do business with your *Generaloberst*.'

8

VENICE, 10 AUGUST 1942

The bed was empty by the time Nehmann finally woke up. He lay still for a while, listening to the muted clamour of the city through the open window: iron-shod wheels on the cobblestones outside the house, the mewing of gulls from the lagoon, an occasional parp from one of the passenger liners he'd seen moored on the seaward end of the Grand Canal.

Back in Berlin, it was impossible to ignore a widespread contempt for the Reich's Axis partner. Only last year, Mussolini had suffered a bad bout of indigestion after trying to gobble up Albania and it had taken German steel and German blood to bail him out. The shortest read in history, went the word on the Wilhelmstrasse, must be the *Book of Italian War Heroes*.

This would guarantee a chuckle in most Berlin bars but here in Venice, Nehmann wasn't entirely sure that the joke wasn't on the Germans. A decade of frantic rearmament, huge rallies and the ever-tighter chokehold of a police state had certainly delivered the spoils of war, but most Italians, it seemed to Nehmann, had altogether different priorities.

Nehmann stretched and closed his eyes. He and Hedvika had got drunk last night in a hotel restaurant she often used. The dining room belonged to an elderly Italian maître d' of immense charm, plainly smitten by Hedvika, and he'd reserved a table beside the window with a dramatic view of the Grand Canal and the Accademia Bridge. Nehmann had bought a bottle of champagne and then another, while he and Hedvika took it in turns to murmur passages aloud from Goebbels' letter.

Hedvika, who'd met Goebbels on a number of occasions, had caught the Minister's voice perfectly. As a gifted public speaker, spot-lit on countless stages, he was capable of an immense range of effects from whispered pathos to chest-beating frenzy, but over the crisp white tablecloth beside the window, Hedvika had cleverly imagined herself into the head of this demagogue, driven to plead his case at the feet of a woman he swore he'd never ceased to love. These laboured endearments had turned heads at neighbouring tables, adding to a surreal sense of theatre that Nehmann knew he'd never forget.

The letter was briefer than Nehmann had expected. It was handwritten, two and a half pages of Goebbels' tightly meticulous script, and it had taken him an hour or two up in the bedroom to decipher every word. The opening passages, they both agreed, belonged in one of the cheap novelettes now available on *Kraft durch Freude* cruise liners.

Goebbels missed his Czech mistress more than he could ever have believed. His submission to his wife, and by implication his Führer, was an act of the most contemptible weakness. He'd treated Lida worse than badly and now – as he should – he was paying the price. But the truest love, the only love that really mattered, was beyond price. It was something immeasurable, something eternal, and he wanted his Czech treasure to know that he would meet any bill, risk any consequence, in order to share time again together. I am your Tristan, he'd written. And you? *Du bist meine Isolde.*

The heart of the letter, its denouement, came on the last page. By now, the maître d' had signalled for their plates to be cleared away and their glasses recharged. Hedvika, hunched over the letter, desperate, intimate, pleading, ignored the scurrying waiters.

'My body was yours to conquer. To you, *Liebling*, I was terra incognita, virgin earth, yours for the taking. You planted your standard and stated terms for the glorious peace that followed our first lovemaking. The land is bare now, the rains long overdue. Nothing grows, not even a single flower. I'm a parched man in a dry land, happy only in our memories. I long for your return. I long for the sun on our faces. I long for you to retrace those old paths, to rediscover the views we shared, to rekindle the flame that warmed those long nights beside the Bogensee. All this could – must – be ours again. Otherwise, my Isolde, all is madness.'

Hedvika, ever the actress, knew she'd drawn an audience. Too much wine had brought tears to her eyes. She was milking this scene, letting the last page of the letter flutter to the tablecloth, burying her head in her hands. Watching her, Nehmann had wondered whether she'd acknowledge the soft ripple of applause and was strangely gratified when she did. Goebbels himself would have expected no less. The wildest life, after all, is the most beautiful.

Now, next morning, Nehmann was beginning to wonder whether last night's performance had been such a good idea. For the dozen or so fellow diners within earshot, there were enough clues in the letter to suggest that a senior Nazi might have been responsible. Conclude that it was probably Goebbels, and everything else would slip into place.

Hedvika spoke both German and Italian with a Czech accent. Lida Baarova, as Goebbels' mistress, had caught the attention of Europe's demi-monde for more than two years. Indeed, Hedvika herself might easily have been mistaken for Goebbels' jilted lover, using the occasion and the company to mock the man who had become the public face of Nazi Germany.

Nehmann's feet found the bare boards beside the bed. He made his way to the window and pushed it wide open. The first lungful of air tasted of fresh pastries from the neighbouring bakery. His head was still thumping and the queasiness in his belly made him feel slightly sick. Something else had been bothering him, too, though it took a moment or two to remember exactly what.

'Here—'

Hedvika had appeared at the open door, swathed in a bath towel. She had a sheaf of white paper in her hand.

'What's that?'

'You told me you wanted to copy the letter.'

'Did I?'

'Yes. Last night. After we got back. So...' she held out the paper '...this is what you need.'

Nehmann nodded. He was looking at the bed. They'd made love twice since he'd arrived, and possibly again last night, though he couldn't remember. In any case, that wasn't the point. Hedvika was noisy. She kept no secrets.

'Your friend downstairs never leaves the house. Am I right?'

'Rarely. And his name's Fabio.'

'And he's really Carlo's brother?'

'He is.'

'So, what might Carlo make of...' Nehmann shrugged '...us?'

'I've no idea. But Fabio won't say a word, if that's what worries you.'

'Why not?'

'Because he knows I'll have the *polizia* here if he does. Avoiding military service is worse than a crime in this country. Many believe it's a sin.'

'And you've told him that?'

'Of course.' She let the towel fall to the floor. 'I spent years in Berlin, remember. I know what buys silence.'

*

Afterwards, Hedvika made a pot of strong coffee and Nehmann sat at the table in the tiny kitchen downstairs, carefully transcribing Goebbels' letter. He knew Hedvika was going to ask him why he was bothering and when she did he saw no reason to lie.

'I may need it,' he said. 'Like it or not we live in a barter economy in Berlin. Is money important? Of course, it is. But knowledge can buy a great deal more.'

'This is the gun you hold to Goebbels' head?'

Nehmann sat back a moment. To his immense relief, the coffee was beginning to settle him down. He picked up the letter.

'No,' he said. 'This is the gun that might save my own.'

'That sounds dramatic.'

'You should know. You're the actress.'

'I am. And you'll need this.'

She circled the table and bent for his pen. Nehmann drained

the last of the coffee, watching her scribble an address on a new envelope and then slip the transcription inside.

Nehmann peered at it. Hedvika said it was an address in Rome. '3/14 Via de'Baullari?' He looked up. 'Have I got that right?'

'Baullari. Emphasis on the last "a". Don't mention my name, by the way, when you see her. She needn't know I run errands for Herr Goebbels.'

*

The train for Rome left in the early afternoon. Nehmann treated himself to a plate of *antipasti* in the restaurant car as the flat green fields of the Po Valley sped by. At Bologna, the war re-entered his life in the shape of four noisy infantrymen who crowded into the otherwise empty compartment. Young, thought Nehmann as a whistle blew and the train began to move again. Young and probably untested. One of them produced a pack of cards and what looked like a bottle of grappa. The bottle did the rounds from mouth to mouth but when offered to Nehmann he shook his head.

'*Genug.*' He tapped his head. Enough.

More troops joined the train at Florence. With all the com-partments packed, they lined the corridor and blew kisses to the women on the platform. By now, the soldiers in Nehmann's compartment were asleep. Sitting by the window, he slipped the copy of Goebbels' letter from his jacket and checked the address on the envelope. At the terminus in Rome, he'd find a taxi to take him to Baarova's apartment. According to Hedvika, Goebbels' ex-mistress was days away from starting a new film at the studios in Cinecittà and he hoped that her stay in Prague, before the move to Italy, would have won her a little peace of mind.

Nehmann returned the envelope to his jacket and gazed out at the passing landscape. Was it really his job to disturb that peace? To trouble her with memories she'd probably prefer to forget? He knew that the answer was no but Nehmann, in a busy life, had never had much time for matters of conscience. Goebbels, he knew, had shown him doors in Berlin he'd never suspected existed. A favour like this was the least his master deserved.

The queue for taxis at the Rome terminus stretched deep onto the station concourse. Nehmann wondered briefly about finding a map and walking but decided against it. The queue shuffled forward, one step at a time. It was nearly six o'clock before Nehmann found himself at the kerbside.

He was about to duck his head and get into the waiting cab when he felt a pressure on his arm.

'Do you mind sharing? It might help these good people behind.' Excellent German. Berlin accent.

Nehmann glanced round. He hadn't been aware of this stranger, not the last time he'd looked. He was tall. He wore a lightweight summer suit, beautifully cut, and had a raincoat folded over one arm. Mid-forties, Nehmann thought. Maybe older. No luggage.

'How did you know I was German?'

'The leather jacket, my friend. I have a jacket like that myself.' He named a specialist tailor with a long list of influential clients.

The driver was getting impatient. Nehmann held the rear door open and stood back to let this stranger take a seat before getting in himself.

'You speak Italian?' he asked.

'Of course.'

'Here.' Nehmann gave him the address Hedvika had scribbled down earlier on the envelope. 'You mind telling the driver? Afterwards the taxi's yours.'

The stranger bent forward and gave the driver the address. His Italian was fluent. The taxi began to move.

'You're here on business?' the stranger enquired.

'Pleasure.'

'Excellent. Rome has turned her back on the war. You'll find it a deeply pleasurable city, if you know where to go.'

Nehmann said nothing, staring out at the swirl of traffic. He knew when he'd fallen into a trap. He could smell danger at a thousand metres. *Der Überlebende*, he thought. The Survivor.

'So who are you?' he asked.

'That needn't concern us.'

'What do you want?'

The stranger said nothing. Then he gestured down at the envelope.

'This is Baarova's address. It would save us both a lot of time if you told me why you're paying her a visit.'

'You've been following me?'

'Of course.'

'From Venice?'

'No need.'

Nehmann nodded. Easy, he thought.

'Someone phoned ahead,' he suggested. 'Someone gave you a train time and a description. That's all it would take. Then you suddenly find yourself in a taxi queue.' Nehmann smiled to himself. 'You're good. I'm flattered.'

The stranger returned the smile. The raincoat was folded in his lap. He moved it slightly, revealing the dull barrel of a Luger automatic.

'Here?' Nehmann was looking at the gun. 'You want to kill me in the back of this cab?'

'I don't think that will be necessary.' The stranger nodded down at the envelope. 'This is the letter?'

'Yes.'

'From the Minister?'

'Yes.'

'He wrote the address himself?'

'No, I did.' Nehmann watched him slipping the envelope into his jacket. Then the stranger leaned forward and muttered something to the driver. The cab began to slow, before drawing to a halt at the kerbside.

'One question,' Nehmann said. 'Do you mind?'

'Not at all.'

'What business is this of yours? Why go to so much trouble?'

The stranger smiled again. The gun had disappeared.

'Sometimes we have to save Herr Goebbels from himself,' he murmured. 'If you're still thinking of paying Fraulein Baarova a visit, I suggest you spare yourself the trouble.'

'You've moved her out?'

'She's decided to live elsewhere.' A parting smile. 'Enjoy Rome.'

9

KALACH, 10 AUGUST 1942

Messner, to his intense irritation, was obliged to spend the night at Kalach. It was the orderly who'd met him who brought the news about the little Fieseler Storch. Messner had asked for it to be refuelled. This had been done but the engineer who'd attended to the aircraft had noticed a crack at the bottom of one of the undercarriage struts. Messner was welcome to risk a take-off but there were no guarantees that the strut would survive any more punishment from an airfield as rough as Kalach's.

The orderly, whose name was Klaus, had contacted the mechanics who were busy repairing Panzer tanks on the battlefield. The pressure to get the tanks back in working order was intense but Klaus had secured a promise that a weld on the damaged Storch would be in place by the following morning.

By now it was late afternoon and Messner had completed the round of meetings Richthofen had ordered him to attend. All of them had taken place inside the tent and he'd been counting the hours until he could finally emerge and take a breath or two of fresh air. Beside the dirt road, the sun was still high, the sky cloudless, perfect conditions for the return flight to Mariupol.

'There's somewhere for me to sleep?' Messner was eyeing the car. The back seat, he thought. With maybe a blanket or two.

'We can do better than that, Herr *Oberst*. Come...'

They got back in the car. On the western edge of the town was a low timber building with a sagging roof and a line of bullet holes beside one window. The front door was missing and two horses were grazing on a patch of nearby pasture. Beside the fence was a child's swing, the wooden seat hanging on a single length of rope.

'This was the school, Herr *Oberst*, until four days ago.'

'So where are they now? The kids?'

'At home? In hiding? Gone? Dead?' Klaus shrugged. 'No one knows.'

'And I'm to sleep here?'

'No. You sleep next door.'

Next door was another building, smaller, neater, in a much better state of repair. This, the orderly explained, had been the schoolmaster's house.

'He still lives there?'

'No. We commandeered the property as soon as we arrived. There's space inside for eight officers. If you're lucky, they might give you one of the armchairs. If you're luckier still, they may spare you a little vodka. Either way, Herr *Oberst*, you'll be in good company. I'll pick you up tomorrow morning as soon as your aircraft is ready. *Gute Zeit, ja?*'

Have a good time, eh? Messner watched the car bumping away, then turned back towards the house. Like the school, it was single-storey but a recent coat of fresh paint on the door and the window frames gave it a pertness that lifted Messner's spirits. Kalach was a world away from the Wannsee but there was something about the house that reminded him of the lakeside property he'd shared with Beata and little Lottie after their marriage. Someone had loved this place, he thought.

The front door was unlocked. He stepped inside, aware at once of the earthy scents of men living together at close quarters. A modest sitting area had room for two armchairs, a folding table and a home-made banquette that ran the length of one wall. Logs were piled in a fireplace. Beneath the single window was an upended wooden box full of books and, when Messner explored further, he found more books tidied neatly in the corner of one of the two bedrooms. There was room here for at least four men, more if you were happy to sleep on the bare wooden floor, and he was about to return to the living room when his gaze was drawn to a line of photographs on the windowsill.

There were four in all, one very faded, the other three more recent. The latter were family shots, one of them taken beside the swing he'd just seen. The swing appeared to be working. A little girl sat on the wooden seat, her legs out straight, her tiny hands gripping the ropes. She wore a twist of ribbon in her hair and she had a big grin for the camera. Behind her stood a tallish figure in a rumpled jacket and dark trousers, and there were other children playing in the background.

Messner picked up the photo and stared at the two faces. Father and daughter, he thought, caught at a moment of brilliant sunshine before the clouds gathered and countless German armies had fallen on the Motherland. Another photo featured the same little girl. This time, she was sitting on what Messner assumed was her mother's lap. Half close his eyes, and Messner fancied he could see a family resemblance in the upward tilt of the two faces. The little girl had a napkin tucked beneath her chin and her mother was offering a spoonful of what looked like soup. The same wide-eyed innocence. The same dimpled smile. The photo had been taken next door: Messner recognised the logs in the fireplace, and he stared at the image for a long moment, trying to imagine what might have happened to these people.

He'd noticed a radio in the living room. Even here, adrift in the ocean that was the steppe, word would have come of what awaited communities such as these. The rumble of heavy artillery in the west. Strange foreign shapes in the sky overhead. Then uniformed figures trudging east as the first ragged formations of Soviet troops fell back before the German onslaught. But what then? Where would a family like this *go*? Would they take their chances with the retreating Russians? Frightened young men who at least spoke the same language? Or would they stand fast, determined to somehow protect their little flock of pupils?

Hours later, mid-evening, he wanted to put these questions to the first of the property's temporary tenants to return. His face and his name were already familiar from the last of the day's meetings. Renke. A man, thank God, with the manners and the intelligence to conduct a half-decent conversation. At that afternoon's conference he'd won over more impatient colleagues with a quiet recitation of the facts. Like Klaus, he had the advantage of age on his side.

Messner refused the offer of a glass of vodka. Even with a fresh weld on the Storch's undercarriage, he said he needed his wits about him for tomorrow's flight. Renke shot him a look, then shrugged and settled in one of the two armchairs. As the senior supply officer, he'd spent the last two months feeding

Sixth Army's insatiable appetite. They'd naturally foraged for local food wherever they could, but the Soviets had become expert at what he drily called 'sustenance denial'. Field after field of crops had been burned to the ground. Wells had been poisoned, livestock slaughtered, butchered and hauled east. In all too many respects, he said, this war was two thousand years old: primitive, vicious, implacable, no quarter offered or taken. The victories in the west had been easy. This campaign, after a promising start, was anything but.

'The Ivans have two cards to play,' he said. 'One is geography. There's too much of this bloody country. It just goes on and on. It never stops. You set another trap, and then another, and you pat yourself on the back but after you've counted the first forty thousand prisoners you give up because there's just too many of them. Yet the next day, waiting over the horizon, there are more, and more, and more, and you realise you haven't even made a start. These people breed like rabbits. No wonder they call it Mother Russia.'

'Some of us think Paulus could move a little faster,' Messner said stiffly.

'Paulus is unusual. I admit it.'

'In what respect?'

'He cares about his men. He hates to waste them.'

Messner was tempted to argue, to somehow pretend that Richthofen was in the room with them, mercilessly applying the lash. Movement is the essence of conquest. Strike hard and strike often. But there was something in Renke's face, a weary acceptance that he probably faced an eternity of days like these, trying to marry an ever-diminishing trickle of supplies to the demands of tens of thousands of hungry men.

Back home the public's image of the *Wehrmacht* was shaped by photos and newsreel footage from the front line: the murderous shriek of a diving Stuka, Panzer tanks pushing aside curtains of enemy fire, endless lines of enemy prisoners stumbling into captivity. But how many people ever thought – even for a moment – about the unsung heroes in the rear? Officers like Renke who somehow managed to keep the wheels of the killing machine grinding?

Messner wondered about putting some of these thoughts into words but decided that he had nothing to add. Renke lived in the world of figures. He spoke the cold language of supply and demand. All too literally, he measured the success of his personal war in kilos and litres. Was there glory in any of this? Would the Führer strike a medal for the Heroes of Resupply? Probably not.

'So how long have you been living here?' Messner gestured round.

'Two days. This is the third. Compared to previous billets this is luxurious, believe me.'

'And the occupants? You met them?'

'No. They'd gone by the time we were cleared to move in.'

'You think they fled? Went east?'

Renke didn't answer. Instead he swirled the last of the vodka in his glass and then swallowed it in a single gulp. The bottle was nearby. He uncapped it slowly and then glanced at Messner.

'You're sure?'

'Yes. I don't drink much any more. It doesn't do anything for me.'

'Did it ever?'

'Yes. Once.'

Renke nodded, expecting an explanation that never came. The two men sat in silence for a while, listening to a growl of thunder in the west. Then Renke recharged his own glass and drew Messner's attention to the sideboard that dominated the room.

'Top drawer,' he murmured. 'You might take a look.'

Messner got to his feet. The wood of the drawer seemed to have swollen and it took him a moment or two to wrestle it open.

'These were here already?' He was looking at a collection of child's toys.

'No. We found them in the daughter's bedroom. They were everywhere, all over the floor, on the bed. You're married, Messner? You have children of your own?'

'One. A daughter. Lottie.'

'Then you'll know that children and tidiness don't go together, which is exactly the way it should be. When we first walked into that bedroom it was like the family were still there.'

'Maybe they had to get out in a hurry,' Messner suggested.

'Maybe they did but I doubt it. What three-year-old leaves her dollies behind?'

Messner took a closer look at the contents of the drawer. Renke was right. Three dolls, one missing an arm, one with a new skirt. These could belong to Lottie, Messner thought.

'Now try the next drawer down.' Renke gestured with his glass.

Messner did his bidding. This time he was looking at a nest of birds, each one hand carved. He lifted out the biggest and ran his finger down the length of its body. A light coat of varnish had given a dull gleam to the spread of its wings and, when he looked closely, he could see the tiny marks that had transformed the bare wood into feathers. A goose of some kind, he thought. Or perhaps a swan.

'Beautiful,' he said. 'Exquisite.'

'How much work, do you think? For each bird?'

'Weeks, months, I've no idea.' Messner looked up. 'These were in the child's bedroom as well?'

'No. Some of them were next door, in the bigger bedroom, and the rest were in here. We put them away in case they got damaged. War can be unforgiving. Don't you find that?'

Messner's gaze returned to the bird. He picked up another, smaller this time, weighing it in his hand, half expecting it to react, to move under his touch, to squawk in alarm and fly away. Renke was right. No matter how urgent the need to leave, you'd take masterpieces like these with you.

'So what happened?'

Renke swallowed another mouthful of vodka. In the last of the evening sun through the nearby window, his eyes were beginning to swim.

'You know about our SS friends in the *Einsatzgruppen*?'

'A little. Perhaps enough. We spend most of our lives in the air, thank God.'

'That makes you lucky. They follow us everywhere. Some-body once told me they're there to keep us honest but that's *Scheisse*. They're vermin. They're worse than vermin. Fighting the enemy is one thing. Battle is never pretty. You spill a lot of blood, often your own, but after a fashion there are rules, things you do do, things you don't. The *Einsatzgruppen* have no time for rules. Rules are for *Untermenschen*. These SS people are fanatics. They want to wipe Poland clean of Jews. Ukraine, too. And now Russia. See them in action and you might wonder what really drives this war of ours. They want to engineer a new world, regardless of the cost.'

'You're telling me they were here? In this house?'

'Almost certainly, yes. As I say, they follow us everywhere. They have their own transport, their own priorities. They move in behind us and do what has to be done. They call it tidying up.'

'This man was a Jew?' Messner was looking at the little bird in the palm of his hand.

'I doubt it. Two other cardinal sins, Messner. Number one, it doesn't pay to be Russian. Number two, this house obviously belongs to an educated man. On both counts that could be a death sentence.'

'And his wife? His child?'

'Them, too. In SS eyes, they're tainted. *Vernichtung*, Messner. Not a pretty word.'

Vernichtung. Extermination. Not just Jews but anyone with a brain and a schoolful of children to educate and the patience to fashion a living thing from a block of wood.

Messner was trying to visualise the scene in this little house once Sixth Army had swept through. The smoke of battle beginning to clear. Tank after tank grinding eastwards. The family emerging from wherever they'd managed to hide, only to find a different set of uniforms at the door.

'So, what would have happened to them?'

'They're taken away.'

'And?'

'Nobody knows. Last year they killed tens of thousands of Jews in Kyiv. A ravine called Babi Yar. Shot in cold blood. We'd gone by then, thank God.'

'They?'

'The *Einsatzgruppen*. With the help of the Ukrainians.'

Messner nodded. A bullet through the back of the head, he thought. And then the long topple onto the mass of bodies below. Rumours from Kyiv had reached *FK VIII* headquarters on occasions over the last ten months, but no one ever seemed to have either the time or inclination to enquire further. Here was different. He was still holding the little bird.

'There was an SS officer at the first of the meetings this morning,' he said. 'Was he part of the *Einsatzgruppen*?'

'Yes.'

'I didn't catch his name.'

'*Standartenführer* Kalb.'

'And he's been with you a while?'

'Behind us, yes. Oil and water, Messner. We don't mix.'

'Socially?'

'In any way.'

'But he came to that meeting.'

'He invited himself.'

'Why? Why was he asking about our plans for Stalingrad? Why the bid for an aircraft?'

'I have no idea. These people are a law unto themselves. You will notice that he left that meeting early, when it suited him. That's the only clue you'll ever need. These people have powerful allies in Berlin. They also appear to have the ear of the Führer. God knows why but that appears to be the case.' He paused, then reached for the bottle again. 'I'd like to propose a toast, Messner. It's a small thing to ask.'

Messner held his gaze, then nodded. Another glass appeared. Renke filled it and passed it across.

'To our schoolmaster,' he said.

Messner slept badly that night. One by one, the other occupants of the house arrived. Klaus stepped in from the darkness around eleven in the evening with a welcome cauldron of stew that might have been horse.

By now, much against his better judgement, Messner had swallowed two more glasses of vodka and done his best to hold his own against one accusation after another that the *Luftwaffe* were becoming notable for their absence as Sixth Army prepared to push even further east. The Stukas had been more than welcome over the last couple of days, but substantial doubts remained about resupply. Was it really feasible to keep an entire army on the move without proper roads or a decent railway? Messner, who shared these doubts, did his best to defend the honour of *Fliegerkorps VIII* but by midnight his eyes were beginning to close.

Both bedrooms were occupied. Three men shared the living room. Renke offered to vacate his armchair for a berth on the floor but Messner wouldn't hear of it. Klaus had left him a greatcoat and a couple of blankets. Messner spread the blankets on the floor and pulled the greatcoat to his chin. The rough serge smelled of tobacco and engine oil but within seconds he was asleep.

He awoke a couple of hours later, pitch-black. Somewhere outside a dog was barking. Closer, from one of the bedrooms, he could hear two men snoring. Messner stirred. His head was bursting, and he could still taste the rawness of the uncooked paprika in the stew. He struggled to his feet and fumbled his way to the tiny kitchen where he palmed water from the dripping tap into his mouth. Feeling a little better, he knew there was no point trying to sleep again. Better to get some air in his lungs.

Outside, huddled in the greatcoat, he settled himself against a corner of the house, his head tipped up. The sky was ablaze with stars, not a wisp of cloud, and a sliver of moon was already sinking in the west. He sat motionless for minutes on end, trying to rid himself of the images that had haunted the briefness of his sleep. Beata, his wife. Lottie, his daughter. And the little lakeside house that had been full of sunshine and laughter until the madness had overcome him and everything had turned to dust.

Her name had been Olga Helm. She was a movie star, nearly famous, and from time to time she'd appeared with Goebbels on one of the Führer Squadron flights. Messner had never seen a film of hers but when a fellow pilot rhapsodised about her Slav good looks he knew exactly what he meant. The wide curve of her mouth. The goddess cheekbones. The way her smile could transform any conversation. When travelling, she always favoured loose-fitting dresses, hints of a seemliness that Messner found mysteriously alluring. What was she like under those folds of cotton? What might a man expect at rather closer quarters?

To his great surprise, Messner found out. She had a stylish apartment off the Wilhelmstrasse and one night she invited him in after he'd given her a lift back to the city centre from Tempelhof. Anticipating a brief cup of coffee, she'd led him straight to bed. She'd flown with him three times. She loved his sternness, his air of command, and for a woman who was terrified of flying she'd never felt anything but safe. Now she wanted to find out whether he could work that same magic in bed.

The magic worked. When opportunities presented themselves, they continued to meet, sometimes in Berlin, sometimes elsewhere in the Reich. Messner, who'd always suspected that she was one of Goebbels' mistresses, discovered that this was far from true. The Minister of Propaganda still enjoyed a pretty woman on his arm but a previous affair – once again with a foreign-born actress – had clipped his wings and so Messner found himself sucked into a relationship that turned his world upside down.

Never truly comfortable with physical contact, he became obsessed by Olga's dexterity, and her repertoire of little tricks, and her shameless appetite for more and more of him. He wrote to her constantly, a letter most days, scribbled in haste but adolescent in the rawness of his passion. He wanted, *needed*, every inch of her, and in snatched moments together she was more than happy to oblige.

In the end, of course, in the words of his one close friend, he'd crashed and burned. He'd hidden Olga Helm from Dieter Merz exactly the way he'd hidden this secret life of his from everyone else. But Olga had been careless with his letters and, in someone else's hands, they'd come back to haunt him. By now, he was in hospital recovering from the blackout accident that had nearly killed him. In every respect, he was a changed man – remote, solitary, frequently aggressive – and by the time he was physically ready to go home it was far, far too late.

A shocked Beata had sensibly changed the locks at the family home. His infant daughter became a near-stranger. And only the offer of a posting with *FK VIII* gave his life any discernible purpose. Hence that single-minded devotion to duty that Richthofen seemed to prize. And hence, now, the churning deep in his gut when he thought of the schoolmaster, and his wife, and his infant daughter, and his drawerful of magical carvings. Since his days in the Condor Legion, flying against the Republicans over the mountains of northern Spain, Messner had paid lip service to how cruel war could be, but only now, marooned deep in this godforsaken steppe, did he begin to sense its real implications.

Renke roused him at dawn with a mug of tepid coffee. Messner peered up at him, rubbing his eyes against the brightness of the rising sun.

'The SS officer?' he mumbled. 'His name again?'

'Kalb.' Renke was frowning. 'Why do you ask?'

10

ROME, 10 AUGUST 1942

Werner Nehmann had never been to the film studios at Cinecittà. His only previous visit to Rome had been back in the early thirties when the notion of a huge movie-making complex had still been a gleam in Mussolini's eye, but he knew that Goebbels had been much impressed and now, once he'd checked Baarova's apartment, he needed to see for himself. There'd been no reply when he rang her doorbell and although her immediate neighbours spoke no German, he got the impression that she had, indeed, moved on. Nehmann, undaunted, still had a telephone number for the publicity executive at Cinecittà he'd talked to from Berlin. Even at this time in the evening, she might still be at her desk.

She was. Nehmann sat in the reception area, waiting for her to appear. According to the receptionist, tonight had been scheduled for the shooting of a key scene on the studio's biggest set. Designers and craftsmen had been working all week to build a replica of a Carthaginian arena and, out on the studio lot, Nehmann could see a team of wranglers trying to corral a rogue elephant with no taste for the limelight. Goebbels, he knew, had a soft spot for the sheer scale of Cinecittà's ambitions. Privately, the Minister regarded all Italians as children – easily amused, easily led – but they certainly knew how to muster the grander effects.

'*Herr Nehmann? Guten Abend. Willkommen in Cinecittà.*' Good German. Wonderful legs.

Nehmann got to his feet as she extended a rather formal handshake and led him to a nearby lift. Her name was Nina. She occupied a corner office on the first floor and Nehmann stood at the window for a moment, glad to have another look at the elephant.

'The second Punic War comes to Rome.' Nina seemed amused. 'We had a big success with *Scipio Africanus*. Let's hope the sequel works. You found your Hedvika? She was pleased to see you?'

'Very.'

'And Venezia? Your first time?'

'A film set. Perfect in every respect. Ten minutes in a gondola and for me the war never happened. If I ever lived there, I'd never leave.'

'Of course. Sadly, the Venetians have let the rest of the world share the secret. Those people worship money. They've never stopped being traders. Carlos's brother tells me it will be their death.'

'You know Fabio?'

'I do. The sweet man won't even *audition* for the army. That might have consequences, too.'

'He was an actor?'

'Yes. But no talent. No talent, no money.'

'And Carlos? He's still in hospital?'

'I'm afraid so. Emilio's thugs broke both his legs and did unspeakable things to other parts of him. That's what Emilio paid for, of course, so be warned.' She smiled. 'How can I help you?'

Nehmann mentioned Lida Baarova. His understanding was that she'd come to Rome to revive her movie career. Was that true?

'Yes. She has an important role in a movie called *Grazia*. She's popular here in Italy.' That smile again. 'Think of it as a thank you for giving us her time.'

Nehmann returned her smile. *Grazia*. Thank you. Clever.

'So, when does she start?'

'In two days' time. Everything is in place. The script, alas, is in Italian but I can find you a copy if you'd like one.'

Nehmann turned the offer down. Studying the face across the table, he sensed that something had changed between them. He was right.

'Why the interest in Lida?' She was frowning. 'Why come all this way when you could have used the telephone?'

Nehmann tried to make light of the question. It was August. Lately the weather in Berlin had been terrible. Constant rain. Unseasonal temperatures. A dark time for the soul.

'You're here on holiday?'

'In a way, yes.'

'And in a way, no? You're a journalist. You don't write like a German and I imagine Herr Goebbels likes that. I certainly do. Are you here on some kind of assignment? Has he commissioned an article on Lida? On his ex-mistress? Is that why you're asking me these questions?'

Lida was a clue, thought Nehmann. Not Frau Baarova. Lida.

'You know her well? You're friends?'

'Yes. She's been here to the studio a number of times recently. I expect it helps that I admire her work.'

'And how is she?' Nehmann's hand briefly closed over his heart. 'In here?'

'She's well. She has a life of her own now.'

'And does she share that life with...' Nehmann shrugged '...anyone else?'

'I'm afraid that's not for you to ask. Nor me to answer. Is this you talking? Or your boss? If it's the latter, I suggest you tell him that Lida is in good hands, that the script will do her nothing but good and that she loves the life here. She survived what happened in Berlin but only just. She'll never go back.'

Nehmann nodded and wondered whether he should make a note or two. *I did my best, but she never wants to see you again. And, to be honest, who can blame her?*

'Well, Herr Nehmann? Has this helped at all?'

Nehmann said yes. He liked this woman. He liked her directness and her guile. She knew exactly what he was doing here and she'd been very happy to pass a message back to Berlin on Baarova's behalf. He glanced at his watch. Maybe a longer conversation over a drink or two? Or even a meal?

He was about to voice the invitation when he heard an alarm bell deep in the building. Seconds later, the phone on Nina's desk began to trill. She picked it up, listened for a moment, then had a brief conversation Nehmann couldn't follow.

The call at an end, she got to her feet.

'We have a problem with the elephant. It's gone berserk. Two people injured on set so far and no one with any idea what to do next. I'm glad you're here.'

She said there were a dozen German children trapped on

114

the set. They'd been on a studio tour all day. Their teacher was one of the injured. Might Nehmann be able to help in their mother tongue?

'Of course.'

He followed her out of the office. The alarm bell was ringing again and the corridors on the ground floor were choked with people fleeing the building. In the distance, very faintly, Nehmann thought he could hear the howl of a siren.

They were outside the biggest of the studio sets now. The huge wooden doors were closed but Nina led the way through a maze of passages until she paused beside a small access door. She inched it open very slowly. Nehmann offered to take her place but she wouldn't hear of it.

Finally, the door was open. The view across the studio was hidden behind scaffolding that held part of the set in place but there was no mistaking the deep bass roar of the elephant. As a kid, back in Svengati, Nehmann had haunted the travelling circus when the Big Top came to town. He'd seen these animals at close quarters, and he knew how volatile and unpredictable they could be. No one in his right mind would argue with three thousand kilos of elephant.

He and Nina crept around the scaffolding. Men were shouting orders to each other and some of the children were screaming. That ripeness in the air, thought Nehmann: definitely elephant.

The moment they rounded the scaffold, the set yawned before them. Nehmann stopped, astonished. He loved magic. In his own small way, he adored casting spells. The business of illusion fascinated him. But what he saw before him defied description. He was looking at one half of a tiny coliseum from the Punic War. The semi-circle of terraced steps, artfully stone-like, seemed thousands of years old. Palm trees flanked an imposing portico and even the sand on the studio floor looked ancient. In the middle of this space, the elephant reared on its hind legs, trumpeting its rage while half a dozen men tried to cage it behind a thicket of spears. Two of them, obviously actors, were dressed as Romans. The rest, equally brave, were scene hands.

Nina was looking at the children. They were trapped halfway up the terrace of steps, the younger ones plainly terrified. Every time the elephant turned in their direction, lumbering towards them, stopping, roaring, they seemed to physically shrink, trying to make themselves smaller.

'You need a gun,' Nehmann said. 'Shoot for the legs. Drop the animal. Put it on the floor.'

Nina spared him no more than a glance. She was off again, hurrying along the back of the scaffolding, looking up at the lattice of steel tubes, trying to find a way of getting the children off the terraced steps, but it was Nehmann who found the solution.

'There,' he said.

He'd spotted a wooden ladder propped against the studio wall. With Nina's help he manhandled it across to the back of the scaffolding. Propped against the top rail, it might be possible to ferry the children down to safety.

Nehmann began to climb. Every time the elephant reared up on the studio floor, he could feel the ladder shaking beneath him. At the top, a panel of painted canvas blocked access to the steps. Nehmann tore at it with his bare hands, pulling as hard as he could, trying to wrestle it free. He was cursing the efficiency of Italian carpenters when it finally gave way, nearly tipping him backwards, but he clung to the ladder, aware of the sweat cooling on his upturned face.

Then, very suddenly, came a shot, and then another, and the entire set seemed to move bodily with the weight of the elephant collapsing against it. The children were screaming again, much closer this time, and Nehmann inched himself onto the topmost step of the terrace, staring down at the elephant lying in a widening pool of its own blood. The bullets had taken it in the chest, not the legs. The animal's eyes were open, but lifeless, and a last breath bubbled crimson onto the sand.

The man with the rifle was wearing a pair of blue overalls. He circled the elephant, keeping his distance, then put a final bullet into its head. Two of the girls on the steps below Nehmann were hiding their eyes. The rest were weeping.

*

Mercifully, there was no need to use the ladder. Nina appeared in the area and climbed towards the children, beckoning Nehmann to join her.

'Tell them everything's going to be all right,' she said. 'Tell them they'll be safe with us.'

Nehmann talked to the tallest boy among them. He checked that no one had been physically hurt and told them to follow the lady out of the studio. When the boy asked about the teacher, Nehmann said that he, too, would be in good hands.

Nina led the way to the dressing rooms. A handful of make-up staff had appeared and fussed over the children. Keys appeared. Doors were unlocked. An older woman arrived with a tray of fizzy drinks and a huge plate brimming with pastries and sweets while Nehmann and Nina moved from child to child, offering whatever comfort they could. Then, looking up, Nehmann noticed the name on one of the dressing room doors. *Lida Baarova*, it read.

The children were beginning to calm down. One or two of them, pale, were plainly in shock and, as they began to talk to Nehmann, to open up to him, it was obvious that this experience had been doubly horrible. First, the rampaging elephant. Then the man in blue who had so casually killed it.

'*Warum?*' wailed one little girl. '*Warum musste er es tun?*' Why? Why did he have to do it?

Nehmann did his best to explain but then felt the lightest touch on his arm. It was Nina. Transport had at last arrived for the children. The studio, she said, was deeply grateful for everything Nehmann had done but now she had to get her charges off the premises.

'And the schoolteacher?'

'Nothing serious. He was doing his duty. He was trying to protect the children. He'll be there at the hostel by the time they get back.' She smiled, then beckoned him closer before kissing him lightly on the lips. 'Thank you,' she said again.

Nehmann watched them all leave. The moment they'd gone, he stepped across to Lida Baarova's dressing room and closed the door behind him. This, he assumed, would be her professional home over the weeks of shooting to come. There was a pile of neatly folded towels beside the single wash basin. A selection of soaps and shampoos. Trays of make-up. Umpteen shades of lipstick. Even a pile of new-looking Czech fashion magazines in case she was feeling homesick.

Nehmann studied himself in the mirror for a long moment. This, he knew, was the moment of decision. Goebbels' billet-doux was still in his jacket pocket. He could leave it beside the magazines and knew that it would be safe here. She'd walk in to find everything ready, everything prepared, and then her eyes would drift to the envelope. Her name on the front. Something personal. But what?

Nehmann tried to imagine her slipping her finger under the flap, easing the envelope open, spreading the pages inside. She'd recognise Goebbels' crablike, schoolboy script. She'd probably weather the first paragraph or two. She might even be curious enough to make it through to the end. But if she was half the woman Nina had implied, there'd be absolutely no prospect of this drivel getting her back to the Minister's arms. Hedvika had been right. Joseph Goebbels had been talking to himself.

Nehmann hesitated a moment longer, then he reached for one of the lipsticks. It was the deepest crimson. It spoke of passion, and abandon, and Nehmann knew that Goebbels would have gone for it without a moment's thought.

He stepped towards the mirror, aware of raised voices outside. He paused for a moment, deep in thought. Then he reached out to the mirror, neat little loops, two perfect lines of text, as close to Goebbels' hand as he could manage.

Gute Jagd, meine Isolde. Immer dein, immer Tristan.
Good hunting, my Isolde. Always yours, always Tristan.

11

MOUNT ELBRUS, 21 AUGUST 1942

The joint twenty-three-man team rose early, an hour before dawn. These were elite mountain troops, some from the First Mountain Division, the rest from the Fourth. Led by *Hauptmann* Heinz Groth and *Hauptmann* Max Gammerler, both veterans of countless alpine ascents, they brewed coffee, struck camp and set off for the last steep kilometres that would take them to the summit of the highest peak in Europe. With them, they carried the Reich War Flag, as well as a pair of divisional standards.

Both Gammerler and Groth knew that the rest of Army Group 'A' were doing less well below them, moving at snail's pace through the mountains, plodding south towards the Black Sea, but the mood among the climbers was buoyant. They'd been acclimatising to the thinness of the air for days but even so it was wise to move slowly, one step at a time, enjoying the first long shadows on the surrounding icefields, cast by the rising sun.

At altitude, nearly five and a half thousand metres, it paid to take regular breaks, huddling against the biting wind, watching the little moguls of powdered snow snaking up the mountainside towards them. From a perch like this, a man could get a very different perspective on this unending war. The climbers nodded to each other, exchanging smiles before heading upwards again. *Wirklich grossartig*. Truly magnificent.

They reached the summit shortly before mid-morning. The mountain peaked on a steep shoulder of rock sheathed in snow. The honour of planting the War Flag belonged to the man who had carried it up the mountain. Steadied by a friend, he reached up and drove the base of the flagpole through the crust of ice and deep into the packed snow beneath. The moment the pole was vertical, the War Flag streamed out in the stiff wind, the swastika and its blood-red background the starkest message against the blueness of the sky.

To the cheers of his *Kameraden*, the mountaineer who'd planted the flag stepped back, raising his right arm in the Führer salute. The climber charged with recording this moment asked for a tiny shuffle to the left to make the most of the endless spread of mountains beyond. Then, to more applause, he pressed the shutter.

Gammerler was carrying a bottle of schnapps. He went from man to man, offering them each a tiny glassful. The schnapps was ice-cold but Gammerler had insisted on 84 per cent proof, the strongest he could find, and each man tipped back his head as the clear spirit burned its way down his gullet and kindled a fire deep in his belly. The bottle empty, he stowed it carefully in his pack. Then, almost as an afterthought, he opened the flap again and produced a tiny wooden aeroplane.

This, like the schnapps, came as a surprise to most of the men. They gathered round, curious, passing the little triplane from hand to hand. Gammerler didn't have the full story but told them it had come from *Generaloberst* Wolfram von Richthofen. As a fighter pilot he'd cut his teeth with his uncle's squadron over the trenches in the last war and – as a favour – he'd asked the climbers from Army Group 'A' to find a niche for the Fokker on the very top of Mount Elbrus. The Red Baron, he said, would doubtless be looking down. Listen hard for his applause.

The men, warmed by the schnapps, loved the gesture. A couple of them dug a tiny hollow at the base of the flagpole while another consulted a map and a compass. The nose of the plane, he said, should be pointing at distant Stalingrad. He gestured at a shapely mountain away to the north, then checked the map again.

'That direction,' he said, 'would be perfect.'

*

News of the ascent of Mount Elbrus arrived at Hitler's Ukraine headquarters long before the photographs. The Führer had spent the afternoon poring over large-scale maps of the Caucasus, demanding to know why Army Group 'A' appeared to be stalling in the face of fierce Soviet resistance. By now, *Wehrmacht* troops – supported by Panzers – should have been pushing over the Terek River towards the oil wells at Grozny but Soviet aircraft appeared to have the sky to themselves and were inflicting serious damage on the German formations below.

Richthofen, at his headquarters at Mariupol, was on the receiving end of the Führer's wrath and despatched Messner to find out why *FK VIII*'s Bf-109s weren't doing their jobs. After an eternity of delays, Messner finally made radio contact with the Fighter Wing responsible, only to discover that the twenty-eight aircraft available lacked both fuel and ammunition. Without cannon shells and full tanks, the Bf-109s would be staying on the ground.

Hitler was in no mood for excuses. He telephoned Goering at his nearby headquarters and demanded his presence. Albert Speer, the Minister of Armaments, had just arrived from Berlin and when the three men got together in the early evening Hitler led them into the map room. His forefinger jabbed at the lines of advance that had stalled in the mountains. His generals had promised to be down on the coast by now. He was counting on Black Sea ports, on Grozny oil wells, and that final thrust deep to the south-west that would deliver Baku, key to limitless supplies of black gold from the Caspian basin. This, according to Speer, would come closer to winning the war than any other single victory. So why was progress so slow?

The question was directed to Goering. When Hitler pointed out that his commanders on the ground were blaming lack of supplies, the *Reichsmarschall* blustered about aircraft serviceability and the lottery that was the weather over the Caucasus. On the steppe, he said, the *Luftwaffe* could guarantee regular flights. Europe's biggest mountains, on the other hand, had a mind of their own. Either way, he'd see to it that normal service would be resumed. On this matter, as on so many others, the Führer had his solemn word.

At this point, the conversation was interrupted by a soft knock at the door. Hitler turned to find the *Oberfunker* in charge of communications with a message that appeared to be urgent. It had come, he said, from Army Group 'A' headquarters down in the Caucasus. The *Oberfunker* had a smile on his face. Goering visibly brightened. Good news at last, he thought.

'*Lass es mich haben…*' Hitler wanted sight of the despatch.

Putting on his glasses, he walked across to the window for the last of the light. He read the message twice, his face visibly darkening. Then he turned back to the waiting faces by the map table.

'Show me,' he barked.

'*Mein Führer?*' The *Oberfunker* was looking confused.

'This mountain. Elbris? Elbrus? Where is it?'

The *Oberfunker* indicated a point of the map some seventy kilometres inland from the coast. His ink-stained finger was shaking. The oil wells at Grozy lay two days march away to the east.

'The biggest, you say?'

'The tallest, *Mein Führer*. Five and a half thousand metres. A monster.'

'Enough. Leave us.'

Hitler couldn't take his eyes off the map. He was bent over the table, each hand supporting the weight of his body. The *Oberfunker* stole away from the room without a backward glance.

By now, Hitler was shaking with rage. Here was the reason all that effort had come to nothing. Expecting an army to fight, they instead wasted their days with stunts like these. All that effort, all that determination, all that *energy* squandered on a lump of rock. This was a theatre of war, not a circus ring. He wasn't blaming the men themselves. No, that's not where the blame belonged. He didn't doubt for a moment that climbing a mountain like that would demand real guts. But that wasn't the point. These men were soldiers. They were in the mountains to kill Russians, to kick open the door to the oil wells, not to get themselves diverted to some profitless adventure that didn't matter a damn.

He paused for a moment to fumble for a handkerchief and

wipe his mouth. Speer was staring down at the table. A thin mist of spittle had settled wetly on the map. Hitler ignored it.

'I ask for victories,' he roared. 'And all they can give me is a mountain top. What use is that? Can anyone help me here? Can anyone explain? Maybe we shouldn't have gone into the mountains at all. Maybe the temptations were too great. War is about concentration of resources, concentration of effort, an agreed line of advance. Get those things right, get the enemy where you want him, and you can smash him to pieces.' He took a step back from the table and drove his right fist into his open palm. 'Is this something we should be teaching our generals? 'Is this something they've neglected to learn? Or should we simply stop fighting and climb mountains instead? Look. Look here.' He stabbed a finger at the map. 'There are hundreds of them, thousands of them. Who needs an enemy when you can climb a mountain instead? Wonderful idea, gentlemen. Let's stop bothering the Russians and climb a few more mountains. Can either of you organise that? Or must I do *everything* myself?'

The question hung in the air, unanswered. Hitler was leaning on the table, his head down again, his voice low. For a second or two he seemed exhausted. Then he stirred.

'So, whose idea was this?' His voice was low.

Goering and Speer exchanged glances, then Speer shrugged and said he didn't know.

'And you, Herr *Reichsmarschall*?'

Goering did his best to compose himself. He'd been waiting for this moment since the *Oberfunker* left the room.

'Goebbels,' he said. 'Who else?'

12

BERLIN, 22 AUGUST 1942

Werner Nehmann was in bed when he took the call from one of Goebbels' secretaries. He rolled over on his side, shielding Maria from the conversation, trying not to wake her up.

'It's six in the morning,' he whispered.

'I know. The Minister presents his compliments. He's out at Schwanenwerder. A car will pick you up in fifteen minutes.'

'This is urgent?'

'I believe it might be. Ask the driver.'

'But it's barely daylight,' Nehmann protested again. Too late.

Left holding the phone, Nehmann could think of nothing but Lida Baarova. A conversation with Goebbels was long overdue but the Minister had been away since Nehmann's return from Rome. Now, it seemed, would come the reckoning.

*

Schwanenwerder, in Goebbels' phrase, was a select little finger of paradise that jutted into one of the wider stretches of the River Havel, beyond Charlottenburg. Among the wooden slopes that overlooked the water there was room for a handful of houses, most of which had belonged to wealthy Jewish families.

Goebbels was one of the first of the Party chieftains to stake his claim to the silence and the view, and a handsome redbrick villa with a little wooden jetty of its own now formed part of his ever-growing property empire. In mid-summer, his wife and family were away in the Austrian Tyrol and Nehmann knew that Schwanenwerder was where Goebbels liked to turn his back on the world and lick his wounds.

Nehmann knew the Ministry driver well. More importantly, he was always first to pick up important gossip.

'So, what's happened?'

'The Führer's chewing the carpet again. It's something to do with a bunch of mountaineers and he wants to kick the Minister's arse.'

'This is about a *mountain*?' Nehmann felt nothing but relief. Not Baarova, after all.

'Out east.' The driver nodded, then glanced across at Nehmann. 'The Caucasus?'

Nehmann began to understand. Mount Elbrus, he thought. He was trying to remember the name of the pilot he'd met out on the airfield at Schönwalde. Wrecked face. Wrecked marriage. But a nice little house out at Wannsee with an ex-wife to match.

'They got to the top, these people?'

'I've no idea. We've been promised photographs, but they haven't arrived yet. The Minister will know. Ask him.'

Goebbels was alone in the house. It was barely half past seven and he met them at the door, barefoot. The red silk dressing gown, a size too big, might have belonged to his wife. He told the driver to prepare the speedboat and invited Nehmann to come in. Already, Nehmann could smell fresh coffee.

Goebbels led the way through to the kitchen. When Nehmann enquired about the mountaineers, he confirmed that the highest peak in Europe was now German property.

'So, they made it up there?'

'They did.' The Minister was pouring the coffee. 'Can you imagine the battle flag? The views? The faces of the men themselves? You can have too much of campaign footage, Nehmann. On this occasion, I'm assured, there isn't a body in sight.'

'And the Führer?'

'The Führer has a mountain of his own to climb. I was with him three days ago, out east, and he couldn't have been happier, but sometimes I think we expect too much of him.'

'I don't understand. What are you telling me?'

'I'm telling you he cares too much, thinks too hard, takes too much on. Russia is the boldest stroke. There are bound to be moments of difficulty.'

'And this mountain? Elbrus?'

'A triumph, Nehmann. By the weekend every newspaper, every magazine, will be carrying the photos. And then the Führer will come to realise exactly what we've done for him.'

'So, no need to worry?'

'Absolutely none. Drink your coffee. Afterwards I'm proposing a swim.'

Goebbels limped away, leaving Nehmann alone in the big kitchen. Through the window he could see the Ministry driver preparing the property's speedboat, tied up beside the wooden jetty. Nehmann knew that every minute of the Minister's time was dedicated to state business. His diary was full for weeks, months, to come. Nehmann knew he owed Goebbels an account of his dealings in Italy but what – apart from the weather – could possibly justify a leisurely swim?

Goebbels was back with a couple of towels. He was still wearing the dressing gown.

'Here—'

Nehmann took the proffered towel, swallowed the remains of his coffee and followed Goebbels back into the sunshine. On the dock, the driver reached up to help them into the speedboat. When he began to cast off, Goebbels told him not to bother. He and Nehmann would attend to it. Go back to the house and wait for us there.

Goebbels took the wheel. There wasn't a whisper of wind to disturb the mirrored calm of the lake. Nehmann sat back, one arm draped over the varnished woodwork, and decided to enjoy himself. Already, the sun had warmed the plush leather seats and he gazed round, marvelling at how money and influence could conjure this tiny pocket of peace in the very middle of a war spreading to every corner of Europe.

A flight of geese appeared overhead, perfect V-formation, cackling softly to each other. Fish rose, breaking the surface, eager for a midge or a mayfly. Did they know about the gathering carnage in the east, wondered Nehmann. About the sun rising on yet more air-raid damage? About ration cards and three grams of meat a week and endless queues of thin-faced *Hausfrauen* waiting patiently for a bakery to open?

'There, Nehmann.' Goebbels was pointing at a yellow buoy, hundreds of metres out from the shoreline. He throttled back and told Nehmann to make fast with a coil of rope in the bow. Once the boat was secured, Nehmann nodded at the towels.

'We swim?'

'We talk, Nehmann.' A thin smile. 'About your adventures in Italy.'

Nehmann knew the question was coming. Sooner or later he'd have to account for his failure to deliver the letter to Baarova. Since leaving Rome he'd explored a number of explanations, some inadequate, some implausible, others frankly baroque. None of them owed anything to the truth but now – for once in his life – he sensed there was no point in lying. This man knew more about lying than anyone else on earth. When it came to deception, no one was in his league. When the next Olympics came around, he could be certain of a gold medal. Truly, the Prince of Liars.

'I fucked up,' Nehmann said.

'I know. Someone from the Foreign Ministry paid me a visit last night. One of Ribbentrop's associates. Very discreet. No prior warning. In my world, Nehmann, that doesn't happen very often.'

'And?'

'He showed me a letter. He seemed to think it was from me. Happily, that can't have been possible, as I was very glad to point out.' Goebbels paused for a moment. His eyes were very black. 'Your handwriting, I think. Not mine.'

'Yes.'

'Might you care to explain?'

Nehmann did his best. He described the queue for taxis at the Rome terminus, the suited figure who'd helped himself to a seat in the back, and his surprise to be looking at a gun beneath the folds of his expensive raincoat.

'He threatened you?'

'He warned me off.'

'Did he explain why?'

'No. I had an address for Baarova. He told me she'd moved. He also demanded the letter. I'm sorry but I had no choice.'

'How did he know the letter existed?'

'I've no idea.'

'And that's the truth?'

Nehmann didn't answer. He knows, he thought to himself. He knows everything.

'There's a hotel on the Grand Canal,' Goebbels said softly. 'I happen to know it. It's called the Al Codega. They serve an astonishing crème brulée. You were there with your actress friend. And you were probably drunk. You're an inventive man, Nehmann. You understand the power of language, of *make-believe*, and so does your little Czech friend. It was a game you were playing that night. You wrote the script. She performed it. Sadly, the audience included one of Ribbentrop's associates. And, for whatever reason, he jumped to the wrong conclusion.' Goebbels leaned forward, intense, his eyes never leaving Nehmann's face. 'Ribbentrop's people will do anything to attack me, to hurt me. You handed them the perfect weapon. Sadly, from their point of view, they were duped.'

'By?'

'You. Why? Because they believed you. Because you caught my tone of voice on the page and your actress friend was clever enough, or drunk enough, to do the rest. Do we understand each other, Nehmann? Or must I go through it all again?'

Nehmann was staring at him. Perfect, he thought. The perfect cover story. The perfect explanation. The perfect way to keep Ribbentrop's attack dogs at arm's length. A work, in its own small way, of genius. He was about to answer Goebbels' question, but the Minister hadn't finished.

'You were never house-trained, Nehmann, and some days I should lock you in a cage, but the fact that you belong in the wild is an asset. That's why I employ you, believe it or not. You're different. I know I can depend on that. You also take sizeable risks. Risks, alas, have consequences. But first we swim.' He gestured at the water. 'Agreed?'

Without waiting for an answer, Goebbels stood up. Underneath the dressing gown he was naked. He put the garment carefully to one side, balanced briefly on the seat in the stern and then dived overboard. Nehmann stripped and joined him. The water was colder than he'd expected but it didn't seem to bother Goebbels. The Minister beckoned him closer, wiped the water from his eyes and suggested they swim to the bottom together.

'A pebble each, *ja*? Last to surface wins.'

Nehmann nodded assent. Goebbels was first to submerge. Nehmann took a tiny lungful of air and then jack-knifed to follow him, smooth, powerful strokes driving him ever deeper into the murky water. He could see the Minister kicking downwards in front of him but as the light faded, and the water grew colder still, nothing remained but the pale soles of his feet. One of them, he noticed, was twisted inwards. Then the darkness engulfed everything, and he was gone.

Nehmann pinched his nose and blew hard to clear the pressure in his ears. He'd learned to swim in the mountains in water far colder than this but there was still no sign of the bottom and he was beginning to feel the first shivers of panic when, out of nowhere, he found it. At this depth, everything was pitch-black. Nehmann's fingers closed over a handful of mud and pebbles and then he pushed hard against the bottom, kicking upwards, fighting the urge to open his mouth and fill his bursting lungs. That way, he knew, lay certain death.

It was getting lighter now, tiny bits of vegetation in the water, the temperature rising, and then came the moment when his head broke the surface, and he lay on his back, grateful for the sun on his face, sucking air deep into what felt like his belly. Finally, he opened his eyes. Goebbels was floating an arm's length away, breathing normally. Nehmann showed him the pebble from the bottom of the lake.

'And you?'

'Nothing.'

'You didn't make it?'

'No.' The Minister smiled. 'You win.'

*

They helped each other back onto the speedboat and then towelled themselves dry.

'Over there?' He indicated a low house among the trees. 'That's where she lived.'

'Baarova?'

'Lida, yes. I used to take a walk every summer evening. The house had been rented by an actor, Frohlich, and I knew she'd moved in with him. It was inevitable we should meet. I think we both knew that.'

He lay back against the stern of the boat, his legs spread, the towel over his lap, his back cushioned by the carefully folded dressing gown. His eyes were closed and he seemed at peace with the world.

'I used to invite them both out in this little boat,' he murmured. 'Other guests came, too. It was innocent. It was fun.'

'And your wife? Magda?'

'Away somewhere.' He flapped his hand, dismissive. 'Always away.'

'Your children?'

'We had help.' He paused, his eyes still closed. 'A name for you, Nehmann. Kurt Ludecke.'

'I've never heard of him. It means nothing.'

'It wouldn't. He was with us in the early days, but then his nerve failed and he fled. In the end, it was that madman Rosenberg who told me.'

'Told you what?'

'About Ludecke. About him fucking my wife. I had to confront her before she'd admit it. Yes, Nehmann. My wife. The mother of my children. Unfaithful. You begin to understand now? About Lida?'

His eyes were open at last and it suddenly dawned on Nehmann that this man probably had no one else in the world to talk to. Surrounded by potential enemies, often of his own making, he'd sentenced himself to an isolation that would, from time to time, be hard to bear. One of the conditions of surviving at the top of the Nazi Party was that you trusted no one, confided in no one, offered no one ammunition of any sort. No wonder he'd needed a mistress.

'She was responsive? Your Lida?'

'She was careful. As she should be. We talked a great deal. Some evenings there was no one else in this little boat, just us. I could make her laugh. She liked that. Maybe it was the sound of my voice. I used to tell her stories all the time, things we used to get up to in the old days, and she'd tell me that the sound of my voice would make her tingle all over. Were we intimate? Yes, but not physically, not at first, and, oddly, that made the attraction all the more powerful. We both knew it had to happen. But not quite yet.'

That year, at the Nuremberg Rally, Goebbels spoke from the podium. Before the speech began, he told Lida that there'd come a moment when he'd briefly touch his face with a white handkerchief. She was to watch out for this gesture because it meant that he was passionately in love with her.

'And you did it? It happened?'

'Of course. It was a promise as well as a confession.'

'And?'

'She said she was flattered. And perhaps a little more than that.'

On one of the evenings at Nuremberg, Goebbels described arranging for Baarova's latest film to be shown for the first time. The story was set in the world of spies and the audience at the premiere included the likes of Himmler and the *Abwehr* chief, Wilhelm Canaris.

'It was a decent script, Nehmann, I made sure of that. She had the lead role, and everyone agreed she was sensational. I also had the film retitled. I insisted it be called *Traitor*. I was sending a message, a personal little billet-doux to my faithless devil of a wife. Canaris understood at once, of course. That man insists on a code for everything.'

Nehmann smiled. He'd once interviewed Canaris. This was a man who spent his life chasing enemies of the Reich yet Nehmann left *Abwehr* headquarters suspecting that their Chief's own support for the Führer was less than total.

Given his role in the Nazi machine, Nehmann had loved the irony.

'And Lida? At Nuremberg?' he asked.

'She agreed to stay on for a day or two. We had a meal that night with some of the film people at the Ufa studios. In my position it isn't easy to hide yourself away but somehow we managed it. A miracle, Nehmann. That night I prayed to God, and God delivered.'

Next morning, he said, Lida insisted on returning to Berlin. Distraught, Goebbels sent a messenger to the station to intercept her.

'He was carrying a huge bunch of roses, Nehmann, and a photograph I'd managed to lay hands on.'

'Of?'

'Me.'

'And?'

'She didn't get on the train.'

He smiled at the memory, and then trailed his fingers in the water.

'Something precious comes into your life, Nehmann, you'll do anything to keep it. Don't you find that? Don't you agree it pays to be Master of the Hunt? Time waits for no man. Hesitate, and all is lost.'

He was looking at the villa again, the low waterside property that Frolich had been sharing with Lida. The summer had come and gone. The Master of the Hunt, in his own words, was besotted.

'I was putty in her hands, Nehmann. Sometimes there's nothing sweeter than an act of total surrender, not just to the moment, but to all the moments to come. I had to write to her.

I had to talk to her. I had to hear the sound of her voice, if only to reassure myself that I hadn't made her up. I used to put calls through to the house there. Actors work strange hours. Frolich was often still at home. He got a lot of calls from Herr Muller.'

'That's what you called yourself?'

'Yes. And I loved it. The excitement. The subterfuge. All that hiding your real self away.'

'Except for the one who really mattered.'

'Of course. Exactly. The one who really mattered. Our secret got out in the end. There were all kinds of unpleasantness. With Frolich, of course, and Magda, and finally the Führer himself. Some days the pressures were unbearable but we both knew we had to be true to ourselves, to what we had. There's a cabin out in the woods at the Bogensee. I still visit it sometimes, even now, although the pain can be intense. We had a big fur rug in front of the log fire. We spent hours there together, summer, autumn, deepest winter, it didn't matter, just as long as we had each other.'

He nodded and lay back in the sunshine, the faintest smile on his face. Goebbels had long struck Nehmann as an actor manqué. Face to face or roaring at tens of thousands at some tribal meeting or other, he could adopt whatever persona the occasion required. His repertoire of tricks – physical gestures large and small – was extensive. He used his voice like a musical instrument. He was the master, as he'd just admitted, of hiding his real self away. But what if this life of constant camouflage, of artful self-concealment, was all there was? What if nothing lay behind it but an emptiness he could never properly fill?

Nehmann reached for his towel and mopped the sweat from his face. Goebbels hadn't moved. His eyes were still closed, and he seemed to be barely breathing. In some ways, thought Nehmann, this was his deathbed pose. He'd loved and, ultimately, he'd lost but he regretted nothing. A life of suffering, of constant harassment from his many enemies, was chaff in the wind compared to those two precious years with Lida Baarova.

Then, quite suddenly, his lips began to move.

'A question, Nehmann.' His eyes opened. 'Where's my fucking letter?'

'The real one? The one in your own hand?'

'The one I gave you. You still have it?'

'Of course, I have.'

'Then when do I get it back?'

'You don't. Not yet. It's safe. Very safe. No one else will ever lay hands on it. You have my absolute word on that. But for the time being it's mine. Why? Because it makes *me* feel safe.'

'From?'

'You.'

Goebbels threw his head back and began to laugh. Finally, he composed himself. Nehmann thought he caught just a hint of admiration in his voice.

'You know something, Nehmann? People are never honest with me. Never. Sometimes I think it's fear. Other days I put it down to malice. But whatever the motive, people always say what they think I want to hear. Everyone, that is, except you. I like that, Nehmann. For a deeply dishonest man, you never let me down. That's very rare. And very distinctive.'

The pebble Nehmann had fetched up from the bottom of the lake lay between them. It had long since dried in the sun. Goebbels picked it up and gave it to Nehmann.

'This may bring you luck, my little Georgian friend. Where you're going, you'll need it.'

Nehmann studied it a moment. The flatness of the pebble was veined with something darker. Then he stood up, steadying himself as the boat rocked. As a kid he'd been good at this. In fact, he'd been the best. Once the boat had settled, he drew his arm back and then – with that little remembered flick of the wrist at the end – he sent the pebble dancing across the water, ever onward, splash, splash, splash.

Then he turned back. Goebbels, from his seat in the stern, had been watching his every move.

'I made that nine, Nehmann. Let's hope it's enough.'

13

KALACH, 22 AUGUST 1942

Messner was back at Kalach. A brisk crosswind had given him problems on landing, but he'd retained a mental map of the deeper potholes and settled the Storch without breaking another strut.

Klaus, the orderly, met him with a battered old *Kübelwagen*. In the ten days since Messner had been here last, the town appeared to have emptied. Messner knew that Sixth Army had crossed the Don River only yesterday, but it was Klaus who had the latest news.

'We secured the bridgeheads OK and the pontoon bridges were in place by dawn this morning. Sixteenth Panzer should begin crossing any time now. Have you seen those boys in action? God help the Ivans.'

Messner had only watched them from the air, an endless column of tanks, half-tracks, self-propelled assault guns, eight-wheeled reconnaissance vehicles and hundreds of trucks that served as a crowbar to lever Soviet defensive positions aside and open the way to Stalingrad. Face an onslaught like that at ground level and you'd know that your days were numbered.

Klaus was grinning. Fellow NCOs were taking bets on the day

the first units got to the Volga. The huge river entered Stalingrad from the north and then flowed hundreds of miles south-east until it emptied into the Caspian Sea. Among Russians, Messner knew that the waterway had an almost religious significance. On the one bank, Europe. On the other, Asia.

'Well?' Messner wanted to know about the betting.

'September—,' Klaus swerved to avoid a goat. 'My money's on the first week, or maybe the start of the second. Either way, the Ivans will be on their knees. No one's seen an army like this. Ever.'

They were heading west. On the outskirts of the town, among the battlefield debris that had yet to be cleared, the going got tougher.

Messner wanted to know where they were going. The message from *Standartenführer* Kalb had arrived at Richthofen's Mariupol headquarters only last night. It was marked *Immediate, Eyes Only*.

'The SS operate from a little church out here on the steppe,' Klaus said. 'They keep themselves to themselves, which suits us nicely.'

Away from the town, the steppe seemed to stretch forever, not a tree or the barest hint of rising ground to disturb the distant line of the horizon. From time to time, an oncoming vehicle would raise a gaggle of little birds, tiny brown dots that would dart away and disappear into nowhere, but otherwise there was no sign of life.

Then, minutes later, Messner saw the outline of a building a little to the left. At first it looked like a child's addition to the greens and greys of this nothing landscape, a poorly formed collection of angles surmounted by an onion-shaped dome that might once have glowed silver in the brightness of the sunshine. Then he realised that Klaus had been right. He was looking at a church.

'I'm told it was a shrine, Herr *Oberst*. Some miracle occurred here. Don't ask me what.'

Messner nodded. He was wondering why the SS had chosen a place like this as a base. A path led from the dirt road to the gaggle of vehicles parked outside. Klaus got out and opened the passenger door. Messner was watching two men in uniform who'd just rounded the corner of the building. They were both wearing masks and one of them paused to tip his face to the sun.

Messner got out of the car. When he asked Klaus whether he was coming with him, the orderly shook his head.

'I'll stay here,' he said. 'These people will thieve anything.'

Messner approached the nearest of the two men.

'*Standartenführer* Kalb?'

'He's in there. Downstairs. And you are?'

'*Oberst* Messner. *Fliegerkorps VIII*.'

The two SS men exchanged smiles. Messner followed them around the corner of the church. Outside an open door was a row of metal ammunition boxes, full of silverware. Messner had time to glimpse a pair of altar crosses before he was beckoned inside. Thieves, he thought. Klaus was right.

The moment he stepped into the gloom of the church, Messner caught the smell. At first it had a sweetness, slightly perfumed, that took him by surprise. Then he became aware of something much earthier, fouler, more pungent, that lay beneath it. The taller of the two SS men was leading the way down the aisle, his steel-shod boots echoing in the confined space. A fresco of thin-faced saints gazed glumly down from the plastered walls, and a huge bible, propped on a wooden lectern, appeared to have survived the rapacity of the shrine's new keepers.

A door in the depths of the nave was shut. When the SS officer pulled it open and announced their presence a bird appeared from nowhere and flapped madly around before finding another perch.

Silence again. Except for the keening of the wind.

The SS man had put his mask back on and the moment Messner stepped through the door he knew why. The stench here was overpowering. He'd smelled something similar in countless postings across the Greater Reich and normally it was nothing worse than blocked latrines, but this smell had a texture of its own. The sweetness he'd first noticed was definitely there but with it came the ripeness of offal. An abattoir, he thought. Dead bodies. And he was right.

Kalb was waiting at the foot of the wooden steps. He hadn't bothered with a mask.

'Herr *Oberst*!'

The stiff salute drew no response from Messner. He was staring at lines of corpses laid side by side on the earth floor. There must have been dozens of them. Most were the size of adults. Others were anything but. Each was wrapped in something that looked like canvas, heavily stained, but their faces were visible, their eyes mostly open.

'You want to take a closer look? Be my guest.'

Kalb stepped aside. He might have been an artist, Messner thought, a painter welcoming specially invited guests for a private viewing ahead of his latest show. Take your time. See

143

what I've managed to achieve here. All you need, ladies and gentlemen, is a little time and a little talent and the courage to break new ground.

New ground.

Messner was gazing at one of the longer parcels of human flesh. The sheer depth of the smell, sweetened by the thin grey curls of smoke from a pair of hanging censers, suggested these people had been dead for a while, days certainly, maybe even longer, but their faces were still intact, entirely recognisable, and Messner knew with a terrible certainty that three of the faces would be familiar.

He was right. He found the schoolmaster at the end of the line, the same strength in his face, the same hint of a smile. His daughter lay beside him, doll-like in death, her head turned slightly to one side, her blonde curls all too familiar. For some reason she'd raised her tiny hands to cover her ears.

Had she been frightened of something? Had something taken her by surprise? Messner didn't know but it was all too easy to speculate. He took a step backwards, shaking his head. These people had probably been shot. The SS, according to Renke, were meticulous about saving ammunition. Just the one bullet. To the nape of the neck.

'You know this couple?' It was Kalb.

'I stayed in their house. There were photographs.' He turned to face the *Standartenführer*. 'What are they doing here? What have you done to them?'

'These people were terrorists. Someone has to deal with scum like that.'

'Terrorists? This man was a schoolteacher. You dealt with his daughter, too. Explain that to me.'

Kalb said nothing. If he felt uncomfortable, it certainly didn't show.

'We didn't invite you here for a debate on Reich policy, Herr *Oberst*. What's done is done, and for very good reason.'

'We have something else to discuss?'

'Indeed. Tomorrow you intend to bomb Stalingrad. Am I right?'

'Yes.'

'Many aircraft?'

'Hundreds.'

'We need just one. A point I think I made when we last met. I'm not a flyer, Herr *Oberst*. I need a little guidance about the kind of loads your aircraft can manage. You'll be using the Heinkels, *ja*?'

'Yes.'

'And the bomb bay?' He nodded at the bodies on the floor. 'How many could you take?'

Messner shook his head. He'd never had to deal with a question like this and he knew that his first impressions of Kalb had been right. The man came from a different place. He was insane.

'What do you intend to do with them?' Messner asked.

'We intend for you to fly them to Stalingrad. I have a map upstairs. We need to have them dropped in the Volga, upstream from the city. The question, Herr *Oberst*, is how many?'

'But why? Why are you dropping them?'

'The current will take them through the city. Each corpse is carrying Russian identification papers. These are doctors, administrators, merchants and – yes – your precious schoolmaster. Once we know how many you can carry, we need to make our preparations.' His gloved hand made a limp circle in the air.

Messner was staring at him. Madder and madder, he thought.

'Preparations, Herr *Standartenführer*?'

'Of course. The bodies will need to be unpacked. We have in mind various mutilations. You want me to be specific? Eyes gouged out. Fingers missing. Stomachs opened. Where appropriate, castration. These bodies will be retrieved from the river and each one will serve as a warning. A city like Stalingrad is full of people like these, people with a position in the city, people with influence, people with a voice. Once they know what lies in wait, the more eager they will be to flee. It's human nature, Herr *Oberst*. And, once they flee, once they pack up their chattels and head east, then others will follow, millions of others, and the city will be ours for the taking. You spill a little blood to save our own. Is that such a terrible thing to contemplate? Or would you prefer a fight to the death?'

Messner shook his head. There had to be an alternative to this obscene rationale but just now he couldn't offer Kalb an answer. Just to engage in a conversation like this filled him with shame. He felt dirtied. He needed to get out of this foulness, he needed to erase the memory of these alabaster faces. He needed to climb back into Klaus's car, and fire up the Storch, and fly away. Nobody he knew in uniform had commissioned people like Kalb to do anything like this. Only when you saw the evidence could you believe that such a thing was possible.

'Well, Herr *Oberst*?' Kalb was waiting for an answer. 'How many can you take?'

'None.' Messner turned to leave. 'We drop bombs, not people.'

146

'They're dead, Herr *Oberst*. That's the whole point.'

'Dead or alive?' Messner was at the foot of the steps. 'What's the difference?'

Kalb wouldn't answer. For a moment, Messner anticipated a farewell salute but mercifully he was spared. Instead, Kalb checked his watch and then stepped closer. Even his breath, foul, pungent, smelled of death.

'Is this a decision you should be taking, Herr *Oberst*? Or might we expect to be hearing from *Generaloberst* Richthofen?'

14

BERLIN, 23 AUGUST 1942

Nehmann loved Sundays and this one, he'd promised Maria, would be special. The spell of fine weather showed no signs of coming to an end and yesterday's encounter with Goebbels, much to his relief as well as his surprise, appeared to have cemented his position as a maverick in the Ministry's stable of reporters. For once in his life he'd relied on the truth to protect him. And, for now at least, it seemed to have worked. In anyone else's world, Goebbels' parting shot – the hint that something unpleasant lay down the road – might have stirred a moment or two of anxiety but Nehmann had never seen the point of worrying himself without very good cause. The Fates had always treated him better than well. And now would be no different.

He left the apartment early to find supplies for a picnic. He had contacts in a number of restaurants across the city and even at this hour he could rely on a favour or two. By mid-morning, laden with cold meats, wedges of Spanish tortilla, warm rolls and a bag of freshly picked raspberries, he returned to the Wilhelmstrasse. Maria, who'd been playing at the club in Moabit past three in the morning, was still asleep. Nehmann sat on the edge of the bed, gazing down at her. Half awake at last, she reached sleepily up for him. They kissed for a while and then he felt her fingers loosening the buttons on his shirt.

'It's Sunday,' she said. 'You don't have to go to work.'

Afterwards, he made coffee. What he loved about this woman wasn't simply her wants, which were commendably varied, but her instinctive ability to meet his own needs. She had a deftness, a lightness of touch, that went way beyond the physical. In a previous life, he sometimes told himself, she might have been a sorceress or a fortune teller. She seemed to have an almost supernatural knowledge of who he really was. That this might extend to his dalliances with Hedvika in Venice hadn't worried him in the slightest. What was beginning to occur to him was the possibility that he'd fallen in love.

Was this something that happened by accident? Did this have to do with a chance alignment of the stars? He'd no idea but the realisation warmed the very core of him, a much-protected corner of his psyche that no one else had ever visited. Women liked him. Some of them enjoyed him. Like Goebbels, he could make them laugh. But Maria was different because Maria, unlike any other woman he'd ever met, was somehow able to control their relationship. When she wasn't there, he missed her. Worse still, he wanted to know what she was up to.

Still naked, he padded around the flat, in and out of the kitchen, assembling plates, cutlery, napkins, a bottle of Guram's fast-depleting stock of Bordeaux claret. One of Maria's seemingly few possessions was a wicker basket she'd picked up in the market in Prenzlauer Berg. They'd agreed that the banks of the Havel, out beyond Spandau, would be a fine choice for a Sunday picnic. They could eat and drink to their heart's content and afterwards, if the fancy took them, they might hire a sailing dinghy at the little jetty at Wilhelmstadt and venture into the open water beyond.

Dressed at last, they were about to leave when the phone rang. Nehmann turned his back on the instrument but Maria suggested he answer it.

Just as well. Joseph Goebbels had never before rung Nehmann in person, but always through a secretary.

'*Ja?*' Nehmann could think of no other response.

Goebbels was in his office. He was alone all day and he needed a conversation.

'You're telling me you're bored?' Nehmann was staring at the phone.

'Far from it.'

'This is important?'

'I think you'll agree it is. There's some kind of problem?'

Nehmann mentioned the picnic. The weather was wonderful. It was Sunday. What else would anyone half-sane want to do but get out and enjoy the sunshine?

'We're just about to leave,' he added.

'We?'

'Myself. And Maria.'

'Ah... then tell her the C minor was wonderful.'

'The what?'

'The C minor.' Goebbels was laughing now. 'Ten minutes, Nehmann. Ten minutes to get here and ten minutes for us to have our conversation. How does that sound?'

Nehmann was about to answer but realised there was no point. The Master of the Hunt had hung up.

He looked round. Maria was sitting in one of Guram's armchairs, the wicker basket at her feet.

'The C minor?' he queried.

'It's a Beethoven sonata. The *Pathétique*. I played the slow movement last night.'

'Where?'

'In the club.' She was staring at him. 'Where else?'

*

Nehmann was at the Ministry within minutes. The sentry on the door, whom he knew well, expressed surprise that Herr Nehmann should be turning his back on this wonderful weather. Nehmann nodded and for once said nothing. His early confidence that all would be well had evaporated. Dread was something new in his life. Not now, he kept telling himself. Not when everything's going so, so well.

The door to Goebbels' inner office was open. A solitary secretary at one of the desks outside was bent over her typewriter and barely spared him a glance.

'Sit...' Goebbels waved Nehmann into the chair that had been readied in front of the desk. Official business, Nehmann thought. This gets worse and worse.

Goebbels had been making notes of some kind. His pen returned to what looked like a film script. A framed photograph was hanging on the wall behind him. Nehmann had seen it before but never in this office.

He was looking at a family group. Goebbels and his wife were there with their three children. Hitler was standing between them, dominating the background. The group was stiffly posed, designed for a particular occasion, and the photo had appeared in newspapers and magazines across the Reich.

Nehmann remembered it well. October 1938, with the

Czech crisis resolved to the Chancellor's entire satisfaction, Hitler's considerable energies were now devoted to sorting out his Minister of Propaganda's family affairs. Send your mistress back to Prague. Dress up the children. Call in the photographer. Assure us all is well.

Goebbels was still working on the script and Nehmann realised that the photograph, so prominent behind him, was for his benefit. The Minister, as ever, was sending a message. No more secret missions. No more intimacies between them.

'You were at the club last night? In Moabit?' Nehmann asked. The last thing he wanted to discuss was Lida Baarova.

'I was, Nehmann. You're right. Transcendence is very rare, especially in someone your young lady's age. Beethoven might have written that sonata specially for her. He'd have cherished every note, every pause, every tiny nuance in that performance. She must have been there when he wrote it. She had us in the palm of her hand. You know how old she is?'

'Twenty-eight. It was her birthday just recently. That's why I bought her the piano.'

'She's twenty-five.' Goebbels at last looked up. 'She was born on 23 October 1917.'

Nehmann was staring at him.

'*When?*'

'23 October 1917. We were starting to lose the war. My father used to talk about how gloomy people were that year.'

Nehmann's heart sank. This man knows more than I do, he thought. And in matters like this he never makes mistakes.

'Anything else you'd like me to tell me?' Nehmann was trying to hide the concern in his voice.

'You said she was Austrian. I think you mentioned a village down near the border.'

'Villach. She was born near Villach.'

'Wrong again, I'm afraid. She's from Warsaw. Her real name's Szarlota Kowalczyk.'

'You're telling me she's Polish?'

'Partly. Her father's German. He used to teach music at the university in Warsaw. The marriage didn't work out. He's living back here. He was already in his forties when Maria was born. He's an old man now.'

'And her mother?'

'Dead, I'm afraid. Gone.'

'When?'

'Last month. You only just missed her.'

'You're telling me she was Jewish?' Nehmann was watching him carefully.

'Alas, yes.'

'And there was other family? In Warsaw?'

'Two sisters. They were on the first transport, too. Treblinka. My sympathies, Nehmann. This business might be necessary, but it will never be pretty.'

Nehmann was lost for words. He knew about what was happening in Warsaw, about the hundreds of thousands of Jews penned in the Jewish ghetto. More recently, he'd heard rumours of mass deportations to the east where he assumed there must be holding camps. Treblinka, he thought. Wherever that might be.

'They died of hunger? They got sick?'

'They died. As I said, you have my sympathies.'

'I never knew them.'

'Of course, you didn't. But your Maria did.'

The silence stretched and stretched. Goebbels had put down the pen and abandoned the script. At last Nehmann stirred. Did Maria know about what had happened to her mother? To her two sisters? And, if not, was it his job to tell her? For once in his life he felt helpless.

'So, what next?' he said.

Goebbels was taking his time. Nehmann had seen him like this before, but always with other people. It meant that he had a plan, that he was in control of the conversation, and that he was enjoying himself. Something had changed between them. Goebbels was very definitely in charge.

'Where might we find Maria tomorrow morning?' he asked.

'At home. With me.'

'Sadly not. You need to be at Tempelhof by eight in the morning. A driver will collect you.'

'Where am I going?'

'An airfield called Tatsinskaya. It's in Russia. It's belonged to us for several weeks now. The battle for Stalingrad begins tomorrow. Sixth Army is a sorry outfit, but *General* Paulus assures the Führer that the city will be in our hands by the end of next month. The Propaganda Companies will be sending footage back, of course, but that won't be enough. As I'm sure you agree, they can be a liability as well as a blessing.'

'You have something specific in mind? For me?'

'I do, Nehmann. Here—'

Goebbels opened and drawer and extracted a yellow file. He briefly checked the contents before sliding it across the desk.

'Read it,' he said. 'Master it. And then bring me something special.'

Nehmann opened the file. The first photo, in colour, was striking. In extreme close up, the cameraman had caught the subject smoking a cigarette. He was wearing a braided *Luftwaffe* cap. His brow was furrowed. He appeared to be deep in thought but what made the image so special was the cigarette. It was a roll-up and it was held between the second and third finger of the left hand. No one could possibly arrange a shot like this, and the effect was startling. Nehmann had rarely seen a senior commander look so intimate, so interesting, so *real*.

'Von Richthofen,' he said. 'The sainted Wolfram.'

'You've met him?'

'Never.'

'You will. The man was a giant in Spain. Then he tore the French apart when we settled their nonsense a couple of years ago. He would have done the same to the British if Goering hadn't been in the way. Sevastopol was his work. Stalingrad will be Sevastopol all over again, but better. Warsaw? Rotterdam? London? The world has seen nothing until Richthofen attends to Stalingrad.'

'You want me to interview him?'

'Yes. He has an aide. *Oberst* Messner. I understand you've met him already.'

'I have. Briefly. Smashed himself up in a traffic accident.'

'*Ja?*' Goebbels wasn't interested. 'Messner will meet you at Tatsinskaya. He knows you're coming. By the time you get there the first day's raids will be over but part of Richthofen's charm is that the man never stops. We can rely on more raids, more bombs. Did you ever box, Nehmann? Were you ever in the ring? Richthofen always opens with an uppercut. He wants the Ivans on the canvas from the start. Then he waits for his man to get up and jabs and jabs until the moment comes for another uppercut and then it's over. Richthofen is an artist, Nehmann. He paints in blood. He delivers for the Reich. Our people love him already, but I want you to turn him into something truly special. You find the words. The rest you leave to me.'

Nehmann held his gaze. The commission, he had to admit, was beguiling but the unvoiced question on his lips mattered a great deal more.

'And Maria?' he said.

'I have plans, Nehmann, as you may imagine. She plays like a goddess. She deserves a much bigger audience and that, may I say, will be my pleasure to arrange.' He glanced at his watch. 'Did I promise you ten minutes?' He smiled, then nodded towards the window. 'And is the sun still shining?'

*

Nehmann was back outside the apartment. He let himself in and climbed the stairs to the first floor. Half expecting to hear Maria at the keyboard, he was surprised by the silence. He hesitated outside the door, and then realised it was already open. He stepped inside. The big lounge was empty. He called her name. Silence. Her wicker basket was exactly where he'd seen it last, on the carpet beside her armchair. He went from room to room, expecting to find her in the bathroom or perhaps in the bedroom deciding on a change of skirt, but there was no sign of her anywhere. Neither had anything been disturbed. Nor, he realised with a sinking heart, was there a note.

Where should he look next? There was a shop that sold milk on the corner. Should he check there? He was heading for the stairs again when the phone began to ring. He returned to the apartment and snatched at the receiver. She was calling from one of the public boxes on the Wilhelmstrasse. She'd be back in no time at all.

He bent to the phone, recognising the voice at once. Goebbels. 'She's quite safe, Nehmann. We'll take very great care of her. You have my word. I'm afraid I misled you about Tempelhof. You're leaving today, not tomorrow. A car should be with you shortly. *Gute Reise.*'

The line went dead. Nehmann rocked on his heels, exactly the way a boxer might. Goebbels, like Richthofen, fought to win. Jab, jab, jab. These men were animals, he thought. Nothing interested them but the taste of victory, and the roar of the crowd. It had been madness on his part to play games with a burned-out mistress, and now Nehmann had to pay the price.

He returned to the bedroom. The bed was still unmade. He gazed down at it for a moment, then shook his head. Szarlota. Polish, not Austrian. And half Jewish, as well. The irony was so sweet it brought a smile to his face.

This was the age of the lie, big or small. Truth filleted for what might be useful and then tossed aside. Deception practised on the grandest scale. Whole nations, millions of *Volk*, misled, manipulated, lied to. Nehmann was part of that. He understood the power of the lie, the artful sleight of hand, the dark sorcery that turned black into white, and good into evil. That's how he'd made his reputation. That's how he'd won the precious freedoms offered by – yes – the Minister of Lies himself. Yet here he was, still staring at the bed he'd shared with a woman he thought he'd known. The duper duped, he thought. The master of levitation well and truly fucked.

Did it matter? Not at all. If anything, he felt even more for her. Lies were the currency of this crazy time. It was the way you got ahead, made your name. And if you had a problem, if you were half Jewish with the looks to match, it might even be the way you stayed alive. He didn't blame her in the least for hiding bits of herself away. In her position, he'd have done exactly the same. Was Maria her real name? He shook his head, knowing that it didn't matter, that he didn't care. Whatever her real name, wherever she'd come from, she'd remain Maria and the fact was that she'd swallowed him whole.

He brightened at the thought. He knew what Goebbels was up to. He'd taken her hostage against the day when he and the Minister would have to settle their accounts. Because he was clever, as well as devious, he might well invest some of the Ministry's resources in her talent, bring her to the promised wider audience, tempt her with flattery and fame, and he hoped she'd have the strength to keep her bearings in the giddy world of Reich stardom. But in the meantime, provided he survived whatever was to come, he had to protect both their interests.

He left the apartment again and began to climb the stairs. On the shadowed landing at the very top of the building, a door offered access to the roof. The caretaker carried a key but Nehmann knew where he hid the spare. On his knees, he felt behind the radiator and retrieved it.

Out in the sunshine again, he made his way across the ribbed lead roof. A pair of pigeons scattered at his approach. A big water tank stood beside the chimney stack, supported by blocks of concrete at each corner. It fed every apartment in the block and Nehmann knelt again, disturbing the scabs of rust beneath it. He knew they'd be back to search Guram's apartment the moment he was en route to Tempelhof. Goebbels wanted his letter back and he had a couple of men he trusted for work like this. And so Nehmann needed to check it was still safe.

He paused a moment, his hand crabbing awkwardly to the right. He'd wrapped Goebbels' letter in wax paper, and then sealed it in an envelope before taping it to the underside of the tank. For a moment or two he thought it might have gone but then his fingers closed on an edge of the envelope and he sat back on his haunches, sweat pouring down his face, knowing it was still there.

Stalingrad next, he thought. More madness.

15

TATSINSKAYA AIRFIELD, RUSSIA, 23 AUGUST 1942

Georg Messner met his boss back at Tatsinskaya. The airfield had been carved out of the raw steppe. A single east–west runway, unpaved, would handle most of the take-offs and landings over the coming days and local people had watched in wonderment as these once-sleepy hectares had suddenly filled with a vast fleet of aircraft.

Messner hadn't seen Richthofen for a couple of days. His briefcase contained the usual paperwork, all of it marked *Urgent/Immediate*, but just now, unless he was mistaken, there was something even more pressing to resolve.

Richthofen wanted to know about aircraft readiness. The first wave of bombers was due to take off within minutes.

'Bombed-up and ready to go,' Messner confirmed.

'Serviceability?'

'Eighty-three per cent.'

'Really?' The figure sparked a rare smile from Richthofen. Eighty-three per cent was high and both men knew it. Flying time to Stalingrad was an hour and a quarter. By late morning, the first wave should be back here at Tatsinskaya and waiting ground crews would have them back in the air, refuelled and rebombed, by mid-afternoon. Two sorties a day? Perfect.

Messner badly wanted to change the subject. He directed the *Generaloberst*'s attention towards two nearby vehicles. One of them was a staff car adapted for service on the steppe. The other was a truck, the cargo area shrouded in canvas. Both carried the flashes of SS *Einsatzgruppen* C.

Doors in the staff car opened as Richthofen and Messner approached.

'*Standartenführer* Kalb, *Generaloberst* Richthofen.' Messner did the introductions.

Kalb snapped to attention, his right arm raised. Richthofen studied him for a moment, then acknowledged the salute. Another SS officer had joined them. Messner didn't know his name.

'Gentlemen?' Richthofen was rolling himself a cigarette.

Kalb took the lead. In the back of the truck, he said, were a number of what he termed 'gifts' for the citizens of Stalingrad.

'Really? You're playing Father Christmas? At this time of year?'

The irony was lost on Kalb. He mentioned a senior SS commander in charge of *Einsatzgruppen* C, and then another who'd evidently controlled everyone in SS uniform since the start of Operation Barbarossa. Today's plan, he said, had the full backing of both men. Indeed, they regarded it as an important initiative with undoubted relevance to the rest of the campaign.

'I'm afraid I don't understand.' Richthofen sealed his cigarette and ignored the offer of a light from the other SS officer. 'I'm a busy man, Herr *Standartenführer*. Today, as you might gather, is far from routine. Time belongs to no man, least of all me.'

Kalb looked briefly nonplussed. Then he nodded towards the truck.

'*Komm, bitte…*'

Richthofen and Messner followed him. The other SS officer had signalled to two men in the truck and they were already dropping the tailgate. As Richthofen approached, they stood respectfully aside.

'One question, Herr *Standartenführer.*' Richthofen paused to light his cigarette. 'What's smelling so bad?'

Kalb had no answer. Instead, he was looking at Messner.

'In the absence of any figure from you, Herr *Oberst*, I took advice. We understand at least a dozen depending on size. Might that be accurate?' He nodded up at the truck. 'In any event, we brought spares, just in case.'

Spares? Messner was watching Richthofen clambering up into the back of the truck. Once again, he refused help. He parted the two wings of canvas and stood motionless, his booted feet apart, hands on hips, the cigarette smouldering between his fingers. Then he turned, braced his body and jumped. Moments later he was back with Kalb and Messner.

'You killed these people?' He was talking to Kalb, matter-of-fact, no hint of surprise.

'Of course.'

'And they are…?'

'Saboteurs, propagandists, agitators, enemies of the state.'

'And you're denying them a burial?'

'We're putting them to good use.'

'By throwing them out over Stalingrad?'

'Indeed. That's exactly what we're doing.' Kalb seemed warmed by the way Richthofen had been so quick to spot the guile of the plan. He began to explain it in detail, exactly the way he'd done to Messner, dropping the bodies upriver, letting the ID they were carrying – their names, their occupations – make a point or two once they'd been recovered, but Richthofen cut him short. Engines were starting all over the airfield. Ground crew were hauling away the wooden chocks that anchored the wheels.

'You see my aircraft, Herr *Standartenführer*?'

'Of course. *Our* aircraft. Might that be more accurate?'

Messner blinked. This man didn't know Richthofen, couldn't possibly anticipate the fire he'd just lit. Anticipating an explosion of wrath, followed by a curt dismissal, he was surprised that Richthofen barely flinched. Instead, he beckoned Kalb closer, the way a teacher might invite a backward pupil to consider the simplest proposition. The gesture was almost friendly, even conspiratorial.

'As you can see, these aircraft will be taking off in minutes,' he said. 'I'm afraid it's too late to call any of them back and, in any event, it would take us far too long to unload the bomb bay.'

'You're telling me I have to wait? *Kein Problem*, Herr *Generaloberst*.' He turned to share a smile with the other SS officer but Richthofen hadn't finished. He checked his watch. 'The next wave will be leaving in less than an hour. I'm happy to put one of those aircraft at your disposal.'

'Excellent. You can take a dozen of these scum? More, perhaps?'

Richthofen shook his head. He seemed to be counting the men Kalb had brought with him.

'There's four of you?' He was looking at Kalb again. 'Would that be right?'

163

'*Ja.*'

'Then the answer's eight. Eight bodies.' He nodded at the truck. 'You choose.'

Kalb looked briefly confused. Then he began to understand. 'But you said twelve.'

'I did.'

'And the other bodies? The balance?'

'You, Herr *Standartenführer*, and your *Kameraden*. Our bomb bays are bigger than you think. The journey will take no time at all. It needn't be uncomfortable.' He offered Kalb a thin smile, and then took a final drag on his cigarette before grinding it beneath his boot. 'Your decision, Herr *Standartenführer*. *Oberst* Messner will be pleased to take care of the details. *Auf Wiedersehen*. Enjoy the flight.'

16

KYIV, UKRAINE, 23 AUGUST 1942

Werner Nehmann arrived at Kyiv in the late afternoon. He was expecting a fellow scribe from one of the Propaganda Companies to meet him at the airfield but instead, to his delight, a figure from what felt like the distant past stepped back into his life. The same scuffed leather jacket. The same hint of menace in his battered face. The same scars on the shaven baldness of his bone-white skull. Even the way he walked, loose-limbed, his whole body moving from the shoulders, seeming to carry the promise of imminent violence. Wilhelm Schultz, a still-rising star among the *Abwehr* spy hunters, and now – it appeared – resident in this huge city.

Schultz had always done important business in bars and this posting was no different.

'You want to fill your belly and keep your money in your pocket?' he growled. 'Welcome to Kyiv.'

Schultz had a car and a driver. He took Nehmann to a bar built into a cliff behind Khreschatyk, the city's main boulevard. Nehmann stared out at the lines of ruined buildings, gaunt in the midsummer sunshine.

'Who did all this?' he asked.

'The Russians. You want to know how? I'll tell you later. First we need a drink.'

Schultz led the way into the sudden darkness of the bar. They'd first met when Nehmann began work for the Promi. Goebbels had a hunch that, despite the ten-year age difference, the two men were probably brothers under the skin and he'd been right. Now Schultz wanted to know everything that had happened to the little Georgian. Interviewees he'd gutted with that clever smile of his. Senior chieftains he'd outraged. Stunts he'd pulled. Women he'd fucked.

'Let's start with the women, my friend.' Schultz had summoned the barman. 'Tell me about last night and then work backwards.'

Nehmann declined the invitation. In real life, as on the page, you always held something back. Except, perhaps, the tease that always carries the reader into the story.

'I'm in love,' he said.

'And?' Schultz was reaching for the first of the tall glasses of lager.

'Terrifying. Little boy lost.'

'You're making it up. You make everything up.'

'I do. I admit it. But not this. And what's worse is I mean it.'

'Both sides? You both mean it? Two fools on the same errand?'

'Yes. At least I think so.'

'*Think* so? What kind of language is that? Your life is a buffet. You need do nothing but help yourself, especially where the women are concerned. And now you're telling me that's changed?' He shook his head. 'Is this woman real? Has she found signs of life beyond that *Schwanz* of yours? Have you given her permission to have a look round, make herself at home? Bad news, my friend. And, may I say it, a disappointment.' He passed Nehmann the other glass. 'She has a name, this woman?'

'Maria. I think...'

'You *think*? Christ, this gets worse. She's asking the questions? She's doing the interview. Is that what you're telling me?'

'Yes. And you know something else? I love her for it. Why? Because she's probably better than me, sharper than me, more ruthless than me.'

'*Ruthless?* That's fighting talk, Nehmann. This vision belongs in uniform. You should put her on a plane, send her here. What else does she do?'

'She plays the piano. Once you've sat and listened, the game's over. Always fight your battles on the territory of your choice. Me? No fucking chance. Beethoven? Schubert? Chopin? Her father taught her how to play the piano when she was still in nappies. She's made me honest, Willi. I'm a reformed man.'

'And she fucks good?'

'Like an angel, Willi.'

Schultz held his glance, then extended a hand in congratulation. No one else called him Willi.

'To your Maria...' He reached for his drink.

'To Maria.' Nehmann was looking wistful. 'I'm afraid "your" indicates possession on my part. I lie for a living but not in this case. I'm afraid "your" would be hope, Willi, rather than expectation.'

They touched glasses, Schultz acknowledging the distinction with the hint of a smile.

*

167

From the bar, a couple of hours later, they strolled a block or two away from Khreschatyk to a backstreet restaurant where Schultz's face was again welcome. In a city in which many of the locals were starting to eat their ration cards, Schultz was insisting on the Wiener schnitzel with dumplings and red cabbage. Unbidden, the waiter brought a bottle of champagne as an aperitif. Schultz hauled the bottle out of the ice bucket, leaving a row of drips over the pristine whiteness of the tablecloth.

'It's Georgian, Nehmann. You'll love it.'

Another toast, to Stalingrad this time. Schultz wanted to know what his master thought Nehmann would bring to the feast.

'You mean Goebbels?' Nehmann asked.

'Of course. Is he still your pet dwarf? Is he still halfway up your arse?'

Again, Nehmann declined to answer. Much as he liked this man, he had no intention of sharing the story of the last couple of weeks. Trust, even within a relationship like this, was something you'd never want to hazard.

'He wants what he always wants,' Nehmann said. 'He wants me to make the turd smell sweet.'

'You mean this fucking war?'

'Of course. So far, no problem. It's skittles, isn't it? Holland? Belgium? France? You knock them over and wait for the applause. Russia? I'm not so sure.' He paused. 'You?'

'Me? A confidence, Nehmann. I've been here since late September, last year. We'd chased the Ivans out of the city and made ourselves comfortable. The bomber boys had done a respectable job on one or two areas of the city but free labour made it easy to tidy up. Then bombs started going off. No reason. No sign of aircraft. No clue why. We were losing people we couldn't afford to. I think the magic fucking word here is targeting. Hotels we'd commandeered for senior command staff. Office accommodation we'd be using. Someone obviously knew what they were doing. And that someone was either Russian or one of the locals. Either way we had to find out.'

'So, they called you in?'

'They did, Nehmann. I was very happy in Paris. They'd promised me a posting that might have lasted years. There are worse places to fight the war, believe me.'

'And here? What did you find?'

'It was hard going. These people are tough. They had nothing left to lose and that makes a difference, believe me. They're good haters, too, the Ukrainians. They hate us and they loathe the Russians but we'd pushed them to the brink during the siege and when the Ivans came up with a plan to leave us with a souvenir or two, little bonbons to keep us on our toes, they saw the point. It's a quaint notion, especially these days, but they seemed to think that the city was theirs by right and they wanted it to stay that way. The Russians were in a position to make life tough for us. And so the locals said yes.'

'The Ivans planted explosives?'

'Lots. All over the city. Thousands of kilos of the stuff. More than you or me could possibly imagine. All wired up to make life just a little difficult.'

'How?'

Schultz shook his head. Enough, he seemed to be saying. All you need to know is this: that the Russians are clever, and tough, and never give in. Stalin, he growled, has made himself the face of Russia. He calls himself the *Vodzh*, the great fucking

Leader. He has absolute power. He's not a performer. He hasn't Hitler's gifts. He can't find the sweet spot and make all those women get silly about him. But that doesn't matter but because Stalin treats his people like dogs and when he says bark they do just that. Ship all your arms factories a thousand kilometres to the east? It happens. Make the women work twelve-hour days turning out shells? It happens. Put people like me behind the front line to shoot deserters on sight? No problem. Result? No matter how many we kill, they just keep coming. The French, according to Schultz, had gone flabby. The Motherland was something you argued about all day in bars and cafés and when it came to a fight they'd forgotten how to.

'You understand?' He was leaning across the table now. 'You see what I'm trying to say? The Russians aren't like that. For Russians, the Motherland, the *idea*, is all they've got. It's like religion. It's their last hope. It's the difference between life and death. Stalin knows that. And what he also knows is that nothing we – or even the fucking *weather* – can do will ever change that. They have to draw a line. They have to defend that line. They have to get through. At whatever cost. Do they understand that back home? Are there people in Berlin who might have the first inkling about this animal we're prodding with our sticks? You, my friend, would know. Why? Because you're Georgian. You've lived under the Russians. You speak the language. So why don't you tell me what they're really like?'

Nehmann felt like applauding. None of this would make the turd smell any sweeter, quite the contrary, but it had the raw stink of truth, a commodity he'd almost forgotten how to recognise.

'Berlin?' he said mildly. 'You think they have the faintest idea about any of this?'

'That's my question. I'm in the chair here, Nehmann, so what's the answer? Let's start with Goebbels. The man's got a brain in his head, unlike some of the others. You play him like the artist you are. Tell me. Truthfully. Tell me what he thinks.'

'*Truthfully?*' Nehmann smiled at the very idea. 'Goebbels is a realist. He thinks this war will go on and on. He also thinks it's going to get harder and harder to win, which is where people like me come in. The problem with propaganda is this: you put shit in one end and it's not hard to guess what comes out the other. People don't trust stuff like that. They can smell shit at a thousand metres. They don't believe a word of it and that doesn't matter as long as you've got them by the throat but then a time arrives when you're depending on these same people for the basics of life – like your shells and your bombs and your bullets – which are going to keep the rest of the world at arm's length. It's August, Willi. Goebbels lives in the world of promises. What he can very definitely promise is another winter. More cold. Less food. And an eternity on the production line. What kind of offer is that? Unless we can keep delivering all those sweeties from abroad?'

Schultz nodded and sat back to make space for the food. The Wiener schnitzel looked delicious. Nehmann reached for a fork and stirred the cabbage into a puddle of sauce.

'And Stalingrad?' Schultz hadn't finished.

'Another bottle?'

'Of course.' Schultz gave the waiter a nod. 'So, what do you think?'

'I think the city has a very big problem. It has Stalin's name

171

on it. Never underestimate the simple things. Hitler wants it for his little collection. He thinks it would keep the Germans happy and he's probably right. Me? I'm here to pat their little square heads, and engage their interest, and tell them not to worry. The Führer will deliver because he always does. Is it a fantasy? I've no idea but you, Willi, will be the first to know. And that's a promise.'

He began to saw at the schnitzel, but Schultz wouldn't let him off the hook.

'And the Russians? Do they get a say in any of this?'

'Of course, they do. You were here last year. You've just told me how hard they can make life. It's gone midnight, Willi. A truce, *ja*? Time for just a mouthful or two?'

Schultz was staring at him, and for the first time Nehmann realised that these reservations of his were genuine. He had first-hand experience of what the Russians could do, of how tough they were and how resourceful. Sheer numbers, he seemed to be saying, may in the end count more than propaganda.

Schultz peered down at his own plate for a moment or two, then looked up.

'You're flying to Tatsinskaya tomorrow morning. Am I right?'

'Yes.'

'And then you're attached to *Fliegerkorps VIII*? Richthofen's mob?'

'Yes.'

'That may not be enough.'

'Enough for what?'

Schultz shook his head. He wouldn't answer the question. Then he glanced round the near-empty restaurant before returning to Nehmann.

'I can get to the front line any time I want,' he said softly. 'Make contact when you need me.'

17

TATSINSKAYA, RUSSIA,
24 AUGUST 1942

Exhausted, hungover, but otherwise undamaged, Werner Nehmann was at Kyiv airfield by six in the morning. Schultz hadn't accompanied him out of the city but had been on hand at Nehmann's quarters before dawn to shake him briefly by the hand and say goodbye. Nehmann wanted to enquire further about what he might expect over the days to come but Schultz wasn't in the mood for conversation.

'You know how to get me,' he said. 'Ring if you have to.'

Have to?

Nehmann was sitting at the back of the big Ju-52 transport. Every seat on the aircraft was occupied, mainly *Wehrmacht* officers with a couple of younger men in *Luftwaffe* uniform. The narrow cabin was airless and seemed shrouded in gloom. Conversation, at this time in the morning, was subdued. Beside the window, Nehmann had the sun on his face and as the lattice of Ukrainian fields below grew smaller with altitude, he fought the urge to doze. Whether he liked it or not, the regime had gathered him up and was shipping him east.

Have to?

Schultz, he knew, had contacts at every level of the Nazi

machine. As an *Alter Kämpfer*, one of the old brawlers who'd brought mayhem to the streets of Munich when power was still a gleam in Hitler's eye, he had the ear of countless Party members who'd done well out of the regime. They trusted Schultz. For better or for worse, they believed he represented something the Party would be poorer for losing. Whether Schultz still carried the authentic whiff of revolution wasn't for Nehmann to judge but what was incontestable were the talents of the man himself. Like Nehmann, he had an acute awareness of when things might get out of hand. And, like Nehmann, he was a survivor.

The flight was much longer than Nehmann had anticipated, the living proof that Schultz might have a point about the sheer size of the challenge that Hitler had set himself. Halfway through the journey, in the middle of nowhere, they landed to refuel. Nehmann, along with most of the other passengers, clambered down the metal ladder to stretch his legs. In every direction he could see nothing but the yawning folds of the steppe. Apart from a cluster of huts and two refuelling bowsers, there was nothing, just a faint sweetness on the wind and the bored near-adolescent on duty advising one of the passengers not to get too close to the refuelling hose with his cigarette. As a metaphor, thought Nehmann, this scene is telling. We're nomads in this wilderness. Our tenure here is strictly provisional. A blink of the eye, a turn of the page, and we'll be gone.

They filed back onto the aircraft. Nehmann felt better now, ready for a proper sleep. He counted his fellow passengers. There were sixteen. The pilot fired up the three engines, pointed the aircraft at the wind, and took off.

Two and a half hours later, a series of bumps awoke Nehmann. They were descending through a layer of thin cloud. From the window, as the cloud parted, he saw another airfield, away to the right, very different from the last. There were aircraft parked everywhere in clusters of four and five. Midget-sized vehicles busied between them, trailing wispy clouds of dust, while a series of small brown dots marked the edges of the airfield. The dots were everywhere. They looked like insect larvae and it was a full minute before they were low enough for Nehmann to recognise them as tents. This is where I sleep, he thought. This is where I must hatch my best ideas.

Messner was waiting at the low wooden structure that appeared to serve as a terminal. He offered a stiff salute and then nodded at Nehmann's bag. It was red, soft leather with a yellow flower pattern around the handles. It belonged to Maria and it was all he'd been able to find in the scramble to leave Guram's apartment.

'That's all you've got?'

'It is. I'm not staying long.'

'You're sure about that?'

Nehmann didn't answer. He followed Messner to a waiting Jeep. Evidently it was American, a gift to the Russians and now part of the spoils of war. Nehmann couldn't see anything like it elsewhere on the airfield.

'It's for our use only.' Messner told him to get in.

'Our use?'

'Myself and the *Generaloberst*.'

Mention of Richthofen prompted a question from Nehmann. He was here to watch *Fliegerkorps'* chief in action. It was

Goebbels' wish that the nation gain some understanding of what it takes to smash the Russians.

'Is that your phrase?' Messner enquired.

'Goebbels'. Normally he's much more subtle but I think the Eastern Front brings out the worst in him.'

'And you're here to correct that?'

'I'm here to watch.'

They were crossing the airfield at high speed, the Jeep shuddering from rut to rut. Nehmann clung to the hand-grab beside him, watching a big Heinkel wallowing in beneath the grey duvet of cloud. Messner drove like a maniac. No wonder his face was such a mess.

Finally, they lurched to a halt beside a tent. Messner unfolded his long frame and got out.

'Pretend it's a hotel room.' He led the way into the tent. 'Use that imagination of yours.'

Inside the tent there was space for three camp beds, each with a neatly folded blanket. Messner drew Nehmann's attention to an oil lamp, the glass sooty, the wick blackened. It stood on a chair beside one of the beds.

'Only use it when you absolutely have to,' he said. 'Fuel out here is precious. There's a bigger tent I'll show you that serves food three times a day. The food's shit but the water is safe to drink as long as you remember the tablets.'

'Tablets?'

'In the bag there, beside the lamp.'

Nehmann nodded. 'I'm alone here?'

'For the time being, yes.'

'And your *Generaloberst*? When will I get to see him?'

Messner frowned. This was the coldest of welcomes but

after their first meeting Nehmann had expected little else. Every army he'd ever known had a suspicion of outsiders.

'The *Generaloberst* may have time for you this evening,' Messner said. 'It depends on events. Meanwhile, he'd like you to take a look at his work.' He nodded at the bag. 'You have something warm in there?'

Nehmann found a heavy sweater he'd packed in case it got cold at night. Messner had left the tent. When he returned, he handed Nehmann a camera.

'Have you ever used one of these? It's a Leica III.'

Nehmann took the camera. It was small, neat, but surprisingly heavy. His fingers found the lens aperture and shutter speed adjustment controls.

'I used one of these in France,' he said. 'Is it yours?'

'It belongs to the *Generaloberst*. He asks that you take the greatest care of it. It's fully loaded, thirty-six exposures. He told me he's pre-set the film speed. You'll need this, too.'

He gave Nehmann a light meter. Nehmann checked the film speed on the camera: 200.

'So, what am I supposed to do with it?'

'We have a little expedition in mind.' Messner's face rearranged itself into what Nehmann guessed might be a smile. 'Yesterday we took care of Stalingrad. There are more raids in progress but yesterday was the big one. We've assigned you to a Heinkel. There are no spare seats so you'll be flying as the ventral gunner. The pilot's name is Rubell. The plane's fully operational so you'll get a taste of the real thing.'

'We're dropping bombs?'

'Of course.' He nodded at the camera. 'The *Generaloberst*

would appreciate some shots of Stalingrad. Might we assume you'll oblige?'

*

The aircraft assigned to carry Nehmann into battle was part of a much bigger force of bombers. Some of them were already on the move on the bareness of the airfield, taxiing slowly towards the end of the grass runway. Messner pulled the Jeep to a halt beside a lone Heinkel and led Nehmann to the foot of a metal ladder. The pilot was waiting with a spare parachute. The rest of the crew had already embarked and Nehmann was wondering whether his presence was altogether welcome. He'd never fired a machine gun in his life and knew that the training took weeks to complete.

'The name's Rubell.' The pilot extended a meaty hand. 'You're the one who organised that photo, *ja*?'

'What photo?'

'Mount Elbrus. The guys with the battle flag. We all got copies yesterday.' He nodded at Nehmann's borrowed camera. 'You're very welcome, *Kamerad*.'

Nehmann nodded, shrugged, and then milked the applause. In truth he'd forgotten about the showy conquest of Elbrus, but he was very happy to share the glory. If a photo could take him to Stalingrad and back, so be it.

'You were on the raid yesterday?' he asked.

'Of course. Two sorties. By nightfall, between us all, we'd dropped a thousand tons of bombs.'

'Any opposition?'

'Nothing to speak of. We lost three planes.' He patted Nehmann on the shoulder. 'Don't worry, *Kamerad*. Forget about the Ivans. We'll give you a little tour once while we do the business. I'll talk you through it on the headphones.' A squeeze of the shoulder this time. 'Just take the shots, *ja*?'

He helped Nehmann into the parachute harness and watched him tighten the straps.

'Not too big for you?'

'No.'

'You've done this before?'

'*Ja.*'

'You know how many seconds to count? When to pull?' He grinned. '*What* to pull?'

Nehmann's hand tracked to the canvas stitching of the handle that released the chute. Rubell, impressed, gave his arm a final pat.

'*Wir gehen, ja?*'

Nehmann followed him into the belly of the plane. He'd been in a Heinkel before and he knew how claustrophobic this space could be. The ventral gunner's position lay beside the open door and he flattened himself against the skin of the fuselage as Rubell squeezed past before pausing to make him comfortable in the gunner's seat. The gun itself, to Nehmann's relief, had been removed.

'You're seeing out OK? Good view?'

Nehmann nodded. He felt like a tourist. Rubell made sure Nehmann's headset was working and went forward to the cockpit. The aircraft began to shiver as he fired up the first of the two engines. Then came another cough, the second engine, and the whole plane shuddered as it began to inch forward.

'You're hearing me, *Kamerad*?'

Nehmann grunted a yes.

'*Gut*. If it gets too noisy, tell me to shout.'

Nehmann smiled. This was like the movies, he decided. The view through the air gunner's blister was perfect, the greys and greens of the runway beginning to blur as they picked up speed. Behind, and to the right, another Heinkel was keeping station, half airborne between bounces, readying for the moment of take-off. Nehmann had already taken a reading on the light meter and he raised his camera, adjusting the focus, filling the frame with the aircraft as the pilot hauled back on the control column and the wheels left the runway for good. Not bad, thought Nehmann, winding the film on.

The flight east took just over an hour. Barely minutes from take-off, still climbing, Nehmann caught an expletive in his headset which he assumed came from Rubell. He was celebrating the view from the cockpit. Nehmann leaned forward, his nose against the cold Perspex. With his neck at the oddest angle, he could just glimpse towering columns of smoke on the distant horizon. Stalingrad, he thought. Still burning.

He was right. As they approached the suburbs of the city, Nehmann began to recognise the heavy footsteps of *Fliegerkorps VIII*: whole areas cratered by bomb blast, street after street of houses reduced to ashes. The ruins were still smouldering, smudges of light grey smoke curling away on the wind, and it took a minute of two for Nehmann to realise that the curious ochre stripes on each plot of land were brick chimneys, the sole evidence that people had once lived here.

'Incendiary bombs by the thousand.' Rubell's voice again. 'No need to blast anything apart down there. Just set the place alight.'

Nehmann could see the river now, the broadness of the Volga dividing the city in two. On the western bank, the tall white apartment blocks threw long shadows and appeared to be intact. Wrong. Rubell's voice again in his headphones.

'We hit them time and time again. If you looked hard enough you could see concrete dust billowing out of the windows. At ground level there was even more of the stuff. My best guess is that the floors inside collapsed.'

'The people got out?'

'Not many of them. Not that we could see.'

'They have air-raid shelters? Like at home?'

'It seems not.'

Nehmann nodded, raised the camera, took more shots, fidgeting with the focus, hunting for the kind of trophy images that might please the author of this wrecked city: huge petroleum tanks on the riverbank, still aflame, their metal carcasses torn apart; a lake of blazing oil drifting slowly down the river, dragging thick coils of smoke that circled slowly upwards in the updraught from the water; a nearby building on the western shore that must have been a hospital, eviscerated by high explosive, dozens of beds plainly visible inside.

Rubell dropped a wing and then steadied the aircraft for the bombing run. They were running parallel to the river now, no trace of anti-aircraft fire or enemy fighters, the entire city at their mercy, a party box of targets that no bomber pilot could resist. The city centre, according to Rubell, was dominated by a huge Tatar burial mound, Mamaev Kurgan.

'This is our second helping, Nehmann.' He laughed. 'When we arrived on Sunday the Russians were out in force, having their picnics. You never saw people move so fast in your life. Now they know better. Which in some respects is a shame.'

Nehmann felt a blast of cold air as the bomb bay doors opened. He sat back from the Perspex, the camera readied, adjusting the exposure for the gloom of the aircraft's interior. The bombs nestled in front of him, eggs crudely sculpted in dull metal, tail fins welded at one end. Someone had chalked a message on one of the cylinders. Nehmann was still familiar with Russian from his early days in Georgia and he brought the Cyrillic characters into focus in the viewfinder. *With love from Berlin*, went the message. *Expect more where this came from.*

Nehmann squeezed the shutter button, then readied the camera for another shot. At the moment of release the aircraft lurched upwards, suddenly lighter, and then he glimpsed the stick of bombs falling earthwards with a tiny wobble that had an almost dance-like grace. He returned to the gunner's blister, peering down through the Perspex, hoping to capture the line of explosions as yet more bombs stitched their way across the ruined landscape, but the aircraft had moved on and all he could see was smoke.

18

TATSINSKAYA AIRFIELD, 24 AUGUST 1942

They were back at Tatsinskaya in time for Nehmann to join the queue for goulash and cabbage in the tent that served as a mess. Of Messner there was no sign but Nehmann recognised one of the cameramen from the Propaganda Company he'd briefly got to know in France. His name was Helmut and he was now attached to Sixth Army for the final push to Stalingrad. Helmut had set up a darkroom at Tatsinskaya, strictly to develop stills rather than movie footage. When Nehmann mentioned the photos he'd just taken from the Heinkel, Helmut said he was welcome to help himself.

'You know how to develop stills?'

'No.'

'Then I'll come, too.'

They walked the five hundred metres to the dank space behind a maintenance facility that Helmut had converted into a darkroom. He locked the door, checked the blackout on the single window, then warmed the inky darkness with the glow of a red lamp. While Nehmann extracted the exposed film from the Leica, Helmut prepared the developing fluids. Within half an hour, they were both bent over the bath of fixer, waiting for the first of the images to swim up through the soup of chemicals.

Nehmann had been witness to this process on a number of occasions and it always fascinated him. The first glimpse of what he'd captured through the camera, its sheer ghostliness, that fog of greys that slowly resolved itself into shapes he recognised, the remains of a city that only a couple of days ago had been intact. This, in Nehmann's view, was a kind of magic.

One by one, he identified the shots he wanted Helmut to print for Richthofen.

'You're seeing him? You've got an audience with the great man?'

'Tonight, as far as I know.'

'And that's why you're here?'

'Yes.'

'One favour? Do you mind?'

'Not at all.'

'Ask him what the SS were doing here yesterday with a truckload of bodies.'

*

The *Generaloberst* was quartered, at his own insistence, in a smallish tent adjacent to the two-storey wooden structure on the edge of the airfield that served as a control tower. Beside the tent Richthofen had parked the little Fieseler Storch that took him to every corner of 4th Air Fleet's enormous area of operations.

Messner had collected Nehmann from the darkroom. Now, with the prints still slightly wet, Nehmann awaited an introduction. Messner, capless, emerged briefly from the tent and gestured Nehmann inside. Richthofen was sitting on a folding canvas chair, bent over a map, enjoying what looked like a chicken sandwich. The tent smelled of cigarettes and warm leather and a single oil lamp cast a flickering glow over the *Generaloberst*'s upper body. At his elbow was a bottle of brandy and three glasses.

Messner poured drinks while classical music played softly in the background. Beethoven. Probably a symphony.

'And you're Nehmann?' Richthofen glanced up. 'Goebbels' little *Waise*?'

Nehmann blinked. *Waise* meant 'orphan'. He didn't know whether this was a compliment or not.

'*Waise*?' Nehmann wanted to be sure.

'Imp. Elf. Some people I know think you belong in a circus.'

'I'm flattered.'

'I'm not sure you should be. That stunt on Mount Elbrus. Your idea or your master's?'

'I helped make it happen. At the time it seemed a good idea.'

'It was an excellent idea. Poorly received by the Führer, alas, but command at his level is seldom easy. Occasionally you go crazy over the silliest things. You've seen the photo? It was developed here.'

Messner fetched it from a box file beside Richthofen's camp bed. Half a dozen men were clustered around a pinnacle of snow. Above them, the War Flag streamed in the wind. Perfect, Nehmann thought.

'I understand Messner here arranged for a little keepsake to be left up there, as well. A Fokker triplane. My cousin would be flattered. And so am I. War can be a burden sometimes. Moments like these lighten the load.' He took the photo, gazed at it for a moment, and then handed it to Messner. 'So, what do you have for me, Nehmann?'

Nehmann returned the Leica. Richthofen put it carefully on one side, then he rolled up the map and asked Nehmann to spread the prints from the developing bath across the table. The prints were already beginning to curl. Richthofen flattened each of them in turn with one thick finger and told Messner to find a magnifying glass.

'So why are you here, Nehmann?' Richthofen was studying the cratered wilderness that had once been the picnic area on the Mamaev Kurgan. A smoker's grunt appeared to signal approval.

'The Minister is hungry for news.' Nehmann said. 'He thinks Berlin needs a bit of cheering up. I was a butcher once. I know how to carve the best bits from the carcase.'

'And that's your skill? Finding little morsels of good news? Then scuttling back to your lord and master?' He was examining a shot of the oil tanks ablaze beside the river.

'The wick in the Stalingrad candle.' Nehmann nodded at the burning oil tanks. 'That's the kind of image he likes.'

Richthofen glanced up. There was surprise in his face, and just a hint of admiration that he didn't bother to conceal.

'Wick?' he repeated. 'Candle? I like that.'

'It's what I do.'

'Then you're a poet.'

'You're too kind. An ex-butcher would be closer.'

'No.' Richthofen shook his head. 'You should leave the butchery to us. That's why we're here. That's what we're good at. That's why we have the medals and the fancy uniforms. You have a different talent. Maybe I should be envious.'

'I doubt it. This regime has little use for poets.'

'You're probably right, Nehmann. Which raises a question or two. I understand that Goebbels gives you free rein. Am I right?'

'More or less.' Nehmann nodded.

'Then tell me why.'

'I think he's lonely.'

'You're his *friend*?'

'I'm someone he can talk to. That's rare, believe it or not. He's surrounded day and night by people who make life sweet for him. He must know thousands, tens of thousands. How many does he trust enough to risk a proper conversation?'

'That's true for all of us. You flew in a Heinkel today. Those men talk to each other, get drunk with each other, would die for each other and one day they probably will. Get above a certain command level and it's never the same. This job is solitary. It has to be. You can't afford it to be otherwise. But solitary can be good while lonely is something else entirely. So...' He sat back a moment and reached for his brandy. 'Where does that leave Herr Goebbels?'

'Lonely. For sure.'

Messner stepped back into the tent with the magnifying glass. Richthofen muttered something Nehmann didn't catch and Messner disappeared again.

'You'll take a little brandy, Nehmann?' Richthofen nodded at the bottle. 'A man shouldn't drink alone. Bad for the liver but worse for the spirit. *Prosit*. Here's to more candles and more wicks.'

Nehmann raised his glass to acknowledge the toast, watching the *Generaloberst* as he took a closer look at the remaining photos. He'd heard a great deal about this man, and the reputation he'd built for himself since the early days in Spain. To chalk up victory after victory, to rewrite the *Luftwaffe*'s combat manual, to command the respect of flyers who could spot a phony at a thousand metres, to be at ease with the likes of Hitler and General Franco, to be able to stir an old woman like Paulus into taking a risk or two, all this spoke of someone deeply unusual.

Messner stepped back into the tent. He'd brought a thick buff envelope, a little battered around the edges. Richthofen grunted an acknowledgement and said they needed a third chair. Messner once again disappeared.

'He tells me you two have met already.' Richthofen was tidying Nehmann's photos into a neat pile.

'That's true.'

'Then you'll know that he, too, is lonely.'

Nehmann felt acutely uncomfortable. This man broke all the normal rules of conversation, a talent Nehmann recognised only too well.

'Messner has been unlucky.' Nehmann touched his face. 'An accident like that has consequences.'

'Indeed. A moment of inattention? A poor decision? Alas, it doesn't stop with traffic accidents. You should talk to Messner when you get the chance. He deserves what you called a proper conversation and officers at his level aren't good at that.' He glanced up. 'I have a name for you, Nehmann. Olga Helm?'

'She's an actress.'

'You know her?'

'We've met, yes.'

'And?'

189

'She's an attractive woman. Talented, too.'

'Indeed. A combination not without consequences.'

He held Nehmann's gaze for a long moment and then shook the contents of the envelope onto the table and began to sift through them, one by one. As far as Nehmann could judge, these images told the story of the last year or so. A convoy of trucks, poorly camouflaged, bucketing along a birch log road that had been destroyed by the passage of heavy armour. The burned-out remains of a Soviet tank abandoned in some far-flung village square. An aerial shot, not unlike the ones Nehmann had shot that afternoon, a town centre reduced to a moonscape. A gaggle of Soviet prisoners, sitting cross-legged in the mud. Moments caught on the way to Stalingrad, he thought. A simple record of events, framed and shot by someone with an unblinking eye.

'These are yours, Herr *Generaloberst*?'

'They are, Nehmann, yes. Me and my Leica. Man and wife. Inseparable. We Germans have been making history for a year. One day it will be important not to forget. Here—'

He'd finally found the photo he was after. Nehmann found himself looking at a thin-faced man in his late twenties. His eyes were deep-set and the greatcoat, open at the neck, looked perhaps a size too big.

'I took that near Smolensk last year. What do you make of him?'

'He's a prisoner,' Nehmann said. 'Which means he's probably Russian.'

'You're right. How did you know?'

'The eyes. He doesn't know what's going to happen next and he doesn't trust you to make the right decision. If you want to know the truth, I've been that way for most of my life. You don't need to be a soldier to feel the edge of things.'

The edge of things. Another phrase that won Richthofen's approval.

'You know who he is?' he asked.

'No.'

'His name's Yakov. He's Stalin's eldest son. We found out by accident from someone else in the compound.'

'And he's still alive?'

'Yes.'

'In captivity?'

'Yes. His real name's Dzhugashvili, like his father. Our friends in the *Abwehr* talked to him at length. No love lost, Nehmann, between father and son. Yakov fell in love with a Jew He wanted to marry her. Stalin threw him out. Later he married another Jew – a dancer from Odessa. She gave Stalin two grandchildren. He didn't bother with either of them.' He reached for the photo and studied it for a moment or two. 'So how lonely is Stalin? Have you ever thought of that, Nehmann?'

Messner was back with a chair. Nehmann watched him settle and reach for his brandy. Olga Helm? He couldn't believe it.

Richthofen appeared to have lost interest in Stalin. He wanted to talk about Goebbels again.

'*Feuertaufe*? You've seen it?'

Baptism of Fire was a film Goebbels had masterminded. It followed the *Wehrmacht* and the *Luftwaffe* into Poland and had been shown in countless cinemas across Europe. If you happened to be living, unbombed, in London or Paris, it was a deeply uncomfortable warning of what might happen if you ever said 'no' to Hitler.

'A masterpiece,' Nehmann murmured.

'And a lie. You were in France, I believe. You have eyes in your head. How many horses did you see on that campaign?'

'You mean ours? *Wehrmacht* horses?'

'Yes.'

'Hundreds. Thousands. Maybe more than that.'

'Exactly. And how many of those horses appeared in Goebbels' little movie? None. Am I complaining? Absolutely not. Watch that film, come out of the cinema, and you know that we Germans have invented a new way of making war. It's all *Sturm und Drang*. Tanks, artillery, Stukas, Heinkels. Lots of noise. Lots of movement. Not a horse in sight. Does Goebbels ever ask himself how we keep feeding this machine? How we carry supplies to the front line? Never. And why? Because there's no point. No one goes to the movies to watch horses and carts. If they're German, they want to know we're winning. That we're irresistible. And foreign audiences? They're shitting their pants. Clever, Nehmann. But a lie.'

'Poland?' Nehmann said softly. 'Belgium? Holland? France? Don't they belong to us now? Or have I missed something?'

'You've missed nothing, Nehmann. Of course, we've won. But that was the easy part. What I'd like to know now is how Goebbels and his people, people like you, Nehmann, are going to cope when things go wrong, when the enemy doesn't fall over within weeks, when the war is still there, day after day, and there seems to be no end to it. Maybe that's when your boss starts thinking hard about the horses.' A thin smile. 'Largely because, by that time, we'll probably be eating them.'

The music had come to an end. Messner was on his feet, tidying the photos. In the distance, Nehmann could hear the cackle of a lone aero engine.

Richthofen drained the last of his brandy and stood up. He looked, Nehmann thought, suddenly old.

'Enough.' The *Generaloberst* checked his watch. 'Bed.'

19

TATSINSKAYA AIRFIELD, 24 AUGUST 1942

Nehmann was in no hurry to go back to his tent. An hour with *Fliegerkorps VIII*'s forbidding chief had confirmed what he'd long believed to be the truth about the realities of being in charge. Capable or otherwise, High Command set you apart. Some, like Richthofen, could cope. Life had sandpapered their souls. They relished the bruising business of leadership, the endless confrontations, the ambushes that lay in wait, the guarantee that your peers – fellow chieftains – were always out to screw you. Others, maybe Stalin, certainly Goebbels, were more vulnerable, more thin-skinned. Richthofen, he knew, had a baroness for a wife and three fine children. He'd never waste a moment even thinking about the likes of Lida Baarova.

'He liked you, Nehmann. I could tell.'

It was Messner. He'd emerged from nowhere, a cigarette between his fingers. The darkness softened his ruined face.

'Should I be flattered?' Nehmann enquired.

'Yes. Getting his time is one thing. Gaining his confidence, his interest, is quite another. He likes people who answer back.'

Nehmann nodded, trying to mask his irritation. This was like having his homework marked, he thought.

'So, what's been happening?' He nodded vaguely towards the east.

'Good news. The best, in fact. Sixteenth Panzer are already on the river. They arrived yesterday afternoon. A good pair of binoculars, and you're peering into Asia. From the Don to the Volga in a single day? Remarkable. A couple of our fighter pilots put on a bit of a display for their benefit. Victory rolls. Other stuff. You should write it up, Nehmann. They're both back on base here. Kurt Ebener's available tomorrow morning. I can fix for you to see him.'

'You're telling me the city's fallen?'

'No. Sixteenth Panzer are out on their own, north of Stalingrad, but it's just a question of time now. The river crossings within the city are still open. If the Ivans are wise, they'll bale out while they can. Otherwise we're going to be taking another million prisoners.'

Nehmann nodded. Yakov Dzhugashvili, he thought. Stalin's son.

'There's a man called Helmut,' he said. 'Propaganda Company. I'm sure you know him.'

'And?'

'Where would I find him?'

'Now?' Messner was frowning. 'At this time of night?'

Nehmann stepped closer, put a hand briefly on Messner's arm, a gesture of reassurance.

'We're journalists, Georg.' He gave Messner's arm a squeeze. 'We never sleep.'

*

Helmut's tent lay in the same quarter of the airfield as Nehmann's. Messner drove him across. Like Nehmann, Helmut had the tent to himself. To Messner's evident irritation, his oil lamp was still casting long shadows over the canvas.

Messner brought the Jeep to a halt.

'You want me to come in?'

'No, thanks.'

'You're sure?'

'Yes.'

'Then tell him it's late. The oil in that lamp won't last forever. You hear what I'm saying, Nehmann? You'll give him the message?'

Nehmann fought the urge to laugh. Messner shrugged, gunned the engine and accelerated away. Nehmann waited until the lights of the vehicle had disappeared behind a line of nearby Heinkels. After a while, he could hear nothing but the soft keening of the wind and he spent several minutes immobile, his head tilted back, gazing at the million tiny lights pricking the blackness of the night sky. He was trying to imagine what it must be like to be a Russian, living in Stalingrad, waiting for the German axe to fall. Shackled to history's guillotine, these people might themselves be searching the heavens, desperate for some sign of a reprieve. A shooting star burned briefly overhead, a leaving a trail of brightness that flickered and then died. Gone, Nehmann thought. *Kaputt.*

Inside the tent, Helmut was lying on his camp bed, fully clothed. He appeared to be dozing. There was a book open on his chest, rising and falling as he slumbered on. Nehmann closed the tent flap behind him and stepped across to the bed. The book was *War and Peace*, a German translation, much thumbed.

'What do you want, Nehmann?' Helmut wasn't asleep.

'Tell me about Tolstoy. Does he help at all?'

'He always helps. This is my second time through. But you didn't come for that, did you?'

Nehmann didn't answer. Instead, he settled into the tent's only chair, low-slung, canvas stretched over a wooden frame. He wanted to know how long Helmut had been with Sixth Army.

'Too long. This bloody war goes on and on. Last winter was a bitch. You can't believe how cold it gets. Minus forty-five degrees? Some days you end up pissing on your hands, just to get them moving again. Loading film can be a nightmare. Your fingers just don't work any more and the only thing to do is keep melting snow, keep drinking, keep filling your bladder because that way you give yourself a minute or two to get a fresh roll in the camera. Sixteen-millimetre film? Those tiny sprocket holes? Piss on your fingers and it's just possible. Believe it or not, we time each other. A minute, maximum, then you're frozen stiff again.'

Nehmann nodded. As a kid, learning the basic skills of butchery, he'd been banished to an outhouse in the depths of winter. The cold in the mountains could be brutal, especially when the wind got up. He'd shared this arctic space with hanging sides of cattle and sheep, and he remembered the rough grain of the big table, scarred and bloodstained, and the long minutes it took to breathe life back into his frozen fingertips. Sometimes you had to saw the frozen meat from the bone and leave it to thaw out once you could find a fire. That bad.

Helmut had a bottle of vodka. He'd been with *General* von Bock when Army Group Centre's advance had come to a halt in front of Moscow, back around Christmas. The news, all of a sudden, had been worse than bad – Zhukov's armies bursting out of nowhere to chase the *Wehrmacht* away – and there were no pictures to feed the Glee Machine that was Goebbels' Promi.

'You called it that? The Glee Machine?' Nehmann had never heard the term.

'We did. In private. It made no difference, of course. When you tell Berlin the truth they don't want to know, and when they insist you send stuff back, good news stuff, you start making it up. We settled on a theme in the end. How to get the better of winter. How to survive January. It was all campfires and huge stews and close-ups of grinning soldiers who badly needed a shave. There was a corporal who played the mouth organ and that helped. *Kraft durch Freude*. Strength through joy. Our guys looked like a bunch of Boy Scouts. Berlin? Delighted.'

Nehmann smiled. They'd done the third glass now. Helmut had coyly admitted to another bottle hidden in his rucksack and Nehmann watched him struggling off the bed to fetch it.

'That truck,' Nehmann murmured. 'The SS truck.'

'Yeah?'

'You mentioned bodies.'

'I did.'

'What bodies?'

'God knows. They could have been Jews. They could have been anyone. I think those bastards have given up counting.'

'But what were they doing here?'

'I don't know.'

'You saw the bodies?'

'Yes.'

'How many?'

'I didn't count. Maybe a dozen? All the faces were the same, even the little ones.'

'The same?'

'Smashed to pieces. Pulped. All over the place. Think of your friend Messner. They were much worse than that.'

'Did you talk to anyone? The SS people maybe?'

'Christ, no.' At last, he'd found the vodka. He returned to the camp bed in triumph, the new bottle held aloft. The first time he tried to refill Nehmann's glass, he missed. 'Kyiv.' He licked the vodka from his fingertips. 'Did anyone ever tell you about Kyiv?'

'Never.'

'We were there last year. September. Most of the Ivans had gone and the rest were prisoners. Things were settling down nicely then bombs started to go off all over town. People were dying, our people, important people, people who mattered. Our SS friends aren't subtle. One good deed deserves another. An eye for an eye. Very Old Testament. Ironic, eh?'

Helmut was swaying, the new bottle cradled in one arm like a baby. Nehmann gazed up at him. He was as keen on looted vodka as the next man but knew he had to remember some of this.

'An eye for an eye?'

'*Ja*. Kyiv was a bad place to be a Jew last year. The Ukrainians didn't like them either. Our SS friends did what they do best, rounded them all up, kicked them into line, took them out of the city. There's a ravine called Babi Yar. You could hear the shooting all over town. It went on for days. Like I say, no one was counting but in the end I think they ran out of ammunition.'

'Hundreds?'

'Thousands. Maybe tens of thousands. Kyiv's a big place but there wasn't a tailor or a pawnbroker left. All gone.'

Nehmann watched Helmut collapsing softly onto the camp bed. Miraculously, he kept the bottle upright.

'More, Nehmann?'

Nehmann shook his head. He was thinking about Maria. What was her real name? And how soon before she, too, disappeared into the darkness?

Helmut had closed his eyes. For a moment, Nehmann thought he was asleep but again he was wrong.

'You know about any of this stuff?' he mumbled.

'No.'

'You should. Everyone should. Tolstoy would, if he was still around.' His face creased into a smile and his fingers crabbed across the bare earth where he'd left the book. 'You ever read Tolstoy?'

'Never.'

'You should,' he said again. His eyes opened. 'There are photos. I took photos.'

'In Kyiv?'

'Here. Yesterday. Of the SS truck.' He tried to hoist himself up on one elbow but failed completely. 'They're in that shithole of a developing room, Nehmann. Box on the floor. Maybe you ought to take a look.'

Moments later, finally unconscious, he began to snore. Nehmann was drunk, too, but it made no difference. Maria, he told himself. For her sake. He sat beside the camp bed until he was sure that Helmut had gone. A key, he thought. I have to find a key. The developing room will be locked and there has to be a way to get in.

He started with Helmut's rucksack, emptying it item by item, clothing, notebooks, a map of Hamburg, half a bar of chocolate, various items of cutlery, a metal cup, three rotting plums tucked inside a sock. No key. Then he found another bag, much smaller, stitched canvas, lying on the other side of the camp bed. More notebooks, a pair of binoculars, two light meters and a small framed photo of a woman sitting on a beach. She had the sun in her eyes and she was squinting at the camera. She looked much older than Helmut, but she was blowing him a playful kiss. Nehmann studied the image for a while, wondering about the life this man had left behind him, then repacked the bag. Still no key.

Helmut was wearing a pair of the loose black trousers favoured by the Propaganda Companies. They had deep buttoned pockets ideal for storing bits and pieces of equipment and he knelt beside the bed, easing the pockets open, slipping his fingers inside. Helmut never stirred, not once. In the second pocket, at the bottom, Nehmann found the keys. There were half a dozen of them on a knotted length of cord.

Outside the tent, the night was darker than ever. Layers of cloud had rolled in from the west and Nehmann could taste rain in the air. He set off across the airfield, making his way through lines of parked Heinkels, ghostly shapes that suddenly materialised from nowhere. Twice he fell, once heavily, rolling over onto his back and staring up at where the stars had once been. The maintenance workshop, with the darkroom attached, felt much further away than he remembered but finally he recognised the pert shape of Richthofen's Storch and knew he was nearly there.

The door he needed was at the back of the building. He had the keys ready for whatever lock he found but to his surprise the door was already open. He paused in the darkness, running his fingers down the wooden frame. Where the tongue of the lock seated into the rim latch, the wood had been splintered. He paused a moment, trying to remember if the door had been this way before, but knew he couldn't be certain. Then he put his face to the damaged frame and sniffed. A hint of fresh resin, he thought. Someone's been here. Recently.

He stepped inside, feeling his way by touch alone. A tiny lobby, then another door into the cubbyhole that Helmut had converted into a darkroom. A box on the floor. Helmut had been specific. Nehmann found it within seconds, bending in the darkness, his arms outstretched. It was a metal box with a flap on top and once again it was unlocked. He knelt beside it, feeling inside.

Nothing.

20

TATSINSKAYA AIRFIELD,
2 SEPTEMBER 1942

Over the next month, Tatsinskaya became a second home for Werner Nehmann. For the first week, when the *Generaloberst*'s hectic schedule permitted, Nehmann spent more time with Richthofen, exploring his past, inviting his views about the Reich's strengths and weaknesses as campaign after campaign unfolded, trying to get a feel for the man. To his surprise, Hitler's favourite airman was remarkably candid. He had no patience for arse-licking of any description. He viewed the upper reaches of the Berlin military as completely out of touch. Time and again, he insisted that only commanders in the field, especially here in the east, could truly be relied on for the truth.

Nehmann wove the best quotes from these interviews into a longish despatch for Goebbels, knowing only too well that he'd reshape them for his own purposes. The Minister had debts to settle with the likes of Goering and Ribbentrop and in both cases Nehmann was more than happy to supply bullets for his gun. Within days, Nehmann received a brisk note – handwritten – from the Promi. 'Excellent material. *Mehr, bitte.*'

More, please. Nehmann needed no encouragement. Over the next couple of weeks, interview by interview, he moved among the airmen and the ground crews, the maintenance teams and the resupply echelons, and began to assemble a series of supplementary reports.

His subject now, all too easy, was the most obvious. Who was this enemy? What were the Russians *like*?

Luftwaffe personnel he sat down with were only too happy to oblige with an answer or two. Many of them hadn't been home for more than a year. They'd mingled with tank crews and infantry as the Reich's armies pressed ever deeper into Russia and picked up a mass of anecdotal stories.

The Ivans are Asiatic sub-human garbage, said one. Thieves, said another. They put on thin German trousers in the winter because they're warm under their own kit, and you'll never meet an Ivan who isn't wearing at least two German watches. They pillage our dead and leave shit and piss everywhere. Look for yellow snow and somewhere nearby you'll find an Ivan.

Ivans, according to a medical orderly, spend most of their time drunk. They call vodka Product 61 because that's the way it's numbered on the commissary issue lists. A brimming mugful of Product 61 is what they drink when they get a medal. The medal's in the bottom of the mug, you open your throat, swallow the lot, and emerge with the medal clamped in your teeth.

Another medic, a nurse this time, was even more graphic. When the vodka's all gone, and they're desperate for anything, she told Nehmann that the Ivans drink anti-yperite liquid from their anti-chemical warfare kit which drives most of them clinically insane. The lucky ones sober up on water drained from central heating systems or scooped up from puddles. These people live like animals, she said. They *deserve* to be put down.

This was excellent copy but on a more personal level, Nehmann was uneasy about 'put down'. Helmut had already confirmed that the shots he'd taken of the SS truck had disappeared but when Nehmann pushed him further – who? why? – he said he didn't know. The photos, he insisted, were graphic: head and shoulders shots in extreme close-up, useless for individual ID, but ample proof that the SS were sadistic as well as merciless. Why they'd bother to bring the smashed-up bodies to Tatsinskaya was beyond him but this act of trespass by some stranger breaking into his darkroom had disturbed him, and he couldn't hide a fear of possible consequences. The SS had powers you wouldn't believe, he told Nehmann. If I disappear one day, you'll know where to look.

Messner, Nehmann decided, might know the answer. By that first week of September, the two men were getting to know each other. Messner never bothered to hide his attitude towards journalists in general, partly mistrust, partly a kind of dismissive contempt, but he seemed to regard Nehmann as an exception. In his busy working days, he'd always find the time to brief Goebbels' pet *Waise* on progress inside the besieged city: how the Stukas were flying from sunrise to sunset, managing as many as eight sorties while the daylight lasted. How the Heinkels were pounding key industrial targets: the Lazur chemical factory, the Red October metallurgical works, the Barrikady gun factory, and the sprawling complex that was the Dzerzhinski tractor assembly plant.

Nehmann dutifully noted this tally of ruins but more interesting was the physical evidence around him. The airfield, it seemed to him, was getting less busy rather than more. Ground crews were still swarming over every returning aircraft, trying to beat the turnaround times and get them back in the air, but of the aircraft themselves there seemed to be fewer and fewer. When he put this thought to Messner, the *Oberstleutnant* shrugged. It was early evening, and Nehmann had joined Messner for a smoke.

'We certainly have problems,' he muttered. 'It's true. Maybe you should talk to the *Generaloberst*.'

'Maybe I should. Can you fix it?'

'I can try.'

'I need to get up to the front line, too. Possible, you think?'

'Anything's possible. You're getting bored here? We don't frighten you enough?'

The two men were sprawled in the grass, enjoying the early evening sunshine. Over the last day or two, Nehmann had been aware that Messner had begun to lower his guard. At first, every exchange with Nehmann had ventured no further than a formal recitation of facts, statistics, the dry leavings of *Fliegerkorps VIII*'s working day. How many sorties completed. The precise weight of bombs dropped. Target damage assessments recounted with a slightly grim attention to detail. Now, though, Messner seemed in the mood for something more intimate.

'That little girl of yours, the one I met at Wannsee.' Nehmann was lying on his back, his eyes closed. 'Do you miss her at all?'

'Lottie?'

'Yes.'

'She's my daughter, Nehmann. A father has responsibilities.'

'That wasn't my question. You had a family once. I met them out at Wannsee. You remember?'

'Of course.' Messner nodded. He was watching a pair of Heinkels wheeling towards them at the end of the landing run. The roar of the engines made conversation impossible for a minute or two, then the aircraft came to a halt and a sudden silence descended. 'She wanted me to call her Noo-Noo,' he said softly. 'Can you believe that?'

'Lottie?'

'Beata. My once-upon-a-time wife.'

'You make it sound like a fairy tale.'

'Never. It was never that. We were sensible people, Nehmann, my wife and I. Sensible in our professions. Sensible in our choice of friends, in what we ate, in how much we let ourselves go. Sensible in every way you might like to consider.'

'Sensible in bed?'

The question brought a frown to Messner's face. He plucked at a tiny blade of grass, sucked it briefly, spat it out.

'I take it you know about Olga,' he said at length.

'I heard one or two things.'

'How?'

'It doesn't matter.'

'Did the *Generaloberst* tell you? Be honest, Nehmann. It doesn't matter. The man is a grown-up. He knows what matters and what doesn't.'

'Did Olga matter?'

'For a while, yes.'

'And Beata?'

'No. Not any more. I wrote letters, lots of letters, schoolboy letters. These matters are always more complicated than you think.'

'These letters were to Olga?'

'Of course. And in the end, they found their way to my wife. She's a scientist, Nehmann. She lives in the world of cause and effect. She believes in evidence, in putting things to the test, and in the name of good sense she decided that the marriage was over. Very wise.'

'And you?'

'I understand her decision.'

'Do you regret it?'

'You mean the decision?'

'I mean Olga Helm.'

'Not in the slightest. A man does what a man does. Everything in life carries a lesson. Perhaps I married the wrong woman.'

'And you and Olga?'

'Gone. Over. Finished.'

Nehmann nodded. He was up on one elbow now, watching the bomber crews sharing a joke as they walked away from the Heinkels. This brief insight into Messner's private life, he thought, was beyond bleak.

'So what matters now?' He gestured round the airfield. 'Is all this shit enough?'

'More than enough. The *Generaloberst* gives me certain freedoms. On one level I'm flattered. On another I'm simply grateful. Take a good look at my face, Nehmann. And then ask yourself what the rest of me must be like.'

'You're carrying other injuries?'

'Yes.' He nodded. 'Most of them on the inside. Accidents like mine either kill you or nearly kill you. And you may have noticed that I didn't die, not properly, not for good.' He got to his feet, his eyes never leaving Nehmann's face. 'Any more questions, Nehmann? Or are you happy, now?'

Nehmann didn't get up. He'd pushed his luck, but he didn't care. Something had been troubling him for days.

'Helmut,' he said. 'The cameraman.'

'What about him?'

'He's gone. The rest of his team are still here but not him. Was he ill? Have you flown him out?'

'Ill? No. And, yes, we made arrangements for him to leave.'

'He'll be coming back?'

'I doubt it.' He hesitated a moment, a busy man checking his watch, then he was looking down at Nehmann again. 'War can be harsh, my friend. It might be wise to keep that in mind.'

*

In the second week of September, the first frost. Nehmann emerged from his tent, feeling the chill and the crispness of the grass beneath his feet. He'd talked to enough veterans by now, men who'd struggled through the previous winter, to know exactly what lay in wait. The fast-melting frost was nature's down payment on the months to come. The wind from the east was blowing the remains of the summer's dust and chaff across the airfield. It would get far, far, colder.

And it did. On 17 September, the temperature suddenly plunged. Nehmann awoke at dawn. He was still alone in the tent. He'd already helped himself to the blanket folded on the next bed but now, shivering, he struggled out to lay hands on a third. Back in bed, he drew his knees up to his chest, his hands between his thighs, desperate to conserve every particle of warmth. He'd tried to sleep like this as a kid in Svengati, with the cold sluicing off the mountains, but it had been January then, the very depths of winter, while here on the steppe it was still autumn.

Last night he'd been summoned to the *Generaloberst*'s

command tent. Richthofen himself wasn't there but Messner, barely raising his head from the usual pile of paperwork, had told him that there might be a possibility of Nehmann making it into the city. Supply flights to the forward airfield at Pitomnik were scheduled throughout the day and Messner himself would be piloting one of them. Weather permitting, Nehmann was welcome to come along.

Nehmann had asked him what he'd be carrying.

'Food, fuel, letters from home, plus the man from the Promi,' Messner muttered. 'What else could a soldier possibly want?'

Back in his tent, the temperature already below zero, Nehmann had wondered what might be lying in wait for him among the ruins of the city. He talked to returning bomber crews every day. They were in the air for as long as six hours, sortie after sortie, clambering down from their aircraft for a snatched meal and a brief check of the maps and air recce photos waiting in the operations tent. Bombing specific targets, they told him, was like bombing in the dark. There was smoke everywhere from burning oil tanks, thick, viscous. The stuff penetrated the aircraft itself, catching in the back of the throat, insidious, evil, and getting even a glimpse of anything on the ground was impossible. The only thing worse than flying through shit like that, said one pilot, would be trying to survive underneath it.

Messner appeared shortly after eight. He stood in the entrance to the tent, stamping warmth back into his feet. He had an armful of clothing which he tossed at Nehmann.

'Put this stuff on.' His breath clouded in the icy air. 'It's been through the treatment.'

The clothing was Russian. It smelled of shag tobacco and the powder used for de-lousing. Nehmann knew *Wehrmacht* veterans who swore by this kit. They said the Russians didn't skimp on woollen serge. These people understood the cold, respected it, unlike the sharks and budget-mongers in Berlin.

Messner said he'd be back in half an hour. When Nehmann asked how long he might be in Stalingrad, Messner offered what might have been a grin. He was wearing gloves Nehmann hadn't seen before, pilot's gloves, the thinnest grey leather, and he seemed – for once – almost cheerful.

'Depends,' he said.

'On what?'

'On whether anyone kills you or not. I'm not sure whether it makes any difference...' he was looking at the mountain of blankets on Nehmann's camp bed '...but you've still got time for a prayer.'

*

They took off nearly an hour later. The ground crews and the pilots called the big three-engined Ju-52s *Tante-Ju*. Auntie Junkers. All the seats had been removed and the yawning space behind the pilot's bulkhead had been packed with a jigsaw of wooden boxes, jerrycans full of fuel, and bulging sacks of mail addressed to the men in Sixth Army. Three more of the big transports were scheduled for take-off and two of them were already bumping across the airfield towards the end of the runway. Snowfall during the night had left a thin, crisp blanket of white that stretched in every direction and once Messner had completed his start-up checks, and fired up all three engines, he set off in pursuit.

Nehmann was riding in the cockpit alongside Messner. There was no one else on board. Earlier, walking out to the aircraft,

Messner had warned that Soviet fighter pilots were becoming keener by the day. They were flying decent aircraft now, thanks partly to the blessings of the Lend-Lease agreement with their allies, and when the weather offered the opportunity they didn't hesitate to get stuck in. The big old transports were sitting ducks to a Hurricane or a Thunderbolt in the right hands but *Fliegerkorps VIII* could still muster a respectable number of Bf-109s and he anticipated no problems en route to Stalingrad.

Nehmann had met some of these fighter pilots. Many of them had tasted combat at the hands of the French, and above all the British, but the war in the east, they all agreed, was a war apart. They said that the Ivans flew the way they drank, with a wild abandon. In the early days after the invasion, appearing in neat little formations, they'd been easy meat, but they had radios now and they'd lifted a trick or two from the *Luftwaffe* rulebook when it came to the intimate violence of a dog fight. Take the enemy by surprise. Stay close. Then get closer still.

Nehmann was shivering again. At ground level he'd been grateful for the warmth from the cockpit heater, but as they climbed away from the airfield the temperature was rapidly sinking and even Messner's extra layers of clothing seemed to make no difference. Already, when he shaded his eyes against the blinding sun, he thought he could see the towering columns of smoke that had to be Stalingrad.

'One of our fighter guys mentioned a friend of yours,' Nehmann shouted.

'What?'

'A friend of yours. Dieter Merz?'

The roar of the engines was deafening but they both had headsets and the name sparked a nod from Messner.

'We called him *der Kleine*,' he said. 'Lovely man until his luck ran out.'

'He's dead?'

'All but. He lives with that wife of mine. Maybe I should be grateful. Maybe she should, too.'

Nehmann blinked. This was a new Messner, someone he hadn't glimpsed before. The sheer act of flying seemed to have transformed him. He was carefree. He'd shed whatever had tethered him before. His gloved hands were steady on the control column. His fur-lined flying jacket was zipped to the neck. Folds of silk scarf were just visible beneath his chin. He's loving this, Nehmann thought. It's set him free.

The Bf-109s slipped into formation around them, half a dozen of the sleek little fighters, the pilots saluting the big old *Tante-Jus* with a cavalier wave. Nehmann watched them a moment, silver-grey fish against the blueness of the sky, throttled back, riding little cobblestones of turbulence with a grace that seemed itself a thing of beauty. The sight was deeply comforting and Nehmann smiled to himself, the icy cold forgotten. Then, without warning, they were gone.

Nehmann looked across at Messner. His eyes were on the move now behind the aviator glasses, his head swivelling left and right. The 109s had peeled away, climbing for height. Then came a blur of movement, right to left, something stubby and fat that seemed to pass an inch in front of the Junker's nose, and Messner swore softly, pushing the Ju's nose down, as another Soviet fighter suddenly filled the windscreen. Nehmann caught the twinkle of cannon fire and felt the airframe shudder as the shells found their target. One of the engines was already trailing black smoke and Nehmann watched as Messner's right hand danced along a bank of switches, triggering the fire extinguishers, trying to minimise the damage. The beat of the engine slowed, and the propeller began to mill in the airstream.

Nehmann could taste fear in his mouth. So sudden, he thought. And so final. This was the violence that the fighter pilots he'd talked to found so hard to describe. One moment you have a seat in the gods, omnipotent, invulnerable. The next, you're the plaything of gravity, probably on fire, a hostage to bad luck or your own lousy judgement. Half a second, that's all it takes. Half a second, and then an eternity of regret.

The dog fight, as far as Nehmann could judge, was in full swing. Looking up through the glass canopy, he could see a Bf-109 chasing one of the Soviet fighters, quarry and hunter, the Bf matching the Ivan's every move, wingovers, stall-turns, and a sudden gut-wrenching dive that nearly worked. Then came a brief burst of fire, the *Luftwaffe*-blue tracers clearly visible, and the powerful little Soviet fighter was suddenly cartwheeling away, one wing severed, a tiny black dot falling out of the cockpit. Moments later came the blossom of the parachute and a grunt of triumph on the R/T.

Nehmann stole a glance at Messner. The grin, at last, was unforced and Nehmann realised what he should have known from the start, that Messner's face had been wrecked for exactly an occasion like this. Go through a windscreen, even at ground level, even in the clutches of the Berlin blackout, and moments like these were what remained of life's pleasures.

'*Kamerad*.' It was Messner. He was nodding at the windscreen, talking to himself. The grin, if anything, was wider than ever.

Nehmann tried to focus. At first, he could see nothing. Then, out of nowhere, came a huge engine, wings, a tailplane, even a face in the cockpit. Messner held his nerve. The Ju was falling like a stone, a nearly vertical plunge that made the airframe beg for mercy. The entire aircraft was shaking. Something had come adrift in the cargo area behind them and Nehmann heard a splintering of wood before the big old aircraft began to level out, Messner hauling back on the control column, every metal panel groaning around them.

Below, almost within touching distance, was the first scatter of buildings that signalled a major city. Bomb craters instead of gardens. The charred remains of house after house. Tottering brick chimney stacks. Tank tracks across a patch of grass that might once have been a school playground. Then, all too briefly, a kneeling figure in *Wehrmacht* grey, crouched over a series of red and white panels. He glanced up, one arm raised as they thundered over.

'*Scheisse*.' Messner's voice in Nehmann's headset. 'We're too far fucking north.'

*

They landed minutes later. The airfield at Pitomnik was fifteen kilometres west of the city centre. Of the Soviet fighters, mysteriously, there was no sign. The storm had gathered and broken and now – apart from curls of oily smoke from the port engine – there was absolutely nothing to indicate how close they'd come to disaster.

Nehmann let Messner shut the engines down before he removed his headset. The edges of the airfield were littered with the wreckage of planes that would never fly again, broken toys in this pitiless war, but here beside the waiting trucks a line of *Tante-Jus* were being unloaded. Already, Nehmann could hear hands tugging open the big door in the rear of the aircraft, then a voice raised as someone clambered inside. The whole plane began to rock as the stack of jigsawed cargo was unpicked and the first wooden boxes found unseen hands below. The entire workforce, it seemed to Nehmann, were wearing items of Soviet clothing.

'Thank you.' He leaned across and extended a hand. 'I mean it.'

Messner peeled off a glove. His flesh was warm to the touch and he held Nehmann's gaze.

'You see what we do?' The grin again, exultant. 'You see what happens? The guy that came at us? That was an I-16. We called them *Ratas* in Spain. They run out of ammunition, but it makes no difference. *Mano a mano*, my friend. You speak Spanish?'

Nehmann nodded. What little he knew was enough. *Mano a mano*. Hand to hand. No quarter.

'He was trying to ram us?'

'Of course.' Messner smacked a fist into his open palm. 'Bam. You wake up in heaven with an aeroplane in your lap. Tell that to your Promi friends. We were lucky, Nehmann. He could have pushed forward, caught us on the dive, taken our tail off. He didn't.'

Luck? Nehmann shook his head, struggled out of his harness, still living those moments when his forward view, the rest of his brief, brief life, held nothing but the certainty of oblivion. The oncoming *Rata*. The manic face in the cockpit. Not luck at all, he thought, but raw nerve, and years of experience, and the fabulous gift of those precious milliseconds that can spare you for another dawn.

'I used to believe in levitation.' Nehmann put a hand on Messner's arm. 'Now I know it's true.'

21

STALINGRAD, 17 SEPTEMBER 1942

Nehmann's contact in Stalingrad was to have met him at the airfield. In his absence, Messner conducted a brief check of his battered Ju, peering at the damage to the engine, pointing out the oil streaks on the bottom of the wing, using his fingers to explore a deep tear at the base of the metal tailplane. The cannon shell, he grunted, had failed to explode. In one side of the fuselage, out the other. Nehmann walked round the tail in the dirty snow to see for himself. Messner was right. The exit hole was even bigger, the aluminium bursting outwards like a flower.

'Didn't believe me?' Messner was stamping his feet again. In the wind, it was freezing.

'Just checking. Life's all small print, my friend. Your *Generaloberst* said that last week and he's right. In my trade, if you get the details wrong it doesn't matter because no one recognises the truth any more.'

'And in ours?'

'You probably die.'

Messner nodded, tight-lipped. Something had changed between them, and they both knew it. Nothing needed spelling out any more. Friendship was a big word but Nehmann was prepared to give it a try.

Already, the plane was half empty. An engineer, according to Messner, would be along to check out the damaged engine. There'd be nothing he could do to mend it but two engines, with a modest load, would be enough to get Messner airborne again and back to Tatsinskaya. Forward maintenance, he said, was a joke. In all probability the plane would have to be returned to the Reich for proper repair, just another reason why Richthofen was beginning to run out of aircraft.

Nehmann nodded. Messner had never been this candid before. *Blutsbrüder*, he thought. Blood brothers.

'Is it like this all the time?' Nehmann was looking east, towards the city centre, where invisible Heinkels were dropping hundreds of bombs and at least two of the gaunt apartment blocks appeared to be on fire. As well, from time to time, he could hear the distant howl of Stuka sirens as they dived through the murk to find targets among the wreckage below. If there's a choir in hell, thought Nehmann, it would sound like this.

'It's a shithole,' Messner said. 'You've talked to any of the Russian prisoners? Come here a year ago and the place was a model city, everything new, everything working. That's why Stalin gave it his name. Now? You wonder what's left to fight for.'

They'd arrived at the edge of the airfield. A handful of men were gathered around a brazier, warming their hands. What might have been coffee was bubbling in a bucket, suspended over the burning wood. Messner bent for the ladle lying in the snow. A corporal in a mix of *Wehrmacht* and Russian uniform wiped his mouth with the back of his hand and gave Messner his empty mug. Messner spooned coffee into the mug and passed it to Nehmann.

'You first, *Kamerad*,' he said.

'*Kamerad?*'

A new voice, rough, amused. Nehmann spun round. There was a smile on the battered face, which was unusual, but there was no mistaking the rest of him.

'Schultz? Willi? What are you doing here?'

Messner was looking surprised.

'You know each other already?'

'We do.' Schultz nodded.

'Then why didn't you tell me?'

'You never asked. You've been with Nehmann for a while? Then you'll know what we all know. The man is a wraith, a phantom, here today, gone tomorrow, which maybe explains his charm. What you see is never what you get, and what you get is often a very big surprise. I thank you for delivering him intact, Messner. He's mine now, and I'll make sure he doesn't come to grief. *Alles gut?*'

Messner nodded and extended a hand to Nehmann. No Hitler salute. Nehmann watched him as he turned on his heel and made his way back towards the aircraft. Nehmann still had the mug of coffee.

'Give it to someone else,' Schultz grunted. 'There's much better where we're going.'

*

Schultz was driving a VW *Kübelwagen*. The canvas top was shredded and where the bonnet and the spare tyre had once been was open to the elements, the ribbed metal floor of the cargo space already rusting. Schultz stirred the engine into life and told Nehmann to get in. A couple of days ago, he said, he'd made the mistake of leaving the *KW* out in the open too close to the bomb line. The Ivans had been busy with their heavy mortars that night and a couple of bombs had straddled the vehicle. Next day, engineers had got the engine at the back running again but the little runaround had definitely lost its looks.

'Much like the rest of us, Nehmann. Whatever they tell you at Tatsinskaya, this place isn't where anyone sane would ever want to be.'

They were bumping along a cratered road towards the towering smoke that marked the city centre. Waste land to the right seemed to serve as a field and Nehmann caught a glimpse of an old woman bent over what looked like the carcase of a horse. She had some kind of blade in her hand, and she was sawing back and forth, pawing at her shawl from time to time to ward off the snow. To Nehmann's surprise, the area seemed abandoned and there was little evidence that most of Paulus's Sixth Army had come to a halt here.

'People go underground, Nehmann. It's human nature. Whether it's rain or high explosive, you get your head down.'

Nehmann nodded. Schultz was driving fast, zigzagging around one pothole after another. It was snowing hard now, driving fresh needles into Nehmann's face. There were bucket seats in the open *KW*, and he hung onto the bare metal of the grab handles, his hands already numb. He knew that Schultz's connections extended to every corner of Berlin's intelligence establishment and guessed that he had a secure line to *Abwehr* headquarters.

'So, what are you telling them, Willi?'

'Nothing. Yet.'

'Because nothing's happened?'

Schultz, fighting the wheel as they skidded on yet another patch of ice, threw him a look.

'We took prisoners last night. One of them was a lad from Georgia, one of your lot. He knew more about Sixth Army than we did.'

'How come?'

'He's in and out of Chuikov's headquarters. He told us they'd intercepted a message from the General Staff main intelligence department.'

'In Berlin, you mean?'

'*Ja.* The lad had it word perfect. He said it made him laugh. You want to know why? Listen to this…' Steering one-handed, Schultz fetched a scrap of paper from the breast pocket of his tunic. He flattened it against the middle of the steering wheel, squinting hard through the driving snow. '*Stalingrad has been taken by brilliant German forces. Russia has been cut in two parts, north and south, and will soon collapse in her death throes.*' Schultz refolded the message and tucked it carefully back into his tunic. '*Taken? Death throes?*' He gestured towards the smoke. 'How does any of that sound?'

Nehmann said he didn't know. Vasily Chuikov was the Soviet Army Commander in Stalingrad, charged by Stalin with holding the city whatever the cost. Gossip back at the airfield gave him gold-crowned teeth and a deep bandit laugh, both of which had endeared him to Nehmann.

'So what's the truth?' he asked.

'The truth is we've got a fight on our hands. The Ivans are still dug in around the Mamayev Kurgan and we can't winkle them out. They're also hanging on in that fucking great grain silo down by the river. We've shelled it non-stop for days. It has to be full of smoke and dust. It must be hell even to breathe in there, let alone fight, and as far as we can tell they've got nothing but a couple of old machine guns, *Maxims*, can you believe that? They must have run out of water by now. They must be pissing in the cooling jackets. We sent an interpreter last night under a flag of truce. The odds they're facing are horrible. Tanks, tanks and more tanks. And then a whole fucking infantry division. We spelled this out. They knew we weren't bluffing. All they needed to do was surrender. And you know what those fuckers did? They tried to shoot the interpreter. You get the feeling we've upset these people. Whatever Berlin says, they're definitely in no mood to give up.'

Whatever Berlin says. The message from the General Staff had Goebbels' fingerprints all over it and yet Nehmann doubted that even the Minister for Propaganda had the authority to draft official communiques like this. More likely, he thought, the seeds that had germinated in the Promi had now taken root in every corner of the Reich's capital. Repeat a lie often enough and it becomes, as if by magic, the truth.

The thought drew a nod of agreement from Schultz. They were slowing for a turn into a biggish building surrounded by an apron of concrete.

'The Ministry of Wishful Thinking,' he growled. 'That little man of yours has a lot to answer for.'

*

Schultz had pitched camp in the basement of what had once been a bus depot. Concrete stairs disappeared into the gloom below. Old route schedules were peeling from the dampness of

223

the walls. Candles in glass jam jars threw a thin yellow light, flickering wildly every time a fresh gust of wind came in from the street outside. A heavy curtain hung over the door at the foot of the stairs. The constant drumbeat of artillery fire was audible through the thick concrete walls and from time to time a near miss made the entire building shudder.

Schultz pushed the curtain aside and stepped in through the door. Now, Nehmann could hear the low chatter of a generator. The basement must once have been used for storage, but Schultz had found a couple of tables from somewhere and these served as desks. Faces looked up at Schultz. Both men wore headphones and were bent over radios. When one of them began to struggle to his feet Schultz motioned him back to his seat. In the far corner, a pot of coffee bubbled on an army field stove.

'You live here?' Nehmann was gazing round.

'We do. Our visitors call this place the Adlon. It's a compliment, Nehmann. If you think this is primitive, you should see what else is on offer. Light and just a little heat? We're blessed...'

Nehmann smiled. The Adlon was probably the best hotel in Berlin, certainly the most celebrated. When he asked about fuel, Schultz said they had enough for another week if they were careful.

'And after that?'

'After that? We're assuming our brilliant German forces drive the Ivans back over the river. If that happens, the city is ours. If it doesn't, we definitely have a problem. But either way we're relying on your man for everything. So far he's delivering. Just.'

'My man?'

'Richthofen.'

'But why my man?'

'Because he's taken a fancy to you, Nehmann. As no doubt he should. *Kaffee?*'

Without waiting for an answer, Schultz poured two mugs of coffee from the pot in the corner. Beside the trestle table was a sofa that might once have graced a respectable salon. Now, sadly, horsehair stuffing bulged through tears in the upholstery.

'We've got a couple of cats, Nehmann. The shelling upsets them and they take it out on whatever they can claw. I'd get rid of them, but you never know when they might come in handy.'

'You've got rats?'

'*Ja.* Them, too. Anything on four legs, eh?'

For a moment, Nehmann was nonplussed. Then he remembered the old woman bent over the horse in the field.

'That bad?' he murmured.

Schultz held his gaze for a moment, then shrugged. In any situation, he said, it always pays to plan for the worst. A wise man always carries water. And maybe a handful of spices. Spices, he said, could soften anything. Even rat.

He invited Nehmann to sit down. He had a proposition.

'Is that why I'm here?'

'In a way, yes. In another, no. Let's start with the proposition. Your Russian is much better than mine. I can understand the lad we picked up last night. I can pick the bones from what he wants to tell us. But intelligence, proper intelligence, *worthwhile* intelligence, as we both know, is all nuance. And nuance, I'm afraid, is beyond an old donkey like me.'

'You want an interpreter?'

'I want someone who speaks Russian. I also want someone who can *think* like a Russian, who can play the child and make that little jump into someone else's head. You've been doing that all your life, Nehmann, whether you admit it or not, and now the time has come to share a little of that talent, that gift, with the *Abwehr*.'

'Do I have a choice? Be honest.'

'Of course, you do. I can let you go now, this minute. I can take you upstairs, out into the snow, and I can point you in the direction of a thousand stories, right there on the front line. Maybe the grain silo. Maybe the Mamaev Kurgan. Maybe, if you're really lucky, the riverbank itself. Just think, Nehmann, one of the first scribblers to dip his toe in the Volga. Your master would love you. Your other friends at the Promi would write you into history. Werner Nehmann. Proof that Stalingrad has been taken by the brilliant German forces. *Wunderbar, ja?* Except that the city isn't our property at all. And in any case, you'd be dead by sunrise. Maybe enemy action. Maybe not.'

Nehmann was eyeing the two figures at the table. One of them had quietly removed his earphones to listen to Schultz at full throttle and Nehmann wondered how many other arms had been bent on this falling-apart sofa. The *Abwehr* man had always had a gift for persuasion, a talent Nehmann much admired.

'So, if the Ivans don't kill me,' he said carefully, 'who else might?'

Schultz declined to answer the question head-on. Instead, he asked Nehmann if he remembered a cameraman from the Propaganda Company at Tatsinskaya.

'Of course. Helmut. How is he?'

'He isn't, Nehmann. He's dead.'

Nehmann, about to swallow the last of his coffee, was staring

226

at Schultz. In a war like this there were a million ways a man could meet his end but already he sensed a complication.

Maybe enemy action. Maybe not.

'Where did it happen?'

'In Berlin.'

'But where?'

'Guess.'

'Prinz-Albrecht-Strasse?'

'Of course.'

'In the basement?'

'In the rear courtyard. A bullet in the back of the head. Very Ukrainian, Nehmann, and the way we hear it, the man had no chance to state his case. The war is getting ugly, my old friend. No time for the smaller courtesies.'

Nehmann sat back, grateful for the warmth of the coffee between his hands. Prinz-Albrecht-Strasse housed the Berlin headquarters of the Gestapo where a team of imported specialists, mainly Hungarian, honed their skills. Maybe Helmut was lucky to have been spared the journey to the basement torture cells, he thought. Maybe a brisk adieu in the courtyard had been a blessing.

'He saw a truck full of bodies on the airfield,' Nehmann said softly. 'The truck belonged to the SS. According to Helmut, the bodies, the faces, were a mess.'

'And?'

'He took photos.'

'Did he have a name at all? An SS officer, maybe?'

'No. Just the photos.'

'And the SS found out?'

'Yes, I think they did.'

'You *know* that?'

'I checked where he kept them,' Nehmann said. 'The photos were in a locked box in his darkroom. They'd gone. As soon as Helmut found out, he was a different man.'

'How?'

'He was frightened. I think he knew they'd come for him.'

'He was right. They did.'

Nehmann nodded. Said nothing. The photos, he thought, of the faces from the back of the SS truck. The sour sweetness of the developing bath that night had stayed with him ever since.

'I have a name for you, Nehmann,' Schultz said. 'Jürgen Kalb. He's a *Standartenführer*, SS of course. You want a guarantee? You'll never meet another fucker as damaged as this one.'

'You know him?'

'I do. He set up shop in Kyiv after we moved in. I told you about the *Einsatzgruppen*? The killing squads? These people are off the leash. Kalb got a leg-up for his contribution to Babi Yar. Help kill thirty thousand people and you're looking at a bigger pension. Kalb also had dealings with a woman I admired. She was English. What a fucking waste.'

Nehmann nodded. He wanted to know more about Kalb.

'He was at Tatsinskaya? At the airfield?'

'Yes. And at Kalmach beforehand. We took a lot of prisoners there, both military and civilian. Not all of them survived.'

'And now?'

'Now's different.'

Nehmann blinked. Suddenly, it was so obvious.

'And you're telling me Kalb's here? In the city?'

'Yes.'

'Why?'

'Good question. The way I see it, the man believes the place is ours for the taking and he can't wait to clean up afterwards. The SS will never admit it but they're the detergent in the Reich bottle. They're here to make Russia safe for us Aryans. It sounds twisted but people like Kalb regard their brand of butchery as a higher calling. It's a priesthood. Except you pledge your oath in other people's blood.'

'That's crazy.'

'Of course it is.'

'And me? We're talking my blood?'

'Possibly. In this life it pays not to upset people.'

'Like?'

Schultz wouldn't say. Goebbels, Nehmann thought. It has to be Goebbels. Just in case Stalingrad doesn't kill me, then the SS would take care of the job.

He was about to put this proposition to Schultz, but it was too late. The *Abwehr* man had already moved on. Time was tight. He wanted a decision about the Georgian lad. They'd wasted far too much time discussing scum like Kalb. Even this corner of the war, he seemed to be implying, could offer unexpected rewards.

'Like staying alive?' Nehmann enquired.

'Like finding out what the Ivans are really up to.'

22

STALINGRAD, 18 SEPTEMBER 1942

Nehmann slept that night at the bus depot, sharing a small basement alcove with Schultz. The chorus of explosions rose and fell, some nearby, some more distant, but gradually he began to accept the *Abwehr* man's word that they were as safe as anyone could be in this abattoir of a city.

Schultz, a scavenger of genius, had laid hands on a small pile of women's fur coats which he shared with his five-man staff. Nehmann dozed fully clothed on a mattress on the floor, warmed by silver fox, trying to fend off thoughts about what the SS might have done to the bodies in the back of their truck on the airfield at Tatsinskaya. An otherwise colourful life had so far spared him the sight of this kind of obscenity, but it was hard to forget Helmut's terror the night they'd both got drunk. It was the act of a decent man to try and make a record of crimes like these, but the SS viewed decency as a mark of weakness and in the end the gesture had got Helmut killed.

Next morning, Schultz despatched one of his staff to fetch the Georgian. He must have been held nearby because the prisoner was back within minutes in the care of a tall, cadaverous *Leutnant* from the *Feldgendarmerie*. The military policeman wore a metal gorget on a chain around his neck and deferred at once to Schultz when he wanted the prisoner's wrists unshackled.

'Of course, Herr *Oberst*.'

The prisoner couldn't have been older than twenty. Like his captor, he was thin and pale. His eyes were deep-set, and he had tiny razor nicks where someone had recently shaved his head. Schultz had assigned another cubbyhole off the main basement space for the interview, two wooden boxes almost within touching distance, both stamped with Cyrillic characters, and Nehmann waited for the youth to settle before he took his seat. Schultz was nowhere to be seen, an absence that Nehmann regarded as a mark of trust.

The prisoner's name was Kirile. He said he came from Tbilisi and the moment he started talking about the city in late autumn, the first snows dusting the heights overlooking the river, Nehmann had no reason to doubt him. He'd been to school in the Rustaveli district. His father had been a cobbler, like Stalin's, while his mother took in washing for the whole street. He'd never known Georgia under anything but Soviet rule and, when war came last year, he'd abandoned his university course and enlisted in the Red Army. As a volunteer in the Great Patriotic War, that made Kirile unusual.

By now, the interview had all the makings of a normal conversation and when the Georgian expressed curiosity about Nehmann's fluency in Russian, Nehmann saw no reason to lie.

'That's because I'm Georgian.' He smiled. 'Like you.'

'Really?' Kirile couldn't believe it. 'So how come...' he frowned '...you end up here?'

'With the Germans, you mean?'

'Of course.'

'Because I made a choice. My uncle wanted me to be a butcher. My family name is Magalashvili. I did the training. We lived in Svengati.'

'I know Svengati. Beautiful, especially in winter. You didn't like it?'

'I didn't want to be a butcher. I didn't want to be tied down. I wanted to travel. I wanted to write. I had to make a living. As a writer in Georgia that was hard to do. Have you ever been to Paris?'

'Never.'

'Paris turns you into many people. A writer, if you're lucky, is just one of them.'

'And now you're a soldier?'

'No.'

'A butcher, maybe?'

'Definitely not.'

'What, then?'

'I'm...' Nehmann shrugged '...talking to you. That's my job. That's what they want, just now. Life could be tougher, my friend. For both of us.'

Nehmann got up for a moment or two, leaving the young Georgian in the care of the *Leutnant* from the *Feldgendarmerie*. He climbed the stairs to the ground floor and stepped out into the fresh air. The thunder of battle was as relentless as ever but much of the smoke had cleared and thin sunshine puddled on the wet concrete. Looking up, shading his eyes, Nehmann could see tiny silver fish high in the sky, then came the roar of heavier aircraft and he watched the big Heinkels positioning themselves for a bomb run. The release point was barely a couple of kilometres away, and he watched the tiny black dots falling earthwards. Then came a series of explosions almost blurring into one and a shiver deep beneath his feet as the bombs found their targets.

'Well, Nehmann? You're making progress?'

It was Schultz. He was smoking a small cigar. When Nehmann expressed surprise at the boy's intelligence, Schultz nodded.

'That's why it's you doing the talking and not me,' he grunted. 'We think he knows a great deal more than he's said so far. According to another prisoner, he's been in and out of Chuikov's headquarters since the man arrived, but we seem to have picked him up by chance, which always makes me wonder.'

'He told me he was studying languages at university. His German is good. I'm assuming Chuikov would be glad of some of that.'

'You think he likes you, Nehmann?'

'Yes.'

'Trusts you?'

'Maybe.'

'Excellent. This shitfest gets more chaotic by the minute. You need to apply a little pressure, my friend.' A rare smile. 'And this is how you do it.'

*

Minutes later, back on his box in the airless cubbyhole, Nehmann insisted on sharing a jug of coffee. The coffee was Turkish and Kirile, it turned out, hadn't tasted anything like this since leaving Tbilisi. He sucked greedily at the scalding liquid and used a dirty finger to scoop up the grounds at the bottom of his mug.

Nehmann waited for him to finish and then enquired about a flood of fresh equipment coming into the city on ferries across the Volga at night. Rumours suggested that some of these tanks hadn't even been painted. Might that be true?

Kirile was frowning. This was the moment he'd obviously been expecting, the moment when a pleasant chat became an exchange of a totally different kind. This fellow Georgian with access to the coffee of his dreams was asking him to share a military secret.

'I can't say.' He shook his head.

'You can, Kirile, you can. Don't tell me you don't know because I don't believe you. This isn't about your courage. You people fight like lions. Everyone knows that. Everyone respects it. Would we do the same defending Berlin? I hope so. No, this is simply a question about the means, not the end. We accept that you mean to fight to the death. But we also believe that such a thing is unnecessary. Why? Because you lack the equipment.'

'That's not true.' The boy was angry, and it showed. 'We have everything we need. Shells. Reinforcements. Even food.'

'Tanks?'

'Yes.'

'Unpainted?'

'Of course. The factories are a couple of days away on the other side of the Urals. Why waste time with a tin of paint? A tank's a tank. This fucking war's no beauty contest.'

The phrase struck Nehmann with some force. *No beauty contest*. He couldn't think of a better way of putting it.

'You hate it, don't you?' he said. 'The fighting? The killing?'

'We hate you. You're the thief who comes in the night. Every Russian has a choice. Fight or surrender. Surrender opens your door. In comes the thief. You lose everything. Your house. Your valuables. Your daughters. Everything. There's a poem going around just now. You want to hear it?'

Without waiting for an answer, he launched into the poem. Evidently, he knew it by heart.

> The tears of women and children
> Are boiling in my heart
> Hitler the murderer and his hordes
> Shall pay for these tears
> With their wolfish blood...

'Blood of the wolf?' Nehmann said. 'That sounds like Stalin.'

'It isn't Stalin. It was written by a soldier.'

'I meant the sentiment.'

'So?'

'Stalin's a fellow Georgian, Kirile. Maybe that's one of history's ironies.'

'I don't understand.'

'You don't? Then maybe you're not old enough. I was in Svengati when the Russians came. It was 1921. I was eleven. There were hotheads in Tbilisi, in your town, who wanted revolution, Communism, all the rest of that Lenin shit, but most people hated the Russians. The country was ours, Kirile. And they were the thieves. Did you ever talk to your father about any of this? Your mother, maybe?'

The boy was looking confused now. The coffee was a memory.

'We've got lots of tanks.' He was looking at his hands. 'Lots of everything. Winter is coming. You know the word *rasputitsa*?'

His head came up at last. 'The moment when the rain and the snow turn everything to mud? When there are no more roads? When life stops completely? Have your generals thought about that?'

Nehmann acknowledged the question with a smile. He glanced at the hanging blanket that offered them just a little privacy and then lowered his voice and said he had no faith whatsoever in generals. The ones he'd met, he said, were an excuse to dress up in fancy uniforms and get pissed on looted wine every night. They spent other men's lives the way a gambler might spend his winnings.

Kirile was frowning again. He looked, if anything, slightly shocked.

'You believe that?'

'I do. Is *General* Paulus, an exception? Yes, he is. He doesn't drink much and he's fussy about losing too many men but he's slow, and he's cautious, and that, too, makes him a liability. War is madness, Kirile. You know it and I know it and that makes us both good Georgians. I like you. You're my countryman. I believe you should have a future.'

'What does that mean?'

'It means that I will arrange for your escape. This very night. You'll be taken out of custody and released.'

'Released where?'

'Just short of the front line. Fifty metres to your brethren, Kirile. A specially chosen place. Pitch darkness. And all those unpainted tanks just waiting to make life safe again.'

'They'll kill me,' he said at once. 'They'll put a bullet through my head.'

'Who, Kirile? Who will kill you?'

'The Commissars. The NKVD. Anyone who comes back they kill. It happens all the time. They trust no one. They'll think I'm a spy, a traitor. I got taken prisoner. You whispered in my ear.' He shook his head, buried his face in his hands. 'This is a death sentence. They'll kill me.'

Nehmann did his best to look concerned. Then he put a hand on the boy's knee. He could feel him trembling beneath his touch.

'I don't believe you,' he said. 'We'll do it tonight. This is a gesture, just us, you and me, one Georgian to another. Liberty, Kirile. Freedom. Is there a better present in the world?'

That evening, Schultz returned from God knows where with a live chicken. Kirile had been handed back to the *Feldgendarmerie* for safekeeping and Nehmann, after a brief discussion with Schultz, planned to talk to him again towards midnight.

Now, the *Abwehr* man tossed the chicken across to Nehmann and told him to get it ready for the pot. He'd also managed to lay hands on a bucket of potatoes and a beetroot he'd liberated from the woman who used to clean the bus depot.

Nehmann hadn't killed a chicken since his days in his uncle's abattoir. He chased it around the makeshift office while Schultz's staff looked on. One was cheering for the chicken. The others were hungry. Nehmann finally trapped it in the corner beside the field stove, gentled it in his arms for a moment or two, and then, with a single twist of his wrist, broke its neck. The bird went limp in his arms and then, in one last spasm, defecated all over his trousers. Even Schultz was impressed.

'This butcher shit.' He was laughing. 'I never believed you.'

Nehmann asked for boiling water from the kettle on the

field stove. He decanted the water into a bucket, added a little cold, then dunked the bird head-first in the water. Some of the feathers came off at once. The rest he plucked by hand, starting with the legs, before putting the chicken to one side to be gutted.

Schultz kept a bottle of vodka for early evenings. He poured two glasses and then checked his watch. There was a small service-issue radio receiver on one of the two desks. The Promi ran a special series of programmes for serving personnel the length and breadth of the Greater Reich and if you had nothing better to do, then it was easy to gather round the little sets and dream of home. Nehmann knew one or two members of the ground crews back at Tatsinskaya whose entire week revolved around a particular show or a favourite radio host. This evening, said Schultz, there was a programme offering a taste of new musical talent and he thought Nehmann might be interested.

Nehmann had his right sleeve rolled up and was deep in the carcase of the chicken. The innards were still warm as his fingers separated loops of intestine from the smoothness of the ribcage; he was only half listening to the radio. The presenter had a Bavarian accent. He said he'd crossed the border into Austria and made his way to a tiny village down near the Italian border. There he was to meet a native of the village, a young pianist now living in Berlin whom he was certain was destined for fame, someone who'd found the time between concert engagements to pay friends and relatives a flying visit on the eve of the harvest festival.

Nehmann paused. Maria had told him she came from a village near the Italian border. She also played the piano. And, as far as Nehmann knew, she still lived in Berlin. Coincidence? He glanced across the room. Schultz was studying him with some interest. Then he put one thick finger to his lips. Just listen, he seemed to be saying. Just enjoy what we've got for you.

Nehmann had missed the introduction to the first piece of music but the moment he heard the opening notes he knew it had to be Maria. Her stool drawn up to the grand piano in the big lounge on the Wilhelmstrasse, he thought, her fingers dancing on the keyboard, her head bent, her eyes half closed.

'Beethoven.' Schultz was smiling. 'She plays well, your friend. I listened to you in Kyiv, Nehmann, and now I think I understand. Is she always this good?'

'Better.' Nehmann pushed the chicken away and wiped his hands. 'How did you know she was on?'

'We got word from the Promi.'

'From Goebbels himself?'

'From a secretary, a woman called Birgit. She said the Minister thought you might be interested.'

Nehmann nodded. The music had faded after the introduction and now the presenter wanted us to meet the young pianist who had Berlin on its feet. He used her full name, Maria Gaetani. She'd been discovered, he said, playing in a Moabit nightclub and now, thanks to the good offices of the Promi, he was able to bring her talents to a much bigger audience. The young *Abwehr* staffer responsible for cooking the chicken had caught on that there might be a connection between Nehmann and this distant goddess. The knowledge seemed to put the little Georgian in a new light.

Maria was describing the thrill of being back home in the shadow of the mountains. Life these days, she said, was full of uncertainties, but she felt truly spoiled to be among the people she'd grown up with. As a child, harvest festival had been one of the highlights of her year, a time laden with plump fruit, and pastries heavy with cream, and the promise of a dance once the village band got themselves in tune. Berlin, with all its promise, all its opportunities, was any woman's dream, but this little village with all the familiar faces was where her heart belonged.

The presenter said he knew exactly what she meant. He, too, came from the country, Franconia this time, and there was nothing warmer in the world than a welcome from the entire village and a visit to the local patisserie. Maria laughed. Then came more piano music, an upbeat jazz version of 'Tea For Two', before Schultz nodded at the radio set.

'Enough?'

'*Ja.*'

'Homesick?'

Nehmann didn't answer. The entire programme had, typically, been a lie. Her name wasn't Maria Gaetani and – as Goebbels himself had pointed out – she'd never been anywhere near any Austrian village. The recording had probably been made in Berlin, maybe in one of the studios in the Promi's basement.

'He's sending you a message? That boss of yours?'

'Of course.'

'And what does the message say? You want to share it with us, Nehmann? Or is it too painful?'

'He's telling me he has everything under control.'

'You mean Maria?'

'I mean Szarlota. That's her real name. She's Polish. And her mother was a Jew.'

Schultz offered a low whistle, and the aide wrestling the

chicken into the pot pulled a face, but oddly enough Nehmann didn't resent sharing any of this knowledge. One of the puzzles of this city, this battle, was the way it brought you together. He could feel it already. No secrets. Only the collective knowledge that, one way or another, you were there to make it through.

'Goebbels and our Jewish friends?' Schultz pulled a face. 'Oil and water. You think he's fucking her? Is that why she's still alive? Famous? Rich?'

Nehmann said he didn't know. The broadcast, he said, meant nothing. Goebbels was clever. He was the Reich's puppet master. He'd learned how to pull life's strings. That's why he was so powerful. He specialised in control. A promising pianist from Warsaw who happened to be half Jewish? An entire *Volk*? It made no difference. Goebbels had set out to take both of them hostage and he'd largely succeeded.

'A hostage, Nehmann? Is that what she is?'

'Yes.'

'Against what?'

Nehmann shook his head. Despite everything, he was prepared to go no further. If he ever got back to Berlin, if he managed to avoid the attentions of Kalb, he'd try and resolve things but in the meantime, thanks to Goebbels' clever little sleight of hand, he knew she was still alive. And that, of course, had been the real thrust of the programme's message. Keep thinking about her. Keep worrying about her. And when the Minster asks for that letter back just hand it over.

23

STALINGRAD, 18 SEPTEMBER 1942

That evening, the temperature rose again. With the snow beginning to melt, the intensity of the artillery barrage grew and grew, a constant soundtrack behind every conversation, but the *Luftwaffe* didn't fly at night and there was no bombing. The chicken seemed to take an age to cook properly but there was plenty of vodka and Schultz warmed the evening with a series of stories about his days in Kyiv. Once the war had moved on, the city was lawless – Stalingrad with functioning trams and a thriving black market for anything you might happen to need – but there was plenty of extra trade in the shadowy margins of the intelligence world and he'd never been bored. Once you understood the darkness of the Ukrainian soul, he said, Kyiv was the kind of place that would never disappoint you.

Nehmann, who was the first to recognise a fellow survivor in the madness of these times, wondered quite what Schultz meant by disappointment, but when he put the question there was no answer apart from the last centimetre of vodka in the bottle.

'Drink up, my friend. We're back to work.'

Schultz had a couple of fur hats he'd acquired from passing prisoners. Nehmann struggled into a greatcoat that was several sizes too small even for him and he joined Schultz among the puddles outside. It was still teeming with rain but there was an icy wind blowing from the east and Nehmann could feel the raindrops turning to snow once again. *Rasputitsa*, he thought. An entire city disappearing beneath an ocean of mud.

To Nehmann's relief, they were spared the open-topped *Kübelwagen*. Instead, Schultz had laid hands on an ancient lorry that appeared to be Russian. They clambered up into the cab, Schultz behind the wheel. Neither of the windscreen wipers worked and Nehmann could see nothing but the blur of the rain through the filth of the glass.

'Where are we going?'

'Not far. Here—' He produced a torn length of what felt like cotton and gave it to Nehmann.

'What do I do with this?'

'It's a blindfold. We take our young friend for a little drive. In this weather he won't be seeing much in any case, but that's not the point.'

'It's theatre.'

'Of course. You know us too well, Nehmann.'

'A pantomime.'

'Hardly. Not where we're going. He'll be handcuffed to you, by the way. Don't let him lead you astray.'

Schultz had yet to start the engine. Nehmann wondered what other surprises the evening might have in store.

'He believes we'll set him free?' Schultz asked. 'The boy?'

'He does.'

'And?'

'It terrifies him. You're right. The Ivans trust nobody. Our smell on his pelt and the boy is as good as dead.'

'Excellent.' Schultz fumbled for a cigarette. Then came a deafening explosion, the loudest yet, and the surrounding ruins were briefly silhouetted against the blinding flash of light on the horizon.

'The grain silo,' Schultz grunted. 'Paulus is losing patience and not before time. You wouldn't want to be an Ivan, not in that building.'

There was the scrape of a match and Nehmann caught a glimpse of Schultz's face as he ducked into the flame. Some men are born for nights like these, he thought, and I'm sharing a lorry cab with one of them.

'So, what do we ask him? The boy? What's the price for not letting him go?'

The question seemed to amuse Schultz. He sucked in a lungful of smoke and then expelled it slowly, tapping ash onto the floor. He'd been talking to an analyst he trusted in *Abwehr* headquarters back in Berlin. He believed that Stalin was determined to hold the line on the Volga for exactly the same reason that Hitler demanded the city for himself. Symbols, for dictators, mattered a great deal and none – it seemed – was more important than this ever-growing pile of rubble beside the river.

'You and me, Nehmann? And every other fucker out here? We're realists. Maybe fatalists. You wake up in the morning. You count the buildings that have gone overnight. And you maybe wonder what all the noise is about. But sit behind a desk in Berlin or Moscow and you're in a different world. You listen to people who only want to put a smile on your face. Everyone takes a look at the map and agrees that feeding an army nearly three thousand kilometres away is a piece of piss.

We happen to know that's not true, but who's interested in us? This is a different game, Nehmann, and just now it's our job to put ourselves in the head of the enemy.'

Stalin, he said, was also a realist. He knew just how tough it was to bite the head off the German snake, even this far from home. To make any kind of stand, and maybe try to push the enemy west again, he'd need lots more troops, more artillery, tanks by the thousands, bridge-building equipment, the whole circus that went with the application of serious violence. Out on the steppe, especially in winter, it was impossible to hide deployments of this size, and by analysing Russian radio traffic, teams in the *Abwehr* had begun to detect a twitch or two in what Goebbels had recently described as the Soviet corpse.

'Our Georgian friend may well have picked up similar rumours.' Schultz reached for the ignition key. 'So that's where you might start.'

*

Kirile had been readied for collection. No coat. Nothing on his feet. The *Leutnant* from the *Feldgendarmerie* was waiting in the draughty shelter of what must once have been a church. Schultz and Nehmann hurried in from the rain, stepping over a drift of shattered glass and the splintered remains of the door. Nehmann had the blindfold and tied it tightly around the Georgian's head, two turns, no chance of the slightest clue to what might happen next. Kirile said nothing. His face, as pale as ever, was a mask. From centimetres away, Nehmann sensed resignation as well as fear.

An exchange of glances between Schultz and the *Leutnant* produced a sub-machine gun and what looked like grenades.

With the machine gun came two spare magazines. Schultz cocked the gun, checked the chamber, then released the mechanism again. This time, Kirile flinched.

'*Alles gut?*' Schultz patted the *Leutnant* on the arm, a gesture of thanks, and made for the door. Nehmann followed him into the rain, leading Kirile by one arm, helping him clumsily up into the driving cab. The wooden bench seat ran the width of the lorry. There was room for the three of them. Just.

'Here—' Schultz had produced a pair of handcuffs.

Kirile, drenched from the rain, had started to shiver. Nehmann shackled the boy's skinny wrist to his own. Schultz restarted the engine, peering through the windscreen, then began to move again. The trick, Nehmann realised quickly, was simple. Five times round the grid of roads that surrounded the church, stop, start, stop, start, right, left, a grinding of gears, a lurch or two, then right again, a jigsaw of turns impossible to follow. At length, they were back where they'd started, the face of the watching *Leutnant* still visible in the vestibule of the church.

Kirile, they both knew, spoke German.

'I know the *Oberst* here,' Schultz grunted to Nehmann. 'He's promised covering fire. You see the remains of the tree there? Just left of the abandoned tank?'

'Got it.'

'Ivans. Explain it all to our friend. Tell him which way to run. They'll have the vodka ready. Seventy metres? Probably less. Good luck, my friend.' He gave the boy's wet thigh a pat. 'Christmas in Tbilisi, *ja?*'

Schultz exchanged glances with Nehmann, then got out of the truck. With the door still open it was even colder.

'Take it off.' It was Kirile. 'Please take the blindfold off.'

Nehmann ignored him. He wanted to know about troop movements the other side of the river, about the reinforcements that Chuikov so desperately needed, about the measures Stalin might be planning to stop the hated Germans in their tracks and drive them out of the city.

'You think I know stuff like that? You're crazy.'

'Try, *tovarisch*. Just try. Any hint. Any rumour. Any clue. You were in and out of the command HQ. I know you were. A fragment of conversation. A message on a desk. A whisper. Anything.'

Tovarisch. Comrade.

Kirile shook his head. This was beyond him. He was so frightened, so cold, so lost, he couldn't think straight, couldn't put a sentence together. Then came the nearby bark of a machine gun on automatic, rat-tat-tat, and he started to whimper.

'I can't,' he said. 'I can't. Please...'

Next came the flat, sharp, percussive blast of a grenade, just metres away. This had to be a blank, Nehmann thought. Even Schultz wouldn't risk the real thing so close.

Kirile was crying now, his spare hand trying to hide the tears. Nehmann could see the child he must so recently have been, and he shook his head, knowing that this pantomime was deeply, deeply shaming.

He bent to the boy's ear.

'Can you hear me, Kirile?'

'*Da*.' Yes.

'You want all this to stop?'

'*Da*.'

'Then make it up.'

247

'What?' The word seemed to catch in his throat.

'Make it up. Invent it.'

'I don't know. I don't understand.'

'There are hidden armies. Armies beyond the river. No one knows about them. Only Stalin. And Chuikov. And a handful of others. Including you.'

'How? How do I know?'

'You saw a message. Messages, plural. You have a friend. The friend loves you, wants you.'

'*Wants* me?'

'Invent, Kirile. It's your life here, your life at stake. Go out there, into the darkness, and it's over. You don't need me to tell you that. You'll be dead within the hour. And they might play games with you first. No mercy, isn't that the phrase? Think about it. Then think about your friend.'

'I can't. I have no friend like that.'

'Let's give him a name, Kirile. Think of a name. Any name. Your favourite name. Go on. Do it.'

'Sergei.'

'What does he look like?'

'Handsome.'

'What else?'

'Big *Schwanz*. Big hands. Big everything.'

'And he loves you, *ja*?'

'*Da.*'

'Wants you, *ja*?'

'*Da.*'

'How badly?'

'Very badly. Very, very badly. But he's kind, too. And he says he loves me.'

'What does he do? This Sergei?'

'He works at headquarters. He knows everything about everything.'

'Good. Excellent. Because he needs to impress you, doesn't he? He needs you to believe that he's big and important. Not just the *Schwanz*. But the secrets he knows.'

'*Da.*' The boy gulped, nodded. 'And it's worked.'

'You've been with him.'

'Many times.'

'And he's told you about the armies? Stalin's armies? The armies no one else knows about?'

'*Da.*'

'Waiting.'

'*Da.*'

'To push the fucking Germans all the way back to Berlin.' Nehmann paused. 'Yes? You can remember all that?'

The boy nodded, said nothing, then Nehmann's fingers were loosening the knot in the blindfold, pulling it off, revealing a wilderness of puddles and the shell of the church beyond.

Kirile stared at it for a long moment, then buried his head in Nehmann's shoulder, wracked by sobs.

Schultz was standing in front of the lorry, his face a blur through the rain on the windscreen. Then, abruptly, he was climbing back into the cab.

A single glance at the pair of them was all he needed.

'*Alles gut?*' he queried.

'*Da.*' Nehmann nodded. 'What else did you expect?'

24

TATSINSKAYA AIRFIELD, 27 SEPTEMBER 1942

Nehmann was en route back to Tatsinskaya a full week later in the hands of a taciturn *Luftwaffe* pilot who'd once flown the Bf-109 and had no time for the big old *Tante-Ju*. In the back of the aircraft were a dozen badly wounded infantrymen judged to be worth the expense of the journey west. They all occupied stretchers and most of them, thanks to hefty doses of morphine, were unconscious. After refuelling at Tatsinskaya, the aircraft would be flying further west to the comforts of a big field hospital.

Also, in the very back of the plane, were a number of mail sacks full of letters home. Nehmann sat among them. The seal on one of the sacks had failed and he stole a look at a number of the letters, curious to take the pulse of Paulus's struggling army. Most of these missives did their best to soften the realities Nehmann had seen for himself. The Russians were getting weaker by the day. The food was OK, and the weather could be better, but everyone agreed that the Führer was right to be pushing so hard to knock the Ivans out of the war.

To a man, these correspondents were looking forward to a Christmas back home around a roaring log fire and a plump goose on the table. Only one hinted that things might be bleaker than they seemed. 'The snow has gone for the time being,' he'd written, 'and yesterday I saw a woman drinking from a puddle in the road. These people know how to live on nothing. One day, if this lasts longer than we think, we might be as primitive as them.'

Nehmann sat back among the mail sacks. He'd written letters himself, all of them to Maria, mainly at night when he had a little privacy and the time to marshal his thoughts. These, in part, were love letters but they were something else, as well, maybe just as important. He needed to have someone else in his life, someone who didn't know Stalingrad first-hand. He needed to be able to visualise Maria, to be close to her, to explain exactly how he felt about this shitty war, and this godforsaken city. Men in battle knew how to get by, understood the lies they had to tell themselves, developed a real talent for turning pain into sardonic laughter. That's how men like Schultz got through. That's what produced these letters of comfort to loved ones back home. The undeceived, he thought, tell the best lies.

Nehmann refolded the last of the letters, slipped it back into its envelope and returned it to the open sack of mail. Then he lay back against the bulging canvas, his eyes closing. This was why writing to Maria was so important, he told himself. She has to understand what's really happening. She has to *know*.

*

Nehmann had brought two bottles of vodka and a cooked ham back to Tatsinskaya, all three items a present from a grateful Schultz. The *Abwehr* man had been delighted with the boy's information and although it lacked real detail it certainly

251

confirmed Schultz's darker fears. Stalin was reacting exactly the way he'd anticipated. Time to open yet another bottle. Nehmann, of course, knew this was a fiction but was glad about the vodka and the ham. Tell people what they want to hear, he thought. And then fill your belly.

Messner was waiting at the airfield, alerted about the Ju's imminent arrival. Nehmann pumped his hand, knowing at once that the bond sealed by the flight to Stalingrad was still there. Messner even risked a joke.

'That plane we went out on? The damage was worse than I thought. I just made it back.' He gestured towards the distant carcase of a Ju-52. 'They've stripped it of everything useful and left the rest for our children to visit after the war. My daddy flew an aeroplane without engines, they'll tell each other. Just imagine that.'

Nehmann gave him the ham and a bottle of vodka. Messner was impressed.

'Tonight, we'll eat like kings.' He was weighing the ham in his hand. 'My place or yours?'

Nehmann crossed the airfield to his tent. The other two beds were now occupied, one by a movie cameraman from the Propaganda Company, the other by an aircraft engineer, but he didn't care. Tomorrow, thanks again to Schultz, he had a seat on another *Tante-Ju*, first to Kyiv, and then to Berlin. Goebbels had been in touch again, this time in person. The Führer was planning a major speech in the Sportpalast and the Minister needed a full briefing before the text was finalised. This came as some surprise to Nehmann but was also a relief. Maybe Schultz had been kidding him about Kalb's murderous intentions. Maybe he was safer in Stalingrad than he'd thought.

The flight to Kyiv was leaving at dawn. Nehmann gathered his few possessions, shared a glass or two of the vodka with his new companions, and then recrossed the airfield to the spotless tent that Messner called home. It was freezing again, a bank of clouds massing in the east, heavy with snow, and in late afternoon the light was already draining from the sky.

Messner had news about the next day's flight. A *Wachmeister* from one of the *Luftwaffe*'s anti-aircraft regiments had been on the airfield for several days. His name was Knaus and he'd become the toast of his comrades in Stalingrad after destroying no less than twenty-one enemy tanks.

'You've met him?' Nehmann asked.

'I have. Twice. He's an ordinary little man, nothing much to say for himself. Hard to believe, really. The *Generaloberst* has recommended him for the *Ritterkreuz* and they're flying him back to Berlin for the presentation. You'll meet him tomorrow on the plane. I gather your people want you to talk to him.'

Nehmann nodded. It was Richthofen who'd first used the powerful 88mm anti-aircraft guns in quite a different role at ground level. These monsters could bring down an enemy bomber flying at seven thousand metres, packing a knockout punch that would equally tear through the thin armour of a Soviet T-34. Nehmann had seen a battery of them at the airfield at Pitomnik, their raised barrels black against the greyness of the sky. If Knaus was as modest as Messner seemed to think, the story would be a gift for the Promi's publicity machine. Wilhelm Knaus, the little man from nowhere, the name on the nation's lips, our hero on the Volga, yet another legend in the making.

Messner had found an old card table from somewhere and set it up in the middle of the tent. A square of torn sheet served as a tablecloth. Two unmatched plates, a glass and a mug, both brimming with vodka, and a metal mess tin containing three eggs he'd evidently just boiled. He tested the eggs with his fingertips, then blew on them.

'Hot,' he said.

He'd already carved thin slices off the ham. Now he arranged them in an artful fan on the plates while Nehmann took the eggs outside. The snow was already lying on the freezing turf and Nehmann tipped the eggs into the beginnings of a drift on the windward side of the tent. Minutes later he was back inside the tent, the eggs shelled.

'Perfect.' Messner looked genuinely delighted. 'Is this some kind of Stalingrad trick?'

'Svengati. Whatever you learn as a kid never leaves you. We kept chickens. Winters especially, we lived on eggs.'

When Nehmann said he was cold, Messner nodded at a neatly folded pile of garments in the corner of the tent. It was nearly dark now, and the hissing lamp threw long shadows as Nehmann picked out something to keep him warm. The sight of the little Georgian in Messner's service greatcoat brought a smile to his face. As did the leather gloves.

'A tent within a tent,' he laughed, reaching for the eggs.

'What's that?'

'This?' Messner held it up. The smile was, if anything, even wider and there was a faintly manic gleam in his eye. 'This is going to make my fortune.'

It looked like some kind of device. There was an egg-shaped indentation in the base and a hinged metal frame on top. The frame was strung with tight strands of wire that gleamed in the flickering light from the paraffin lamp.

'It's my own design. It came to me in the middle of the night. I had one of the engineers in the maintenance bay knock it up for me. Watch.'

He selected one of the eggs and put it on the base. Then, in a single movement, he closed the frame over the egg and Nehmann watched, fascinated, as the strands of wire carved through the outer white, and then through the yolk, and the egg fell neatly apart. Seven slices, all perfect. Nehmann counted them again, just to make sure.

'That's magic.' He didn't quite believe it. 'Do it again.'

Messner was happy to oblige. First another egg, then the third. Messner arranged the little discs of egg on the plates, framing the slices of ham. A meal in the middle of this godforsaken steppe had just become a work of art.

'Magic.' Nehmann was looking at the slicer. 'Patent that thing and you're right, you'll make a fortune.'

'I know. Something decent has to come out of this fucking war and I think I may have found it. Here's to my slicer… *prosit*.'

They drank a toast. And then, at Messner's insistence, another.

'To survival,' he said. 'And the blessings of sliced egg.'

Messner wanted to know about Stalingrad and Nehmann did his best to do the ruined city justice. They'd both seen the kind of chaos that an army could bring to any location – hundreds of thousands of men all bent on destruction – but Stalingrad, said Nehmann, was in a league of its own. The Heinkels and the Stukas had levelled whole areas of the city, returning day after day to add a top dressing of incendiary bombs, while tanks and artillery, in the hands of craftsmen like Wilhelm Knaus, were finishing the job. Add the blessings of an early autumn, nights so cold you wouldn't believe, and you were left with the makings of a gigantic tomb.

'You live underground,' Nehmann said. 'You rarely see daylight because out there someone or something might kill you. The Russians have a word for it. *Rasputitsa*. I learned it from a Russian prisoner. The time of no roads. The time of shit and slush. The time of nothing. That's Stalingrad. *Rasputitsa*. You've seen it from the air. That's bad enough. For real, it's even worse. We've been looking for a proper fight for a while. I'm afraid this is it.'

Messner wanted to know about Schultz. They'd finished the ham and eggs and were working their way through the rest of the vodka.

'He's my guardian angel.' Nehmann pulled the greatcoat more tightly around him. 'He keeps me safe.'

'From who?'

Nehmann sat back. The SS truck, he knew from Helmut, had been parked only metres away from this tent. Messner must have known about it. He was Richthofen's eyes and ears on the airfield. He knew everything.

'There's an SS man called Kalb,' he said carefully. 'A *Standartenführer*.'

'I know Kalb.'

'You do?'

'*Ja.*'

'And?'

'He's a monster. A sadist. The SS breed them. I dare say he's a credit to that fucking uniform. We should have nothing to do with those people, nothing at all. No one loves you if you invade, if you steal their country, but the SS will be the end of us. One day the world will take a good look at what they're up to and blame us. All of us.'

'So what are they up to?'

'You mean here? On this airfield?'

'Yes.'

Messner looked briefly troubled. He toyed with his mug a moment, circling the rim with a single finger, then tossed the vodka down in a single gulp before reaching for the bottle.

'He's gone now,' he said at last.

'I know. He's in Stalingrad. Schultz told me. You know about Kyiv? What happened in that ravine?'

'No.' Messner shook his head.

Nehmann described the killings at Babi Yar. More than thirty thousand Jews marched out of the city and despatched in a matter of days.

'Open the window and Schultz says you could hear the gunfire in the hotel where he was working. Single shots. Machine guns. Thirty thousand bodies.'

'And that was Kalb's doing?'

'He was part of it, yes.'

Messner's head sank. He seemed to be brooding. Then he was on his feet and Nehmann watched him walk unsteadily across to his camp bed. Two blankets, carefully folded, lay at the foot of the bed. Messner lifted the toe of the thin mattress, revealing a service-issue envelope.

He returned to the table and gave it to Nehmann.

'Twice daily after meals,' he muttered. 'These people are

out of their cages now and we need to remind ourselves what they can do.'

There were a handful of photos in the envelope. Nehmann slid them out onto the table. The first showed what had once been a child's face. The fleshy part of her nose had been crudely removed, probably with a bayonet, and the bone beneath was clearly visible. One eye socket was empty while a still-glistening orb hung on a tendril of white nerve tissue from the other. Her face, otherwise unmarked, made the image even more grotesque. Beautiful lips, still intact. And just a hint of perfect teeth.

Nehmann swallowed hard. Disgust was far too small a word. Anger was much closer. He looked at the next shot, and then the next, until he'd seen them all. Some faces were pulped beyond recognition, the work of a man with a rifle butt, and on another he could trace the imprint of a heavy boot. Finally, he pushed the photos away and sat back.

'Kalb?' he said.

'Yes.'

'You *know* that?'

'Yes.'

'How?'

'He told me. This stuff was part of his job, he said, part of his duty. No one in his position was there to make life pretty.'

Messner explained the plan to drop these mutilated corpses in the Volga upstream from the city, and what had happened when Kalb's demand for an aircraft reached Richthofen. The story, grim as it was, made Nehmann laugh.

'No parachute?'

'None. Word will get back to Berlin, of course. The *Generaloberst* made a fool of Kalb. That will be treason in their eyes. I dare say Himmler will have a shooting squad up his sleeve. Maybe he'll bring one out here. Let's hope so, eh? Then we can teach these bastards a lesson.'

Nehmann wanted to know about the cameraman from the Propaganda Company.

'You mean Helmut?' Messner asked.

'Yes. He took those photos, and that made him a brave man. Schultz told me they cost him his life.'

Messner nodded. He said he'd done his best for Helmut, argued his case in front of Kalb, but the SS had already put a search team into the darkroom and found the prints.

'They knew he'd been sniffing around the truck. They went through everything and found these. Next day they arrested him and put him on the plane. They had the evidence. They'd done their job. That's the kind of people they are. Funny that, the two things going together. I never realised you could be meticulous and evil at the same time. A credit to the Reich, eh? We Germans break new ground every day. Maybe that's a thought for your boss, Nehmann. I wish you luck, *Kamerad*.' He nodded at the table. 'And by all means show him one of these.'

'But how do you come to have them?'

'They were a little present. From Kalb. Just a selection. And you know something else? He was *proud* of what he'd done. Can you imagine that?'

*

Nehmann left the photos with Messner and returned to his own tent, tramping across a fresh blanket of snow on the airfield. The newcomers were both asleep, oblivious to the cold. Nehmann, still wearing Messner's greatcoat, slipped under his single blanket, doing his best to ignore the chorus of snores. He had a repertoire of tricks to get to sleep but tonight none of them seemed to work. However hard he tried, the faces from Helmut's photos returned to haunt him.

In the small hours, shaking with cold, he must have drifted away because the next thing he heard was a voice whispering in his ear and a rough hand giving him a shake. It was the *Unteroffizier* from the despatch team, telling him he had just thirty minutes to make his way across the airfield to the plane for Berlin.

Nehmann nodded, grunted his thanks, then lay back, trying to make sense of the nightmare. He'd been a kid again, back in the mountains around Svengati. It was winter, bright moonlight, the theatre of the surrounding peaks shrouded in snow. Then came a low rumble he first mistook for artillery but then realised were footsteps. They grew louder and louder, thump-thump, and he looked up, terrified. A giant, he thought, striding over the Caucasus, pitiless, hungry for flesh of any kind, and then a head appeared, dwarfing the frieze of peaks, and a slender neck, and bare shoulders, and he saw only darkness where the eyes had once been, and he knew he was looking once again at the little girl in the back of the SS truck.

Kalb's work.

Nehmann pushed the blanket away. His booted feet found the bare earth. He stood up, aware that he was trembling, hoping that Messner would forgive the theft of his greatcoat. God willing, I may be back here one day, he thought, slipping out of the tent, trying to remember how to find the plane.

25

BERLIN, 28 SEPTEMBER 1942

Nehmann was last onto the aircraft. The pilot had already started all three engines and Nehmann tried to duck the icy blast from the propeller on the port wing as he clambered up the ladder with his single bag. There was one seat remaining and the plane was already on the move when he finally made it up the narrow aisle.

He sank back, groping for his seat belt, but something had happened to the buckle and it wouldn't work. He shrugged. He suspected that the little figure across the aisle with the dumpling face and the ready smile was Wilhelm Knaus, but he didn't care about that, either. The flight to Kyiv would take hours, and after that came the even longer leg to Berlin. Just now he wanted to close his eyes and bask in the warmth of the cabin. Within seconds, still bumping towards the runway, he was asleep.

He awoke five hours later. The aircraft was still droning west above a carpet of fluffy cloud. Sunshine streamed in through the window and when Nehmann took a second look he recognised the two silver shapes high in the sky behind them. Bf-109s, he thought. Just in case I think this fucking war is over.

They landed at Kyiv in time for a snatched lunch in the

windowless room that served as a cafeteria. While ground crew refuelled the *Tante-Ju*, Nehmann found a table and took advantage of the peace and quiet to have a word with the Reich's new hero. Messner had been right. Knaus was a small, unassuming figure, a one-time baker from Koblenz, and he seemed oblivious to the place in Nazi folklore that Goebbels was preparing for him.

Faced with Nehmann's racing pencil, he confirmed that he was a flak gunner. He'd enrolled with the *Luftwaffe*, half intending to become a pilot, but his mum had been right about his eyesight and he'd ended up in the *Luftwaffe*'s Flak Regiment. He had good mates there. He also had a mongrel dog he'd christened Gustav for no particular reason that he could think of. He'd tried to smuggle Gustav aboard the plane at Pitomnik but had been caught out. The mutt was white with grey patches which sometimes made life tricky trying to find him in the snow.

Nehmann underlined the name Gustav. Readers loved nonsense like this. As Goebbels was the first to point out, it made them feel better about the war.

Nehmann looked up.

'Twenty-one tanks? Have I got that right?'

'Twenty-two really. One got away but it was trailing smoke and I blew one of the tracks off it. We found it later that day.'

'And the crew?'

'Still inside.'

'Dead?'

'*Ja*, very.' He was eating a plate of pickled cucumbers. He chased the smallest one with a corner of his bread and then sucked at the vinegar. The bread, he said, was *Scheisse*. Kyiv needed a decent baker.

Nehmann tried to tease out a quote or two about the 88mm flak gun, about blowing all those tanks apart, about what it took to be in a battle, and hold your nerve, and steady your aim, and chose exactly the right moment to squeeze the trigger.

'Trigger? Have I got that right?'

'Lanyard. It's a kind of rope. You lay the gun first. Then give the rope a yank.'

Nehmann wrote the word down. *Yank*. The Reich's new hero might have been preparing a tray of *Brötchen*.

'Did you shoot before? As a kid, maybe?'

'Never.'

'And the funfair? As a kid? Did you ever try for the coconuts?'

'My father hated the funfair. He locked us up, me and my brother.'

'Did you ever go to the movies? American films, maybe? Westerns?'

'No.' He reached for the last of the cucumbers. 'You think Gustav's going to be OK? You think he might find his way back to those mates of mine?'

*

The departure of the plane for Berlin was delayed by a problem in one of the engines. At first it was a question of hours but then a Ukrainian engineer appeared and announced that the plane wouldn't be taking off until early next day. By now, Knaus was dozing at the table, his head pillowed on his folded arms. Nehmann stared at his pad, flipped a page and then got to his feet to find somewhere more private to start writing.

Next door to the cafeteria was a bare, empty room with a single folding chair propped against the wall. Nehmann unfolded the chair, found a pencil and began to write. Present tense, he told himself. Make it *real*.

His mates, he wrote, call him Billy the Kid. His real name is Wilhelm Knaus. On the battlefield he's known as the fastest gun in town and his fame in this little corner of the Wild East extends to even the Soviet trenches. When little Willi Knaus appears, enemy tank crews know their days are numbered. Why? Because Billy the Kid and his trusty 88mm flak gun never miss.

Nehmann smiled and sat back a moment. He especially liked 'the Wild East' and he knew that Goebbels would, too. It was funny. It would raise a laugh or two. And only the handful of veterans who'd made it back to the Reich in one piece would understand the irony. Wild, indeed. And not in a good way.

Half an hour, and the profile was complete, a cheerful confection of falsehoods, another rung in the ladder that would take this little gunner to heights he'd never dreamed about. For a moment or two, he toyed with letting Knaus have a peek at what he'd written but then decided against it. The man was a peasant at heart, and most peasants – uncursed by imagination – had a respect for the truth. Nehmann doubted whether their paths would ever meet again, and even if they did he'd mutter something about the editing process and blame the whole thing on his boss.

What was left of the day slipped past. A truck arrived from the city and drove the marooned passengers to a nearby army barracks where they spent the night. Nehmann, keen to avoid Knaus, spent a pleasant hour or so with a surgeon from the biggest of Sixth Army's field hospitals, returning to Berlin to plead for more resources. He took a wider view of what was happening in Stalingrad and agreed with Nehmann that even a hundred ack-ack regiments wouldn't guarantee any kind of victory. We're overextended, he said. Geography and the weather have a brutal logic of their own. And that's before we even start discussing the Ivans. It was only at this point in the conversation that Nehmann admitted working for the Promi. This confession prompted a shake of the head.

'That boss of yours has a lot to answer for,' the surgeon murmured. 'As you doubtless know.'

*

Goebbels, as it turned out, had sent a car to Tempelhof to meet the incoming flight. Expecting to be driven straight to the Promi, Nehmann found himself drawing up outside Guram's apartment on the Wilhelmstrasse.

'You're going to drop me here?'

'That's right. The Minister's office will be in touch. I'm told there's *Weisswurst* in a cupboard in the kitchen. That makes you a lucky man, Herr Nehmann.'

Nehmann let himself into the apartment, relieved that the key still worked. The Bavarian sausage was a favourite of his, as Goebbels well knew, and the weather in Berlin was fabulous, a perfect autumn day. Late afternoon sun was streaming in through the windows and wherever he looked there were stands of fresh flowers. He could smell perfume, too, a scent he recognised, and for one giddy moment Stalingrad had never happened.

'Maria? *Liebchen?*'

Nothing. Not a sound. He was looking round. On the wall above the piano was a picture he'd never seen before, not here in the apartment. It was the front cover of a magazine called

NS-Frauen-Warte, one of the Reich's top sellers, and it showed a black and white photo of the half dozen soldiers who'd scaled Mount Elbrus. The shot was beautifully framed, no expense spared, and Nehmann sensed at once that it was here for his benefit. A thank you? A ministerial pat on the back? He'd no idea.

Shaking his head, he explored the rest of the apartment. In the bathroom he found a collection of soaps and lotions he knew Maria liked. They, too, were expensive – way beyond the means of a Moabit nightclub singer – and when he opened the bathroom cabinet he found a small, square bottle of French perfume, Shalimar by Guerlain, Maria's favourite. The bottle had been here since Nehmann arrived at the flat. It had belonged to a girlfriend of Guram's and Maria, at Nehmann's invitation, had helped herself. When he'd left for the east, it had been a third full. Now there was barely any left.

She's moved back in, Nehmann told himself. He'd left the bathroom now, and he was looking down at the bed where they'd slept. On one pillow was a carefully scissored rectangle of newsprint. Nehmann picked it up, recognising the font, the layout, even the trademark style of clipped, flat reportage. He'd last seen prose like this in Paris, he thought, in the pages of the *Wehrmacht* newspaper published locally for German occupation forces in the capital and the major provincial towns beyond, a publication that never raised its voice, never risked a joke, but relied solely on a bland diet of foreign victories and news from home. Goebbels, he knew, had been itching to get his hands on it. He'd put fire in its belly, rouse the *Wehrmacht* from its torpor, give the idle captors of France a bit of a shake.

Nehmann went to the window and read the report. It seemed

there'd been an unfortunate incident at Montparnasse Metro station in central Paris. A man in his early forties had fallen in front of a train and been killed. This individual, unnamed, had an important role with the occupation forces, reporting directly to Ambassador Otto Abetz. Suspecting the involvement of French terrorists, ten hostages had been seized and shot that very afternoon.

Nehmann settled on the bed. He knew that there was a tariff that applied in circumstances like these. Kill a German in occupied France, or Brussels, or Amsterdam, or anywhere else in the Greater Reich, and you'd normally expect fifty hostages to be taken and held under sentence of death. In this case, only ten had faced the firing squad. Was there some doubt about the circumstances of this man's death? And, in any case, who on earth was he?

Nehmann read the report a second time. Like the framed photo hanging on the wall next door, he suspected that it must have been deliberately left for him, part of a carefully composed tableau he couldn't fail to notice. Goebbels, he thought to himself, trying to send some kind of message. He frowned, trying to understand the implications, then he shrugged and ducked his head to sniff the pillow. Shalimar by Guerlain, again. Maria.

Nehmann was in the kitchen, wolfing the last of the *Weisswurst*, when he heard a knock on the door. It was the Promi driver who'd picked him up from the airport. The Minister presented his compliments, he said, and would welcome Nehmann's company for a drink or two. Nehmann finished the sausage and accompanied the driver down the main staircase to the street. It was nearly dark by now.

Expecting a lift to the Ministry, Nehmann found himself being driven north, over the Spree. Beyond the suburbs, the houses thinned, the land rising and falling, dark stands of pine trees in every direction. Already he'd asked the driver where they were going, getting no response. Now he had a suggestion of his own.

'Bogensee?'

'*Ja*,' the driver laughed. 'Where else?'

The recently built villa at Bogensee was yet another of Goebbels' residences, his country retreat, and already a national byword for the kind of indulgence to which a senior Party member could treat himself. It was alleged to have seventy rooms, though Nehmann had never met anyone who'd counted them, and the Minister used the place to brood, to write and to entertain. It was here that he'd courted Lida Baarova and doubtless others, and it was here, too, that he'd probably penned the letter Nehmann had taken to Rome.

The entrance gate, hard to spot, was hidden in the gloom of the pine trees. The driver led Nehmann to the big front door beneath the white stucco of the arch. Goebbels himself welcomed his visitor.

'The Wanderer' – he had a pencil in his hand – 'returns.'

The driver stepped back into the darkness while Nehmann followed the Minister into the house. It was cavernous, an uneasy mix of Third Reich kitsch and something altogether more modern. Through a pair of open doors halfway down the hall, Nehmann caught sight of what he assumed was a huge reception room, black and white diamond chequers on the floor, the ceiling boxed in varnished wood, a long rectangular table set for a single place.

At the end of the hall, among a selection of looted French Impressionist paintings, was a framed photograph Nehmann had never seen before. He paused beside it. Goebbels, in a military greatcoat and a cap, was on the right, his gloved hands clasped in front of him, about to address an unseen figure. Behind him, at the very centre of the photo, was a woman in a three-quarter-length white fur coat. She had a flower in her hair and her gown extended to her ankles. She, too, was looking at someone on the right. An occasion of some kind, Nehmann assumed. He was right.

'*Olympia*?' Goebbels had stopped, too. 'You've seen it? That was the night we launched Leni's masterpiece.'

Nehmann nodded. Leni Riefenstahl was the Reich's favourite film director and *Olympia* was her record of the 1936 Berlin Games. Nehmann had loved it at first sight, mainly because it broke all the rules: smash cuts, weird camera angles, extreme close-ups. Riefenstahl, he often thought, achieved on the screen effects he himself tried to put on the page. She understood, above all, how important it was to reach out and compel attention.

'And that's Baarova? In the fur coat?'

'Lida.' Goebbels barely spared her a glance. 'Yes.'

He opened a nearby door and stood aside to let Nehmann through. This had to be the Minister's study, in many ways a replica of his perch in the Wilhelmstrasse. The same neatly organised desk. The same side table stacked with film scripts. The same nest of family photographs. Nehmann noticed that door was still a centimetre or so open.

'A seat, Nehmann. You must be weary.' Goebbels waved his guest into one of the two armchairs. 'Wine or whisky? I suggest the latter.'

Nehmann said he was happy with either. Goebbels busied himself with a cut-glass decanter, pouring two large glasses of what he said was single malt.

'I expect a man can get sick of vodka.' He smiled. 'It's very good to see you in one piece, my friend. Is it equally good to be home?'

Nehmann was noncommittal. Goebbels, as ever, was setting the conversational pace, pointing Nehmann in the direction they both understood. 'Home' meant the apartment on the Wilhelmstrasse.

'I liked the flowers,' Nehmann said. 'And the *Frauen-Warte* cover was a nice touch.'

'Excellent. The Elbrus edition broke every circulation record. Men in uniform have a wonderful effect on women. Put six of them on top of a mountain and millions of *Frauen* are ours for the taking. You'll be glad to know that even the Führer approved in the end.'

Nehmann nodded. The first sip of whisky was burning his throat.

'Someone left a cutting on my pillow,' he said slowly. 'In the bedroom.'

'Really?' Goebbels feigned surprise.

Nehmann outlined the story: the crowded platform in the Metro, the approaching train, doubtless a scream or two from the women who witnessed what followed.

'So, who died?' he asked.

Goebbels wouldn't answer, not at first. Instead, he wanted to know about Stalingrad, about the state of Paulus's army, about the sturdy bridge Goering's Ju-52s had built to the supply dumps in the west.

'The whole thing's a shit heap,' Nehmann said. 'The Ivans fight like tigers. We don't have enough aircraft. If anyone tells you different, they're lying.'

'But is that a surprise? Everyone has his breaking point, his line in the sand. This happens to be Stalin's. That helps us, Nehmann. That means the gloves are off. Every play, every novel, every opera has its final act. This is the moment we have to prevail. Stalin knows it, and the Führer knows it. It's simply a question of will.'

'*Schwerpunkt*,' Nehmann said lightly. 'The military swear by it.'

'Exactly. We gather ourselves. And we fall on the enemy. Remember when we went into France? Remember Sevastopol? The impregnable fortress? Stalingrad is simply more of the same but happily, once the city has fallen, we can turn our attentions elsewhere. You're right about the Ivans. To give them a little credit, they're tougher than we anticipated. But once the Volga is ours, we can deal with Leningrad. And then Moscow. You know what the Führer thinks?' Goebbels leaned forward, his voice lower. He wanted to beckon Nehmann into the inner sanctum. He wanted to share a secret. 'The Führer is convinced Stalin will sue for peace. That partly comes from something Ribbentrop said and partly from somewhere else. Ribbentrop's a fool, of course, but at least he understands how to negotiate with these people. Stalin will be on his knees and then the whole Bolshevik racket will collapse like a pack of cards.'

'Somewhere else?'

Goebbels nodded, said nothing. The past month or so had deepened the hollows in his face but there was a strange gleam in his eye. Nehmann was still waiting for an answer. Goebbels lifted his glass.

'A toast, Nehmann.' He smiled. 'To Providence.'

'Providence? This is where the message came from?'

'Indeed. Our people are primitive. With a little of the right kind of help, Nehmann, they believe in the sublime. They acknowledge a higher calling. In a setting like this, words fail us. Even you, Nehmann, even you with all your gifts might be challenged. Is it a deity we reach out to? A god? Or should we simply be grateful that he's taken human form and moves among us?'

Nehmann held his gaze, appalled. Madness, he thought.

'You're talking about Hitler?'

'About the Führer, Nehmann. About the voice of Providence.'

'And that will take care of Stalingrad?'

'Of course, Nehmann. And of everything that follows. I've known it since the early days. Our apostle of truth, Nehmann, our helmsman, our voice in battle, our exemplar, our *Leader*. In two days' time he will launch the Winter Appeal in the Sportpalast. It will be an opportunity, Nehmann, for the nation to draw its breath and check its bearings. Do we need clothing? Sturdy boots? Woollen greatcoats? Of course, we do. But we need something else, Nehmann, infinitely more precious. We need faith, a shared belief in our destiny.' He got up and stepped behind the desk. From a drawer, he produced a handful of typed sheets. 'The first draft, Nehmann. That's why I've called you back. I want you to be the first to read it. I need your thoughts, your opinions. Then, together, we can start work on the second draft and – if need be – the third. The Führer will have a day or so to make his own mark. He may decide to rip the whole thing up. He might want to make a fresh start. But something tells me that won't be the case. Listen, Nehmann. Bear witness. Be with us when we conquer our demons.'

His body shifted slightly behind the desk, a tiny movement that Nehmann only remembered later, and then, through the still-open door, came piano chords from somewhere deep in the house, sombre at first, then more playful, teasing out this first theme before exploding in a wild cascade of notes. Nehmann listened, spellbound. Beethoven, he thought. The sonata Maria called the *Pathétique*.

'Go and find her, Nehmann.' Goebbels gestured towards the door. 'Reintroduce yourself. Make yourself known. Enjoy...'

Nehmann left the study. Another passage led deeper into the house. The music was growing louder and louder, the playing as deft and delicate as ever, and finally he came to another door, likewise open, and he pushed softly, making no noise, no disturbance, as the music built to a crescendo and then died.

This was the far end of the big dining room. There was a mirror on the wall and Maria had watched the door opening. She got to her feet and stepped across to him. She was wearing an embroidered waistcoat over the same blue skirt he remembered from that final Sunday when they were to take a boat and sail away across the Wannsee.

He kissed her, held her, ran his fingers through her hair, kissed her again. Then he nodded towards the piano.

'Don't stop,' he murmured. 'Play the rest for me.'

They rejoined Goebbels half an hour later. He was still in his study, bent over the speech Hitler was to make in the

Sportpalast. He barely lifted his head as Nehmann appeared at the door.

'The car's still outside.' He gestured at the draft speech. 'Come to the Ministry tomorrow.'

Nehmann nodded. He had one question.

'The article,' he said. 'On the pillow.'

A frown briefly clouded Goebbels' face. He seemed to have forgotten about the death at Montparnasse. Then he looked up.

'It was Guramishvili, Nehmann, that friend of yours. I understand he upset some of those French swine. If it's any consolation that apartment of his belongs to us now. Consider yourself our guest, eh?'

*

The driver took them back to the Wilhelmstrasse. Nehmann and Maria sat in the back of the big Mercedes. He held her close, his hand in hers, her head on his shoulder, saying very little, knowing that whatever passed between them would find its way back to the Promi.

He still didn't quite believe that Guram – so enterprising, so clever, so *aware* – could have found himself under a train in the Paris Metro. Georgians knew how to look after themselves. They recognised the smell of danger. Emptying French cellars of countless cases of fine vintage wine would never have endeared him to the Resistance but Guram would have known that from the start. So, if he was really dead, there had to be another explanation.

Did it involve Goebbels? Was this scrap of newsprint yet another piece of theatre he'd conjured out of thin air? Did it serve his purposes to gradually, item by item, strip Werner

Nehmann of everything he held dear? First the woman he loved? Next, his oldest friend? And now the apartment he'd dared to call home?

Nehmann didn't know, could never be sure, and what made this bombshell so especially painful was the knowledge that he and his master were fellow practitioners in the same dark arts. What was true, and what was false? Was Guram really dead? And if not, would he – Werner Nehmann – ever be certain where the truth lay?

The truth.

He and Maria were back in the apartment. It wasn't late, barely ten o'clock, but Nehmann had opened one of Guram's few remaining bottles and taken it to bed. She lay in his arms. He was right about the broadcast he'd heard on the radio. She hadn't set foot in Austria. The whole interview had taken place not in the Promi, as Nehmann had suspected, but in another facility in the Ufa studios across the city.

'And that village of yours? Down near the border?'

'A fiction. It exists, of course, but not in my life.'

'You're really from Warsaw?'

'I am.'

'And your name?'

'Maria. It's on my ID. I can prove it.'

'Your family name?'

'Gaetani.'

'So who gave you the ID? Who sorted out your papers?'

'Goebbels, of course.'

'And you're happy being Maria Gaetani?'

'Of course. She was my idea from the start. Szarlota Kowalczyk would have put me in a camp.'

'Like your mother?'

'Yes.'

'You saw that coming?'

'My father did. He gave me the new name, the Austrian village, everything. He got me out, too. He taught music at the university in Warsaw, but I think he really wanted to be a novelist. He told a good story when he'd had enough to drink and when it came to this one, he put me in the middle of it. I saw him last week. He's an old man now. What happened to my mother broke him.'

'The Nazis broke him. We broke him.'

'Not you, Werner.'

'How can you say that? I work for these people. I tell lies for them every day. I make all that shit of theirs smell sweeter.'

'No.' She moistened a fingertip and traced the shape of a heart across the bareness of his chest. 'You belong to no one. I knew that from the start. No one.'

'I belong to you.'

'You think you do. For now.' She laughed softly.

'Forever,' he insisted.

'No.' She shook her head. 'You're a beautiful man and I'd like to think you're my beautiful man but if there's one thing this war teaches you, this city maybe, certainly this life of ours, is never make assumptions. Assumptions bring nothing but grief. Do you believe me? Do I sound Georgian enough? All you have to say is yes.'

'Yes.'

Her face was very close. Nehmann kissed her, told her he couldn't help himself. Whatever the word meant, he loved her.

'That's nice.'

'That's everything. Believe me. Without it, without you, here, you, me, us, there's nothing. Ask Goebbels. He knows.'

'The man's so lonely. And it shows. He's been kind to me, believe it or not, and I appreciate that.'

'Because he's made you famous?'

'Because he's been honest with me. I haven't got the talent he needs, not to get to concert standard.'

'That's not the purpose you serve.'

'I know. He's honest about that, too. That's why he brought me out to Bogensee this afternoon, had the piano installed, and the buzzer thing, too.'

'Buzzer thing?'

'The button under his desk. It rings a buzzer in that huge reception room. It told me when to start playing.'

Nehmann nodded. He remembered Goebbels seated behind his desk, the spell that Hitler still cast on him, and then that tiny moment when he'd delivered his speech, appeased the gods of Providence and pressed the buzzer with his knee. So theatrical. So perfectly contrived. No wonder the man was fascinated by the movie business.

'He says you've got a letter of his.' Maria had abandoned the love heart on Nehmann's chest.

'He's right.' Nehmann nodded.

'What sort of letter?'

'It's a letter he wrote recently to Baarova. She was his mistress once.'

'I know. He talks of no one else. Why you? Why have you got the letter?'

'He asked me to take it to her. In Rome.'

'And?'

277

'I failed. The letter is deeply compromising. This is a man the Führer has ordered to be in love with his wife. The letter suggests he doesn't obey orders. That's a capital offence in this city.'

'You've *read* it? The letter?'

'Of course, I've read it. At Goebbels' level you'd never survive by playing the rules.'

'And?' She was up on one elbow now, hungry for more.

Nehmann kissed her again, said it didn't matter. Just here, just now, there were more interesting things to do than discuss Goebbels' love life.

'Tell me.' She pushed him gently away. 'Just tell me what's in the letter. Is it passionate?'

'Of course.'

'Romantic?'

'Very.'

'Undying love?'

'Definitely.'

'And does he mean it?'

'I don't know, and that's the point because I don't think he does either. If you want the truth, the letter is pathetic. It's not about love at all. It's about loneliness, about lostness, about need. In the hands of his enemies, it would kill him. That's why he wants it back so badly. It's like I have a gun, pointed at his head. Goebbels can't live with that. No man could.'

'*Kill* him?'

'In here' – Nehmann took her open hand and placed it over his heart – 'where it matters.'

Maria nodded. She seemed to understand.

'So where is it?' she said at last. 'This letter?'

Nehmann looked at her for a long moment, and then smiled.

'There's a water tank on the roof,' he murmured. 'If anything happens to me, look underneath.'

They made love. In the middle of the night, Nehmann awoke. Maria's face hung over him, concerned, even fretful.

'And the East?' she said. 'Stalingrad?'

Still groggy, Nehmann thought about the question.

'Horrible,' he managed at last, closing his eyes again.

26

BERLIN SPORTPALAST,
WEDNESDAY 30 SEPTEMBER 1942

Nehmann had never liked the Sportpalast. Recently, talking
to Schultz in Stalingrad, he'd likened it to something you'd
find in Goebbels' kitchen. It was a cooking pot, he said.
It was a favourite utensil you'd fetch out for those special
occasions when you wanted to whip up something irresistible
to keep everyone happy. You put together the recipe from what
you knew and trusted. A little of that intimate frenzy from
the Bürgerbräukeller days in Munich. Plus a huge helping
of spectacle and mass adoration from the Zeppelinfeld at
Nuremberg: hanging banners, roving spotlights and a sound
system that would put Hitler's rasp and Goebbels' chest-
thumping roar into every German heart. When the national
pulse showed signs of faltering, a couple of deafening hours
in the Sportpalast always did the trick.

The trick.

Nehmann had spent the best part of an entire morning
with Goebbels in the ministerial office, going through the first
draft of the speech line by line. It was about the war in the
east. At first, foolishly, he'd assumed he was there as an act of
reconciliation. For the sake of the Promi's credibility, he told

himself, Goebbels needed to find a compromise between the usual torrent of visionary drivel and the smaller truths about what was really happening in Stalingrad.

Wrong. The Minister's starting point turned out to be the way the British had consistently managed to turn defeats into victories. First at Dunkirk, and more recently after the botched attempt to land a force of Canadians to create mayhem at Dieppe, London had refused to be humiliated. On both occasions, as Goebbels knew only too well, German forces had chased the Allied troops back into the sea, and yet London had somehow managed to repackage both events as magnificent examples of pluck and resilience against impossible odds. Nehmann was already aware of Hitler's quiet admiration for the British. What came as a surprise was Goebbels' envy of their propaganda talents.

'Stalingrad's a mess,' he'd told Nehmann yesterday. 'So far this war has been too kind to us. We need to take a lesson from the British.'

And so the draft was written, and rewritten, and Goebbels prevailed upon Nehmann to add a little of his trademark lustre to lift the speech where it was in danger of sagging. Nehmann did his best to retain a cautionary note or two about the unexpected depth of Soviet resources but was ignored. In late afternoon, the most senior of the secretaries in the outer office typed up the final version which was hand-delivered to the Chancellery. Would the Leader take the slightest notice of any of this? Probably not but – as Goebbels was the first to point out – it paid to keep a finger in the Führer-pie. If the demanded note of triumph was misplaced, so be it. No one prospered in this regime by telling the truth.

Hitler, to Goebbels' considerable relief, appeared to be on form. A week or so ago he'd received a personal note from the Führer's operational headquarters in East Prussia. The handwriting, he told Nehmann, was that of an old man: scratchy, wayward, senescent. Now though, back in Berlin, he seemed buoyant and newly energised. The weather out at Rastenburg, Goebbels' concluded, was bleak enough to put years on any man. Why should the Führer be exempt?

The Sportpalast was packed, an audience of thousands, all of them devotees of their adored Leader. Hitler stood at the rostrum, flanked left and right by Party chieftains, and beat the drum for the Fatherland's military prowess, each savage chop of his hand tallying yet another triumph. German troops occupying the Black Sea port of Novorossiysk. German troops on the French Channel coast tossing the Canadians back into the sea. And now a German U-boat dropping mines in the busy sea lanes leading into Charleston, North Carolina, taking the war to the very edge of the vast American continent. Nowhere on earth, the Führer seemed to be saying, was safe from the reach of the Greater Reich.

Nehmann knew that much of this was old news. The winter, in reality, had been full of disappointments and the campaign in North Africa was going badly wrong but the vast audience didn't care. They'd come to hear the Führer exultant, the Führer all-powerful, the Führer mocking the drunks and warmongers among the nation's enemies, and he didn't let them down. Churchill was a buffoon. Roosevelt sat in the lap of the Jews. The British lived on a thin diet of defeat after defeat, fooling themselves that a disaster like Dunkirk was somehow the path to victory. This was a line that had survived from the final Promi draft and Nehmann sat back, wondering whether Goebbels' hunger for recognition, for some tiny crumb from the Führer's table, had been satisfied.

But then Hitler turned his attention to the east where, he assured the doting multitudes, only time stood between the Fatherland and the untold riches of the Caspian basin. Army Group 'A', he promised, would thrust down through the Caucasus and cut the Soviets off from their precious oil. In the meantime, he roared, the battle for Stalingrad was virtually over. The city on the Volga, the diamond in Stalin's crown, lay in German hands. He paused, mopping his face with a handkerchief, his body slightly bent as if he, too, had been part of this monumental feat of arms. Then he stiffened and looked out at the sea of faces. He wanted his people to celebrate. And he wanted to offer a guarantee. 'If you can be sure of anything,' he roared. 'You can be sure of this. That no one will ever get us away from this place again!'

The auditorium erupted. Thousands were on their feet, their arms outstretched, bellowing the Führer's name. Textbook Nuremberg, Nehmann thought, noting the broadness of the smile on Goebbels' face.

Minutes later, after an appeal for clothing and other comforts to carry the nation's warriors through the coming winter, the speech was over. The Führer departed, attended by his Minister for Propaganda who half turned and signalled for Nehmann to follow.

He caught up with them in a smallish anteroom behind the stage. Space was tight and Nehmann found himself beside Hitler. He was still perspiring after the speech and Nehmann caught the rank sourness that came in waves as he shifted his weight from foot to foot. It was a smell that would stay with Nehmann for the months to come, the smell – as he interpreted it – of a body in revolt, of a man taking leave of his senses, of the stench of megalomania seeping ever outwards.

Goebbels was on hand with a fresh handkerchief. He introduced Nehmann, who had never met the Führer before.

'A colleague from the Ministry, *Mein Führer*,' Goebbels said. 'I think I mentioned him earlier.'

Hitler nodded. His eyes were still glazed, a man in a trance. Then he blinked and gave his forehead a final wipe with Goebbels' handkerchief. He seemed to recognise Nehmann's name.

'Stalingrad, Nehmann. The Minister passed on your impressions. He told me how well we're doing out there. I'm grateful. Keep up the good work, *ja*?' His hand briefly fell on Nehmann's shoulder. Then he was gone.

*

Maria had listened to the speech at the apartment. A car from the Ministry was already waiting at the kerbside, waiting to take her out to the airfield at Tempelhof. Goebbels had secured her a seat on one of the Führer Squadron's Ju-52s. She was flying down to Munich where this evening she'd be playing at a special concert to launch the Winter Appeal in Bavaria.

Nehmann kissed her. She looked radiant and she smelled even sweeter. Shalimar by Guerlain, he thought. The bottle must be nearly empty.

'Our Leader?' Nehmann held her briefly at arm's length. 'What did you think?'

'I thought of all those letters you wrote me.' She nodded

towards the bedroom. 'They're in one of the drawers. I've kept them all. Show them to Goebbels. Make Hitler read them. Maybe there are two Stalingrads and you were in the other one. There has to be an explanation. Might that be possible?'

She smiled at him. She said she had to go. With luck she should be back in Berlin tomorrow, or perhaps the day after, certainly by the weekend. Whatever happened, the weather might be kind.

'Wannsee?' She'd half turned to leave. 'Maybe a sailing boat?'

Nehmann nodded. He told her he needed to find a decent bookshop. He'd been away for a while. Things changed so quickly in Berlin. Any ideas?

'Ja.' She paused at the door. 'There's a little place called *Lies mich*. It's in Kopernikusstrasse, off Warschauer Strasse. It's easy to miss but there's a tree outside. I was in there recently. *Wiedersehen, ja?*' She blew him a kiss and left.

*

Lies mich. Read me. Sweet. The bookshop was a couple of minutes' stroll north of the tangle of railway lines that fed the *Hauptbahnhof*. It was small, dwarfed by the five storeys of apartments above it, but the tree was the clue. Nehmann waited for a horse and cart to pass before crossing the street, enjoying the slant of late afternoon sun on his face. Schultz had asked him to lay hands on a German–Russian dictionary, nothing fancy. We're going to be here for a while, he'd said. His Russian was barely adequate, and it would certainly pay to learn a little more.

At first, Nehmann thought the shop must have closed. There were a couple of dusty-looking novels propped up in the window, and a much thumbed guidebook to the glories of Potsdam. He lingered a moment, and then tried the door. A bell sounded deep inside as he stepped in. The place smelled musty. Bookshelves packed with titles receded into the gloom. Then he heard the faintest meow and a cat materialised from nowhere. It was plump, old, well-fed, three words you'd rarely attach to any animal in this city.

The cat wound itself around Nehmann's ankles and he bent to fondle the little bony recess beneath its cheek. The cat responded at once, lifting its head and starting to purr.

'Can I help you?' An oldish voice.

Nehmann looked up. A man had appeared beside the little desk that served as a counter. He was in his sixties at least. He wore a pair of old corduroy trousers and a grey flannel shirt loosely tucked in. He hadn't shaved for several days and the grey felt slippers were fraying at the heel. In the breast pocket of his shirt, a pair of gold-rimmed glasses.

Nehmann asked about dictionaries. The books here looked second-hand.

'Which language?'

'Russian.'

'Ah...' The old man had a lovely smile. 'An accent like yours, I'm surprised you need one.'

'It's not for me. It's for a friend.'

'But you're Russian, *nein*?'

'Georgian.'

'Same thing, isn't it? Your age, you'd speak Russian from the cradle. Or did you say *Niet*?'

Nehmann laughed. He'd always liked the informality of Berlin, but this ageing bookseller already seemed to regard him as a family friend. Under the regime, conversations like this could quickly become uncomfortable but the old man had a companionable sense of mischief that Nehmann rather liked.

'You have a choice of dictionaries, I'm glad to say.' He left Nehmann beside the table and disappeared towards the back of the shop. Moments later, he returned with two books, one big, one small. The smaller one looked brand new.

'You might recognise this.' He weighed it in his bony hand a moment. 'If you want a dozen, I'm happy to oblige. For an order like that a Georgian gets a handsome discount. Please, see what you think.'

Nehmann had seen the dictionary before. The regime had printed nearly a million of them in the days following the start of Barbarossa. In the aftermath of last year's operation, went the logic, any enterprising German would find themselves in the wake of the invading armies, doubtless keen to make the most of this sudden windfall.

Nehmann leafed through the opening pages. There were cartoons of German troops being nice to Russian peasants. Underneath, three sample questions that might prove invaluable.

Wie weit nach Moskau? How far to Moscow?

Ist das Ihr Haus? Is this house yours?

Wir kommen in Frieden. We come in peace.

'You think that's funny?'

'I do, yes.'

'And your friend?'

'He'll think it's funny, too.'

'You know the east?'

'My friend does.'

'But you, do you know it?'

'Yes, a little.'

'Where?'

'Stalingrad.'

'You're in the *Wehrmacht*, maybe?'

'No.'

'You're homesick for Russians? You miss the language? The food? The music? The good manners?'

'Of course. But no.'

The old man apologised. He was curious, that's all. He didn't want to offend his new customer.

'Maybe the proper dictionary? This one?'

He offered the bigger of the two books. Nehmann shook his head. The small one was fine. It would keep his friend amused for weeks.

'Good.' A nod of approval. 'Laughter and a new language often go together. A good student is a happy student, didn't you always find that? In your Russian classes?'

Nehmann ignored the question. For the first time, he'd noticed the small, boxy radio wedged on a shelf between rows of books.

'You listened to the speech this afternoon?' he asked. 'From the Sportpalast?'

'Yes.' He nodded.

'And what did you think?'

'Me? What did I think about that speech? About every speech that man makes? You don't think there's a reason I keep the radio on the fiction shelf?'

Nehmann blinked. The questions were beyond reckless. In Berlin, like everywhere else, it paid to hold your tongue when it came to strangers. Nonetheless he liked this man and viewed the trust he'd vested in Nehmann as a compliment.

'You know about Stalingrad?' Nehmann asked. 'You know the way it really is?'

'I have a daughter,' he said. 'And she has a boyfriend.'

'In the army?'

'In Stalingrad.'

'And what does this boyfriend say?'

'He says the Russians are good fighters. He says the Russians will never give in. He also says that there are millions of them, billions of them. The city doesn't belong to us and he doubts that it ever will. If he was here in this shop now, I'd suspect he'd buy the bigger dictionary. Does that answer your question, young man?'

Nehmann laughed. He loved this man's courage, his refusal to bend to the regime, and above all he loved his wit. The bigger of the two dictionaries, he thought. Perfect.

'I'll take them both,' he said. 'You've been in this shop long?'

'Just over a year. I bought it for a song. The previous owner had died. His wife turned out to hate him. The sale was a small act of revenge.'

'For what?'

'The man had got the shop for free. 1938? *Kristallnacht?* The previous owner was a Jew. The SA chased him out and the woman's husband helped himself.'

Nehmann nodded. *Kristallnacht:* the Night of Broken Glass. Synagogues, shops and other Jewish properties had been smashed up in the wake of an incident in Paris. A young Jew had killed a German diplomat and Hitler had unleased the thugs of the *Sturmabteilung* to do their worst.

At Hitler's elbow, masterminding this orgy of violence? Joseph Goebbels.

'He really got it for nothing? This woman's husband?'

'Nothing. *Nichts. Nada. Rien.* And you know the irony? He hated books. He didn't even know how to read. She couldn't wait to get rid of the place. Which made me lucky, too.' He stared at Nehmann, contemplative, then he nodded towards the window. 'You know what I still find when I get busy with my duster and my dustpan and brush?'

'Broken glass.'

'You're right, my friend. Tiny fragments. And you know something else? That's all this war is worth. That's all we'll be left with once it's over.'

Nehmann nodded. He accepted the old man's embrace and then stepped backwards.

'So how much? For the books?'

'A Reichsmark for the big one, my friend.' The old man was smiling again. 'And you get the comic for free. You're going back to Stalingrad?'

'Yes.'

'Your choice?'

'Yes.'

'Then take care.' Another embrace, briefer this time.

Nehmann opened the door and was about to step out onto the street when the old man called him back. He had something for him, something he wanted him to have. Not a gift, exactly. More a memento of their conversation.

The old man was flicking through a pile of magazines. Finally, he found what he was after. Nehmann was looking at a copy of *Das Reich*, Goebbels' monthly magazine.

'It's the May edition. Have you read it?'

Nehmann was trying to remember. He sometimes wrote for *Das Reich* but did his best not to take the relationship any further.

'I doubt it.' He took the magazine. 'What am I looking for?'

'The editorial, of course. Self-indulgence is a Goebbels speciality. Feast yourself, young man. And then take it to Stalingrad and show it around.'

*

Nehmann didn't want to go home, not yet. It was dusk now, but still warm. Street sweepers were out in force on the Warschauer Strasse, tidying up beneath the tall elms, and Nehmann found himself a seat at a pavement café table as the offices along the broad boulevard began to empty out. He ordered a beer and lit a cigarette, watching two women, arm in arm, as they paused at the kerbside, waiting to cross to the tram stop on the other side. They were laughing at some joke or other and one was carrying a tiny bunch of what looked like roses. Half close your eyes, Nehmann thought, and the war might be over.

Goebbels, it turned out, had addressed the same thought. His editorial was headlined *What's It All For?* A tall glass of beer arrived, and Nehmann sat back, the magazine open on his lap, thinking of Goebbels' face on the dais while his precious Führer was in full flow. This afternoon, Hitler had firmly established Paulus's victorious army on the banks of the Volga. Afterwards, once Hitler had departed, Nehmann had enquired whether he was supposed to return to Stalingrad and Goebbels had nodded. The battle, as the Führer had confirmed, was as

291

good as won. The Russians were beaten, and it was now the Promi's job to make good on that promise.

Both Goebbels and Nehmann, master and servant, knew that 'make good' was a slippery little verb, just short of an outright lie, and there'd once been a time when Nehmann would have been baffled about what he was supposed to do. Could he summon battalions of infantry? Columns of tanks? Squadrons of Richthofen's heavy bombers? Or was it really possible to marshal public opinion with nothing more than pen, ink and an untroubled conscience? The latter, of course, had now become a way of life and when he and Goebbels had parted on the pavement beside the Minister's sleek Mercedes, he'd asked whether or not to expect more detailed instructions.

'Not at all, Nehmann.' Goebbels was in the best of moods. 'Do what you always do so well. Make us *happy*.'

And so, there it was. Happy. A quarter of a million men digging themselves deeper and deeper into the frozen steppe, into the wreckage of a ruined city, into any hole that would offer shelter from Russian fire. Happy.

Nehmann turned his attention to the editorial in *Das Reich*. The war, in Goebbels' eyes, was virtually over and now it was time to imagine the kind of world in which the entire nation would undoubtedly find themselves.

'We are dreaming of a happy people in a country blossoming with beauty,' Goebbels had written, 'traversed by wide roads like bands of silver which are also open to the modest car of the ordinary man. Beside them lie pretty villages and well laid-out cities with clean and roomy houses inhabited by large families for whom they provide sufficient space. In the limitless fields of the east, yellow corn is waving, enough and more than enough to feed our people and the rest of Europe. Work will once more be a pleasure and it will be marked by a joy in life which will find expression in brilliant parties and a contemplative peace.'

Nehmann reached for his beer, only too aware of the thinness of the lie. A busy man, he thought, reaching for a handful of straw to toss to his readership. Pretty villages? Fields of waving corn? Brilliant parties? These were clichés. The writing was perfunctory. Neither Goebbels nor anyone else would ever believe this shit. It might draw a nod of assent, and even a smile, from the likes of Hitler and Goering, an important audience for the tricksters at the Promi, but no one else would be fooled for a moment. Certainly not the old man in his bookshop. And certainly not anyone with a moment's experience, first-hand or otherwise, of life on the Eastern Front.

Nehmann closed the magazine and was about to toss it aside when he had second thoughts. Maria, he thought. When she comes back from Munich.

That night, he listened to her on the radio. Since he'd been away, she'd added to her repertoire. She played Liszt and Mozart, as well as a Beethoven sonata, and he smiled when the moment of silence at the end of her performance was swamped by applause. Acclamation like this, thought Nehmann, was genuine, a response to the music, something way beyond the reach of the Third Reich. This afternoon, so different, had been orchestrated for the groundlings in the Sportpalast, a very different audience, almost a sub-division of the Promi. They wanted to be lied to. They thrived on fantasy. Hence the near-hysteria in the hall at the end and the sour reek of the Führer's efforts backstage afterwards. Brilliant parties, he thought. And the blessings of a contemplative peace.

Maria returned two days later. Nehmann, alerted by the Promi, was about to leave once again for the long two-stage flight back to Stalingrad. He'd harvested a couple of handfuls of chillis from his pots on the windowsill, a present for Schultz, and he was about to pack the three remaining bottles of Bordeaux from Guram's cellar when he heard Maria's key turning in the door. He met her in the hall. She looked exhausted. He tried to hold her close and said he was proud of the performance in Munich. She could see his bag readied by the door. She understood at once what he was really saying.

'You're going back?'

'I am.'

'Because you have to?'

'Partly. Partly not.'

'You *want* to go back?'

'I have to go back.'

Nehmann was looking at her. The question he expected was 'why?' but it never happened. Instead, she wanted to know whether he'd managed to lay hands on a Russian dictionary.

'Yes.'

'At the bookshop I mentioned?'

'Yes.'

'And you met the bookseller?'

'I did. Fabulous man.'

'Good.' At last she kissed him. 'That's my father.'

27

STALINGRAD, OCTOBER 1942

Schultz was delighted with both dictionaries. He and his tiny staff were still occupying their basement quarters in the bus depot, and when Nehmann enquired about the state of the battle the *Abwehr* man simply shrugged. The young Georgian prisoner, Kirile, was now part of the team. With his help they'd been monitoring Soviet command transmissions and it was obvious that the Russians, like Sixth Army, were exhausted. They'd fired too many bullets, too many mortar bombs, too many artillery shells. They were running out of targets, as well as munitions, and the following day – as if by some psychic act of collaboration – the shooting more or less stopped.

A sudden silence descended on what remained of the city, punctuated by occasional small-arms fire and the sharp bark of exploding landmines, often triggered by horses. In the aftermath, as Nehmann discovered, ration parties would descend on the corpse of the dead animal, men with axes and combat saws, everything muffled against the cold but their eyes. They'd kneel over the still-steaming entrails, hacking at the body, stealing away at the half-crouch, a foreleg or a haunch on each shoulder. At moments like these, Nehmann longed for a camera. This strange hiatus, this moment of frozen calm, had an almost biblical quality and in the long evenings he tried to do justice to it with words on paper.

Schultz read his work from time to time, puzzled by the intended readership.

'You're going to waste this stuff on *Goebbels*? You think that piece of shit will know what you're trying to say?'

The answer, of course, was yes. Like it or not, the Minister of Propaganda was deeply cultured. He understood the impact of an arresting image or a well-turned phrase, but Schultz was right, as well, because the Reich had turned its collective back on the developing catastrophe in the east and didn't want to be bothered with truths either large or small.

'I'd be wasting their precious time,' Nehmann admitted. 'I'm here to write fiction.'

Next morning, after soundings around a tepid bowl of wheat and corn syrup porridge, Nehmann wrote a seven-hundred-word despatch about lice. He wanted, he said, to let the nation into one of Sixth Army's more closely guarded secrets. Its real enemies weren't the Ivans at all. It wasn't even the cold, which was starting to make life a little difficult. It was lice, those tiny little presents from the devil.

Like the men themselves, lice loathed the weather. Lie in the snow all day, hunting for targets, and they'd never bother you. Come back in from the cold, with your reddened hands and your chattering teeth, and they'd wake up at once and make themselves known. In the words of a *Feldwebel* from Essen, they were like the Russians. Kill one, and ten more appear.

Another man, a machine-gunner from Koln, called them 'the little partisans'. They lurked out of sight, he said, in the deepest seams of the warmest part of your clothing and then laid ambush to you when you were least expecting it. In reality, none of these men said anything of the sort, largely because Nehmann had invented them. The stories themselves were true but their authors had a deep mistrust of being quoted and only one, a slightly crazed former brewer from the Black Forest, was prepared to see his name in print. He had, he said, come up with a fool-proof antidote to the curse of the louse. 'Read them anything by Goebbels,' he told Nehmann, 'and they'll all die laughing.'

'You'll get the man killed.' Schultz thought it was funny. 'He survives a couple of months out here and then gets shot in Berlin for insubordination. How's that for bad luck?'

'I'll change it,' Nehmann promised. 'Instead, he'll read them last night's orders.'

'That's worse. You think any of Paulus's people have a sense of humour? They'll shoot the poor bastard here.'

The story was flown out next morning in one of the special Promi envelopes marked *Dringend*. Urgent mail like this was still guaranteed to arrive in Berlin within thirty-six hours. While he awaited a reply, with battle yet to recommence in earnest, Nehmann did a piece on a trench dog whose admirers swore could tell the difference in engine note between *Luftwaffe* aircraft and the Soviet planes that were beginning to appear over the city in some numbers. The men in the trench had acquired the dog over a thousand kilometres ago, west of Kyiv, and it had been with them ever since. They fed it on a diet of viscera scraped from the bellies of dead cattle and horses and its keeper called it 'Wulf'. To Nehmann, who loathed dogs of any kind, it appeared to sleep most of the time, but when he insisted on a demonstration, the keeper managed a very credible impersonation of one of the Soviet Yakovlevs. The dog was on its feet within seconds, barking and barking, drawing a fusillade of oaths from a *Kamerad* trying to snatch an hour's sleep before turning out for sentry duty.

Nehmann took the story back to the bus depot where Schultz, as it happened, was interrogating a Soviet pilot who spoke German and who'd crash-landed after an attack on the airfield at Pitomnik. Nehmann, amused by the coincidence, settled on a wooden box beside Schultz and introduced himself in fluent Russian.

'I'm here for you to tell me stories,' he said. 'The truer and the dirtier the better.'

'You mean secrets?' The pilot, a youthful looking maths graduate from Moscow, wouldn't hear of it.

'Stories,' Nehmann insisted. 'They're not the same thing.'

The pilot was confused. Schultz did his best to help him out. Herr Nehmann, he said, was a journalist. He was also a comedian. His job was to make people either laugh or cry. Make life simple for him. Tell him something funny.

The pilot seemed to get the point. He turned back to Nehmann.

'You want to know about one of our aircraft?' he said. 'You want me to tell you about the Polikarpov? It's a biplane, two wings, very simple. We make it from wood and canvas. It's an old woman, very slow, and at night we switch the engine off and glide over your trenches, your front trenches, and drop bombs.'

Nehmann nodded. He'd heard of these shapes that came ghosting in from Soviet lines. They were flown by female pilots and some of these women had become trench legends because they sang to the men below before dropping their bombs.

'*Nochnyer ved'ma*,' Nehmann said. 'Night witches.'

'*Da*.' The pilot was grinning.

'And the plane? You've got a story about the plane?'

'*Da*. We pilots call them *kerosinka*. And you know why? Because they catch fire in no time at all.'

Kerosinka. Nehmann wrote it down. A kerosene lamp.

'You liked being a pilot? Going home every night? Getting a good night's sleep?'

The pilot nodded. Sometimes it was fine. Other times it wasn't. The food, he admitted, was better than the men in the front line got and you weren't shelled and bombed all the time, but the planes weren't looked after properly, especially the engines, and you lived in dread for the moment when the propeller stopped and you looked down from the cockpit and the Volga was more than a glide away.

'That's what happened today?'

'No. I got shot down. That was my fault.' He looked at the blood still caked on his hands. 'You know what we pilots say? Here? In Stalingrad?'

'Tell me.'

'We say that our life is like a child's shirt. Short and covered with shit.'

Schultz had been doing his best to follow the interview, now it was in Russian. This bit he appeared to understand. He checked with Nehmann and then rocked with laughter before giving the pilot a pat on the shoulder.

'Any more stories like that,' he said, 'and we might have to give you something to drink.'

*

299

Nehmann despatched this story, too, but over the days to come he heard nothing from the Promi. When he caught the familiar beat of the *Tante-Jus* landing at Pitomnik, he occasionally wondered whether one of the envelopes in the *Luftpost* bag might have his name on, but nothing turned up, neither from Goebbels nor Maria. By late October, both sides had re-engaged, and the battle was as fierce as ever and, as the days slipped past, Nehmann recognised the way this city, this experience, closed around you, making everything else so remote that it became meaningless.

By now, he was translating regularly for Schultz in prisoner interrogations, especially when the captives were officers, and he began to detect a pattern in their guarded accounts of life on the Soviet front line. They called the political officers Commissars. These were the party fanatics who'd dedicated their lives to the Bolshevik cause and their task was to root out the slightest hint of deviance from the Communist line. By and large the officers agreed that the Commissars were a pain in the arse and completely unnecessary because the very presence of the Germans on Soviet soil was enough to persuade most Russians to fight to the death, but one of the consequences of the battle was an outbreak of genuine equality between the men and their officers. They faced the same risks, ate the same shit food, suffered together, laughed together, and all this in a world where rank seemed to matter less and less. The key word was *tovarisch*. Comrade? Yes. But mate, first.

'The Commissars hate it,' one officer said. 'They think standing by your fellow soldiers is some kind of conspiracy. Share a cigarette with some Tatar animal from fuck knows where? That's grounds for arrest. And why? Because the

Commissars haven't been through it, not the way we have, day after day, night after night. The Tatars are the best fighters we have. They're like the night witches. They get the harmonica out and sing at night before they crawl into your trenches and slit a throat or two. Be honest. Germans are terrified of them. How do I know? Because we are, too.'

More notes. More stories. Then, in early November, Nehmann – via Schultz – got wind of a dinner party to be held in the church the *Feldgendarmerie* had made their base. The thickness of the church's walls was as close to a guarantee of safety as the remains of the city could guarantee and Schultz had heard rumours of foal's liver dumplings with boiled potatoes. As the *Abwehr*'s senior officer in Stalingrad, he proposed to acquire an invitation and thought that Nehmann should come, too. The dinner, he said, was being held to celebrate the anniversary of the Russian Revolution. Toasts would naturally be drunk to the death of Stalin and the defeat of Ivans everywhere.

That same day, Nehmann at last got a letter from Berlin. Expecting a missive from the Promi passing judgement on the reports he'd so far submitted, he found himself reading a letter from Maria. The news, she said, wasn't good. She'd come back to Berlin from a concert tour in Franconia to find everything in Guram's apartment torn apart: mattresses and chairs sliced open, floorboards lifted, cupboards emptied. Worse still, the piano had been attacked with a sledgehammer, the top stove in, the keyboard splintered.

Naturally, she'd made contact with Goebbels who'd promised to send an aide to see for himself. Maria had slept that night on a nest of blankets and torn sheets in a corner of the bedroom and the aide had arrived the following morning, making a brief tour of the apartment, stepping from room to room, shaking his head in disapproval. Berlin, he told her, was in the middle of an epidemic of burglaries, evidence that morale in the city was beginning to sink. He promised to find her somewhere else to stay but her concert bookings had mysteriously come to an end and she'd heard nothing from either the aide or Goebbels since.

In the meantime, she'd moved in with her father in a tiny room at the back of the bookshop and she was glad to report that life was sweet again. He really liked you, she wrote at the end of the letter. Which makes two of us. In a brief postscript, she told him not to worry about anything because she'd taken care of it. Potsdam, she added, was a trip she knew they'd never forget.

Anything? Taken care of it? Nehmann thought hard about the postscript. They'd never been to Potsdam, not once, but he knew this had to be code as well. Maria was clever. She'd fled Warsaw and she'd survived. She knew that letters to and from certain correspondents were routinely screened by a special department at Prinz-Albrecht-Strasse because he'd told her so, and she must have suspected that Nehmann's name, and maybe her own, would be on that list.

Nehmann took a hard look at the envelope. The postmark was smudged, possibly on purpose, but he thought he could make out the figure 10 which would indicate it had been posted in October. Now, it was already 6 November. He held the envelope up to the light, looking for evidence that it might have been opened, but he knew they routinely used steam to loosen the glue and had special techniques to reseal the flap without leaving any trace.

302

Schultz was curious. He wanted to know who Nehmann had upset in Berlin. Nehmann wouldn't tell him. I'd need a really big sheet of paper, he said, and I know you're easily bored. Schultz laughed and checked his watch. The dinner was tonight. Half past seven, he said. Death to the Ivans.

In the early evening they made their way to the church on foot, hugging the shadows, moving carefully from one ruined building to another, following the tracks of others in the crusted snow. It was cloudless, very little wind, and a huge yellow moon was rising in the east. Overhead, a million stars.

At the corner of a street, Schultz paused to get his bearings. Lately, civic-minded troops had taken to making signposts out of the leg bones of dead horses, the flesh stripped off, the knee joint immobilised with a nail. The top of the bone, where it hinged into the animal's pelvis, had been split to make room for thin wedges of wood daubed with directions. Tonight's sign read '*Pozhaluysta*'.

'It's Russian,' Nehmann said. 'It means "you're welcome".'

The church lay at the bottom of the street. Nehmann recognised the remains of the orthodox onion dome, silhouetted in the moonlight. There was very little activity on the front line and in the silence he could hear a door opening and closing as shadowy figures made their way inside. Tonight, according to veterans who'd been with the campaign since last summer, the entire Soviet Army retired for the night to get blind drunk, often literally if they'd run out of vodka and had to rely on industrial alcohol. It would, of course, have been the perfect moment to mount a crushing attack but Nehmann drew some comfort from the fact that Sixth Army, on this of all nights, also preferred to party rather than kill.

303

They were at the church now. Schultz led the way inside. Nehmann had been expecting something a little select, even decorous. A menu and wine list had circulated earlier in the day. The meal was to begin with fish from upriver, where the Panzers had broken through. The fish had been slaughtered with a volley of grenades tossed into the water mixed with little parcels of high explosive and would be served with a medley of wayside weeds. The fish came with chilled Chablis, and alongside the foal's liver dumplings and prime cuts of steppe pony, guests would be offered a choice of burgundies. That, at least, may have been the intention.

Alas, no. The moment Nehmann stepped into the church he sensed they were in for a rough evening. The nave had been cleared of pews, making space for the long silver wing of an aircraft. The wing was propped upside down on three wooden trestles. The large red star suggested it must have come from a downed Soviet fighter and now it served as a table, littered with bottles and the odd glass. Everywhere there were candles: propped in jars, in cups, even on battered Orthodox bibles.

The rest of the nave was a swirl of bodies, most of them wearing oddments of clothing and equipment lifted from Russian prisoners or perhaps the Soviet dead that littered the front line. Men affecting shawls and bonnets under their helmets. Men sporting gaudy ochre stars scissored from canvas and soaked in animal blood. Men dressed as wayside hags, clad in rags, ash rubbed into their faces. Men offering themselves as campaign wives, their lips daubed in something scarlet and sticky, arm in arm with fellow grotesques, already insensible.

The last time Nehmann had seen anything like this was in a Tbilisi bar on New Year's Eve when he was barely out of his teens. On that occasion he'd abandoned himself to the mercies of three women, all of them older, who'd led him up a narrow flight of stairs to an attic room at the very top of the building and taken their turn to fuck him. Watching two men waltzing drunkenly to the lilt of a mouth organ, he could still hear their laughter. The ugliest of them had stayed with him all night. One day, she promised, you'll thank us for what we've done. And, in a way, she was right.

In the far corner of the church, under the watchful eye of an orthodox priest, a fire was burning on the tiled floor. From a huge iron frying pan came the warm, yeasty smell of fresh griddle cakes, flour, milk and a little salt. Despite the fire, and the sheer mass of people, the temperature was dropping by the minute and every shouted conversation was wreathed in white as warm breath clouded in the freezing air.

'Here—'

Schultz had brought one of the bottles of wine Nehmann had lifted from the remains of Guram's cellar. He dug out the cork with a hunting knife and passed it across. Nehmann had never drunk red wine so cold but it didn't matter. He could smell madness in this place, and he knew it was no time to be sober.

Within minutes, more bodies were pressing in through the door. One of them, with a touching faith in his own immediate future, was dressed as Santa Claus, his cheeks and chin sprouting clumps of glued-on upholstery stuffing, a red bobble cap on his head. Another sported a pair of horns he'd acquired from somewhere while other newcomers wore crude paper masks with big Stalin moustaches and an extra large hole for a mouth. The hole had to accommodate any size of bottle or glass. Vodka passed from hand to hand, pursued by roars of laughter.

Then, from nowhere, came the keening of a violin and the bedlam paused. This wasn't a gipsy fiddle, far from it. The notes were long, beautifully held, plangent, mournful, and Nehmann recognised the opening bars of 'Das Wolgalied', the Song of the Volga, the anthem adopted by Sixth Army as the nights got ever colder and the river began to freeze.

> Es steht ein Soldat am Wolgastrand
> Hält Wache für sein Vaterland...

Some of the men were linking arms now, swaying left and right, while others picked up the melody.

> There stands a soldier on the Volga's shore
> Standing the watch for his Fatherland.

Nehmann stole a look at Schultz. He'd never met anyone less sentimental in his life, but in the candlelight he swore he could see the gleam of a tear on one battered cheek.

Motionless, the steppes lie dormant...

Abruptly, the music stopped. Nehmann looked round, feeling a blast of even colder air. The church door was open again and from the shadows emerged four figures. Their greatcoats and peaked hats offered not the slightest concession to the evening's theme but what turned them into figures from a nightmare were the four identical balaclava woollen face masks, black, holes cut for eyes and lips. The crowd seemed to melt in front of them. They stood in a loose semi-circle, eyeing the pageant, unmoved and unmoving. Then one of them, the biggest, seemed to respond to a signal from another and he gestured the violinist towards him. The crowd parted, making way. The violinist looked at first confused, then rueful, then frightened.

Schultz beckoned Nehmann closer.

'SS,' he murmured.

Nehmann, drunk, was looking at the one who seemed in charge. He was maybe five metres away. His eyes were flicking left and right. Then he gestured to the musician. That violin of yours. Give it to me.

The violinist was uncertain. He tried smiling. He tried backing away. Then the biggest of the SS men took a step towards him and seized the instrument, handing it to his boss. His boss studied it a moment, plucked a single string, let it fall to the floor. The violinist muttered an oath and bent to retrieve it but two of the SS men had closed on him, pinioning his arms, making room for the boss.

For the first time, Nehmann caught the gleam of silver in the mouth of the balaclava. Messner had told him about the silver tooth. Kalb, he thought. Kalb from Tatsinskaya. Kalb with the truck. Kalb the keeper of the bodies.

Kalb was still gazing at the violin. Then he took a half-step forward and stamped on the body of the instrument with his boot. Nehmann heard the wood splintering, and a gasp from the violinist. Then came the pipe of another instrument, a flute this time, a penny whistle. The fourth SS man was playing the *Badenweiler*, the Führer's favourite march. Kalb had picked up the rhythm, stamping with the same foot that had just destroyed the violin, gesturing to everyone else to join in. No one moved. No one said a word. They were staring at men in the balaclavas. They showed neither fear nor respect, only curiosity. The SS were the real grotesques. These were creatures from another planet. They came from deepest space. They belonged in the coldest, darkest place imaginable. There wasn't an ounce of music in their bones and everyone knew it.

Schultz was closest. Kalb held his gaze, unblinking.

'Get out of here,' Schultz growled. 'Before these men eat you alive.'

Kalb ignored him. He'd spotted the *Leutnant* from the *Feldgendarmerie*. Like the SS, he was still wearing service uniform. He wanted to know the whereabouts of the prisoner. No name, no rank, just 'the prisoner'.

'Down there, Herr *Standartenführer*.' He pointed at the floor.

'It's locked?'

'Of course.'

'*Komm mit uns.*'

Kalb turned on his heel, gesturing to his SS colleagues. The *Leutnant* followed them out of the church, closing the door carefully behind him. The moment of silence that followed was broken by Schultz. The pistol he carried in the waistband of his trousers had appeared in his hand. He glanced at Nehmann and then nodded in the direction of the door.

Outside, it was colder than ever. Beneath the building was a damp basement room that had served as a vestry. A door on the side of the church was open. A flight of stairs led into the darkness and Nehmann could hear murmured fragments of conversation from below. Then came something sharper, the slap of flesh on flesh and a sudden gasp of pain.

'Kirile,' Schultz said. 'That's where they keep him. That's where I pick him up every morning. Poor little bastard.'

Schultz was checking his automatic while Nehmann tried to imagine how this scene could possibly end. The mathematical odds, five to two, were hopeless. Every SS man would be carrying a weapon, probably the *Leutnant* as well. He knew what these men were capable of. He'd seen the evidence with his own eyes. Were matters to be resolved downstairs? In the vestry? Or might it be better to stage some kind of ambush up here, in the open, where they at least had the advantage of surprise?

Schultz was evidently determined to intervene. Kirile was getting a beating now, the SS staging a little anniversary celebration of their own, and Schultz had taken a first step into the darkness when other figures appeared. There were dozens of them, then more. They were streaming out of the church, still wearing their Stalin masks and their crude make-up, and they'd paused only to pick up whatever weapon came to hand. Some had the knives they always carried, the blades unsheathed and gleaming in the moonlight. One or two had firearms. Several had paused to pick up half-bricks or small rocks from the drift of debris outside the church. One of them, wearing a trophy fur hat, had seized a candlestick from the altar.

The beating had stopped now and Nehmann could hear footsteps ascending from the vestry. First into the open air was Kirile, his wrists tied together, his face webbed with fresh blood. Schultz had the gun in one hand. With the other, he pushed the Georgian towards Nehmann.

'Yours, my friend. Tell him it's going to be fine. Tell him we'll take care of everything.'

Kalb was next to emerge. The sight of Schultz's automatic brought him to a halt. He demanded to know what was going on.

'We have custody of the prisoner,' Schultz growled. 'That's all you need to know.'

'We?'

'Myself and my *Kameraden*.' He gestured at the watching faces. 'The Bolsheviks turned the world on its head. Maybe we're doing something similar.'

'That's treason,' Kalb said. 'And you know what happens to traitors.'

'Treason is your word, my friend. I can think of a number of others. The prisoner will be safe in our hands. Any complaints, I suggest you address them to Admiral Canaris in Berlin. This man is an important intelligence asset. These last few weeks he's earned the Reich's gratitude. I think you'll find it pays not to waste men like that.'

There came a murmur of agreement from the ever-growing mob of partygoers. Yet more had appeared around the corner of the church.

Kalb glanced back at his men, then shrugged. His body language spoke volumes. Not now, he seemed to be saying. We'll take care of this later. He stepped past Schultz, then stopped again, barely centimetres from Nehmann.

'You're Goebbels' little monkey, aren't you?' Dead eyes behind the mask. 'He told me you'd be here.'

28

STALINGRAD, NOVEMBER 1942

Two days later, the temperature plunged to minus eighteen degrees and forecasters warned of an impending storm. Frozen clumps of horse dung, rock-hard, littered the streets. Nehmann watched men from a bicycle company wheeling their machines past the bus depot, needles of ice hanging from their nostrils. Listen hard between spasms of artillery fire, and you could hear the grinding of ice floes drifting down the river.

Then, overnight, the wind picked up, and Nehmann awoke to the metallic clatter of corrugated iron sheets, torn loose by the gale, cartwheeling away across the apron of asphalt where the buses had once parked. Soon the falling snow became a full-scale blizzard and when he ventured out again, accompanying Schultz to yet another interview, the corpse of the city lay under a thick white shroud.

Schultz was worried about *Standartenführer* Kalb. He'd done his best to locate SS headquarters but had so far drawn a blank. Just the mention of the men in black was enough to seal most lips and, in the end, he'd had to resort to a long conversation with Nehmann. Nehmann was reluctant to talk about Goebbels but Schultz had picked up enough to know that the little Georgian had incurred some kind of debt to his Minister, and that Kalb had probably been tasked with obtaining settlement. Himmler and Goebbels, he said, were on the best of terms. Which in turn put Nehmann in a position of some danger.

'You think Goebbels has the ear of the SS?' Nehmann asked.

'Yes.'

'How do you know?'

'Because in the *Abwehr* we follow their every fucking move. Himmler knows where the power lies. That means Hitler. Hitler has always had a soft spot for Goebbels' wife, the saintly Magda, whore that she is, and as for the man himself, Hitler has him in the palm of his hand. Your little boss has always been halfway up the Führer's arse, which happens to suit the Führer very nicely because the man is clever, too. He's a believer. He makes things happen. And when he needs a favour, he knows he can rely on Hitler's backing. Believe it or not, that puts the whole of the fucking SS at his disposal. Something you'd be wise to bear in mind.'

Schultz, ever practical, had laid hands on a bodyguard for Nehmann, an enormous infantryman called Ernst Grimberger. The Bavarian was a dog-handler by trade and had somehow taught an Alsatian called Mitzi to detect anti-vehicle mines laid during the chaotic days of the Soviet retreat. Most of the mines had now been located and dealt with, leaving Grimberger at a loose end. Schultz, who had highly placed contacts at Sixth Army headquarters, secured Grimberger's service in turn for a guarantee that Werner Nehmann would continue to put *General* Paulus and his men in the best possible light.

'Go nowhere without Ernst,' Schultz told Nehmann. 'This man's like his dog. He can smell shit like Kalb at a thousand metres. He's as close as you'll get to safe.'

And so Nehmann, after his brief interlude in Berlin, began to write again. Mitzi was an obvious place to start and Ernst was delighted with the results. The story centred on a truckload of badly injured men from the front line en route to the airfield at Pitomnik where they were to await evacuation. Mitzi loped ahead, nose to the ground, tail wagging, and despite several centimetres of frozen snow she still managed to find the anti-tank mine that would have blown the truck apart. The wounded men were on special rations and every single one of them insisted on sharing their good fortune with Mitzi. The story was, of course, a fiction but Ernst didn't seem to care. Had a mine really been there, he insisted, then she'd definitely have found it. So, who's making a fuss about whether it's true or not?

*

On 11 November, in a last spasm of violence, Richthofen's Stukas and battle groups newly organised by Sixth Army HQ made a final bid to winkle the Ivans out of their positions in the ever-shrinking pocket that was their last remaining hold on the city. The Russians, as ever, fought like tigers. A handful of them were forced back to defend a narrow strip of land barely seventy metres from the riverbank.

That evening, Nehmann talked to a tank commander from Bremen who'd been in the front line, baffled by the odds the Ivans were facing. 'In the end,' he told Nehmann, 'their ammunition ran out and you know what they did then? They got their own artillery, on the eastern bank, to shell us. We were that close...' his hands were a centimetre apart '...and they all died under their own shells. If you think that was some kind

313

of accident, you'd be wrong. They called in fire knowing that was the only way of stopping us. And you know something else? It worked.'

*

Two days later, Nehmann met Georg Messner at the airfield at Pitomnik. Messner had brought a *Tante-Ju* with supplies from Tatsinskaya and he looked gaunt with exhaustion. Richthofen, he said, was beginning to despair about the prospects for any kind of victory at Stalingrad. Ice floes on the river were threatening Soviet efforts to keep their front line in food and ammunition yet somehow the Ivans still managed to improvise night after night and keep the supply lines open.

'If Paulus can't finish this business when the Volga's icing up and supplies are down to a trickle,' Messner said, 'then the game's up.'

Nehmann would have been glad of a longer conversation. He wanted to tell Messner about Kalb, about Kirile, about the madness that was settling on the ruined city, but he never got the chance. The weather forecast for the afternoon, said Messner, was dire. Already they were having to light fires under the aircraft engines every morning at Tatsinskaya to thaw out the oil before start-up, and if he didn't take off within the next fifteen minutes he wouldn't get home at all.

Home. The word had ceased to mean anything. That night, Nehmann sat up with Schultz and Ernst Grimberger over a bottle of vodka. Kirile, much to his relief, now had a corner of his own at the bus depot and accompanied Schultz during the day when Nehmann was otherwise engaged. He'd made a primitive chess board with a full set of pieces and he played a series of games with Grimberger most evenings while Schultz and Nehmann talked.

'This is a paper war for our Leader.' Schultz was toying with his glass. 'His maps tell him there's a pocket or two he needs to clear out. To do that he has to lay hands on more infantry because Paulus, believe it or not, is running out. So that means that cooks, medics, signals staff suddenly find themselves in the front line. Even tank drivers, fucking *Panzers*, are given a rifle and a spare magazine and told to kill a few Ivans. Can you believe that? Just to make Hitler's map look neater? The man's obsessed. He thinks it's his city already and no one's got the balls to tell him different.'

It got worse. The following night, after a lengthy radio conversation with *Abwehr* headquarters in Berlin, Schultz appeared to call Nehmann aside.

'I shouldn't be telling you this,' he said, 'but I'm going to. We just got the latest production figures. Two thousand two hundred a *month*.'

'Of what?'

'Soviet tanks. They come out of factories out beyond the Urals. Can you imagine that? Over two thousand? Month after month? The figures went to the Chancellery and guess what? The bloody man doesn't believe them. He thinks we're making them up. He's convinced it's some kind of plot. It shouldn't happen, therefore it hasn't. What chance do we have, Nehmann? Be honest, for once.'

Honest. Nehmann thought about the conversation overnight. He didn't know what 2,200 tanks might look like. Kilometre after kilometre of tanks. Hectares and hectares and hectares of Soviet armour. An eternity of low shapes on the unending steppe, and muzzle flashes, and huge explosions where men had once been. Hitler had given the Russian bear a poke and now hundreds of thousands of men – underfed, frozen, stoic, resigned – were about to pay the price. Should he write about the real betrayal? Should he risk the truth for once? Would Goebbels even *read* stuff like that?

*

The following day, in the late morning, a special prisoner arrived. He'd been sent back to the bus depot by a front-line *Oberst* who knew and respected Schultz. The prisoner had been only lightly injured but his nerve had gone. He said he'd discovered God and he wanted to talk.

'About God?' Nehmann was looking at the man. He was tall and he had the pallor and the blank-eyed listlessness that comes with too many days and nights under fire. He'd already been talking to Kirile and he indicated that he'd like this conversation to continue.

Schultz, for once, seemed uncertain what to do. Nehmann made the decision for him. Kirile, he knew, was deeply grateful for the part Schultz had played the night he'd fallen foul of the SS. Maybe now was the moment he'd repay that debt.

Schultz agreed. Kirile and the Russian prisoner retired to the privacy of Nehmann's sleeping space. Within the hour, he was back again. Nehmann was alone in the room that served as an office.

'He's got a desk at Chuikov's headquarters.' Kirile nodded at the prisoner, visible through the open door. 'He knows most of the same men I knew.'

'And?'

'There's a huge attack in the offing, armies north and south.' He cupped his hands, brought his fingers together. 'It's an encirclement with us in the middle. Zhukov's in charge. That man knows what he's doing, believe me.'

'When is this supposed to happen?'

'Tomorrow morning. He's even got the code name. Operation Uranus.'

'Tomorrow *morning*?' Nehmann checked his watch, wondering where Schultz might be. 'And you believe him?'

'I do, yes.' Kirile looked away. 'If you want the truth, I've known since you took me prisoner.'

*

Soviet armies fell on the flanks of the German bridgehead the following morning. Within four days, the twin arms of the Soviet thrust had closed the circle sixty-five miles west of the city. It happened to be a Sunday, *Totensonntag*, the one day in the year that Protestants all over the Fatherland remembered the dead, and more than a quarter of a million men of Sixth Army were now cut off. Over the days to come, as Berlin slowly admitted the truth about the battle for Stalingrad, the German bridgehead on the Volga was renamed a *Kessel*.

Kessel. 'Cauldron.'

29

STALINGRAD, 28 NOVEMBER 1942

Kirile disappeared five days later. He'd been sleeping in a nook in the basement where boxes and boxes of passenger tokens for use on the city's buses were kept. There was barely space for a couple of blankets on the floor, and a nest of field pouches for a pillow, and there was a door that really wasn't a door but that didn't matter because everyone knew where Kirile's real interests lay. The last thing on his mind was a life outside the bus depot. He feared the SS and he feared his fellow Russians. Two good reasons to stay safe in his new home.

At first Nehmann assumed he'd gone out for some fresh air. It happened sometimes. He'd get up for a piss, still fully clothed after a night's sleep, and Nehmann would meet him on the stairs that led up to the freezing concrete space that had once been a waiting room upstairs. Kirile had the knack of acquiring supplies of the harsh Russian tobacco from newly taken prisoners and always smoked outside because he knew everyone else loathed the smell. But when Nehmann went upstairs to look, there was no sign of him.

By mid-morning he still hadn't returned. Nehmann and Grimberger were due to meet a supply flight from Tatsinskaya at Pitomnik. The flight was carrying sacks of *Luftpost*, including a special package for Schultz. The plane was late, wallowing in to land through yet more flurries of snow, zigzagging across the airfield to avoid shell craters. Nehmann knew the pilot, a friend of Messner, and he listened to him moaning about Goering while Nehmann's gaze settled on a nearby bunch of prisoners, two of them barefoot in the snow, unloading the aircraft. The big plane was only half full and Nehmann watched the boxes passing from hand to hand, wondering whether Kirile might be planning to somehow make it onto a plane out.

The pilot was checking his watch. Goering had evidently promised Hitler aircraft and supply flights he knew he couldn't possibly deliver. Worse still, the fucking man had now gone off to Paris to buy yet more fucking pictures, leaving *Fliegerkorps VIII* to pick up the pieces. The staff sergeant on the airfield had been keeping a tally of deliveries over the last week and yesterday he'd threatened to jump on a plane to Tatsinskaya and have it out with Richthofen personally, and the pilot didn't blame him. A bare handful of tons a day when the army needed ten times that? Madness.

Back at the bus depot, Nehmann met Schultz in the empty shell of the waiting room. Schultz was looking up at the fading map of the city's bus routes that dominated one wall. He drew Nehmann's attention to a black daub on the bottom right-hand corner of the map, within easy reach of someone standing amid the litter of broken glass. Two letters. SS.

'Was that here yesterday?' he asked.

Nehmann said he didn't know. Might have been. Might not.

'You're thinking…?' Nehmann took a closer look.

Schultz shrugged. Kirile had gone, and the black daub explained why.

'Fuckers', he grunted, looking at the route map again.

*

Nehmann didn't give up. He blamed himself for not keeping a closer eye on his fellow Georgian. Schultz was probably right about the SS. People like Kalb were fanatics. They lived in a world of their own making and they never gave up. Would they use Kirile the way Schultz had? Would they put his perfect Russian to work when they conducted their own interrogations with Soviet prisoners? Was that why they'd bided their time, and hatched the plans, and waited for the moment when Kirile – sleepy, badly needing a smoke – had emerged into yet another grey Stalingrad dawn? Nehmann rather hoped so. That way, the poor bastard would at least stay alive.

Grimberger had a different take on the incident. He started carrying an extra gun, a Walther P38 with a nine-round magazine. In his view, Kirile's disappearance was a declaration of war. Nehmann, for whatever reason, would be next. He'd been at the church on the night of the party. He'd witnessed the scene at the top of the vestry steps. He knew these SS people and he knew that a moment of humiliation like that wasn't something they'd ever tolerate. Sooner or later they'd be back.

Nehmann said he didn't care, which wasn't strictly true. The weather was getting worse. Day after day, Nehmann awoke to freezing fog and plunging temperatures and seven kinds of grey masking the view from the bus station, but wherever he and Grimberger went, whatever the reason for their journey, he was still thinking about Kirile. He knew that looking for someone gone missing in the city of the lost was absurd, surreal, a non-starter. People were muffled against the cold, their heads down, only their eyes visible. Kirile would be wearing the same ragbag of German and Soviet clothing as everyone else. How would he recognise him? Where would he start?

It didn't matter. Paying a visit to the front line was dangerous, and Grimberger was visibly unhappy about the prospect, but Nehmann insisted he needed to talk to infantrymen in the very eye of the storm and so they made their way towards the sullen hump of the Mamaev Kurgan, taking advantage of the ruined buildings and mountains of debris, following the black telephone lines that snaked ever onwards.

The trenches here were mere scrapes, minor adjustments to the chaos of the battlescape, fought over, died for, abandoned and retaken within the same half-hour. The Russians were barely twenty metres away, equally exposed, but somehow they seemed to have the upper hand.

A *Wehrmacht* staff sergeant with a weeping infection in one eye talked of Stukas dropping bombs barely metres away, of the incessant rain of Soviet mortars, of a local sniper who could pick your teeth from a thousand metres, of taunting melodies from a Russian harmonica in the darkness, of close-quarters fighting with knives, sharpened spades, bare hands, anything. Worst, he said, were the Siberians. They were born hunters. They stole into your little world from fucking nowhere. This was the *Rattenkrieg*, he said. The War of the Rats. The dead of night was a phrase he never wanted to hear again.

Nehmann nodded, said he understood, peeled off a glove to scribble a note or two, and then – as if the thought had just occurred to him – enquired whether anyone had come across a young Russian with perfect German, name of Kirile. The staff sergeant, who was a difficult man to fool, stared at Nehmann.

321

'You've come here to ask me a question like that?' He was incredulous. 'You're risking your life for a fucking *deserter*?'

The answer was yes, as Grimberger was the first to point out once they were back in the safety of the bus depot, and after that there were no more expeditions to the front line. But it didn't matter because Nehmann's mood had darkened. There were no more attempts to make the turd that was Stalingrad smell sweet, no more bids to confect amusing stories, fictitious or otherwise, about the small print of this sorry enterprise. On the contrary, Nehmann began to brood.

One evening, in a snow-dusted dugout near the airfield as homely as the conditions would permit, he had a long conversation with an artillery man from Bielefeld. Smoke from a homemade stove curled through the frost-stiffened tarpaulin. The walls were lined with hessian and there was a wonderful smell of horse rissoles and cakes baked on mess-tin lids.

A couple of weeks ago, said the artilleryman, his battery had been deployed to target a Soviet stockpile of artillery shells. The shells were shipped across the river at night. Women carried them eight at a time, in groundsheets, for six kilometres and then went back for more, night after night, six kilometres, twelve kilometres, eighteen kilometres. This was what the intelligence told us, the artilleryman said, and it turned out they were right. We knew where the target was. We had the coordinates. We were told to wait for days and days until the women had built a decent pile and then came the order to fire.

'So, what happened?'

'The biggest bang you ever saw. A huge explosion. Our *Leutnant* thought he was up for a medal. Maybe even a *Ritterkreuz*. Me? I could have wept for those women, for all that effort, all that pain, all that *fear*. The killing in this city never takes time off. Have you noticed that?'

The killing in this city never takes time off.

Nehmann made a note of the phrase. It was as close to the truth as anything he'd heard. Death was a physical presence: conscientious, reliable, scrupulous, even-handed. It came for you without warning, and it ignored any objection you might have. People said that bullets never hit brave men but Nehmann had seen enough now to know that this was bollocks. Death was everywhere, first cousin to the weather, and Stalingrad had become the *Schicksalsstadt*, the City of Fate.

A couple of days later, with still no word on Kirile, Nehmann picked up the November edition of *Das Reich*, the magazine Goebbels used to explore his changing thoughts about the war. The key to his thinking was always the editorial and that afternoon, with time to kill, Nehmann settled down to read it. Goebbels, he quickly realised, was keen to make a distinction between *Stimmung*, meaning 'mood', and *Haltung*, meaning 'bearing'. The first, he said, was frivolous, a plaything, an indulgence, of no consequence, while *Haltung* was something weightier and altogether more seemly. With the right *Haltung*, the nation could do anything, share any burden, survive any trial. *Haltung* might one day be the only path to victory, which meant that the days when *Stimmung* mattered were well and truly over.

Nehmann sat back, remembering the afternoon when Hitler returned to Berlin after his triumph in France. The flowers along the Wilhelmstrasse. The crowds desperate for a glimpse of their Führer. The swelling roar of acclamation as the cavalcade approached from the Anhalter station. And

Hedvika's arse moving sweetly beneath him. *Stimmung*, he thought. Another world.

*

That night he declined Grimberger's offer of a cigar and a glass or two of vodka and worked hard on a piece about their visit to the front line. For once, he let the facts speak for themselves, no embellishments, no easy punchlines, not a single opportunity for the reader to arrive at anything but the obvious conclusion: that battle was an experience beyond most people's imagination and that this one was probably lost.

The draft complete, he wound a fresh sheet of paper into the *Abwehr* typewriter and then showed the results to Schultz. He took his time to read it. Lately, he'd had to find a pair of glasses from somewhere, a tiny detail that told Nehmann a great deal about this war. Not even a stayer like Schultz could survive undamaged.

'It's the best thing you've done here.' Schultz looked up. 'Goebbels will wipe his arse with it.'

'Maybe not.' Nehmann nodded at the *Luftpost* pouch readied on the desk. 'I'll try and get it out tomorrow.'

It went next day. The following week, mid-December, the river froze over completely and a machine-gunner returning from the front line reported that the Soviets were broadcasting announcements day and night for the benefit of the listening Germans. One of you will die every seven seconds on the Eastern Front, a voice would say. We'll be pleased to maintain this service as long as you're here. Propaganda like this, accompanied by a loudly ticking clock, naturally prompted an instant response – volleys of mortar shells to silence the loudspeakers – but supplies of the shells, said the machine-gunner, were fast running out. Shit music, too, unless you liked the tango.

Nehmann was impressed by the story but it seemed to have made little impact on the machine-gunner. In the relative warmth of the bus depot, he took his helmet off. He'd wrapped a Russian foot bandage around the bareness of his shaven scalp and when Nehmann offered his compliments on the choice of insulation, the machine-gunner showed him his gloves. They were crudely made, an odd piebald colour, but apparently effective.

'We had a dog called Fritz.' The machine-gunner grinned. 'I got to skin it.'

That night, by radio, Schultz received word from the Promi. Goebbels had read Nehmann's piece about life in the front line and wanted more of the same. Not only that, but he also needed Nehmann back in Berlin in time for Christmas.

'I was wrong about Goebbels,' Schultz said. 'All credit to you, my friend, but this means we're definitely fucked.'

Nehmann stared at him. Schultz never apologised. Neither was he ever wrong.

*

Next morning, Nehmann and Grimberger set out once again for the airfield at Pitomnik to enquire about the possibilities of Nehmann getting a flight out to Berlin. By now, Soviet fighters and anti-aircraft guns dug in around the edges of the *Kessel* were making life tough for Richthofen's fleet of *Tante-Jus*. According to Schultz, who'd seen the *Abwehr*'s figures, Sixth Army would need 300 flights a day to keep fighting yet barely a trickle of the big tri-motors made it safely into the city.

A small city of bunkers and tents had sprung up at the edge of the airfield. In the biggest of the tents, Nehmann found the *Luftwaffe Leutnant* in charge of compiling passenger lists. A general field hospital had been established nearby and the *Leutnant* was trying to calculate how many badly wounded men could be loaded onto the return flight. Nehmann had already seen these evacuation candidates outside, each man secured to a stretcher, some of them groggy from too much morphine. Was his claim to a place on a *Tante-Ju* really more urgent than theirs? He wasn't at all sure.

The *Leutnant*, whom he knew, made a note of his request. Christmas was coming and pressure on the ever-fewer flights out was intense. Nehmann would be wise to have a bag packed ready in case a place on the plane was suddenly free.

'Here—' He opened a drawer and slipped out a copy of a newspaper. 'This came in yesterday. Congratulations. Much better than that usual shit you send them.'

Nehmann was looking at a copy of *Völkischer Beobachter*, the Party's daily paper. Millions of copies were sold all over the Reich. His front-line piece was on page three and a quick scan suggested that Goebbels hadn't changed a word.

'There's someone else you might like to talk to,' the *Leutnant* said. 'His name's Dr Gigensohen. He arrived from Tatsinskaya yesterday and as far as I know he's still over in the field hospital at Gumrak.'

'What does he do?'

'He's a pathologist. He deals with the dead, not the living so he's spoiled for choice here.' He shrugged, returning to his passenger list. 'See what you think, eh?'

Nehmann and Grimberger departed with the copy of the

newspaper. The field hospital was half an hour tramp away through the rutted snow. Beyond the airfield, a horse had been hit by a Soviet shell. Its head was hanging by threads of frozen flesh, and shrapnel from the explosion had scored a neat excision the length of its belly. The coils of viscera inside gleamed purple and yellow in the thin winter sunshine and Nehmann tried hard not to imagine the smell when spring finally arrived, and the city's countless bodies began to thaw.

The pathologist occupied a wood-lined bunker just metres from the hospital. An iron stove took the edge off the intense cold but sitting at the desk, he was still wearing gloves as he made notes from a pad at his elbow.

Nehmann introduced himself. It turned out that Gigensohen, too, had read the front-line report in the *Beobachter*.

'An outbreak of realism,' he said drily. 'More than welcome.'

Nehmann asked him what he made of what he'd seen so far.

'Remarkable,' he said. 'I'm here to cut up bodies. That's not as easy as it may seem. You wear gloves, of course, but they're made of rubber and the rubber's as frozen as everything else. I'm managing a couple of autopsies a day at the moment but under normal circumstances I could double that figure.'

'You're trying to work out who killed these people?' Nehmann was confused. 'Might the Russians have anything to do with it?'

'Of course they have. It's a battle. People get shot. They die. But these folk…' he nodded down at the pad '…are different. There are no wounds that I can see.'

'So, what killed them?'

'Hunger. And stress. And lack of sleep. And, dare I hazard a guess, despair. These people have starved to death. If you want a headline, there it is. Give a man five hundred calories a day and you open his door to all kinds of nastiness. Hepatitis? Dysentery? All you need is a vector, a means of transmission, and as it happens lice are perfect. If this goes on much longer, we'll be looking at typhoid and typhus, too. In the end we're just flesh and blood. This kind of fighting feasts on us.'

Feasts on us.

Nehmann stayed at the doctor's side for nearly an hour while Grimberger stood guard beside a pile of frozen bodies stacked outside. The pathologist was only too happy to share his findings and his fears with a journalist who reputedly had the ear of the Minister of Propaganda, and they parted on the best of terms. When Nehmann mentioned that he might be back in Berlin in time for Christmas, Gigensohen wished him well.

'I dare say you'll be pleased to see the back of all this.' The pathologist gestured around. 'You've been here long?'

'Long enough,' Nehmann said. 'Everyone here has a job to do. I suspect that can make a difference.'

'And you?'

'I watch. And listen. That can be hard, believe me. I'm not religious, far from it, but God never designed us for something like this.'

*

The thought stayed with him for the rest of the day. That evening, alone for once, he made his way back to the church where hundreds of cheerful drunks had celebrated the Russian Revolution. The wing of the Soviet fighter had been removed from the body of the church and now, propped up outside, it gleamed in the light of the moon. Nehmann paused for a moment, looking at the outline of the Red Star. These people are winning, he thought. As maybe they should.

Inside the building, candles flickered at the far end of the nave, casting the long shadow of a kneeling figure onto the folds of cloth draped over the table that served as an altar.

Nehmann approached, aware of tiny shards of broken glass beneath his feet, and phrases from the liturgy buried deep in his childhood began to surface for the first time in his adult life. The Body and Blood of Christ Jesus, he thought.

Nehmann paused, just metres away from the figure bent in prayer. At last, he stirred. It was the priest. He'd been at the party, a watchful presence behind the dense tangle of greying beard, happy to welcome laughter to the house of God. Nehmann had heard that he occasionally played the organ on days when he could make the bellows work properly, mainly Bach toccatas.

'You're here for me?'

'Yes, Father.'

'You want to pray?'

'I want to take communion.'

'I see.' The priest struggled to his feet. He was in his fifties at least, much older than Nehmann had imagined. His face was clouded with a frown. He seemed to be considering Nehmann's request. 'That may be difficult,' he said at last. 'We have very little wine, and what's left is frozen.'

Nehmann shrugged. He said he was happy to do without the wine.

'No wine?' The frown had deepened.

'No wine,' Nehmann confirmed. 'We'll just pretend.'

'Pretend?' The ghost of a smile. 'And assume that God won't notice?'

In the end, they prayed together. The priest made no mention of the battle, of the injured, of the dead. To Nehmann, mumbling 'Amen' when each prayer came to an end, the war might never have happened. They might have been in some city or other, surrounded by the blessings of peace, praying for the usual list of propositions: good health, humility, wellbeing. After a final recitation of the Lord's Prayer, the priest made the sign of the Cross and indicated that their conversation was over.

Nehmann thanked him and turned to leave. Then the priest called him back. He looked weary, almost resigned.

'We had visitors last night,' he said. 'You might like to take a look at the vestry.'

Nehmann nodded. Once again, he was heading down the nave.

'There's another way down,' the priest called. 'You needn't go outside.'

He collected a candle from the altar and gave it to Nehmann. Then he led the way to a door half hidden behind a brick pillar and gestured at the wooden steps that led into the darkness.

'God be with you,' he murmured.

Nehmann thanked him. The candle was dripping hot wax onto his hand and he paused on the first step to adjust it. Then he began to make his way down, following the spill of light on the rough brickwork, step after careful step. At the bottom, his boots found a solid floor. Another door, he thought. He pushed it open, holding out the candle, wondering whether he should have gone back to the bus depot to collect Grimberger. Then his eyes found the body on the floor.

He knew at once it was Kirile. The same thin wrists. The same falling-apart boots with different coloured laces. But where

330

his face had once been was a criss-cross of deep wounds, the features smashed, the eyeballs empty, shattered teeth between pulped gums. Nehmann's hand began to shake. The flame wavered, spilling onto the floor beside the wreckage of Kirile's face. The spade looked new. Frozen blood, a deep ochre, had crusted on the gleaming blade and there was more of it on the wooden shaft and on the worn floorboards around Kirile's head.

Nehmann knelt briefly. The flesh of Kirile's hands was icy. He brought one hand to his lips and kissed it. Then he left.

30

TATSINSKAYA AIRFIELD,
23 DECEMBER 1942

Nehmann flew out of Stalingrad on a stormy morning, two days before Christmas, trying hard not to think of Kirile's ruined face. The Ju-52 was overweight on take-off, packed with walking wounded from the field hospital at Gumrak, and the airframe groaned as the aircraft hit a final rut before getting itself airborne. The pathologist, Dr Gigensohen, was also on board, his work among the city's many dead complete. He and Nehmann were at the rear of the plane, squashed against a bulkhead.

The weather, thankfully, made any interceptions from Soviet fighters unlikely. One of the Junkers' engines quickly developed a fault and the pilot was unable to nurse the aircraft into clean air above the turbulence. As a result the *Tante-Ju* was at the mercy of the storm, tossed around by the violence of the gusting wind. Many of the men, already white-faced from the pain of their injuries, began to be sick and by the time the pilot managed to slam the aircraft onto the airfield at Tatsinskaya, the metal floor of the fuselage was pooled with blood and vomit. For once, Nehmann was glad when ground crew wrestled the door open and let in the icy air. The heavy sweetness of the fug inside the aircraft had become unbearable. After Kirile, he thought, comes this. Life can't possibly get worse.

Wrong. Messner was on hand with a *Kübelwagen*. While the pilot conferred with a technician about the engine he'd had to close down, Messner drove Nehmann and the pathologist across to the makeshift building *Fliegerkorps VIII* were using as a squadron mess. The *Tante-Ju*, he assured them, would be repaired and cleaned up for the next leg of the flight west. With luck, they'd be back in the air before dusk.

It didn't happen. From the mess, Nehmann was able to watch engineers working feverishly to replace parts on the malfunctioning engine. After darkness fell, they became half a dozen torches, their fading beams criss-crossing in the darkness. By now, after days of raids by Soviet bombers, the airfield was threatened by a Soviet tank army pushing in from the west. According to Messner, Richthofen had begged permission to pull out and save the aircraft that were still serviceable but High Command had issued Goering with a 'stand-fast' order. Only if the airfield came under direct attack from forces on the ground, insisted Hitler, was Tatsinskaya to be abandoned.

This, Nehmann knew, was exactly the fate that awaited Stalingrad itself. Never retreat. Never surrender. Fight to the last man, regardless of the odds.

'Well?' He was looking at Messner.

Messner was chewing a crust of black bread smeared with jam. He said he'd talked to Richthofen on the radio only minutes ago. The *Generaloberst* had ordered every crew of every serviceable aircraft to be at instant readiness to leave. Boxes of precious spares had already been packed into dozens of the Ju-52s. Every available fuel can had been filled to the brim. As for *FK VIII*'s personnel, each individual had been allotted an onboard allowance of just a hundred kilograms, to include body weight. The news put a smile on Nehmann's face. Very Georg, he thought.

By midnight, the booming of heavy artillery fire from the west was impossible to ignore. Nehmann braved the cold for a minute or two. He could see the distinctive outline of Messner's nearby tent in the throw of brilliant light from the bigger explosions, and he wondered what it must be like to make an exit like this after months on the steppe. A movement beside him revealed the abrupt presence of the pathologist. Like Nehmann, he was helpless, a mere spectator as the Soviets tightened their chokehold on the airfield.

'This is history,' Gigensohen murmured. 'Let's just hope we live to bear witness.'

At half past three in the morning, Soviet artillery batteries opened fire on the airfield and shells began to fall among the parked aircraft. Ground crews abandoned loading and ran for cover. Minutes later, word arrived that Russian tanks had broken through the airfield's flimsy defences. Messner, it seemed to Nehmann, was enjoying this moment of drama. He moved from group to group, calm, unhurried, issuing a sequence of orders. Visibility on the airfield, he said, was down to five hundred metres. The cloud base was a bare thirty. Both figures would sink lower, making take-offs even more of a hazard. Time to leave.

Air crew and personnel began to run towards their respective aircraft. Nehmann watched them for a moment, aware of the shrill whine of incoming shells. The guns on the tanks had a sharper bark than the big artillery pieces, and he ducked instinctively as the frozen earth erupted just metres away. Then came a push from behind and he turned to see Messner. He was pointing at a nearby aircraft at the end of the line of *Tante-Jus*.

'Yours,' he shouted. 'Go.'

'And you?'

'I'll be with you.'

Nehmann bent for his kitbag and began to run, collecting the pathologist on the way. The aircraft was already half full, a blur of faces desperate for the engines to start. Nehmann helped Gigensohen up the metal ladder, then hung back waiting for Messner. He could see the tall *Oberst* directing the last of *FKVIII*'s ground crews to another aircraft. Then he began to hurry towards Nehmann. Moments later, in mid-stride, he paused, changed direction, made for his tent, tore open the flap, disappeared inside. The pilot of the *Tante-Ju* had begun to fire up the engines. Then came the shriek of an incoming shell and Messner's tent seemed to physically levitate, hanging in the air, shredded by the blast.

Nehmann didn't hesitate. He ran towards the smoke of the explosion, shouting Messner's name. Where the tent had been there was nothing but torn strips of canvas and the sour sweetness of expended cordite. Nehmann found Messner sprawled on the freezing turf. His throat was torn open and half his head had gone.

Nehmann crouched over him a moment, aware of more explosions, some of them close, and the roar of aircraft engines. There was a face he recognised at the door of the *Tante-Ju*. It was Gigensohen.

'Run,' he was yelling. 'We're off.'

Nehmann knew he was cutting it fine. He took a final look at Messner, then he noticed the object in his hand. It was the egg slicer. That's what he'd come back for. That's what had killed him.

Nehmann bent quickly, easing the fierce grip of Messner's fingers. Then he began to run.

*

Nehmann's memories of leaving the stricken airfield at Tatsinskaya were, he thought later, cinematic. In the crush of bodies as the aircraft lurched drunkenly into the air he could see nothing but occasional glimpses of the Soviet onslaught through the Ju's big square windows: the sudden yellow blossom of an explosion, a deep scarlet at its core; the aircraft's own shadow, briefly visible, racing over the shell-pocked outer airfield as the pilot fought for altitude; then the relief as shreds of cloud closed around the aircraft and everything went grey. The atmosphere in the cabin was sombre. People avoided eye contact. They'd tasted defeat and they knew that worse was probably to come.

They landed first at Rostov, which had mercifully been spared the attentions of the Soviets. Then, after a brief pause for refuelling, they were on their way again, still standing shoulder to shoulder as they droned west. Cinematic, Nehmann thought. Goebbels would doubtless be proud of him.

They arrived in Berlin nearly ten hours later after another refuelling stop. By some miracle, the Promi had anticipated his arrival and sent a car out to Tempelhof. The driver met Nehmann at the aircraft steps. It was Christmas Day, already late afternoon. The driver was under orders to whisk him out to the villa at Bogensee where the Minister and his family were celebrating together. Nehmann insisted that Gigensohen be dropped off first but the pathologist declined the lift. He

336

said he was grateful for the offer but, in all truth, he needed an hour or so on his own before he could face the real world.

Nehmann knew exactly what he meant. The big Mercedes had been, according to the driver, a recent present from the Chancellery, a mark of the Führer's gratitude. It was heavily armoured and could survive any attack. Hitler, it seemed, had also presented his Minister with no fewer than four bodyguards, a tribute to his importance. Nehmann sat in the back as the car purred away, aware of the smell of new leather, wondering whether centimetres of armour plate and a huge engine was meant to offer him reassurance.

Nightmare, he'd already decided, was too small a word. First Stalingrad, just the word itself, a tocsin for the soul, a synonym for everything hateful about the world. Then Stalingrad's weather, the bitter cold that stole into your very core, and the frozen parcels of flesh and blood, some animal, some not, that littered every ruined street, every pile of roadside debris, every next line of footsteps that might once have been a road.

These images, Nehmann knew, would stay with him forever but what was far, far worse was the journey he'd made at the priest's invitation, the descent into hell, the moment of purest horror when the image he'd kept in his head of Kirile melted in front of his eyes and became a child's papier-mâché apology for a face, scarlet daubs, obscene hollows, eyeless, broken, the work of someone deeply evil. Kalb, he thought. Kalb had done that. And whatever else happened in this bitch of a war, Kalb would pay.

31

BOGENSEE, BERLIN,
25 DECEMBER 1942

Nehmann had never met Magda. Frau Goebbels was waiting in the dim fall of light at the open front door to greet the family's Christmas Day visitor. Nehmann had seen photographs of this woman, erect, handsome, stern-faced, always exquisitely dressed. In her previous marriage, to a wealthy businessman, he knew she'd acquired a taste for the finer things in life, a passion Goebbels had been happy to indulge, but this afternoon she was wearing a plain dress in a sea-green velvet and for that Nehmann was deeply grateful. A middle-of-the-night escape from the Soviet Army and two days on a *Tante-Ju* did nothing for your peace of mind, let alone your appearance. In a word, he felt rough.

Goebbels, to his surprise, had readied a change of clothes. He escorted Nehmann along a corridor he recognised from his previous visit. He could hear the piping of children's voices, the patter of footsteps, and a delicious smell hung in the air. Goose, he thought. And wonderfully waxy potatoes. And spiced sauerkraut. And – if he was really lucky – even a dumpling or two. He noticed, to his amusement, that on the wall at the end of the corridor the framed photograph featuring Lida Baarova had gone.

Goebbels led the way to a guest bedroom. The replacement set of clothes that awaited Nehmann might have been lifted from Guram's apartment. The same heavy pullover with the same zigzag motif. A pair of trousers, freshly ironed, that fitted like a dream. Even the triangle of red silk scarf that Nehmann liked to knot around his neck.

'We took advice.' Goebbels was beaming. 'We got word that you were losing weight, so we acquired a tighter pair of trousers. That was Maria's doing. Don't tell me you're surprised.'

'Not at all. How is she?'

'Well, my friend. And as eager as ever.'

'For?'

'You, Nehmann.' The smile was even wider. 'Who else?'

The family, he explained, would be eating later, before the evening's entertainments began. For their guest, the cook had prepared a cold platter from last night's Christmas Eve celebrations. Nehmann would be dining alone in Goebbels' study over a drink or two while together they did their best to resolve certain matters. Nehmann was very welcome to take advantage of the facilities. A bath had already been run. Afterwards, soaped and lotioned, he would doubtless be able to remember his way to the study. A glass or two of Gewürztraminer would be waiting for him once he'd had time to collect himself.

Certain matters? Collect himself?

Nehmann lay full length in the bath, his eyes closed. He couldn't remember when he'd last enjoyed water this hot. It seeped into him, a reminder that life in the Third Reich could have its moments of purest pleasure. The temptation was to tally this against the countless images he'd just left behind him, to remind himself that everything in this weird regime came at a price paid by millions of others, but he shook his head. With luck, he'd be back on the road to the city within a couple of hours. Maria, he thought. Waiting for him.

Goebbels, when Nehmann joined him a full hour later, was showing signs of impatience.

'You slept,' he said.

'How do you know?'

'I checked. You're a guest Nehmann. You live here by our rules, not yours.'

Goebbels was, as ever, sitting behind his desk. Nehmann settled in the proffered chair. None of this matters, he told himself. I'm still alive.

'You have something for me?' Goebbels couldn't have been blunter.

Nehmann nodded. He'd typed up his encounter with Gigensohen, the pathologist, and now he handed it across. Goebbels, it turned out, knew about the pathologist's visit to Stalingrad already. Indeed, by his own account it had been partly his own idea.

'We need focus, Nehmann. We need to acknowledge the reality of things. And, in my view, there's no better place to start than the findings of a man like Gigensohen. He's a scientist. He deals in facts, not fictions. People will trust him.'

He bent his head and scanned Nehmann's account. Then he read it a second time, a green pen in his hand, making notes in the margin.

'He told you about having to thaw out the bodies? Before he carves them up? How difficult that can be? How long it takes?'

'Yes.'

'And he told you about the time he left one poor man to roast for too long? Charred him down one side? Like some *Schwein* on a spit?'

'Yes.'

'Then use it. Make it graphic. Make it *real*.' He lifted his head at last and adjusted his reading glasses. 'What's the matter, Nehmann? Why do I have to tell you all this? Has Stalingrad done bad things to you? Robbed you of your appetite for that killer phrase we know and love?'

'Not at all, Minister. Stalingrad has taught me many things, not all of them pleasant.'

Goebbels caught the change of mood at once. Nehmann very rarely called him 'Minister'. Indeed, a faux-camaraderie had always been the very essence of their relationship: two buccaneering artists pushing propaganda to its limits.

'What's the matter, Nehmann?'

'Nothing.'

'You still regard me as a friend? A colleague? A *supporter*?'

'Of course, Minister.'

'Then read this.' He pushed a magazine across the desk. It was an advance copy of the January edition of *Das Reich*. The article, authored by Goebbels, was headlined *Totaler Krieg*. Total War.

The article was brief. Nehmann understood the thrust of it in seconds. The nation had to understand that war could be ugly, and costly, and painful. The quicker the whole business was over, the better. Wise, therefore, to devote every particle of the nation's effort to winning. At whatever cost.

'Total War, Nehmann.' Goebbels rapped the top of the desk with his knuckles. 'There's no other way. People have to understand that this war will never be won in Horcher's or the Rivoli. It demands total commitment. From every single one of us. You agree?'

Nehmann nodded, said nothing. Horcher's was Hermann Goering's favourite Berlin restaurant and he knew Goebbels had been trying to close the place down for months. The Rivoli was a cinema that specialised in screening lavish movies, many of them sponsored by the Promi, to packed houses.

'You agree, Nehmann?' Goebbels said again.

'Of course. And the answer is yes, Minister.'

'Then attend to this shit. Make it bolder. Use the bodies. Make us *feel* the bite of those bone saws the pathologists use. I've cleared a space in next week's *VB*. The Führer is half convinced but he needs a little push and that's where you come in, Nehmann. What a way to launch the New Year, eh?'

'How many words, Minister?' *VB* was the *Völkischer Beobachter*.

'Five hundred. Anything longer, people lose their way. Come on, Nehmann, for God's sake, you used to know all this.' Goebbels pushed the text of Nehmann's account towards him. His gaze was unwavering. 'Well?'

'You want me to do it *now*?'

'I do, Nehmann. I do. I want you to do it now, here. I want it sharper. I want it better. I want to imagine half of Germany reading it and nodding and realising that there's no other way. Total War, Nehmann.' He rapped the table again. 'Or nothing.'

Nothing. Nehmann reached for the text and took the proffered pen. He'd finally realised what was going on. He'd finally recognised the sub-text to this conversation, the reef buried beneath the pleasantries, and the readied bath, and the change of clothes, and all the Third Reich nonsense afterwards. This was humiliation on a subtly grand scale, a reminder of just where he, Werner Nehmann, wordsmith and jester, belonged in the ranks of the mighty. He was back at school, master and pupil, here to do Goebbels' bidding. And then what? He shook his head, trying to dismiss the thought.

He began to go through the text, changing a word here, adding a detail there, trying to catch the pathologist's turn of phrase, trying to remember exact anatomical details, trying to do justice to yet another stack of Stalingrad corpses. Goebbels watched him, affecting indifference, toying with his glasses. Soon, it was done. The Minister scanned it quickly, nodding when a new phrase caught his eye, then smiling at the end where Nehmann had added the line about death never taking time off.

'Excellent.' He sat back. 'You never let me down, Nehmann. I'm glad to say your work is done.'

'Done?'

'Indeed. Will the Reich need you again? Of course, it will. No nation wages Total War without a great deal of effort and, dare I say it, wit. That's your job. That's where little Werner Nehmann comes in. But for now, my friend, you and your lady must enjoy the rest of Christmas. I'm glad Stalingrad was kind to you. Best to forget the worst of it, eh? My driver will be glad to take you back to the city. That little bookshop on Kopernikusstrasse? Am I right?'

He got to his feet, one hand outstretched. But then came the creak of the door opening. For a moment Nehmann thought it might be the promised meal, but it turned out to be Magda. She said she felt a little guilty. It was, after all, Christmas. Was there anything she might be able to find for him in the way of a present? Nehmann gazed at her for a moment then mumbled that it was a kind offer but that he had nothing to offer in return.

'Nonsense, Nehmann.' This from Goebbels. 'You've brought yourself, graced us with your presence, what more could we possibly want?'

Nehmann held his gaze. Goebbels had always been half in love with sarcasm, but this was far too clumsy.

'Well, Herr Nehmann?' Magda was still waiting for an answer.

'Yes.'

'Yes, what?'

'Yes, I'd like a present. Could you manage a little collection of spices? What your cook has in the kitchen? A little salt? A decent pinch of pepper? Hungarian paprika, as hot as you can manage? Cayenne, maybe? Nutmeg? Cloves? And some herbs, too? Dill? Chives? Parsley?'

'That's quite a list, Herr Nehmann.' Magda was looking surprised.

'I'm sorry.' Nehmann started to apologise but Goebbels cut him short.

'He gets carried away, darling. That's part of his charm.' He tore a sheet of paper from the pad on his desk and reached for a pen. 'Give me that list again, Nehmann, and we'll see what we can do.'

*

The Mercedes was waiting, as promised, outside. Nehmann, clutching a bag of herbs and spices, went through the pantomime of farewells, first a courtly kiss for Magda on both cheeks and a murmured thank you for the present, and then a stiff handshake for the Minister. Goebbels gave his hand a little squeeze before letting go, the significance of which was lost on Nehmann.

'Be good at New Year, Nehmann.' He was beaming again. 'Take care of that lady of yours.'

Nehmann got in the car. He was starving. Beside the driver sat one of the bodyguards. Another was in the back beside Nehmann. Both were impeccably suited and barbered. Not a trace of the brutal SS haircut for the Minister's retinue.

They drove back to the city in silence. Nehmann wondered whether to offer directions to the bookshop but knew there was no point. Goebbels was a master of taking care of the smallest details. This little scene, like much else in his life, had been carefully stage-managed.

By now it was mid-evening, the streets of outer Berlin deserted. There was a 20 kph speed limit during the blackout, ruthlessly enforced, but Goebbels' driver took no notice. He was driving with his headlights on, ignoring the occasional red lights at major intersections, sounding the ministerial klaxon when a lone cyclist wobbled into view.

Nehmann sat back, aware of the warmth of the bodyguard beside him, thinking of Georg Messner. It was the Berlin blackout that had sent him through the windscreen and so nearly killed him. He'd managed, in the end, to put most of his life back together again but for what purpose? To fly handfuls of food into a besieged city without a future? To try and snatch some kind of victory from the jaws of a humiliating defeat? Nehmann shook his head, remembering the shriek of the incoming artillery shell on the airfield at Tatsinskaya and the moment Messner's precious tent, his pride and joy, exploded. I must get out to Wannsee, he thought. I must present my sympathies and tell that wife of his that she had, in the end, married a good man.

They were in Mitte now. Nehmann recognised the turn that would take them into Kopernikusstrasse, and then the ghostly shape of the tree outside the bookshop. The big Mercedes came to a halt at the kerbside. Nehmann grunted a thank you for the lift, picked up his kitbag, and got out. The street was deserted but very faintly he thought he could hear a woman's voice singing a carol. *Stille Nacht*. Beautiful.

There was no sign of life in the bookshop. He crossed the pavement and knocked lightly on the door. Nothing. He knocked again, waiting patiently in the darkness, aware that the Mercedes hadn't moved. All three faces were watching him from the car. A third knock. He was trying to imagine the living arrangements inside. Was there a little room at the back, part kitchen, part living space, where father and daughter ate their meals together? Might there be a couple of bedrooms on the next floor where they slept? The prospect of a bed and a little privacy put a smile on Nehmann's face. Then he heard footsteps inside, and a voice he recognised.

'Who's there?'

'Werner. Werner Nehmann. Maria's friend?'

'Ah...'

The door opened. It was her father. He peered down at Nehmann, saw the car at the kerbside, frowned, gestured for him to come in. As Nehmann stepped past him, he heard one of the car doors open and he glanced back in time to see one of the bodyguards buttoning his jacket and making his way towards the corner of the street.

'*Komm*, Herr Nehmann.'

The old man led the way through the bookshop. In the darkness he seemed to know every hazard, every creaky floor-board, but Nehmann was more cautious, inching his way forward, his hands outstretched, one small step at a time.

'Maria?' he whispered. 'She's here?'

The old man seemed not to hear him. When Nehmann at last found a door at the back of the shop he was already in the next room, bent over a lamp, trying to coax a flame with a wavering match. The smell of paraffin took Nehmann back to Stalingrad.

'Maria?' he repeated. 'She's here?'

The old man glanced up at him. The wick was burning now and he turned it down, his face shadowed and seamed in the throw of light.

'Those people outside? They belong to Goebbels?'

'They do, yes.'

'And you've come from his place? Out at Bogensee?'

'Yes.'

'Then you must have seen Maria. That's where she is. She plays for the family this evening.' He put a bony hand on Nehmann's arm. 'It's an honour, my friend,' he said heavily. 'We should all be very proud, *ja*?'

Nehmann was staring at him. The entertainment, he thought, after the family have eaten their fill, and the children have opened their presents, and the staff have cleared the plates away. After the goose and the dumplings, a little light relief, maybe even a song or two.

Nehmann felt a sudden surge of anger. This, he realised, was Goebbels' masterclass in humiliation. Everything scripted. Everything pre-planned. Not a single detail left to chance.

You're anticipating a plate of something delicious, something *festive*, to fill that belly of yours? Alas, no.

'You're expecting her back? Afterwards?'

'No.' The old man shook his head. 'She'll be staying the night. Again.'

'She's there often?'

'*Ja*. Too often.'

Nehmann nodded, said nothing. He knew he had to get out of this place, this trap, this life. There was a door beside the big square sink.

'There's some kind of courtyard at the back? Maybe a way out?'

'Of course. Live in this city and you have a bicycle. Where else would you keep it?' He paused, frowning. He seemed to have remembered something. Nehmann was already at the door. 'Wait, my friend. Please…'

He stepped back into the bookshop and Nehmann heard him rummaging in the darkness. Then he returned to the kitchen, a book in his hand. He examined it carefully in the light from the paraffin lamp before giving it to Nehmann.

'From my daughter,' he said. '*Frohe Weihnachten, ja?*'

Happy Christmas. Nehmann was looking at the book. It was the guidebook to Potsdam he'd last seen in the bookshop window. He opened it. Inside was an envelope he recognised, brown manila, carefully sealed. The water tank on the roof of Guram's apartment block, he thought. Goebbels' precious fucking billet-doux. She must have been up there, she must have retrieved it, kept it safe, knowing that one day I'd be back.

He lifted it to his nose, sniffed it. Nothing. Just a faint

mustiness, the fug of the bookshop, the scent of a thousand stories.

His gesture made the old man smile.

'She'll be back tomorrow,' he said. 'You want to stay the night here?'

'No.' Nehmann shook his head. 'One favour? Do you mind?'

'Of course not.'

'Please tell her I love her.'

'Just that?'

'I'm afraid so,' he smiled. 'Is there anything else?'

*

Outside, in the tiny courtyard, Nehmann could make out the shapes of three bicycles propped against the back wall. He still had the letter, but he'd left the book with the old man. He slipped the letter into the breast pocket of his jacket. There was a wooden door beside the bicycles. The bottom bolt was stiff beneath his fingers and it took a moment or two to wrestle it free.

His hand found the handle and latch and he half turned to take a final look at the back of the terrace before he left. One of those windows, he told himself, belongs to Maria's room. Her world. Her bed. Her smell. He half closed his eyes, trying to imagine what it might have been like if he hadn't put her in harm's way, if she hadn't played like an angel, if she hadn't been taken hostage by the little dwarf out at Bogensee. Then he shook his head, knowing that what-if games like this were the shortest cut to madness, and he pulled the back gate open to make his escape.

For a split second the bulky shape of the waiting bodyguard

confused him. Then he realised that this little movie had arrived at its final reel.

'*Komm*, Nehmann,' the bodyguard grunted.

Nehmann nodded, said nothing, feeling the huge hand tighten around his upper arm. Game, set and match, he thought vaguely. 'Happy fucking Christmas. So much for *Der Überlebende*.'

*

The bodyguard took him along the narrow lane that ran the length of the terrace. Back in Kopernikusstrasse, the Mercedes was still waiting, the rear door already open. Nehmann paused on the kerbside. He thought he could see the paleness of a watching face in the darkness of the bookshop, but he couldn't be certain.

'Get in, please.' The bodyguard was losing patience.

Nehmann felt pressure in the small of his back. He glanced up and down the street, tempted to make a run for it, but then the bodyguard pushed him into the back of the car and the opportunity had gone. The driver half turned behind the wheel. They were to drive him to the airfield at Tempelhof. There, said the driver, he would be put on an aircraft and returned to Stalingrad.

'To do what?'

'I have no idea, Herr Nehmann. Hasn't the Minister told you?'

Nehmann didn't answer the question. Instead he said he wanted to go first to Wannsee.

'Why?'

'I need to see somebody. I have something for them. Call it a gift.'

'A Christmas present?'

'Yes.'

The driver had turned back to check his watch. Now he was staring out at the street. Nehmann could see his eyes in the rear-view mirror.

'He's close, this friend?' he asked.

'She.'

'*Ja?* Someone important to you?'

'Very.'

'OK.' He nodded and reached for the ignition key. 'Five minutes only. You give me directions, *ja?*'

*

The drive out to Wannsee took less than half an hour. Nehmann was trying to remember the exact location of Messner's house and, once they'd found the road that skirted the lake, he asked the driver to slow down and give him a good look at each property as it slipped past. The tree in the corner of the front garden, he told himself. Where the pet rabbit had been buried.

Finally, he recognised the house and told the driver to stop. The property was in darkness but that meant nothing because the blackout rules applied out here, too.

'It's late,' the driver muttered. 'And it's Christmas Day. What kind of time is this to pay a visit?'

'You want to bring me back tomorrow? The next day?' Nehmann was searching deep in his kitbag. 'I'd be very happy with that.'

'*Ja.* And pigs might fly.' The driver tapped his watch. 'Five minutes. And Hans goes with you.'

'Lucky Hans.'

The driver ignored the comment. Nehmann's fingers had closed over his present for Beata. He pulled it out. Hans was the bodyguard beside him. He got out and circled the car, holding the door open for Nehmann. Nehmann stepped out and stood motionless for a moment on the icy pavement, enjoying the chill of the wind. He was past mere hunger, now. Far out on the lake he could hear the throaty chatter of what sounded like ducks.

'You still want to do this?' It was Hans.

Nehmann nodded. Hans followed him down the path to the front door. Nehmann rapped twice, then again. Stepping back and looking up, he caught a twitch in the blackout curtain and the brief hint of a face. Then came footsteps from inside and a male voice.

'*Ja?*'

'My name's Werner Nehmann. I'm a friend of Georg Messner.'

'You are?'

'Yes.'

'So, where is he? Tell me something about him. What does he look like?'

Nehmann realised his story was being put to the test. Very sensible.

'He's tall. He flies airplanes. His face is a mess. Was.'

'*Was?*'

'Please open the door. I need to talk to his wife.'

There was a brief pause. The door opened.

'You mean my wife. Her name's Beata.'

'Werner Nehmann.' Nehmann extended a hand. 'Happy Christmas.'

'Dieter Merz. What's that in your hand?'

Nehmann wouldn't say. Merz was as small as he was. He was wearing pyjamas under a dressing gown that was several sizes too big. His feet were bare and when Nehmann asked whether he was cold he nodded.

'Of course, I'm cold,' he said. 'What's this about?'

'It's difficult. Can I talk to your wife?'

'She's in bed.'

'Can you get her down? It's important.'

Merz was frowning. He wanted to know about the other figure at his front door.

'He's a friend of mine,' Nehmann said. 'He's doing me a favour.'

'You said "was" just now. What does that mean? Has something happened to Georg? Something bad?'

Nehmann was beginning to lose patience. Five minutes was nothing. Then another face appeared, and he recognised Messner's ex-wife. She must have stolen down the stairs without making a sound, Nehmann thought. He extended a hand. In the other he still had the present.

'Happy Christmas, Frau Merz,' he said. 'I'm sorry to call like this.'

She brushed aside his apology. The children were asleep.

'What's happened?' she asked. 'Why are you here?'

Nehmann explained briefly about the tent, and Tatsinskaya, and the Russian tanks, and the shells exploding everywhere. Beata was looking confused but he at last had Merz's full attention.

'You were there? At Tatsinskaya?' Merz asked.

'I was. You know it?'

353

'Very well. I'm a flyer, too. Georg was my best friend. Tatsinskaya's a shithole. The Russians have taken it now and in my book they're more than welcome.'

'Georg?' It was Beata. She didn't care about Tatsinskaya.

'I'm afraid he's dead. I'm very sorry. I got to know him a little out east. He was a good man.'

She nodded, biting her lip, saying nothing. Then Merz had his arms around her heaving shoulders, holding her close. Nehmann heard a scrape of movement behind him as the bodyguard shifted his weight from foot to foot.

'One minute,' he muttered. 'Then we go.'

Beata had regained her composure. She'd found a handkerchief in the pocket of Merz's dressing gown and she blew her nose.

'You were at Stalingrad?' It was Merz.

'Yes.'

'How was it?'

'Don't ask.'

'That bad?'

'Worse.'

Merz nodded. Nehmann at last offered the present to Beata. She took it, turned it over, examined it from all angles. Finally, she shook her head.

'What is it?' she asked.

'An egg slicer,' Nehmann said. 'Georg invented it himself. He told me you have chickens. These days eggs maybe need to go further. Make a thousand, and Georg thinks you'll both be rich.'

'Thinks?'

'Thought.' Nehmann offered a parting nod. '*Frohe Weihnachten.*'

354

The airfield at Tempelhof was no distance at all. The first flights out would be departing at dawn but the ground floor of the terminal was already busy with servicemen in uniform, mainly *Wehrmacht* and *Luftwaffe*. A *Standartenführer* in SS uniform was waiting for Nehmann and his bodyguard beside the desk that checked every outbound passenger. A secure room, he said, had been prepared for Herr Nehmann. He would, from now on, become the responsibility of the Gestapo.

A prisoner, Nehmann thought. In all but name.

Hans offered him a curt nod of farewell and strode back out to the waiting Mercedes, while the SS *Standartenführer* demanded a look through Nehmann's kitbag. Nehmann emptied the contents onto a nearby table, aware that he still had Goebbels' billet-doux in his pocket. Among the litter of stinking underwear and sundry other items on the table, the *Standartenführer* found a brown paper bag.

He opened it, sniffed the contents, frowned.

'What's in here?' he asked suspiciously.

'Herbs. Spices.' Nehmann held his gaze. 'Where I'm going the food is shit.'

32

STALINGRAD, 12 JANUARY 1943

That first week of the New Year in Stalingrad was quiet. At night, Nehmann sat in the *Abwehr* office in the bus depot, mostly alone, smoking. From time to time he caught the flat bark of a sniper rifle or a distant burst of machine-gun fire, but he got the sense that, post-Christmas, the orchestra was still tuning up. Sixth Army was surrounded. Walk in any direction and you'd finally bump into a Russian. Both armies were restive but the final onslaught, that last yank on the rope that would strangle the German presence on the Volga, had yet to come.

Did it matter? He wasn't sure any more. After his brief visit to Berlin – hot water, proper food – Stalingrad had closed around him again. This was an outpost of hell he'd come to regard as normal. The bread ration had been reduced to seventy-five grams per day, less than a couple of slices, and even Schultz was running out of food. Blankets, proffered by peasant women in felt boots, had become the new currency. Infantrymen turned up at the bus depot complaining that frostbite had done them in. Their forefingers were so swollen, they said, that they could no longer get them through the trigger guard.

An army incapable of firing a rifle? Nehmann simply added

this tiny detail to the grotesque tapestry that had become his world. Once he'd have made a note, worked it into one of his stories, used it at the end of a paragraph to make the reader close his eyes and shake his head and wonder who'd commissioned madness on this scale. Now, though, Nehmann had put his pen away. The Promi didn't need him any longer. His readership had gone. And even Stalingrad, with its inexhaustible horrors, couldn't penetrate a growing sense of apartness. If Nehmann felt anything, he concluded, he felt numb. Nothing mattered. Except somehow finding Kalb.

Then came the moment when he and Schultz were sharing a cigarette on a patch of dirty snow outside the *Abwehr* office. Crows were circling overhead, black against the grey shroud of cloud that never seemed to lift. Schultz watched them for a moment then told Nehmann they were looking for fresh corpses.

'They're running out of eyes to peck,' he grunted. 'That's what those bastards have for lunch.'

Eyes, thought Nehmann. The hostages trussed in the back of the SS truck. Kirile sprawled on the floor in the vestry, nothing left of his face. Kalb had done that.

Kalb.

*

In the second week, Russian envoys crossed the front line with a demand that the Germans surrender. Their position was hopeless. Sixth Army was running out of food and fuel. Almost all the ammunition had gone. On days when the weather was kind, permitting supply flights, Soviet fighters were causing havoc among the lumbering *Tante-Jus*. In short, the game was up.

Schultz knew about the Russian offer. The good *General*, he said, had just twelve hours to make a decision. Naturally, Paulus consulted Hitler. The Führer dismissed any thought of retreat. Sixth Army would have to fight on.

With what?

*

In the middle of the month, Nehmann found himself once again at Pitomnik airfield. Schultz had done his best to locate Kalb's SS detachment but was beginning to suspect that it had gone. Commandeering a place on one of the handful of departing flights would be easy, he said, for someone in Kalb's position. He'd use the uniform, and perhaps a word or two from Berlin, to pull rank and save his life. That's what any sane man would do, Schultz insisted, but Nehmann had disagreed. Kalb, he muttered, wasn't sane. That was the whole point. And that was why he was probably still here.

'You *have* to believe it, don't you?' Schultz had said.

'Yes.'

'Then find the fucker.'

Nehmann had done his best but in a city where no one ever exposed more than a centimetre or two of bare flesh, the search was almost impossible. Grimberger had been reassigned to his infantry unit. Alone, for day after day, Nehmann set out to find Kalb among the endless torrent of broken warriors falling back from the front line, many of them wounded, all of them nameless, anonymous, indistinguishable. Pointless, Schultz kept telling him. Spare yourself the frustration, the misery, the pain. The man's gone. Either that or he's dead. You're living with a ghost.

Schultz, of course, was right but it made no difference. Nehmann had to find out, he had to be sure, and so this morning he found himself back at Pitomnik, scanning the mob of lightly wounded soldiers desperate to force their way onto one of the departing aircraft, only too aware that bad had abruptly become worse.

The Russians, according to Schultz, were now only kilometres away, pushing hard from the south-west. It was only a matter of days, perhaps even hours, before the airfield would have to be evacuated. Trucks had arrived from the front line full of wounded men. There was nowhere for them to go because the trucks had run out of fuel, and the flights out were already full, and so many of these men, their faces blue-black, had already frozen to death. More bodies were stacked like cords of timber, no names, no obvious injuries, no indication of what might be done about them next.

Then, as Nehmann watched, a Ju-52 appeared against the western sky, drawing thick black clots of anti-aircraft fire, and somehow managed to land. The pilot taxied as fast as he dared, weaving left and right to avoid the bigger shell craters, finally coming to a halt. Nehmann, his body hunched against the fierce cold, had a clear view of what followed.

Someone inside the aircraft kicked open the door and began to heave wooden crates onto the frozen turf. One of them splintered on impact and was attacked at once. Hands tore at the contents, desperate for food, and the moment someone emerged with a case of something tinned he disappeared under a mass of bodies, kicking and clawing at each other. A burly looking *Unteroffizier* in a *Wehrmacht* greatcoat emerged from the melee, a single tin held aloft, and Nehmann watched as he plunged a bayonet through the lid. The tin was full of frankfurter sausages and he tipped it to his lips, sucking greedily at the liquor before prising the metal open, plunging his fingers in and swallowing the sausages whole.

The plane was empty within minutes. The Chain Dogs from the *Feldgendarmerie* had arrived with drawn pistols. When no one paid them the slightest attention they began to fire blindly into the tangle of bodies and at last some kind of order was restored.

Men were on their feet again, brushing themselves down, ignoring the scatter of bodies. With the *Feldgendarmerie* was another figure. He wore a grey Russian army greatcoat, full-length, wide lapels, with the yellow shoulder boards of a tank captain, but his head was covered with a standard issue *Wehrmacht* helmet. He moved from body to body, stooping to inspect one who still appeared to be alive. Moments later, he drew an automatic and shot the man twice through the head. The circle of watchers around him stared at the fountain of blood and then began to back away.

Nehmann was still very close and his eyes never left the face above the Russian army greatcoat. It was largely obscured by a black balaclava and the moment the lips parted in the oval hole around the mouth he knew his search hadn't been in vain.

A single silver tooth. Kalb.

The empty plane was beginning to take on passengers. Kalb seemed to have put himself in charge. He stood beside the ladder propped against the metal body of the fuselage, subjecting each exemption card to detailed scrutiny. One in three of the walking wounded he turned away. When desperation drove them to argue their case, or even try and force their way aboard, he simply signalled to the nearest Chain Dog. The gesture, barely a lift of an arm, had Kalb's trademark indifference. Under arrest, the unlucky ones were handcuffed and marched away to God knows where. Within minutes, the plane was full.

Nehmann was within touching distance of the SS *Standartenführer*. Might now be the time to find a way of killing this man? Of settling the debts he owed to the bodies in the back of the truck? To Kirile? And to the thousands of Jews Schultz had told him about in Kyiv? Watching his every movement, every cloud of expelled breath that condensed in front of the balaclava, every brief order he issued to this man or that, Nehmann knew that the answer was no. It wasn't simply a question of killing him. He had to make Kalb bleed.

The plane began to move. Kalb was checking his watch. He beckoned the nearest Chain Dog closer. Nehmann recognised the *Leutnant* that had been responsible for keeping Kirile under guard. The man was nodding. The conversation over, he drew himself up, offered a smart Hitler salute and hurried away. Kalb was watching a distant Heinkel running the gauntlet of Soviet flak as it lined up for its approach run. The Russian gunners appeared to have the range at last. A pair of explosions bracketed the aircraft, left and right. For a second or two it seemed to hang in the air, wreathed in coils of dirty black smoke, then one wing disintegrated, sending the Heinkel into a flat spin. Nehmann turned away, knowing the aircraft was doomed. Kalb watched it until the end, the eyes behind the woollen mask giving nothing away.

The *Leutnant* was back moments later. Nehmann heard him apologising for the lack of transport. If they were to go now, it had to be on foot. Kalb offered a curt nod and then checked his watch again before setting off at a brisk pace, leaving the *Leutnant* in charge of the next incoming aircraft to make it safely onto the airfield. Nehmann, his head down, his hands plunged deep into the pockets of his borrowed *Wehrmacht* greatcoat, set off in pursuit. Finding Kalb had been a miracle but what was especially sweet were the odds so suddenly stacked in his, Nehmann's, favour. Just as Stalingrad had hidden Kalb all this time, so the city would make Nehmann equally invisible. All he had to do now was stay close.

Nehmann was back at the bus depot by dusk. Schultz was at his desk in the office. He barely lifted his head to acknowledge Nehmann's return.

'You're late,' he growled. 'We've been worried. Where the fuck have you been?'

'Kalb,' Nehmann said simply. 'I've got him. I've found him. I know where he's quartered.'

Schultz's head finally came up. If he was pleased, Nehmann thought, it didn't show.

'How? Where?'

Nehmann described the scene out at Pitomnik and the way that Kalb seemed to have materialised from thin air.

'One minute I'm looking at a Russian tank captain,' he said. 'The next I realise it's Kalb. He's with the Chain Dogs. I should have worked that out weeks ago.'

'You're right, you should.' Schultz had got to his feet and crossed the office to the big map of the city that showed all the bus routes. 'So how do we find the fucker?'

'Here.' Nehmann's finger settled on an area called Tsaritsyn. 'I followed him back from the airfield. The building is only half demolished. He must have commandeered it.'

'How do you know he lives there?'

'There's a well nearby. It still works. There were a couple of old women dropping rocks to break the ice at the bottom.'

'And?'

'I talked to one of them. Pretended I was a journalist. Asked all those sweet questions that disguise your real interest.'

'And?' Schultz had never learned how to mask his impatience.

'The man dressed like a Russian lives in the house I mentioned, draws his water from the same well.'

'He's alone in the house?'

'She thought not. She thought there might be more men in there. They might have something to do with the field hospital at Gumrak. It's a forty-minute walk away.'

Schultz nodded. He was still staring at the map.

'And the terrain?' he asked at last.

'Flat. Like everywhere else.'

'Any cover?'

'Not much. Except for a little stream about six hundred metres away.'

'Frozen?'

'Of course. But there are banks on both sides, maybe about this high,' Nehmann's hand briefly hovered at waist height.

'You checked?'

'Yes. Why does that amuse you?'

'Because you've been thinking snipers, Nehmann. Just like I would.'

*

That night they emptied the last bottle of vodka. Schultz, Nehmann realised, had only half believed that he'd really found the *SS Standartenführer* but when Nehmann sat him down and made him listen to a detailed description of what had happened beside the *Tante-Ju*, he acknowledged that it must be Kalb. More importantly, he began to visibly warm to the script Nehmann had written for himself. His entire professional life, Nehmann had always stood a challenge on its head. First work out what you want to achieve. Then work backwards until you know how.

'I want him crippled,' he told Nehmann. 'I want him injured enough so we can take him to Gumrak.'

'The field hospital?'

'Yes. He'll need attention. Happily, we'll be in a position to take him there.'

'And you think they'll have the time to deal with him? Have you been inside that place? It's a tomb, a charnel house. They have nothing. No drugs. No anaesthetic. No bandages. No plaster of Paris. On a good day they scrape lice off uniforms and skin with a spoon and throw them in the fire, but mostly they don't bother. They have no food, either, nothing to keep these men alive. Most of them die from starvation. I'm told the busiest man in the hospital is the Catholic chaplain. He gives extreme unction hundreds of times a day. They call him the *Tote König*.'

The Death King.

'It's not important,' Nehmann said.

'It's not? We pick up the bastard? He's bleeding all over us? We take him to this place? And it's not *important*?'

'Not in the slightest, Willi. Because the trick is he never arrives.'

'This is some kind of kidnapping?'

'It is. We'll need a place to take him. Somewhere private. Somewhere out of earshot.'

Schultz reached for his glass, not saying anything. He swallowed the vodka in a single gulp and told Nehmann to fill the glass again. There was a darkness around his eyes that Nehmann had seen in a thousand Stalingrad faces. He looked exhausted. And old.

'You've thought this through, haven't you, Nehmann,' he muttered at last.

'I have, yes.'

'The sniper takes the shot while he's at the well?'

'Yes. He aims for the legs, preferably the knee.'

'Why?'

'Because it will be agony.'

'And us? What do we do?'

'We wait. In the *Kübelwagen*. And then we turn up and play the patriot.'

'Good.' Schultz nodded. 'Very good. One more death? Who's counting?'

'Death?' Nehmann made light of the word.

'You're telling me you won't kill him?'

'I'm telling you we'll have lots of time. Plan it right and you won't believe what might be possible.'

Another silence. Nehmann thought Schultz might be having second thoughts but it turned out he was thinking about the sniper. Over the past few months, he'd met most of the men who were making themselves a reputation in the front line. The sheer brutality of close-quarters combat left little room for heroes but the ongoing battle between Soviet and German marksmen had caught the imagination of both armies. Indeed, a long interview Nehmann had done with one of these magicians, had been a Goebbels favourite. The man, now sadly dead, had ended the interview with a quote Nehmann would remember for a very long time. My job, he'd said, is to make the cleanest of kills on the dirtiest of battlefields. Perfect.

'I know two,' Schultz said at last, 'who'd gladly do it. One of them lost his brother to the Gestapo. An SS *Standartenführer* would make a very acceptable target.'

'And the other?'

'He owes me a very big favour. You'll love the man.'

*

His name was Schmidt. He was small, even smaller than Nehmann, and he had a smile that must have won him an assortment of beautiful women. With the smile went a peaceable acceptance that life was always going to be shit in this war, and that once you understood that, then neither Stalingrad, nor the weather, nor the Ivans, nor any other of the torments of this hideous city mattered in the slightest.

Schmidt was here to master the challenge of the long-distance ambush, to plot the rise and fall of his bullet, to take into account a breath or two of God's wind, and finally – if he got everything exactly right – to watch the face in his telescopic sight explode. It seemed that the latter image, a thin film of crimson that hung in the air after the body had dropped, had become a bit of an obsession. That may or may not have been true, but it was said that Schmidt always slept with a smile on his face; after getting to know him a little, Schultz believed he knew the reason why. The man was an artist.

The favour, according to Schultz, had to do with Schmidt's

sister. She lived in Berlin. She was as small as her brother and –
said Schmidt – perfectly formed in every respect. She'd attracted
a number of admirers and one of the least welcome and most
persistent had been a highly placed diplomat in Ribbentrop's
Foreign Ministry. The man had used his standing to make life
deeply uncomfortable for little Hannelore, and Schultz, in turn,
had used an *Abwehr* colleague to warn him off.

'He has a name? This man you want me to kill?' Schmidt
had paid the bus depot a visit.

'Kalb,' Nehmann said. 'And please don't kill him. A knee
shot is all we need.'

'Range?'

'Six hundred metres. I paced it out.'

'No problem. Right knee? Left knee? You have a preference?'

Schultz was sitting with them. The question made him laugh.
Nehmann, on the other hand, gave it some thought.

'Left knee,' he said. 'That's the one he dreams of bending
if he's ever awarded the *Ritterkreuz*.'

*

The next three days, while the roar of Soviet artillery grew
louder and the slender thread of resupply flights threatened to
break entirely, Nehmann made his way to the empty stretch of
steppe in Tsarytsin. On each outing he wore a different set of
clothes in case anyone was watching. On foot, especially when
the going got treacherous, the journey seemed to last forever,
and on the third morning, when heavy snow arrived, he had to
depend on the handful of waypoints that were already familiar.
Three eyeless horse cadavers, blown apart by the same shell. An
abandoned tank, the lid of its turret still open. The frozen body

of a young girl with blonde plaits, inexplicably undamaged, her tiny ears full of snowflakes.

Once he'd found the frozen stream, Nehmann made himself as comfortable as he could, belly down on the freezing gravel bank, only his head exposed. The binoculars belonged to Schultz, who'd stolen them from a captured Russian tank commander, and the optics, Nehmann thought, were a tribute to Soviet science. From his perch beside the stream, he tried to put himself in the head of a sniper, and as the hours ticked slowly by, his admiration for Schmidt's patience grew and grew.

Despite five layers of clothing, he was freezing cold, a deep chill that had stolen into the very middle of him. He had two pairs of gloves but after a while even holding the binoculars steady became impossible. His teeth ached. His nose was full of icicles. How would you manage with a sniper rifle? How could you possibly keep something as small as a knee in the scope under these conditions?

On the first day, to his astonishment, a thin bundle of fur emerged from nowhere. It was a hare. Nehmann tried to track it through the binoculars as it hopped around, suddenly pausing, erect, attentive. Did it hear the Russians coming? Did it feel the shake of the earth as yet another shell exploded in the middle of nowhere? Would it be a pair of gloves by the time spring arrived, and the melt came, and the city began to smell like the abattoir it had already become?

At the well, very little happened. Civilians appeared, mainly women, not very many and not very often. On the first two days, there was no sight of the long Russian greatcoat, and it was only on the third day, after the snowstorm had gone, that Kalb paid the well a visit.

It was mid-afternoon. Kalb was carrying what looked like a canvas bucket. He attached it to a rope and lowered it into the well. The bad news was that he was gone within a minute. The good news was that he seemed to favour the side of the well that faced the stream, thus presenting his back to Schmidt's rifle. But how on earth do you gauge the whereabouts of a knee beneath an ankle-length coat?

'Leave it to me.' Schmidt, that same night, seemed untroubled. 'You want him crippled but alive? My pleasure.'

Nehmann said he was grateful. He'd finally thawed out and when the little sniper disappeared into the night he retreated to the bare comforts of the basement storage where he slept. He'd been back in Stalingrad now for nearly two weeks. He'd done his best to put Berlin, all of Berlin, behind him. He didn't want to dwell on Goebbels, or Guram's wrecked apartment, or the moment he'd knocked on the bookshop door and found Maria elsewhere. All that, he told himself, was part of a life that had gone. Stalingrad was where he'd ended up, and the very lack of a future was – in some strange way – a comfort. His whole life he'd tried to resist making assumptions. Assumptions – about anything – were the shortest cut to disappointment. Make the very best of whatever happens. Do what Georgians have always done. Live a little.

Until now, he'd resisted opening Goebbels' letter. For once, because Schultz had finally run out of vodka, he was completely sober. The letter was still in the breast pocket of the jacket he'd worn the night he'd flown back from Berlin. He fetched it out and stared for a long moment at the envelope.

How much of the last few months, maybe much longer, had been shaped by this letter? Without this gun to Goebbels' head, what else might have happened? Would he and Maria still be together in Guram's apartment, untroubled by a Nazi chieftain desperate to reclaim his mistress? Had he been crazy to bend the knee, and play the messenger, and take the train south to Italy? To all of these questions he knew there was only one answer, the Georgian answer, the answer of the apprentice butcher who'd turned his back on the mountains and sought a life elsewhere. You do what you do. And face the consequences.

He used a penknife he'd acquired from Schultz to open the envelope. Inside, as expected, he found three folded sheets of paper. He slid them out and flattened them in the flickering light of the paraffin lamp. Anticipating paragraph after paragraph of Goebbels at full throttle, he found himself looking at three sheets of music. This was a language he didn't speak. His eyes tried to follow the notation at the top of the first page. Hopeless. There were no clues to what this music, this tune, might be, but the implications were only too clear, and he realised at last why Maria, in Berlin, had been so close, and yet so far.

For whatever reason, she'd betrayed him.

33

STALINGRAD, 16 JANUARY 1943

Nothing to lose, Nehmann told himself.

The sniper, Schmidt, reported to the bus depot an hour or so after dawn. He was wearing camouflage, entirely white. His journey on foot, he said, had taken more than two hours and every next step had revealed more evidence of the army disintegrating in front of his eyes. Infantrymen pissing on each other's hands. Reinforcement companies turned away from the field hospital, limping towards the front line. How strange a man looked when he'd lost his ears to frostbite.

Nehmann, only too aware that the battle might be over within days, was impatient.

'We have to do this thing,' he told Schultz, 'before the Ivans get here.'

Schultz agreed. There was half a tank of fuel left in the *Kübelwagen*. They went outside into the cold. Snow was forecast and the first flakes were swirling in the wind. Schmidt was looking dubious. With no visibility and a wind like this, a clean shot would be impossible.

'Then get closer,' Nehmann said. 'Give me the rifle and I'll do it myself.'

They drove to Tsarytsin. The snow was still holding off.

Schultz followed Nehmann's directions and brought the *Kübelwagen* to a halt fifty metres from the remains of Kalb's commandeered quarters. It turned out that Schmidt had already paid this place a visit, noted the well, paced the distance to the frozen stream. Impressed, Nehmann extended a hand over the back of his seat.

'Good luck,' he said.

Schmidt checked his rifle, wiped a smear from the telescopic sight, and got out of the car. Nehmann watched him walking away, back down the road. Schultz wanted to know where the fuck he thought he was going.

'He'll circle round,' Nehmann said. 'He thinks of everything.'

Schultz grunted something Nehmann didn't catch, then got out of the car and propped up the rear flap that exposed the engine. No one in this city cared any more about a broken-down *Kübelwagen*, but if the Chain Dogs arrived Schultz needed a reason to be here.

'And now?' He was back in the car, blowing on his hands.

'We wait.'

Nothing happened. From time to time, not often, Nehmann caught the distant bark of anti-aircraft fire and then the distinctive drone of a *Tante-Ju* that must have made it through to the emergency airfield at Gumrak. Once, a horse and cart appeared, heavily laden with wounded. The horse plodded past, the lone driver barely lifting his head to acknowledge the presence of the *Kübelwagen*. Most of the soldiers, lying prone in the back of the cart, appeared to be dead.

'Seventeen.' Nehmann smothered a yawn.

'Bodies?'

'Ribs.'

Schultz gave him a look. Lately, thought Nehmann, he has the eyes of an old man.

'You *counted* them? The ribs of the horse?'

'I did.'

'*Verrückt.*' You're crazy.

Nehmann nodded. He agreed with crazy. Maybe nineteen, he thought. Maybe twenty. Maybe a hundred ribs. Who cares any more? He tried to stretch his legs in the cramped chill, staring out through the windscreen. A film of ice blurred the view but it seemed to him that the sky, full of snow, was getting darker by the minute.

To the right, across the whiteness of the steppe, he could see no sign of Schmidt but he expected nothing less because the man had mastered the arts of invisibility. In his white camouflage, he could literally disappear, become one with the savage emptiness of this ruined landscape until the moment came to steady his rifle on its little tripod, and settle the cross-hairs on the folds of Kalb's greatcoat, and take the lightest breath before squeezing the trigger. Who would ever notice in a city like this? Just one more rifle shot? Just one more body in the snow? Who's counting any more?

Except that Kalb wouldn't die. Not out there in the snow. Not yet. Nehmann had found a spade in the workshop at the back of the bus depot. Very similar to the spade that had maimed Kirile, it looked nearly new, not a trace of rust on the gleaming blade, and he'd tossed it into the back of the *Kübelwagen*. Anticipation, he told himself, bred excitement and with excitement came a fierce adrenaline rush that kept him warm. Events had become unreal.

Nehmann had loved the theatre all his life. He loved sitting in the darkness with the play unfolding before him. He adored the clever feints of a good script, the cut and thrust of well-shaped dialogue, the dangerous surprises that lay in wait for cast and audience alike. And here, now, in the moonscape that was Stalingrad, he sensed that the final act was at last upon them.

A Soviet victory, regardless of whatever might follow, was now inevitable. The men of Sixth Army would stumble into captivity and most of them would probably die. Not from the kindness of a Russian bullet but from exhaustion, and starvation, and disease, and most of all from the merciless embrace of the weather. But in the meantime, in the precious hours and days that were left, there might still come just a flicker of redemption.

'It's snowing.'

Nehmann blinked. Schultz was right. The windscreen was suddenly white with snowflakes.

'You think he's in there? At home?' Schultz nodded in the direction of Kalb's quarters, now invisible in the blizzard.

Nehmann said he didn't know. All he could think about was Schmidt, flat on his belly as the snow fell, blinded by white. White through his sniperscope. White when he lifted his head to peer over the rifle. An eternity of whiteness, a shroud falling over everything, obliterating everything. Schmidt would know what he and Schultz knew: that the forecast was promising two metres by midnight, and that the blizzard was here to stay.

'We have to take him.' It was Schultz again. 'And we have to do it now.'

Nehmann didn't even bother to agree. Schultz had brought a machine pistol. He also kept a Luger under his seat. He checked the magazine, worked a round into the chamber and gave the gun to Nehmann. Outside, the wind tore through every layer of clothing in seconds.

Nehmann had the spade from the back of the *Wagen*.

'You're going to *bury* the fucker?' Schultz was shaking his head.

Step by step they made their way towards the well. From there, Nehmann would know exactly where to head in order to find Kalb's quarters. The blizzard was becoming heavier, more violent, visibility down to a couple of metres. Then, abruptly, Nehmann caught sight of a shape looming before them, something dark, formless, sprawled in the snow. He stopped for a moment, Luger in one hand, spade in the other. There was fresh blood pinking the snow around the folds of the Russian greatcoat and, as he stared at it, Nehmann caught a flicker of movement and what might have been a groan. One arm raised, then fell again, the gloved fingers flexing.

'*Hilf mir.*' Help me. An order, not a plea. It was Kalb. It had to be.

Schultz bent to check, grunting with the effort as he rolled the body over. Kalb's pale face stared up at them.

'In here.' He gestured helplessly at his abdomen. 'I've been shot.'

'Schmidt.' Schultz shook his head in disbelief. 'And we never heard a fucking thing.'

Nehmann nodded. A canvas bucket with a rope handle lay beside Kalb.

'The *Wagen*, *ja*?' He looked across at Schultz. 'Follow our footsteps back.'

Schultz muttered something Nehmann didn't catch and

disappeared into the blizzard, his head down. Nehmann was already kneeling beside Kalb. He'd never seen the face beneath the balaclava. The *Standartenführer* was freshly barbered, his chin and cheeks perfectly shaved around the stamp-sized moustache, and as Kalb struggled for breath Nehmann thought he caught a hint of something sour, foul-smelling, with just a hint of menthol, that seemed to come from deep within him.

'Hang on,' Nehmann said urgently. 'We can take you to Gumrak. Hang on. Don't give up. Don't die. *Verstehst Du?*'

Kalb seemed to nod but Nehmann knew he was bleeding out. Not a knee shot at all but something far more serious.

Moments later, a figure emerged from the driving snow. Assuming it was Schultz, Nehmann got to his feet but of the *Kübelwagen* there was no sign. Then he realised he was looking at the *Leutnant* from the *Feldgendarmerie*. He'd come to give Kalb a hand at the well.

'What's going on?' He was staring down at the blood in the snow, at Kalb.

'Fuck knows. We can get him to Gumrak. We'll need a hand.'

The *Leutnant* was a policeman. He was looking now at the Luger, at this stranger, at the tiny black-rimmed hole in the greatcoat.

'So who are you?' he demanded.

Nehmann was spared having to answer. Schultz had arrived in the *Kübelwagen*. He opened all four doors and struggled towards them through the snow.

'*Heil Hitler!*' He snapped the *Leutnant* a salute. '*Oberst* Schultz. *Abwehr*. This man is badly injured. We need to get him to Gumrak.'

Without waiting for an answer, he hooked his big hands beneath Kalb's armpits and told the *Leutnant* to take his feet. The *Leutnant* began to protest but Schultz cut him short with a look.

'You want the man to bleed to death?'

They carried Kalb to the *Kübelwagen* between them. Kalb's eyes were closed but he appeared to be still breathing.

'*Schnell, ja?* As quick as you can.'

They folded Kalb into the back of the *Wagen*. The *Leutnant* was demanding Nehmann's details.

'He's with me,' Schultz grunted. 'That's all you need to know.'

He gestured for Nehmann to get back into the *Wagen*, offered the *Leutnant* another salute, and then settled heavily behind the wheel. Moments later, the *Wagen* was on the move again and, looking back, Nehmann could see nothing but whiteness.

Schultz was adjusting the rear-view mirror with his right hand. When he'd finally got a proper look at Kalb, Nehmann, twisted in his seat, had failed to find a pulse.

'He's dead,' he said. 'We haven't got much time.'

'To do what?'

Nehmann shook his head, wouldn't say. He wanted Schultz to keep driving away from the well, just a couple of minutes, no more. Schultz nodded, tense at the wheel, his face inches from the windscreen. The single wiper had broken, a thin black stripe heaped with snow. They were moving at no more than walking pace, the *Wagen* ploughing slowly onwards, lurching from tussock to tussock.

'Here,' Nehmann said.

The *Wagen* came to a halt, rocking in the blast of the wind. Nehmann forced his way out. Kalb, he judged, had probably been dead for less than ten minutes. His body would be cooling already and once out in the snow his exposed flesh would quickly freeze.

'Help me, Willi.' Nehmann had got the rear door open and was trying to extract Kalb by his booted feet.

'You want him out?'

'*Ja.*'

'The fucker's dead.' Schultz was looking up at the rear-view mirror. 'Isn't that enough?'

'No.'

Schultz shrugged and struggled out. Between them, they laid Kalb's body on the snow. Nehmann knelt beside him, undid the buttons on his greatcoat, pulled it back. Underneath, Kalb had been wearing his SS field uniform. Beneath the stiff serge, God knows what else.

'You've got that knife of yours?' Schultz nodded. He'd given up asking questions. He dug beneath the belt of his trousers and Nehmann found himself looking at the hunting knife Schultz kept sharpened for every kind of emergency. The top edge was serrated with saw teeth while the cutting blade, lightly oiled, was razor-keen.

'You don't have to watch, Willi.' Nehmann nodded towards the *Wagen*. 'Just pass me the bucket and the spade.'

Schultz did what he was told. Nehmann was already unbuttoning the front of Kalb's uniform jacket. Beneath, he used the blade to slide through the layers of wool and cotton, peeling them back, exposing Kalb's bony chest. He did the same with the trousers, cutting down the line of the crease then folding back the material. The blade had already scored a line through the flesh beneath and blood was seeping out among the black hairs on Kalb's skinny legs. Within minutes, in a nest of torn clothing, the *Standartenführer* lay naked beside the *Kübelwagen*.

Schultz hadn't moved. Without a word, he passed Nehmann the canvas bucket. Nehmann looked up at him for a moment, wiping the snow from his eyes.

'Thank you,' he said.

Nehmann ran this thumb the length of the blade, the lightest touch. He was back in the abattoir his uncle owned in Svengati. Both cattle and sheep were suspended from meat hooks before the *coup de grâce* and moments afterwards, as an apprentice, Nehmann had always paid special attention to that first thrust of the butcher's knife, the one that split the animal's belly from top to bottom.

He remembered the spill of guts onto the tiled floor, the brightness of the yellows and greens and shades of indigo violet you never saw in any book. He remembered, too, the hot gust of shit and offal that stayed with you for hours afterwards, clinging to your hands, to your hair, to everywhere. This, he knew, was going to be different. There were no hooks. He couldn't rely on gravity to loosen Kalb's guts. And, when the moment came, the cold might steal away the stink of the man.

Aware of Schultz still standing beside him, Nehmann straddled the body, paused a moment, and then plunged the hunting knife into the tiny depression beneath Kalb's breastbone. The thrust was perfect, no obstructions, nothing solid, and he used both hands to rip the blade towards him, cutting cleanly through the layers of fat and muscle, until he found the hard ridge of the pelvis. Exposed to the driving snow, Kalb's guts were steaming. Schultz's big hand covered his nose but he didn't look away.

Nehmann had abandoned the knife for a moment. With gloves on, he knew that what he had to do next would be difficult, maybe even impossible, and so he pulled them off and left them in the snow before plunging his right hand deep into Kalb's body, up beneath the ribcage, feeling his way through the tangle of blood vessels and connective tissue until his fingers found the twin sacs of Kalb's lungs. They were still warm, slippery to the touch, and nestling between them he recognised the shape of what he'd come to find.

'Here—' Schultz was ready with the knife.

Nehmann reached up for it. Then, one by one, he slashed through the major vessels and moments later he pulled Kalb's heart free. He held it in the palm of his hand for a moment. Blood was still seeping from the chambers inside. That, too, felt warm.

'In the bucket?' Schultz needed no prompting.

Nehmann gave him the heart. Next came the liver. This, to Nehmann's relief, was easier. He could see it glistening, webbed with fatty imperfections, and he carved it out with a deftness that would, he suspected, have impressed his uncle.

'Legs? Thighs? Something to chew on?' Schultz had put the liver in the bucket.

Nehmann nodded. The temptation was to separate both legs from the pelvis but even under perfect conditions this operation would call for patience as well as skill. Kalb's temperature was dropping fast. Better for Nehmann to carve off as much as he could before the flesh froze solid. His lightly muscled thighs yielded three decent slices each to the hunting knife, and Nehmann took more from both calves. Finally, with the addition of handfuls of intestines from Kalb's abdomen, the bucket was full.

Nehmann got to his feet, admiring his handiwork. There'd been moments when life had tapped him on the shoulder and delighted him, but he'd seldom tasted anything as sweet as this. First he'd helped kill this man, and now he'd torn out his heart. For a moment, euphoric, he tried to find the words to describe the way he felt, and he decided that a kind of primitive bliss was the closest he'd ever get. The American Indians did this on the plains of the Midwest. And now he knew exactly why.

Schultz, unprompted, had produced the spade. Nehmann took it. The blizzard seemed to have eased a little, but he could still hear the wind keening over the rough pelt of the steppe. His mouth, his nostrils, his ears, were full of snow. Kalb's body had become a smear on the face of the earth. Only his face remained intact, frozen in surprise, or perhaps anger. Nehmann stood beside him, staring down, tallying the faces in the back of the SS truck, remembering Kirile sprawled in the vestry. Then he raised the spade high before driving it into Kalb's face, splitting it cleanly in two. He'd never felt better in his life.

34

STALINGRAD, 17 JANUARY 1943

Nehmann cooked the remains of Kalb that night, tossing the guts to the two cats. He used the remains of the wood in the bus depot, fired up the *Abwehr* stove, borrowed Schultz's biggest pot, and scraped a thin layer of fat from Kalb's thigh to grease the bottom of the pan. He sliced up the heart and liver and put them carefully to one side. The meat from Kalb's legs would take longer to cook and, after flash-frying chunk after chunk, he added fresh snow from a drift at the back of the building. Once the snow had melted, he added generous spoonfuls of salt, pepper, paprika, cayenne, plus a selection of herbs from the supply Magda Goebbels had given him at Christmas. By the time Schultz returned to the bus depot with an armful of more wood, stamping the snow from his boots, the pot was bubbling nicely.

Schultz peeled off his greatcoat and gave it a shake.

'He smells a lot better dead than alive,' he grunted.

*

Nehmann let Kalb simmer all night. He threw together a makeshift bed on the floor beside the stove and for the first time in weeks he slept like a baby. Next morning, he awoke to find Schultz inspecting the contents of the pot. The roar of battle felt very close.

'More water,' Schultz said. 'And more pepper.'

'You've tasted it?'

'Of course.'

Mid-morning, the meat tender, Nehmann put a lid on the pot, wrapped it in a blanket, and then carried it carefully out into the snow. Schultz had told him more than enough about the field hospital at Gumrak. The pot was nearly full. There was enough, certainly, to feed at least a dozen men. It would be Nehmann's pleasure to put SS *Standartenführer* Kalb to the service of the Greater Reich.

The storm had blown itself out overnight and a weak sun threw long shadows across the virgin snow. For whatever reason, both armies appeared to be catching their breath and a silence had settled on the emptiness of the city. Under any other circumstances, thought Nehmann, it might almost have been beautiful.

At Schultz's suggestion, they took a longer route to the field hospital, avoiding the *Feldgendarmerie* HQ. Nehmann was disappointed not to be able to see Kalb's body for one last time but the best bits of him, the useful bits, the tastiest bits, were in the pot between his feet. Wild dogs, he guessed, would be nosing at the rest of Kalb by now, tearing off frozen chunks from his face, eating his brain, lapping at the torn remains in his body cavity, starting on the bones, and in any case it was best to avoid the Chain Dogs. Kalb might be unrecognisable by now but his Russian greatcoat most definitely wasn't.

The field hospital announced itself with piles of bodies stacked untidily beside the rutted tracks in the snow that served as an approach road. Closer, some of the bodies, on stretchers and planks of wood this time, appeared to be alive. A flicker of movement in a man's eyes at the sound of the *Kübelwagen*, a head turning as it bumped slowly past, a hand lifting in a plea for it to stop.

The hospital itself was smaller than Nehmann had imagined. Smoke curled from a brick chimney. He smiled, glancing down the saucepan. They could warm Kalb up. Everything would be fine.

A male orderly met them at the hanging blanket, scabbed with something brown, that did duty as a door. Under what remained of his uniform, he was skeletal. He was wearing gloves and a torn field jacket. The cuffs of the jacket glistened with fresh blood and there was more blood clotting on his trousers. His eyes were bright in the gauntness of his face.

'You're hurt?'

'We've brought food.' Nehmann nodded down at the pot. 'We can warm this up?'

'What is it?'

'Stew. Casserole. Call it Ragout Stalingrad.'

'It's got *meat* in it?'

'Of course.'

'*Komm.*'

He led the way inside. Despite the fierce cold, the stench was overpowering, a thick, sour sweetness that reminded Nehmann at once of Kalb. Every horizontal space – beds, mattresses, wooden pallets, the floor itself – was littered with bodies, most of them bandaged. Men lying on their backs, their sightless eyes open, their chests barely rising and falling. Men lying sideways in the foetal position, their knees drawn up, their hands buried between their thighs. One of them had a hideous facial injury where a bayonet must have plunged into his cheek. A big flap of flesh was hanging down, revealing tobacco-stained teeth and the whiteness of bone beneath, and the bloodstained length of bandage barely hid half the wound.

'We've nearly run out.' The orderly was nodding at the bandage. 'We're down to half a metre a man. By lunchtime, we'll have nothing.'

He'd taken the pot from Nehmann. He lifted the lid, peered inside, dipped a finger, licked it.

'*Gut*,' he muttered, slipping off a glove and scooping up a mouthful with his bare hand. Then he put the lid back on and led the way down a corridor to a kitchen. A small pile of wood from smashed-up delivery pallets lay beside the stove. The cast-iron top of the stove glowed red-hot. The orderly put the pot on the stove and disappeared. Seconds later he was back with a battered metal spoon. He gave it to Nehmann.

'Stir,' he said.

Nehmann and Schultz stood beside the stove while Nehmann stirred the stew, grateful for the warmth. Within minutes, the thick, brown concoction began to bubble. Schultz had been right. Kalb smelled delicious.

The orderly returned. He wanted Nehmann to go from patient to patient, feeding each just a little of the stew. A couple of spoonfuls would be enough to keep most of them alive for an extra day or two. Any more, and their stomachs would never cope.

'*Komm*,' he said again. 'We feed only those who might survive.'

Nehmann didn't move. He was looking at Schultz.

'You want some, Willi?' he asked. 'Before we go?'

Schultz took his time in answering. Finally, he shook his head. The orderly was staring at him, amazed.

'No?' he said. 'Meat? You don't want any? You're really saying no?'

'No.' Schultz patted the flatness of his belly. 'Enough.'

Nehmann left Schultz warming his hands beside the stove. As they entered the main ward, the orderly turned to Nehmann who was carrying the pot, wrapped once again in the blanket.

'Your friend is a true Christian,' he said. 'How many of those does this army have left?'

'A man of faith.' Nehmann was looking at the pot. 'And a privilege to be his *Kamerad*.'

They moved from bed to bed, Nehmann spooning the stew into the mess tin while the orderly coaxed each broken body into some semblance of a sitting position. Most of the men could barely chew, let alone swallow, and every one of these small acts of mercy left a great deal of Kalb on the fronts of greatcoats or tangled in a week's growth of beard. Yet these men, tormented by the unctuous smell still wafting up from the pot, still did their best to get the stew inside them. Some darkly primitive survival urge, Nehmann thought, had prompted a belief in survival, or maybe even salvation, and here it was.

With barely a spoonful of Kalb left, Nehmann found himself perched beside a man who looked older than the rest. He had, he said, been the sole survivor of a Panzer crew hit by a Katyusha rocket. He'd been in the hospital for nearly a week while both his legs had been amputated. The pain, he admitted, was grim but there was no infection in either wound, itself a small miracle, and he'd been promised priority on the evacuation list for the next flight out.

He swallowed the last spoonful of stew and insisted on wiping out the pot with his finger afterwards. Crudely taped to the wall above his bed was a magazine cover that Nehmann recognised. The *Frauen-Warte*. He pointed the photo out to the amputee: half a dozen of the Reich's finest, bestriding the top of Mount Elbrus.

'*Gut, ja? Wunderbar.*' The amputee was still sucking his finger. 'I look at it at nights when I'm lonely. You know where I come from? Berchtesgaden. I used to do that as a kid. Show me a mountain and I'd climb it.'

Show me a mountain and I'd climb it. Nehmann nodded and reached for the man's hand. He came from the mountains himself, he said, and he knew exactly what they meant. He wished him luck on the flight out and gave his hand a squeeze.

The pot empty, Nehmann got to his feet to follow the orderly through the tangle of bodies. The smell in the ward was, if anything, worse and Nehmann was still wondering what it must take to work in conditions like this when he stepped back into the warmth of the kitchen. It took him a moment to realise that Schultz was no longer alone. Three other figures, all Chain Dogs, had joined him. One of them was the *Leutnant*, who was in the process of handcuffing Schultz. The moment he saw Nehmann he told him he was under arrest.

'For what?'

The *Leutnant* didn't answer. He was staring at the empty pot.

'What was in there?'

'Stew.' Nehmann shrugged. 'For the men here.'

'What sort of stew?'

'Stewy stew. Ragout. Weather like this? Very sustaining.'

There was a moment's silence. The *Leutnant* sniffed the pot, studied the smear of liquid at the bottom.

'Delicious.' It was the orderly. 'Don't you agree?'

Nehmann and Schultz were driven back to the half-demolished building that had served as a joint SS/*Feldgendarmerie* headquarters. It turned out to have been a school. The two prisoners were separated the moment they arrived, and Nehmann found himself in a biggish room flooded with afternoon sunshine. Rows of tiny desks and midget chairs occupied most of the floor space and the remains of a lesson on elementary addition was still chalked on the blackboard. There was a scatter of picture books, too, and Nehmann made himself as comfortable as he could on the floor, handcuffed to a radiator that didn't work, listening to the roar of battle barely kilometres away. There was no glass in the windows at all. It was cold but bearable and Nehmann sat with his back to the wall, his knees drawn up, dreading the moment when the sun would dip below the window and the temperature would plunge.

The *Leutnant* arrived nearly an hour later. He eyed Nehmann warily, the way you might view an animal you didn't entirely trust, and he finally settled on a nearby desk. Nehmann had only ever been in the company of this man when Kalb had been present. He'd never talked to him, never had a chance to form any kind of opinion. He didn't even know his name.

'Mikhail Magalashvili.' Nehmann extended his free hand.

'You're Georgian?' The *Leutnant* seemed surprised.

'Yes. From Svengati. Ever been there?' Nehmann gestured up at the window. 'This kind of weather but with mountains.'

'You have papers? ID?'

Nehmann nodded.

'Put them on the floor. Let me see them.'

All Nehmann had was his Promi pass. He put it on the floor. The *Leutnant* got off the desk and picked it up, never taking his eyes off Nehmann. He inspected the pass at arm's length.

'Werner Nehmann?'

'That's me, as well.'

'You work for Goebbels?'

'I do.'

'As a Georgian?'

'As a journalist.'

The news seemed to give the *Leutnant* pause for thought. He was back on the desk now, the Promi card put carefully to one side.

'*Standartenführer* Kalb,' he said. 'You were taking him to Gumrak. What happened?'

'He died. In the car.'

'And then?'

'We stopped, obviously. We tried to revive him. When that didn't work, we left him in the snow. It seemed the kindest thing to do.'

'Kind?'

'We had to get back. You know the bus depot. You've been there. It's quite a way. We had very little fuel. The least weight on board, the better. That's what we thought. That's why we left him.' Nehmann forced a smile, knowing how lame the explanation must sound.

The *Leutnant* had produced a pad. He scribbled himself a note and got to his feet.

'Wait,' he said, and then left the room.

Wait? Bizarre.

Nehmann knew about the *Feldgendarmerie*. They had a reputation for taking matters into their own hands. They rarely bothered themselves overmuch about evidence. Normally, the word of their senior officer was enough to earn a man a bullet. In this place, Nehmann suspected that the senior officer had probably been Kalb but now he was dead. Not just dead but hacked into pieces and left for the dogs. Something like that would never go unpunished, not even here, where sudden death had turned the world on its head. The *Leutnant* would have them both shot, himself and Schultz, of that Nehmann was certain. The only question of any interest was when.

The *Leutnant* was back within minutes, his arms full. When Nehmann saw the spade, and the canvas bucket, and the bag of spices and herbs from Magda Goebbels, his heart lurched. This man is behaving like a proper detective, he told himself. Thousands are still dying by the day and yet here he is, back in the world of evidence and probably motive, trying to establish a sequence of events. Absurd.

He was showing Nehmann the spade. His gloved finger was pointing at clots of something brown on the wooden haft.

'Blood, *ja*? You agree?'

'*Ja.*'

'We found it in your *Kübelwagen*. On the back seat.'

'*Ja?*'

'*Ja*. And this?' He picked up the bucket. 'You want to look inside?' Nehmann shook his head. 'You don't? You don't want to take a look? Have a sniff, maybe? That bucket belonged

390

here, in this place, and now we find it in that shitty bus depot of yours. And these?' His hand settled briefly on the bag of spices. 'What are these for?'

'Cooking, I imagine.'

'Of course. Cooking. Making food taste sweeter, nicer. So what happened, Herr Nehmann, Herr whoever you are? What happened to *Standartenführer* Kalb? Don't take me for a fool. Just tell me the truth.'

'You think that matters?'

'What, Herr Nehmann?'

'The truth. Here. In Stalingrad. You think the truth matters in a place like this?'

'Of course. The truth always matters, wherever you are.' He was frowning now. 'What could possibly matter more?'

The question brought a smile to Nehmann's face. This man was full of disgust, he could tell, but he was unsettled as well because he seemed to have worked out exactly what had happened, and his conclusions disturbed him deeply.

Nehmann looked at his free hand, flexed his fingers, then glanced up.

'You're right, Herr *Leutnant*. I killed him. I killed Kalb and then I chopped him into pieces and put him in the pot. Not all of him, just enough to make a difference to those men in the hospital. You might say I put the bastard to some use. You want to know why?'

'Tell me,' the *Leutnant* said stiffly. 'If you think it makes any difference.'

Nehmann took a deep breath. After a confession like that, he knew he was a dead man, but he welcomed this one chance of putting a question of his own.

'You were at Tatsinskaya, Herr *Leutnant*. You saw the bodies in the back of that SS truck? You know what Kalb had planned for them?'

'*Ja*, of course. This is war. Certain measures might be necessary.'

'Might be?'

'Are.'

'You saw the state of those bodies? What Kalb had done to them? *Had* done to them? Maybe that was your work? Your colleagues? Was that what happened?'

'Not at all.'

'So, who did it? Who mutilated those people?'

'That's none of your business.'

'But it is, Herr *Leutnant*, because I'm curious, because I'm a journalist, and because I'm proud to ask questions on behalf of the *Volk*.'

'The *Volk*? The people?' The *Leutnant* didn't bother to hide his contempt. 'They were terrorists, those scum at the airfield. They were a threat to the Reich. We have the complete support of the people in everything we do.'

'They were ordinary. They were local. They were mothers, fathers, daughters, little *girls*. One of them was a headmaster. He belonged in a room like this. Yet you shot him. And then smashed his face to pieces.'

'Not me. I didn't do that.'

'Who, then? Who did it?'

The *Leutnant* wouldn't say. The thunder of yet another artillery barrage rolled across the whiteness outside, giant footsteps coming ever closer, making the earth itself tremble. Clouds of tiny birds exploded from the remains of a nearby tree and Nehmann realised that it had been many hours since he'd last caught the growl of a landing aircraft.

'The Russians are all over us,' he said softly. 'You think another couple of deaths will stop them?'

'What you did to the *Standartenführer* was wrong. It was worse than wrong.'

'Killing the bastard?'

'Cooking him. Eating him.'

'And I die for that?'

'Of course. Death is what a cannibal deserves. Even in this city.'

Death is what a cannibal deserves. Nehmann studied him for a long moment.

'Are you a religious man, Herr *Leutnant*? Do you go to church? Do you pray to your God?'

'Yes.'

'And do you take communion?'

'Yes.'

'The body and blood of Christ?'

'Yes.'

'Because it sustains you?'

'Because it makes me a better person.'

'Then think of poor Kalb. And think of the men in that tomb of a hospital. He's kept them alive. And that was my doing.'

'You're telling me it was an act of *redemption*? Killing Kalb?' The *Leutnant* was staring at Nehmann.

'Not at all. I'm telling you I put him to some use. I'm beyond redemption, and so is Kalb. I expect I'll die, as well, but before you shoot me, might I ask one favour?'

'What? What favour?'

'That you eat me, too.'

The *Leutnant* didn't answer. He thinks I'm mad, Nehmann thought. He thinks I'm clinically insane and he's probably right.

The interview at an end, the *Leutnant* left the classroom without a backward glance. The sun was sinking towards the horizon, a huge orange ball wreathed in the smoke of battle, and Nehmann began to shiver as the temperature fell. A couple of books lay within his reach and he opened one of them with his spare hand. 'A' for 'Apple'. 'B' for 'Boy'. He stared at the cartoon faces, the sweetness of the smiles, at the way that every object triggered a thought, even the beginnings of a story. At the end of a lifetime devoted to telling stories, he thought, my days are ending where they began. 'A' for 'Apple'. 'B' for 'Boy'.

Had his questions made any impact on the *Leutnant*? Had they touched a nerve or two? Prompted a ripple in the cess pit that was his conscience? Had he gone away to think? To reflect? Or was he even now slipping a fresh magazine into that machine pistol of his?

Nehmann didn't know, and he was so cold, so numb, that he didn't really care. Why not now, he thought. Why not get it over with? Why not spare himself another night on this earth?

Darkness fell. The battle seemed to intensify. Then the classroom door opened, and a uniformed figure loomed briefly over him. It wasn't the *Leutnant*.

'Here—'

Expecting to be released from the radiator, expecting to be hauled to his feet and dragged out into the snow, expecting to find himself on his knees, the cold muzzle of a gun to the back of his neck, Nehmann felt something rough settling around him.

'What's this?'

'Blankets.' A soft laugh. 'They belonged to Kalb.'

The figure disappeared. The door of the classroom closed. The noise of battle seemed to have diminished. Curled awkwardly beside the radiator, Nehmann slept.

He awoke at dawn, shivering. Another cloudless day. Nehmann pulled the blankets more tightly around him. He smelled of Kalb, he knew he did. He smelled of camphor, of mothballs, of menthol. He smelled sour. He smelled of death.

From the corridor outside the door came a murmur of voices then a thump as something heavy was dragged across the floor. The voices receded. A door opened and closed. Then came the soft crunch of footsteps in the snow outside and, perhaps a minute or so later, Nehmann heard a single shot, very close, followed quickly by another. Schultz, he thought. Dawn. The hour of our passing. The moment of execution. Me, next.

He closed his eyes, tried to still the raging in his empty guts. Please let it be quick. Please let me think of nothing. In this city of nothing, nothing.

But nothing happened. No more footsteps. No more voices. Nothing. Slowly, over the next hour or so, the sunshine grew stronger and the temperature in the freezing classroom began to inch up. And then, for the first time, Nehmann saw the hunting knife. It belonged to Schultz. It was the same one he'd used on Kalb. Someone had left it on the floor beside the radiator. Someone had stolen into this room during the night and measured the space by eye and given Nehmann a little parting gift.

He struggled free from the blanket, rubbing his eyes, trying to ease the cramp in his legs, and reached for the knife. It was close, tantalisingly close, teasingly close, maybe ten centimetres beyond his closest foot. Someone, maybe the *Leutnant*, was playing games with him. With the point of the knife he might be able to force the lock on the handcuffs. With the serrated top of the blade, and a little time and effort, he could certainly saw through a link in the chain. But how could he reach the fucking thing?

A challenge, he thought. For the journalist from the Promi, for the little Georgian cannibal, one last test. He stared fiercely at the knife, concentrating every gramme of psychic will, trying to make it move, trying to make it levitate. Hopeless. He looked round for a stick, a child's ruler, anything to bring the knife within reach. Then he realised the answer. The blanket, he told himself. Use the blanket.

And so he did, casting it out towards the knife one-handed, like a fisherman spreading a net. The first couple of times, it didn't work, but the third cast snagged the knife and he heard a scraping on the rough wooden floorboards as he tugged the blanket towards him. Nehmann, all his life, had loved irony. Kalb, he thought, may have saved my life.

For most of the morning, Nehmann worked to get himself free. When he failed to unpick the lock itself – the angle too awkward, the lock too well made – he began to saw through the chain. He chose a particular weld in one of the links, hoping to find a point of weakness, but the metal was tough and it was difficult to keep the chain steady. Expecting the return of the *Feldgendarmerie* at any moment, he once lifted his face to find himself looking at a rat, large, brown, plump, crouched peaceably among the schoolbooks on the floor, watching his efforts. He's waiting, Nehmann told himself, returning to the tiny groove in the link. He's waiting for me to give up and die.

But he didn't give up. By what he judged to be noon, he was nearly through. Another minute, and another minute after that, and the serrated edge of the knife was sawing at empty air. In the golden pool of sunshine, Nehmann had even worked up a light sweat. Redemption, he thought. Who'd have guessed?

He used the knife to lever the broken link apart and then pulled the chain from the radiator, trying to keep the noise to the minimum. He was still wearing a single handcuff, but he was free. He stood up, uncertain of his balance, watching the rat scurrying away. He did his best to massage the pain from his aching arm, and then he stole across the classroom towards the door, aware of the noise of battle ever louder.

The door was unlocked. He stepped into the corridor beyond, alert for the sound of movement, the murmur of voices, but the thunder of exploding shells masked everything. He moved quickly from room to room, beginning to realise that these people had gone. The Chain Dogs had shipped out. Was the airfield at Gumrak still operational? Had they forced their way onto a departing flight? Were they even now droning westward over the steppe? Thinking about the bodies they'd left behind?

Nehmann ventured outside. He could see Schultz lying in the snow. He approached him carefully. He'd heard rumours of bodies booby-trapped with a live grenade. Take care, he told himself. Now is no time to die.

He was standing over Schultz, swamped with a fathomless grief, staring down at the big face cushioned by the snow. Then, very slowly, he realised that something was wrong. The snow had melted around his nose and mouth. He was breathing.

He was still alive. Schultz opened one eye. Not dead at all, but asleep.

'They play games with us, these fuckers.' Schultz was chained to an iron ring embedded in a huge block of concrete.

'They've gone, Willi. It's just us.'

Nehmann was looking at the chain, at the ring, at the block of concrete. The grunts of effort at dawn, he thought, as the Chain Dogs wrestled this thing into the snow. And then the two shots, so terrifyingly final. A game, indeed.

The lock, this time, surrendered to the point of Schultz's hunting knife. Nehmann hauled him to his feet, asked him if he was OK.

'I'm starving,' Schultz grunted. 'There has to be something to eat.'

There wasn't. Not in the wreckage of the kitchen. Not in any of the cupboards littered around the school. Not in the big room the Chain Dogs seemed to have used as a dormitory. Then Nehmann found himself in the little cubbyhole that must have belonged to Kalb. The smell of the man still lingered in the cold air. A camp bed occupied most of the available space and there was a wardrobe wedged into the corner beside it. The wardrobe was locked but Nehmann prised it open with the knife.

Inside, he found an SS-issue kitbag. He pulled it out. It was much heavier than he'd expected, and he could hear the clunk-clunk of objects inside. He emptied it on the camp bed, staring down at tins and tins of US Army-issue spam, of beans in tomato sauce, and at tube after tube of menthol pastilles. Kalb, too, had been packed and ready to go.

*

Nehmann and Schultz slowly made their way back to the bus depot, their bellies full of spam. They shuffled along like the two old men they'd become, ignoring everything on the way, the frozen bodies, the smashed-up vehicles, the occasional face peering out of this ruin or that, even the roar of the approaching juggernaut that was the Soviet Army.

The bus depot was empty. There were no signs of Schultz's tiny *Abwehr* staff. Schultz rubbed his face and used his hunting knife to prise open another tin of spam while Nehmann fetched snow from outside.

Schultz hoped his men would get through OK.

'Get through where?'

'Fuck knows.'

Nehmann tried to kindle a flame from the remains of the wood but gave up the attempt. He told Schultz he wanted to pay a visit to the priest at the church.

'Now?'

'Yes. You've got something better to do?'

Schultz shook his head. He'd finish the spam first, but why not?

'What's that in your hand?' he asked.

'Nothing.' Nehmann folded the sheets of paper into the pocket of his greatcoat, and then nodded at the tin of spam.

'Do I get any of that?' he asked.

*

They set out for the church. It was mid-afternoon by now and the battle seemed to have paused. Nothing stirred in the ruined landscape. Even the crows had given up.

Nehmann found the old priest sweeping the tiles in front

of the altar. Watching him from the emptiness of the nave, it seemed a crazy gesture, readying an empty church for a non-existent congregation, and Nehmann remembered the lines from Goebbels' editorial in *Das Reich* that had lodged in his memory. Above his head, he could see sky through the gaps in the roof.

In the limitless fields of the east yellow corn is waving, enough and more than enough to feed our people and the whole of Europe. Work will once more be a pleasure and it will be marked by a joy in life which will find expression in brilliant parties and contemplative peace.

'Brilliant parties and contemplative peace,' he told Schultz. 'Remember all that shit?'

The priest had put down the broom and was on his knees at the altar rail, praying. At the sound of a voice, he half turned. Nehmann was shocked by how much weight he'd lost. A bag of holy bones, he thought.

The priest limped very slowly down the aisle. His breath clouded on the freezing air and his beard, Nehmann noticed, had turned the colour of fresh snow. No longer grey, but white.

Nehmann dug in his pocket and gave the priest three sheets of paper. The priest studied them one by one, his head nodding as a finger moved from line to line.

'You want me to play this?'

'Yes please, father.'

'You'll help with the bellows? Nothing works any more.'

'My friend will.'

The priest slowly led the way up a flight of wooden steps to the organ loft, explained what Schultz had to do, and then settled himself at the keyboard. Nehmann heard the sigh of the bellows as Schultz began to pump. Then came the opening chords of the music Nehmann remembered so well. He could see the priest from the nave, a hollowed-out figure, a stick of a man clad entirely in black, plucking at the instrument's bank of stops, urging more and more volume from the foot pedals as the music briefly filled the church. Then came the first of the faster virtuoso passages, and the priest slumped back on the stool, defeated.

For a long moment, absolute silence, then Nehmann heard Schultz enquire whether the priest liked American spam. The priest whispered something Nehmann didn't catch, then one of the big doors of the church swung open and Nehmann spun round to find three black figures silhouetted against the still-bright afternoon.

They stood motionless for a second or two before the tallest of them strode down the aisle towards Nehmann, his boots echoing on the flagstones. He was wearing a neatly buttoned, full-length greatcoat but he'd removed his cap and his head was bare. Nehmann was staring at his shoulder boards. A captain in the Russian artillery? Kalb, he thought. *Redux*. Was this levitation? The blackest magic? Had the SS *Standartenführer* risen from the dead?

The captain was cradling a machine gun, the leather strap looped around his neck. He looked around, taking his time, and gestured up towards the organ loft. Nehmann understood his Russian perfectly.

'Again,' he said. 'Play it again.'

The priest gazed down at him, then shrugged. A nod to Schultz on the bellows, and he squinted at the first sheet of music and bent to the keyboard.

The Soviet Captain listened to the music for several seconds, his boot tapping on the flagstones, and then told the priest to stop.

'Beethoven.' The Russian seemed amused. 'The *Pathétique*.'

Nehmann nodded, and then slowly raised his arms. He couldn't take his eyes off the machine gun.

'я подчиняюсь,' he said. I surrender.

About the author

GRAHAM HURLEY is the author of the acclaimed Faraday and Winter crime novels and an award-winning TV documentary maker. Two of the critically lauded series have been shortlisted for the Theakston's Old Peculier Award for Best Crime Novel. His French TV series, based on the Faraday and Winter novels, has won huge audiences. The first Spoils of War novel, *Finisterre*, was shortlisted for the Wilbur Smith Adventure Writing Prize. Graham now writes full-time and lives with his wife, Lin, in Exmouth.

www.grahamhurley.co.uk